on

b

JAMESIE'S PEOPLE

JAMESIE'S PEOPLE

JOHN BURROWES

MAINSTREAM
PUBLISHING

Copyright © John Burrowes, 1984
All rights reserved

This edition published in 1984 by
MAINSTREAM PUBLISHING COMPANY (EDINBURGH) LTD.
7 Albany Street
Edinburgh EH1 3UG

ISBN 0 906391 71 7

Typeset in 10/11 point Andover by Studioscope
in conjunction with Mainstream Publishing.

Printed in Great Britain by
Forsyth Middleton & Co. Ltd., Kilsyth.

For Lilian, Kyle, Janie, Robin . . . His People.

GLASGOW STREET

Out of this ugliness may come
some day so beautiful a flower
that men will wonder at that hour
remembering smoke and flowerless slum
and ask
glimpsing the agony
of the slaves who wrestle to be free
"But why were all the poets dumb?"

—William Montgomerie.

Most of the places and many of the events in this book, particularly the role of the Glasgow Highlanders in World War Two, are based on historical fact and every effort has been made to adhere to those facts. There were people like Jamesie's People but all of the characters depicted are the author's creation and bear no similarity to people living today.

Contents

1

JAMESIE IS DEAD

JAMESIE Nelson died the way he had lived . . . brutally, savagely, violently. Just as he himself had slashed, knifed, chibbed and booted his way to the height of fame among his contemporaries and those who admired him and to the depths of infamy among those who respected and loved the city. Jamesie and his like were the fag-end products of a community which bore the brunt of the industrial revolution and wallowed in the unhealthy wash of man's progress, a human factory farm whose blight was filth and disease and where minds were convulsed in a conformist imprisonment from which there was little escape.

Jamesie and his brother Sammy were taken to the Royal Infirmary in one of the big wood-panelled St Andrew's Ambulance Service wagons, They had been assailed by a hyena-crazed gang, 20-handed, and left for dead on the slate-slabbed pavement of Crown Street, with Jamesie's blood dripping into the fetid cesspool beneath the metal stank grill. Jamesie Nelson, at only twenty-eight, had had his day. Others, just as he himself had done as a younger man, were out to prove that they were better . . . meaning harder, more ruthless, more mindless. And they did.

Only fate had involved Sammy in what happened that Friday in June 1927. For Sammy Nelson was what they called "respectable". Not for him the ways of his brother. He had a regular job in a big city emporium, and even earned enough for he and his wife Peggy to have achieved their life's ambition by moving out of the Gorbals.

Better places, it seemed, were always over the railway tracks. Over the Cathcart Road Bridge and the main Glasgow to London railway line and you were in Govanhill, the first suburb immediately south of the Gorbals. They had what they called "a lovely wee room and kitchen" on the high part of Carfin Street and although it was at the rear of the building, they could see all the way to the distant Cathkin Braes. The houses in the Gorbals didn't have a view like that. All they saw were other black and decaying tenement houses like their own, long black walls with slits, vertical letter boxes for humans which the English called entrances and the Scots called closes.

Sammy had been on an errand from work and had stopped to buy an evening paper in Crown Street, busy Crown Street, busy as a whole town itself where man, woman and family could get every earthly need and necessity they desired, from midwife to undertaker, and all that was in between from the delights of heaven to the horrors of hell.

"Gonnie get warmer. . . so it said in the papers this morning,"said the vendor, rattling the coppers bulging in his jacket pocket.

"Aye, melt ye so it would," Sammy replied.

The shriek of loud women's screams ended their brief exchange and the two men looked round sharply.

Earlier that morning Jamesie Nelson had been released from Barlinnie, the grim prison fortress atop the hill in Riddrie in the north eastern edge of the city, having just completed his third sentence of a year's imprisonment for street fighting. With a turnover of over 100 prisoners a day, only special cases were brought before Governor Donald Macrae on the day of their release. Nelson, always a model prisoner, was one of them.

"Well, Nelson," he said in his soft Hebridean tones, "You're for the outside and your freedom once more. You know it won't be the Sheriff the next time, laddie. Three in a row and all for using weapons. That's the High Court in future and a long one up at Peterhead. And if you go there you know what they call you . . . convict. That's the name they give to you there, James. Convict. Not very nice. And you'll get no regular visits like you do here. A year is easy at Barlinnie. It's not like that up there in Peterhead. The warders have cutlasses and won't think twice about drawing them. Aye, and there's the cat as well. Know what they do when they give you it, James? They tie you to what they call the triangle by the ankles and wrists. Like something from the Middle Ages. And they give you a right good flogging. Eighteen you'll get on your bare back . . . and the cat's got nine tails, stout whipcord tails. Not a nice sight, James. Not nice at all. You're a bit older than the first time you came here. A bit more sensible too. Time for you to be settling down and changing your ways. I know you're not a fool, James Nelson."

The big Governor knew his words were more than likely a lost cause but he felt he had to say something to Nelson because of his reputation. There was no reply, except the Glasgow man's nod, a fractional movement of the head that a blink would have missed but which said a lot and in James Nelson's case it meant, "Aye pal. Got your message . . . but nothing's changed."

He collected the statutory £2 which good behaviour prisoners got on their release together with the dark navy suit, muffler and cloth cap he had been wearing on the contrastingly cold and wet day he had been admitted the previous June.

The heat of the morning was oppressive and strange for it was rarely as warm as that in Glasgow where a summer could pass without a summer's weather, a wet spring stretching out to meet a cool autumn. He sweated profusely as he walked the two miles down the long straight Alexandra Parade. Its handsome red sandstone tenements had gone the same dreary soot black as the honeyed freestone of the Gorbals dwellings. He would have loved a pint in one of the many pubs he passed on the wide Parade but the drink could wait till he got to what mattered . . . a pub in the Gorbals. For he wanted them to see him and to know he was there and among them again. That was important to men like Jamesie Nelson; the men who they said were mindless were forever mindful of the violence which they knew and understood so well and which if they didn't give, they would get. Re-establishing his presence as the hardest man in the South Side and doing that as quickly as possible was the only thought on his mind. The drink could wait till the Gorbals.

He anticipated too the men who would be waiting for him in the Rutherglen Road pubs, ready to demonstrate to all and sundry that they were his old chinas . . . old and trusty friends.

He pushed wide the swing doors of Marr's, as he always had done, and walked briskly to the polished walnut bar backed by a high mirrored gantry. He shot a catarrhal spit at the sawdust under the brass foot rail and before he could order a drink, two men were by his side. Georgie Sproul and Davie Steedman had fought with him in his last great battle over in Nuneaton Street, across the Clyde in the East End of the City, the one for which he had just served 365 days as a guest of His Majesty at Barlinnie.

Without even asking, three whiskies and three bubbling pints of the rich, nuggety 90 shillings ale were put in front of them. Tommy Faulds, the head barman, said, "Welcome home, Jamesie". The men accepted the drink as a rite; it would have been unthinkable for any head barman to have acted otherwise in their district on such an occasion. Nelson pulled one of the glasses towards him and gave an

unsmiling nod in the direction of the barman who smiled in
appreciation; he had been blessed by the *spirito santo* himself, he felt; his
card was marked, his membership paid up. He could say he was a
friend of Jamesie Nelson . . . Jamesie, never Jim or Jimmy like the other
men who had been christened James. He hated Jim and Jimmy for they
were the names of the ordinary and anonymous men. The punters,
who were the mass of the men, would call others Jim or Jimmy if they
didn't know their names; sometimes they would use it in a derogatory
fashion; it was their Diego. And there was to be nothing derogatory
about James Nelson's name; nor was there to be anything ordinary
about it.

His mother, Mary, a kindly soul, had doted on him and had called
him, her firstborn child, Jamesie, to be different from the others. To
call him anything else, or even to refer to him by any other name was
an invitation for him to unleash the most terrible retribution; at least
one man had died for taunting him with the insult . . ."Jim". And such
had become the effect of the name Jamesie in the Gorbals, it outdid all
the other gangleaders and individual hardmen who had to wrap
themselves in weird titles like Gorilla, Animal, Blades, Big Shot and
Razor King, the one who had become such a legend they had written a
book about him. Jamesie Nelson didn't need their nicknames and
titles. He knew that. They knew that.

The three men spoke animatedly about current events, tittle-tattle
of no great consequence except to them.

"Mind o' Robina Brody? You know the big, red-haired hairy from
Portugal Street? Well, Tam McFarlane stuck her up the puddin' . . . and
her going wi' one of the Clanton boys. Anyway, they got McFarlane.
He's still in the Royal. Face like Carstairs Junction. Daft bastard. And
Stewie McConnell? Was doing a runner for Izzy Feldman, the Cally
Road bookie. Skipped it wi' the money . . . twenty quid. They found
him wi' four whores in a pub in Tradeston. They say he'll no walk
again. Did something wi' his back."

"What?" said Jamesie."Break it!"

They were still laughing at the aside when a little man in a coat that
had once been a gaberdine nervously left through the side door at the
far end of the pub by the Family Department counter. He was anxious
not to be seen by them for they would have thought it strange that a
person like him, Bum Beaton, should leave the pub so quickly after
Nelson's arrival. The Bum was one of a variety of parasites who
festered in the Gorbals. They were small-time pilferers, police narks,
bookie cheats, who could and would demean themselves flagrantly,
almost proudly. The Bum would tour the pubs where he was least
known and steal men's beer and spirits when they went to the toilets.
He would never try it in Marr's for if anyone lost a pint there and Bum

was in the bar it would be a sore face. But there were places where it was easy and they said he once got eight whiskies, two rums and seven pints of ale in the swanky Grant Arms, getting himself so drunk in the process he couldn't even lift another drink.

Bloodsuckers have to move fast to live. Their eyes can never stay still, forever casting for the chance that means something to them, nothing to others. The sight of the newly-freed Jamesie Nelson was such an opportunity. The news that he was out and had been seen celebrating in Marr's would be worth a drink in any of the other Rutherglen Road pubs . . . and Bum knew them all: The Struan, Robb's, The Ivy, The Moffat Arms, The Oval, The Challenge, The Railway Tavern, The Ferry, Hanlon's and The Coronation. Move fast enough before the word got right around and there would be a half and a half pint in four or five of them. If his luck was in he might even make it as far along as the Coronation at the corner of Caledonia Road.

After being deprived of drink for a year Jamesie Nelson was feeling the effect of the four whiskies and pint chasers he had been plied with by admirers in Marr's.

A year was a long time to be missing from the streets. Men of his type had come and gone. Patsy Gallagher had been kicked to death within sight of Lawmoor Police Station, Dancer Dolan slashed to death in the Bedford Parlour dance hall, Tank Gorrigan found bludgeoned in a close in South Portugal Street. And there were new men on the scene; men who had been mere boys when Nelson had gone to the jail they nicknamed The Place. They could find their manhood quickly in the Gorbals: a street duel, a man vanquished, and youth in a night became adult.

What he needed, he said, was a quick barney, a right good barney, to get him back into form and to let them know, the new ones, the ones who might not know, that Jamesie was back and there was no one better.

Sproul and Steedman tried to reason with him. They tried not to be too direct and didn't tell him there were other younger men who had been boasting they were ready for anybody, even this Jamesie they all spoke about, whereas before there was no one locally who ever dared talk like that. If they had told him about such challengers, Nelson would have left Marr's there and then to go looking for them. As it was, they parried with his plans, cautioning that the Busies, as they called the police, had been more active than they had ever been; there was even talk of bringing in the best Chief Constable in Britain to deal with the gangs.

But Jamesie was not for cautioning, not even when Davie Steedman

said . . . "Christ, have ye no' been marked enough?" Nelson turned on
him with a terrifying stare. He knew he was badly scarred but no one
was to say that. The last man who did had been kicked unconscious
and had Steedman not been such a loyal lieutenant he would have
been turned on too.

In the Ferry Bar, further along Rutherglen Road, the Bum's news
had its greatest effect. The brothers Steve and Jackie Holden —
Snakey and Jakey, but only to those who were their closest chinas —
had come to the prime of their fighting careers when Nelson had been
in Barlinnie. Jakey was the oldest but it was Snakey, just turned
twenty, who was feared the most. He had an unpredictable temper
and had even turned on gang mates because they had called him
Snakey.
     The brothers were the leaders of the Cumbies, a new gang named
after Cumberland Street where the Holdens lived. Snakey had known
about the prowess of James Nelson ever since he could remember.
Before he had left Camden Street School he had been involved in gang
fights and in these early battles he styled himself on the stories he had
heard about him. Eventually he had even fought alongside him and
Nelson acknowledged him as a good "sticker" and one of his boys.
Now he had heard enough of him. It was Snakey Holden they should
be talking about. And brother Jakey, even though he was a bigger and
more powerful man, encouraged his beliefs that he was the best. Bum
was bought his drink for the news . . . then they jeered at him for being
an informer. "Hey, Bum . . . d'ye ever rat to the polis?" asked Jakey
Holden.
     "No' me, Mr Holden," said Bum, slurping his drink fast. "Ah'm no'
like that. Ah've heard of some that does, but no' me. Naw, no' me."
     "Ye're a lying wee cunt, Bum. You would shop yer auld Granny for a
tumbler o' Keystone. Tell ye what, Bum. When we get Jim Nelson we'll
tell him who sent us."
     "An' he'll no' miss you when we're finished wi' him," said Snakey.
"Know how? For you'll be all he's fit tae fight."
     Snakey laughed at his jest, at the same time looking around at the
faces of the crowd that stood with them in the bar.
     Everyone of them was laughing their loudest. But the laughter
stopped abruptly when Snakey's face went deadpan. And pint glasses
quickly sloshed to eager mouths to hide the obvious change of mood
dictated by the man they were saying would one day be the next king
of the streets.
     "Right," he said. "Get the rest of the boys. We're going for Nelson . . .
Jimmy Nelson."

Jamesie Nelson was to be done. Finished. And quickly before he could get his old team around him and established again as the most feared man in the Gorbals.

Jamesie still enthused with Sproul and Steedman about the next battle. He badly wanted revenge for the last conflict in which he had received his most recent scars . . . as well as the year's sentence. "We can get two hundred. The best men in the Gorbals. Some good boys over in Oatlands as well that'll come with us. We'll get the Thompsons, the Prentices and the Shanes. And there's the Holden boys as well, Snakey and Jakey. They fought well with me at the Green a couple of years ago. Good boys them. And we'll take on the Briggait Boys and the Calton Entry . . . thegether."

He expected them to spread his intentions to the others of their "team". His first mission of freedom completed, he indicated there was some urgent business and he would have to leave. What he didn't say was that the business was a visit to the Beehive Store along the road to buy a gift for a child of which he was the father and from which one brief sighting had given him the strange and unusual sensations of tenderness and compassion. But others were not to know he harboured such gentle thoughts. With a hurried shake, the remains of his fourth double whisky were emptied into the big tumbler of ale before him and downed in a long gulp. Then he turned and left the bar, his only farewell to the others a faint nod and a mumbled "See ye'se". The world now knew that Jamesie was back. With the child in mind, he hastened his normally quick pace, a confident athletic stride, so unlike the more common short step used by others and called the "flyman's walk".

A group of children playing whips and peeries suddenly surrounded him and his feet scattered one of the upright spinning tops into a drunken demise. "Hey, d'ye know who that is?" said one of the younger boys. "Jamesie so it is." "Aye, but did ye see a' his scars?" said another as he hurried down Rutherglen Road towards Crown Street. "Big red ones, so they are. One went right down the whole length o' his face, so it did." And at that they gasped in astonishment as they stared, mouths gaping at the man who was to them one of the most famous people in the whole world. He pretended not to hear their loud gasps and shouts to one another that it was him, Jamesie, the one and only Jamesie, that was walking past. But the recognition from the children of the street after such a long absence was gratifying. Even they knew he was the very best street fighter in all of Glasgow . . . which really meant all of Scotland. And if the children of the street knew it, then it would be right.

He hurried, fast as a Cameronian, along Rutherglen Road, past South Shamrock Street, Florence Street, where Jock Wilson was king because he was the bookmaker there, to the Beehive Store where he purchased his gift, asking them twice to make sure it was well wrapped, then continued on his way again in the direction of his house in one of the tenements in Adelphi Street which faced on to the Clyde. From Rutherglen Road he turned right into the short stretch of Crown Street, which ended at the Albert Bridge. Like the rest of Crown Street, it was crammed with traders, Scots, Irish and Jewish, the principal ingredients of the Gorbals mix . . . Mary Bell's for the Woodbines and *Noon Record*, Andrew Cochrane for the Belfast and Typhoo, Paddy Devine's for the Johnnie Walker and McEwans, and Sameroff's and Lizerbaum's who would tell anyone who entered to look at their clothing . . . "For you my friend, a special deal".

It had only taken minutes for the Holdens to assemble the gang of twenty men ready, if it was necessary, to take on another group of that number, and fearless enough to take on twice that amount.

They walked in groups of six and eight, two on one side of Rutherglen Road, two on the other. At Marr's they were told that Nelson had just left and when they learned he was heading for his house they broke into a fast trot. The fox had been scented. And it was on its own . . . single-handed. But that was of no consequence to them. Honour was no part of their life. It was winning; not the way.

When they got to the corner of Crown Street, the groups had formed into one pack. They swarmed past Sammy Nelson as he spoke about the weather with the vendor and then charged across the road, causing a white-banded, Springburn-bound tramcar to slither to a screeching halt, sparks flying from the bogeys, its bells clanging desperately. A coal cart's Clydesdale reared in fright at the commotion. James Nelson, walking purposefully, looked up with a startle. He had always anticipated trouble, whether giving it or receiving it, and the first man that got to him got the the first of his instant reflexes on such occasions, the pointed toe of his boot viciously driven deep between his legs with such intensity he was instantly paralysed.

"Christ . . . it's Jamesie," said Sammy, desperately, dropping his paper to sprint towards his beleaguered brother. In an instant he was in the middle of the fray, head butting the first man he contacted. Sammy, two years younger than his brother and without his powerful physique, wasn't a fighting man. Despite that, however, he had never shirked conflict in his younger days and could handle himself well. But it needed more than that on that warm Friday in June.

The weapons were out and flailing wildly, silver blades mirroring the high sun in brilliant flashes. Clubbed from behind, Sammy sank to his knees on the cobbles. When he fell forward two of his assailants, as they would glory to their admirers later, "put the boot in". There were ten of them around James Nelson, their faces a blur as he bobbed and weaved, parried and struck with fist and feet at the seemingly endless bodies that came at him, each ferociously competing for a strike of their own at the quarry. The action momentarily froze as he recognised two of the faces, the nearest ones to him; faces that had snarls of delight on them, faces that were flushed with the thrill of the shining and brutal weapons, their beloved blades, and the power they gave them; the power to maim and disfigure and, if they fully accomplished what they had set out to do, to kill. It was in that fractional snapshot of time that he knew all was lost; if only he had gone straight home from the prison to collect a knife, or his razors; if only he hadn't wanted to make his presence known; if only he hadn't been thinking about that gift and the sweetness of the little person for whom it had been meant; if only!

"Youse," he screamed at the recognition of the Holdens, the Sheffield blades of Snakey curving wildly towards him.

"Fall . . . ya bastard," sneered Snakey as he drew his weapon down Nelson's cheek, slicing criss-cross the other scars that were there. The blade arced and glinted once more in the sun before furrowing open a long slice on his forehead, temple to temple. There was no pain as the razors carved him; there never is with razors at the time, just a cold sensation as the blood spills. The pain was always later; hot, searing hot agony along the full length of the wound. But James Nelson was never to feel those wounds, or the others that slashed across the hands and fingers feebly trying to protect his face.

The pack was in full bay now and from behind two of them with heavy joiner's hammers beat him on the shoulders and on the head. He fell slowly, first on to one knee, vainly continuing to fight back, then, when another hammer blow struck him on the base of the skull, toppling sideways, one arm still raised as though in a semi-conscious act of defence. But they still weren't finished with him. The crumpled, lifeless body had to receive the final ritual of the Glasgow street man . . . the kicking. Snakey Holden, gloating in triumph was first, followed by his brother. They weren't particular where they booted him; it was their merciless *coup de grace*, their expression of the victor's triumph and totality, the victim humbled and humiliated. And they fought with each other for just one kick, a horrific and primitive rite proclaiming that violence was victorious. And thus another generation, who knew not why, would be enslaved by the men who were the heroes of the street.

It didn't need the cries and screams of the brown-shawled housewives shouting "messin" and "bastards" and "polis" for the gang to disperse. They ran off in all directions, some towards Adelphi Street by the Clyde, others up Crown Street, some through closes to be lost in the maze of back courts. It was twenty minutes before the ambulance arrived. Sammy Nelson had regained consciousness and knelt beside his brother.

His head rested on a purple velour cushion they had bought from Jacob E. Gordon's, the furriers of number 75 Crown Street, on whose pavement he lay. A towel had also appeared and was wrapped around his face. It made him appear mummy-like, only a small area around his nose uncovered in order to allow him to breathe, however feebly. He died the next day, never having regained consciousness. The knife and razor wounds had mainly been superficial, although his face would have been horrifically disfigured. But the kicking had ruptured his liver and spleen, and they couldn't stop the internal bleeding. Mr Kyle, the white-haired surgeon, had told Jamesie's wife, Nell, that he would never have recovered from the terrible head injuries. She had sat by his bedside throughout the night and the next day, hoping against hope that the doctors might be wrong, that there would be some sign he was going to recover. She sobbed throughout her vigil, so deeply shocked at the prospect of losing the first and only love of her life that she was unable to communicate to anyone, or even accept the tea brought to her by the nurses.

About ten o'clock the following morning they folded the sheets over the swathed face of Jamesie Nelson, the news making the later editions of the evening papers, together with all the other events of that Friday, June 24, 1927: Tommy Milligan was in the final stages of training for the world middleweight championship scheduled for the following week; a Dennistoun man had been slashed; police had been called to break up a fracas at a wedding in Stevenson Street in the Calton; four men were each fined £10 after a betting raid at Parkhead Cross; the Salvation Army were looking for 320 boys to work on Canadian farms; filming had begun on Buchan's *Huntingtower*, starring Sir Harry Lauder, and everyone was singing the chorus from the story:

"See that's wet, see that's dry
I'll cut my throat if I tell a lie,
We are the Gorbals diehards."

When they first escorted Nell from the Infirmary on the hill where the first men had come to settle in the dear green place they called Glasgow nearly a thousand years previously, she was a broken woman. She had idolised her Jamesie. She had even fought alongside him in a battle at Glasgow Green, primitive and despicable to those

not of them, heroic and courageous to those who were. She had
suffered but never complained, on the nights he had stayed away from
home. She knew he was laying with other women. That was Jamesie,
her Jamesie and his ways . . . virile and dominant and she would have
had him no other way; at least she did have him and she was part of
him and that made her a queen. He had been her very own Shining
Knight and such was the warped respect for the gang fighter who at
his best had no equal, Nell had been the envy of her neighbourhood
when she had courted and married him.

The funeral was at the Southern Necropolis in Caledonia Road, its
long blackened boundary wall broken only by the impressive entrance
archway dominated by the Charles Wilson romanesque watchtower.
    With the old Gorbals Cemetery filled to capacity — "There's no'
even standing room in it," they would joke — the Southern Necropolis
became the burying place for the Gorbals people. They all ended there,
rich or poor, famous and infamous. Millionaire Tommy Lipton, the
world's grocer, had his mother and father laid there. And when it was
his turn he followed them. Old James Nelson, Jamesie's father, had
gone there in 1920 followed by Mary, the mother, three years later.
And just four years after that their son James was laid beside them.
    There were only a handful there: the big and fanciful funerals were
for the gang leaders and gangsters of other places. The Glasgow
gangster was a poor man who fought not for material gain. His fight
was initially for survival and a desire to gain the kind of recognition
that only masculine supremacy could bring amid the hodden mass that
was the Gorbals. They carried him over to the west end of the big 21-
acre burial ground to his parents' lair.
    "They keep this bit for a' the newcomers," joked Harry Connelly, a
Florence Street patter man who had been one of Nelson's corner boy
crowd. Tommy McNab, another of the same crowd, nodded a smile,
pointing to the gravestone in the next lair to the Nelsons. "The
Property of Masonic Lodge Clyde No. 408" it said. "Christ, yer man's
in good company anyway".
    When they lowered his light oak box into the dark loam and just as
the Rev Ninian Anderson got to the climax of his short service where
the men would pick up handfuls of earth to scatter in the grave,
Sammy Nelson threw two objects which clattered metallically on the
coffin lid, causing the minister to look away scornfully. They were the
faithful razors which Jamesie fought with in countless battles in the
South Side of Glasgow . . . the ones he hadn't been carrying on the day
of his last battle of all.
    The same crowd were back at the Southern Necropolis that autumn

to bury his wife Nell in the same lair. The shock of the death of the man on whom she doted had been too much for her. The only oblivion she knew from the agony of a life without him was an alcoholic stupor.

The Nelsons had lived in the Gorbals for generations. At one time there were several branches of the family but they had moved away. Now only Sammy lived on as the one direct male descendant of the clan . . . and he was away from the area. With Nell's death there were now no Nelsons left in the Gorbals.

Although Nell had borne him no children, Jamesie had fathered two girls. The first was to Betty Beggs, one of the best looking women in Rose Street. Like so many, the child was conceived in a drunken fumble in a back close, a fetid, rat-infested passage-way which led to the refuse shelters in the rear court of their blackened tenement building. To legitimise the child she had married Joe Driscoll but the baby died at six months of whooping cough.

The other child was born to Isa Lawson, a red-haired beauty and one of the few who could match the girl Beggs in looks. A month after she knew she was pregnant to Jamesie Nelson, he had received his third sentence to Barlinnie. Isa had visited him there and he had told her to get herself married. "Nothing worse than a bastard wean," he had said abruptly, coarsely. Isa, like Betty Beggs, had no problem in finding another man, despite the child she carried within her. For she was a prestigious catch; any woman who could boast they had been courted by the famous Jamesie Nelson was. And there were scores of weaker men only too eager to be with a woman that Jamesie had been with for that, to them, was something that would make them talked about; some of his shine would rub off on them. It was the way they were. And so, for Henry Baird, a pasty faced £2-5/- a week plasterer, marrying Isa Lawson, impregnated with the sperm of the man he had boasted about to others and others had boasted about to him, was an achievement that would give him a distinction he thought he would never achieve.

People would speak about him and point to him and give him some respect. And they didn't do that for being a plain and ordinary 45/-a week tradesman. The child, a girl, which Baird was to accept as his own, was born on January 25th, 1927 in their single roomed house at 188 Florence Street, and the neighbours said that she would be something in life, for not only was she Jamesie Nelson's only living child, she was also born on the same date as Robert Burns, the poet, their only poet.

When she was but a bundle, Isa took the long trip on the blue-banded tram car to the far north-eastern side of the city where the big prison was, to show Jamesie his infant daughter. He laughed when Isa uncovered the white shawl in which she was wrapped inside her own brown plaid shawl. Nelson was not a man of words. He would have loved to be able to say that the baby was the most beautiful little thing he had ever seen, which was what he felt, but sentiments like that stayed within you when you were inured to a life of violence and being violent, hardness and being hard, when even one soft or sweet expression might betray a quality that would rank with weakness and weakness was to be despised.

"Wee, isn't she?" and he laughed sheepishly again. Isa nodded and smiled. "Like a wee star, so she is . . . aye a right wee star you've got there, Isa, What are you calling her?"

"We've still to christen her, but I'm thinking about Margaret for my mother."

"Aye . . . that's nice. But I'll call her Star."

The baby was christened Margaret Star Baird and they called her Star. But when she was five and was registered for Miss Kennedy's Penny Buffs infant class at Camden Street School, her mother gave her name as . . . Star Nelson. The name Nelson had returned to the Gorbals.

2

THE UPS AND DOWNS OF A BROTHER

SAMMY Nelson was still off work with the injuries he had received in the gang attack in which his brother James died when a message boy came to the door of his house in Carfin Street, Govanhill. "You've to come and see Mr Booth right away," said the boy, fresh-faced and fourteen, like Sammy had been when he had started in the same job. "Aye, fine," replied Sammy . . . "so it's Mr Booth is it!"

William Knox Booth was fat, forty, described himself as an upright Christian and to prove it he was in the pews of his local United Free Church every Sunday, never missing a meeting of the Sons of Faith Loyal Orange Lodge. He had been in every July Orange Walk since he could remember, and they didn't come much more upright than that. But not even his wife, Ella, a leading light in the Eastern Star, the women's Orange movement, knew that he was a secret drinker, although some at work did because of his carelessness with the little whisky muskins which he drank. Ella Booth was frigid and had been for ten years, frustrating her husband to the point where his only sexual outlet was a bizarre morning promenade. He would leave home earlier than necessary so that he could walk round city offices, particularly the ones with stair entrances, lusting for the sight of the rear of a scrubbing woman exposing an expanse of thigh or knicker leg whereupon he would find a vantage point from which he could stare while masturbating underneath his raincoat. William Knox Booth, or Billy Booth as they called him at work, was one of the chargehands in Myer's, the big Argyle Street Emporium, not far from Glasgow Cross. Sammy Nelson had worked there since leaving school. And Billy Booth was Sammy's boss.

Myer's was one of the best known warehouses in the city with a reputation of having the most varied stock and offering the best prices available . . . and of treating their staff badly.Old Nathaniel Myer himself had laid down the rules. For hiring staff, there was just one condition . . . get them as cheap as possible. For keeping them . . . make them scared. Sammy Nelson had a chequered career with Myer's. When he had got the job after leaving school they predicted a bright future for him because he had a much better school report than most of the other youngsters who would come to them twice a year looking for jobs as ten shillings-a-week messengers, hours 8 till 5.30 with half an hour for a break to eat the wrapped pieces they brought with them and a cup of ha'penny tea, a service which chief accountant, Herbert MacKinnon, had proudly told the last directors meeting had provided the company with a profit over the year of £34 and 4 shillings, after wages, breakages and capital set aside for new equipment, that is, a spare teapot, canteen size.

Sammy had felt very proud to be working at Myer's for everyone knew the store and, although it was generally known about the way they treated their staff, their prices were good and, anyway, it was nothing unusual for workers to be treated contemptuously. His job as an errand boy involved running to various parts of the city for the office staff, delivering bills and invoices, receipts and circulars. After eighteen months of doing that, and still wearing the same short trousers he had worn in his last days of school, he became a junior assistant in the hardware department, being trusted to take cash from customers, fill out the appropriate bill for the goods and sending the lot in one of the cylindrical carriers which sped across the department on pulleys like miniature mountain cable-cars, to the raised cash desk overlooking the entire floor from one end of the department.

It was a great system, Sammy thought. It meant that someone else did all their sums for them and all they had to do was check the cash when it returned on the overhead carrier again. It was also the best thing Myer's had done to prevent pilfering from the big brass cash registers which once merrily tinkled away all day from each counter. Now all the cash on each floor went to one central point where one of their most trusted cashiers supervised the staff.

After hardware, Sammy spent some time in the paint department, then floor coverings, learning all there was to know about lino and wax cloth, and then being transferred back again to be in charge of the nails section in hardware. Harry McClintock had taken exception to that. McClintock was from Mathieson Street and knew all there was to know about the Nelson family. He was also a year older, had been with Myer's longer than Sammy and thought the job in charge of nails should have gone to him. So he went to Billy Booth to whisper: "Did you know about Sammy Nelson's brother? He's Jamesie, the hardest man in the Gorbals. Was him that ripped that fellow in the Gorbals Cross battle last week."

"Is that a fact?" said Mr Booth, running his right hand over his bald crown, as was his habit when speaking to staff. "The one and only Jamesie, eh! Imagine that! Protestants, aren't they?" McClintock nodded reluctantly having overlooked that vital point. "Aye, well . . . is there anything else to worry about then, Harry?" Booth looked him straight in the eyes. McClintock's face flushed and he made to leave the office. He was just about to close the door when Booth spoke again: "Eh, Harry . . . I wouldn't mention that to anyone else. You know, things like that can get around . . . might even get to the ears of the Jamesie boy himself." And he smiled as the look of terror came over McClintock's face.

The nails were kept in galvanised iron bins. When the customer asked for a quantity they would weigh them out on a pair of hanging Salter scales. Sammy had this process speeded up by using the quieter periods in the department to make up 2-ounce, quarter pound, half pound and one pound bags of the various makes of nails and stacking them neatly beside the appropriate bins. He took great pride in knowing, and letting it be known, that he had the entire stock of nails at his fingertips. He could rhyme them off, virtually without taking a breath: round plain head, round lost head, extra large head clout or felt, convex head, pipe, panel pins, round shank and square shank, plastèr board jagged shank, oval broad head and oval lost head, tile pegs, spring head twisted shank and square twisted shank flat head, annular ringed shank flat head, helical threaded shank flat head, duplex head, dowels and tenter hooks.

"See nails," he would say, "people just don't realise about them. But there's more to learn about nails than some folks learn in a lifetime. And it doesn't stop with the various types. That's just the beginning. For after that you've to know the material they're made with and the materials they're meant for. And then you've to learn to count them . . . and there's rules for that as well. For instance, see the big ten-inch round plain heads . . . well there's five of them to the pound. And the 2.5-inch, same make, has 140 to the pound. Two-inch round plain heads give you 129 to the pound, the one-inch 650 and the half-inch 6125. And unless you know all these sums it can take you ages to serve a customer." But there was little waiting at Myer's nail counter after Sammy got his simple, but effective, pre-pack system established.

News about his idea and the increased efficiency — and profit — it had brought to hardware had reached Mr Booth and when they were looking for a new canvasser for the wholesale department, it was he who recommended Sammy for the job. That promotion had enabled Sammy to be able to afford the luxury of moving with his wife Peggy away from her parents' room-and-kitchen house in Sandyfaulds Street where they had stayed since being married, to their own house in the Govanhill they had desired so much. It was commonplace for young couples to move in with either of their parents, invariably the one with the most room, a factor dictated by the number of other children they had. In their case it was Peggy's parents, the McGormans, who had more space: their single bedroom was shared by Sammy and Peggy, who used a fold-down settee bed, the springs of which had long since expired, little brother William on a thin floor mattress which was stored during the day under the other bed in the room in which Peggy's sister, Susan, slept. Mr and Mrs McGorman used the bed recess in the kitchen and never once did any of them think they were overcrowded. There were too many families round about them sharing less space.

Being promoted to canvasser had opened up a whole new world to Sammy and Peggy. His wages with sales bonuses once a month gave them earnings in excess of the average worker. That was sufficient for Peggy to be able to leave her job as a washerwoman in the Richmond Park Laundry in Rutherglen. The bourgeoisie didn't like their wives to work and Sammy knew all about the bourgeois and their ways. In appearance and speech he could be taken for one of them. He wore his new soft hat at a jaunty angle, a neat blue suit and a light fawn raincoat which Peggy had gone with him to buy and insisted that it be bought from Paisley's, the gents' oufitters where the real gents went. Sammy too knew the value of speech in his new job as representative of Myer's. But then, everyone knew the value of speech in Glasgow. The way you spoke was your caste-mark. Every nuance of the accent delineated your social status. While other accents were principally geographical, the Glasgow accent was purely sociological. Its variance was such that it catered for every strata and the educated listener could tell you within a sentence or two whether you were from an ordinary close or a wally close, whether you were scheme or slum clearance, Corporation or owner-occupier, and many could even tell Protestant from Catholic . . . all by the way particular words were pronounced. There was even a great variance of the accents within the Gorbals themselves, the lower the' social strata the more the glottal stop, water becoming wah...er. There were many with a lower order of accent than the Nelsons in the Gorbals and while his own accent had sufficed in the hardware department, Sammy considered he would do better in the shops along Victoria and Pollokshaws Roads, both wally close areas, if he had a better accent; the kind they spoke there, an accent called "pan loaf" because that was the kind of bread they ate in the more salubrious areas of the South Side, the more traditional plain loaf being the stuff of the working man and his class.

But the new accent and appearance were only a front for Sammy. For behind the adopted image, he still liked to think of himself as something of a Communist and a bit of an intellectual, or, at the very best, an intellectual Communist. In real terms he was neither. But he had read on the subject and did have sympathies with the movement which was creating a new order on the biggest landmass in the world. The little bookcase by his kitchen fireside was crammed with books on politics he had bought from the handcart book hawkers who traded in the lanes off Renfield Street. And within the confines of his own house he would often lecture visitors on the struggle of the working class, quoting his favourite extracts, although not revealing he was in fact quoting, from the Communist Manifesto. One he knew by heart was: "The bourgeoisie cannot exist without constantly revolutionising the instruments of production and thereby the relations of production and with them the whole relations of society." There wasn't a better conversation stopper: the wives in particular would look at each other and nod slowly as though they had a real sage in their midst. And when he got even more warmed to politics he would always speak about John Maclean, the man who "was Scotland's greatest ever martyr . . . for Socialism that is". What they didn't like about Maclean, he would say, was the fact he asked too many of the wrong questions. From one of the books he would pull a series of clippings on Maclean and read from them. "Wait till you hear this one from the *Glasgow Herald*. This is it! 'Bolshevism, or to call it by its old familiar name, Anarchy, is not only a disease, it is a crime, which, like other forms of morbid and unnatural offences, invariably brings a host of weak-minded and degenerate imitators in its train.'" Then he would pass round the well-fingered cuttings so that they could read it for themselves. "Aye, the wee Maclean man got the capitalist press steamed up alright . . . and there's the evidence before you about what they're like when they get steamed up."

The week after the pay increase that took him to a £3-a-week man, Myer's issued its 500 workers with the shock announcement that their wages were to be cut by ten per cent. The statement posted on all the staff notice boards said that they were being forced to make the cut because of the sharp fall in prices which, in turn, had brought down their profits. And everybody would be affected, said the statement boldly in a painful attempt to illustrate just how democratic their masters were. "The directors' fees will have an appropriate adjustment," said the announcement.

"An appropriate adjustment," repeated Hughie Donnelly, one of Admiral Beatty's veterans from the Battle of Jutland and a chargehand at the tools counter. "See when they use fancy words like that . . . that means they're up to something. You can guess fine what their appropriate adjustment will be . . . bugger all."

Sammy and Peggy were spared the worst of the blow, the ten per cent reduction bringing their wage to about the same level as before the rise he had been given three weeks previously. Nevertheless, it reminded them of the precariousness of their position in life.

Before he had gone out on the road to represent the company, Sammy had been known to many of the workers as a man with a clever political tongue and he had often expressed his feelings about the capitalists and particularly the Myer family and their enormous wealth which, he said, had come off their backs. Although he hadn't spoken like that for some time, they had remembered and when the wage cut was announced he was the first man they turned to for guidance. But without as much as telling them that he would be no party to any kind of action, Sammy dodged the issue saying he was "in a hurry". Sammy might have had his Communist sympathies but he had rationalised that they were better in his mind than his mouth: his wife and their little house in Govanhill came first. The hostility over the decrease subsided quickly and within two or three weeks it was virtually forgotten.

Then the week after Jamesie had got his third one year sentence to Barlinnie the Myer directors announced yet another ten per cent cut in the wages at the store. This time it was a real blow to the Nelsons with no recent wage increase to cushion it. Sammy had been in the warehouse at the time the notices were posted on all of the staff-room boards on each of the five floors. There was a big crowd of workers round the notice on the ground floor. Sammy pushed his way through to the front and read the announcement, going over it three times as though in disbelief at what he was learning: "The management regret that because of the economic conditions it has been found necessary to make a further ten per cent reduction from all wage earnings. The Directors of the Myer Emporium Company Ltd. wish it also to be known that this is an all-round reduction and that the Board of Directors will also be imposing an appropriate decrease in their fees."

"Bloody swines, so they are," said Sarah McColl from floor coverings. "That'll be one and sevenpence off o' my wages bringing me down to about sixteen and a tanner. Christ, that widnae keep me in fish suppers. What do you think then, Sammy?" Others nodded and repeated her question to him: "Diabolical is it no'?"

He was furious at the threat to his and his wife's livelihood. "Aye, it's diabolical . . . and a lot of other things," Sammy replied, turning to face the crowd that had gathered. "This is the typical example of modern bourgeois society with its relations of production of exchange and of property, a society that has conjured up such gigantic means of production and of exchange it becomes like a bloody sorcerer who cannae control any longer the powers that he has found to make all his magic spells. Liberty-takers, that's what they are."

This little speech was almost word perfect from the part of the Communist Manifesto he had memorised but none of them knew that. They broke into spontaneous applause when he was finished, some even cheering him for the words. "Telt ye he knew his stuff our Sammy." "Aye, don't let his soft hat kid you," said two of the men as they applauded.

"Right then, Sammy," shouted Hughie Donnelly. "Are we gonnie tell the gaffers they're not on?" They cheered at the prospect of that.

"Myer's have always told us they lead the way. Aye, in more ways than one. If they get off with cutting the workers' wages it will give all sorts of other bosses the same idea. Any stand that we take now is on behalf of the British working classes." The small assembly cheered him wildly.

"What do you want us to do then, Sammy?" asked Sarah McColl. "Strike?"

"No . . . I'm not going to use that word. They'll just sack the lot of us. What we should do is get some public sympathy . . . organise some marches with placards letting the people know. They won't like that. No they won't like that one bit."

McClintock, the clipe, was in Billy Booth's office within minutes of the meeting having broken up.

"Strike," fumed Booth. "Strike you say. There'll be no bloody strikes in Myer's."

"No . . . well . . . you see they say they are not going to use that word . . . but they are all going out to have a protest march. And they tell me that a lot of them, including Sammy Nelson, say they will be . . . taking a holiday or going sick."

"There'll be no strike OR holiday OR sickness OR demonstration OR wretched trade union activity, as I hear them call it, at Myer's. You get back there on the shop floor and keep me fully informed about what Nelson's getting up to."

Booth then ordered some clerical assistants to look out the job application files. There were three filing cabinets crammed with them and he gave instructions for two hundred names to be readied. "We might be hiring a lot of new staff," he said.

About half the staff, including Sammy, didn't turn up for work that Monday. Over the weekend they had finalised the plans they had been formulating all that week for the big demonstration march to take them from Glasgow Cross, past the store in Argyle Street, then up Queen Street to George Square, culminating at the City Chambers where they planned to meet the Labour Party Group. It would be something really rare for the staff of a store like Myer's to demonstrate and the strikers thought it would really create an impact in the city.

But others were having different thoughts on the subject. The bosses of Myer's were also at work every night that week preparing a plan of campaign to counteract the anticipated disruption to normal trading. Nathaniel Myer relished the prospect of the battle as he did all forms of competition. He gave no thought to the workers' struggle. It was just one more of the many impediments, obstacles and challenges he considered part of the daily life of being the most competitive and aggressive store owner in the City of Glasgow. The rights and wrongs of the workers' case were of no importance to him. The one thing that mattered was the success of Myer's. He had known big challenges in the past mainly from rival stores. Gromberg's had copied his tactics once with sensational advertising and had declared Glasgow's "First Huge Sale"; Myer's countered with the "Monster Sale" and stole their thunder. Simpson's thought that a great idea and six months later announced their own "Monster Sale". A week prior to the commencement of the sale, Nathaniel got a copy of their price list and published it in the weekend papers alongside Myer's specially reduced prices for the "Magic Monster Sale". It cost Simpson's thousands and Myer's profits soared. And when Woolworth's started shouting about their "3d and 6d stores," Myer's retorted with: "All the same 3d and 6d bargains are on sale in Myer's . . . 2d and 5d."

Nathaniel Myer knew all the tricks of the trade. He had come from Crown Street, one of the big Gorbals Jewish community. His father, Nathaniel Senior, had fled in one of the early Russian pogroms and at Rostock on the Baltic had bought a ticket for California via New York. Together with the other passengers he had been put off at Leith in the East of Scotland and told to start walking towards the West and California. Five days later they were in the Gorbals and never got any further. They had been befriended by the Lipton family who ran a small provision shop across the road from them at No. 13 Crown Street, and Nathaniel would often speak about his father's memories of that family's illustrious son, Tommy. "Old Dad remembered the day Tommy returned as a boy from the States where he had gone to make a fortune. He was barely twenty and came back with a hundred pounds in his pocket, riding in a hansom cab with a rocking chair on top of it as a present for his mum." As he was warming to the story he would suddenly stop and change the course of the conversation. For he rarely spoke about the Gorbals. He had made his escape from it and he would treat it as an event that had never happened in his life. His lifestyle was that of the Pollokshields and the imposing baronial mansion he had there, mock turrets, bartizans, crowsteps and all. And it was his enterprise that had got him there.

A special meeting of the directors was called for the Friday morning, Mr Nathaniel being in the chair. Suggestions were called for to meet the threat of the workers' demonstrations, but it was a new situation which the company faced and none of them had an effective proposal . . . until, that is, the chairman had his turn. "Right," he said authoritatively, "this is what we will do. The workers are going to have a demonstration as they call it. That's the message. We're going to have a demonstration. A Demonstration Sale. We'll get the biggest block advertisments we can get in the *Evening Times, News* and *Citizen,* one in the *Glasgow Herald* as well and they'll read: 'Myer's Demonstration Sale'. Beneath that, in smaller print, it will read 'Myer's Demonstrate Yet Again They're Glasgow's . . . no better make that Scotland's . . . best bargain store. All prices cut in the MYER'S DEMONSTRATION SALE . . . BEGINNING MONDAY.' "

The other directors and Billy Booth couldn't contain themselves as he read out the words for the big block advertisement and chuckled in glee at what it would do to the protestors. "Silly beggars," said Myer. "When the general public see them waving their stupid placards they'll think they're out advertising our big sale. They'll probably pull in more customers with their march than our advertisements. That's the trouble with workers . . . they're a brainless lot. But then I suppose that's why they're workers, eh?" And Billy Booth and the others nodded visibly.

The protest was a disastrous flop. And the Myer's Demonstration Sale broke all records in turnover for one day. Of the members of staff who had stayed away from work on that first day, ninety per cent turned up the following day to plead for their jobs. Only a handful were taken back. Hughie Donnelly, the Jutland veteran, was sacked but Sarah McColl, her wages down to sixteen shillings and sixpence exactly, was given her job. Sammy Nelson stayed off work for a week and didn't return until the following Monday. He was told to report to Billy Booth's office the moment he arrived.

"We had a lot of faith in you," Booth told him. "You were the one that was going places . . . then you start all this trade union stuff. Mr Myer got a full report about you and said what you did amounted to treachery. That's how bad he feels about it. Your jotters are made up, Nelson. You'd better not hang about any longer."

Their eyes never met as Booth spoke. Sammy had looked at him but he had never taken his gaze away from a pile of papers he nervously shuffled before him, rubbing his bald crown now and then.

It was still before ten o'clock that morning when Sammy returned home. When she saw him at the door Peggy knew the worst had happened. She broke down and wept. "Oh Sammy, Sammy. It's the end of our dream . . . our ain wee house. We'll have to give it all up."

And she wept bitterly again. He tried to console her with optimistic words like "It'll all be for the best" and "Don't worry, I'll get another job", but it wasn't the time for words. That week he tried some of the rival warehouses for work, thinking that his expertise in the trade would be an asset, but the word had got round the small-knit community of owners. Strikes and strikers and trade unionists were to be treated like the plague. Peggy went back to her old job at the Richmond Park Laundry, where her wages were sufficient to pay the rent in Carfin Street but little else.

"There's no going back to the Gorbals, Sammy," she vowed. "We'll stick it out here even if we starve."

"I'd have given it up had it not been for you, Peggy. But you're right . . . we're away from the Gorbals and we're staying away no matter what. Something will turn up . . . you'll see."

Just after Easter in 1927, after more than six months out of work, including a long and hard winter, Sammy Nelson returned in desperation to Myer's where he asked for Mr Booth. The clerkess asked for his name and he was more than surprised when she returned to say, "Mr Booth will see you now."

"So you've come back, Nelson," said Booth as he was shown into his room. Normally he didn't like eye to eye contact, but this time he didn't avoid Sammy's eyes. He knew he was back to beg and he was enjoying it. "Aye, and so you want your job back again. Well as you know Mr Myer would never stand for that. However, I am given a free hand in the staffing of various jobs. I'm not a vindictive man and Myer's is not a vindictive organisation. It's the contrary. We have a benevolent attitude towards staff, particularly ones who have been loyal to us."

"Mr Booth," interjected Sammy, "there'll be no more agitation. I'm finished with all of that. I learned my lesson." What he meant, but didn't say, was that the lesson he had learned about freedom and democracy, was that you could have as much of them as you liked in this country . . . but you had to keep your mouth shut.

"Yes, Mr Nelson, I suppose you have learned your lesson." He paused for a moment, looked at a file on his desk, ticking off some of the names on it. "Yes, there's a vacancy. You can start on Monday, 8.30 sharp. It's as a messenger-porter. The wages are twenty-five shillings a week," and he raised his head again from the papers to look directly at Sammy's eyes.

"Thank you very much, Mr Booth. You have my word about . . . er, trouble and that."

Just over two months later the young message boy called at the house to tell Sammy that Mr Booth wanted to see him urgently. The interview was predictable and lasted for less than two minutes. He tried to protest his innocence over the fight which had caused the death of his brother. But every single person, including the directors, said Booth, knew of the scandal. He was never to ask the company for work again.

3

A STEPFATHER PAYS THE PENALTY

HENRY Baird, the man who had gone to the altar with Jamesie
Nelson's pregnant lover, Isa Lawson, bore many of the hallmarks
of a hard upbringing in the Gorbals. He was a small, undernourished
man, his pale face accentuating vivid lips. He had long since
surrendered the merest vanity of trying to keep his thinned fair hair in
place and it straggled over the balding areas of his high temples and
the rear of his head. His light red moustache had, over the years,
grown increasingly stained in the middle from the bubbling ale he
called "special" and the nicotine from the spiky Woodbine cigarettes,
five to a slim green paper packet which was decorated with the yellow
flowers of the honeysuckle and which fitted neatly into a top
waistcoat pocket without as much as a bulge. He would smoke them
until they were so small he couldn't remove them to exhale, discarding
them only when they singed the untrimmed hairs of his moustache.

There was plenty of work in the building trade, with MacTaggart
and Mickel, John Lawrence and William S. Gordon all competing with
each other in new sites they were opening up in farmland at Giffnock,
Williamwood, Clarkston and Stamperland, southern suburbs of the
city. With overtime, Baird could earn more than £3 a week, all of
which went on his "special" and Willies, the nickname for Woodbines.
He didn't need to give his wife Isa any housekeeping money. She
worked too and it was his opinion that her wages should pay the rent
and food. Anyway, he hardly ever ate at home, his main diet consisting
of the four slices of plain loaf, corned beef on one half, cheese on the
other, which he took with him each day for the lunch break they called
dinner time. And if he felt like food after filling himself with "special"
at night, he preferred a tuppenny poke of chips from the Deep Sea fish

and chip shop in Crown Street, eating them as he swayed along
Cumberland Street to their single-end house in Florence Street.

Isa had to leave home every morning for work. She would tuck her
baby daughter snugly into her dark brown plaid shawl, wrapping it
tightly round her, then walk to her mother's house, two up on the left
in the Clock Bar's close at 37 Bedford Street. The walk meant crossing
from one side of the Gorbals to the other, from Florence Street along
Cumberland Street, down Main Street, through Bedford Lane, where
the men could hire their green Elliot's barrows to go street hawking,
and into Bedford Street, towards the Parlour Dance Hall where she
had first met Jamesie Nelson.

Isa's mother was known to everybody as Maw Lawson, for she was
the archetypal granny and the Gorbals was full of grannies and other
women who weren't real grandmothers but were called so, who
willingly took over the responsibility of rearing the children of
mothers who worked or mothers whose miniscule one-roomed
houses hadn't the space for another body. Maw Lawson was a widow,
her man Archie having been one of the 1460 sailors drowned when
the *Aboukir, Hogue* and *Cressy* went down in a Great War sea battle. That
had left her with a family of six to rear on her own. When they grew
up and left the house she helped other struggling wives of the district
by rearing their children and it gave her the greatest of pleasure to
take in Isa's daughter, Star . . . "one of our ain," as she would say. Like
she had done for other little babies she had reared, she emptied one of
the half drawers from the single bedroom's tallboy to make up a cot
for her new granddaughter. Little Star slept and gurgled her days
away in the makeshift cot atop the kitchen table while Maw, a
handsome woman, her auburn hair grey-streaked, fussed over her
kitchen range, the pride of her house, zebo-ing the grease and soot of
its day's exertions from the black cast iron facing, emerying the
stainless steel of its frame and maker's lettering, so that it sparkled,
even in the dim light of the gas mantle and in stark contrast to its
sombre and humble surroundings.

From her grandmother little Star learned her first words: "Maw. . .
Maw . . . Maw . . . that's right, that's what you call your granny. And
Da is for your faither and Mammy for your mother." And when
Frances Congleton up the stair had no further use for the many-
handed Churchill pram she had bought at Paddy's Market in the
Briggait, it was Maw Lawson who bought it from her for the three
shillings and sixpence she took from her savings of silver threepenny
pieces that she kept in her only valuable possession, an early Victorian
floral teapot given to her by her own grandmother as a wedding
present which sat in the centre of a high mantelpiece above the
range. She would fuss with her like a new mother as she walked down

Bedford Street to Main Street for the daily shopping she called "the messages". The pram saved her wrapping Star in her own shawl, the same dark plaid as Isa's. "Aye, the daughter Isa's wean," she would say to the other women of the street, whether they knew it or not. "Wee Star we call her . . . gonnie be a beauty like her Mammy so she is."

The years passed and Star outgrew the pram and, like the other children around, went out to play in the street on her own when she was three, although many were left out even younger than that. Maw would supervise her on her daily "hing", watching the world go by, arms folded at her open bedroom window. She saw the signs that little Star was indeed going to be a beauty like her mother. There were also the strong features of her father, James, although Maw preferred to overlook that and think of her as the entire image of her firstborn.

The streets and the back courts where the children played were their breeding ground. There character was revealed and there other mothers and fathers, having their own ritual window "hing", could see all the traits and manners, the signs of resilience, the fortitude and enterprise or the lack of it, of their own and other offspring. The small girls would play mammy to the smaller ones, like Star on her first unsure steps on the slabbed pavements, their playground, and later, as the years passed, she played mammy herself to other younger ones, then "shops" and "nurses" and later still peever and "beds" and "actors and actresses", pacing out across the road with each point gained in the game. The other children came to admire Star through such games, juvenile tests of awareness, intelligence and athletic prowess, for Star was always tops; she was their first champion, the one they would remember even when they were long grown up and far removed from Bedford Street and the Gorbals. They liked her too for her strength of character, never bowing to the bully—and she was always the first to succour the weak and frail, of whom there were plenty also. The older wives in their gossips after their hings would say she was "just like the faither" and they all knew who he was. "Got his eyes," they would say, and they knew that didn't just refer to their dark colour but to the menacing stare which delivered a message words couldn't equal. "Others use their eyes for seeing, Jamesie Nelson used them for penetrating," they would say. His daughter did the same, they noticed, and the hidden menace it served to aggressors had more effect than those who resorted to fists and feet.

Maw was motherly and Maw was wise and Star found it easier to confide in her than with her mother for Maw always had an answer, a reason, an explanation for the enquiring and active mind of her granddaughter.

"Maw, why is it the boys are always fighting? Are they like that all over the world?"

Maw smiled. "Well I don't know about the rest of the world, hen.
But I know that's the way of it here. It's always been the way. The boys
fight and the men fight even worse. Do you know that hundreds and
hundreds of years ago when Glasgow was just like a wee fishing
village, the boys from the Gorbals used to go down to the Clyde to
meet the boys from the other side of the river and they would stone
each other. And they're still at it, only it's worse things than stones
now. They want to show that they're men. That's their way and it's
the way it's always been here. You see, hen, you are what you grow up
among. That's the way of the world."

After she left Star with her grandmother in the mornings, Isa had an
even longer walk from Bedford Street to Govanhill, past the
screaming steam valves and the rumbling thuds which came from
Dixon's Blazes Ironworks, up the slope of Cathcart Road that led past
a row of old miners' houses called Lower English Buildings around
which there was a weeded field which was almost a breath of country,
then across the bridge which went over the main Glasgow to London
railway line. Isa worked in Duncan's Dairy at the crest of the hill in
Batson Street and had to be the first in the shop in the mornings
to take in the milk and rolls, sort out the orders for the delivery
boys, then make up stacks of sandwiches, cheese on the left pile,
gammon on the right and corned beef in the centre, ready for the
workers.
    Isa had what she said were "nice customers" as well as the ordinary
workers who came to the dairy early in the morning for their pieces
and milk and yesterday's pies and bridies. The nice customers she
spoke about didn't wear the dungarees or cloth caps of the tradesmen
and labourers. They wore suits, mainly dark blue and pin-striped,
gaberdine coats, soft hats, some with bowlers and some too with
spats, that being the sign of a real toff. Govanhill had its good end and
its not so good end, the latter being the end nearest the Gorbals and
with the standard tenement building of its neighbour suburb over the
railway line. In the good end the houses were a more substantial and
handsome red sandstone, with tiled closes and inside toilets. These
were the homes of the office workers, the clerks and book-keepers,
those who worked in the shops and the big stores, assistants and
salesmen, as well as small-time managers and gaffers and penny-a-
week collectors for the life insurance they called "industrial policies".
    Some of the families of the workers who dirtied their hands would
think of those on the other side of the district as snobs because they
had a less pronounced glottal stop than their own. And, in reverse,
some of the others would think of them as ruffians because their

glottal stop was so marked. And if a man went to work in a suit with an umbrella and a soft hat or a bowler, well he had to be some kind of a toff for that made him really different from them. Yet apart from the fact that they lived up a close which was tiled, a "wally close", the families of the men with the suits didn't really have such a different lifestyle from the others. Wages only varied slightly and if one lot were earning £2-10/- for their working week, the other lot only got about £3. But to Isa Lawson they were her nice customers and, still being an attractive woman, the occasional nice customer would say nice things to her. She would cheerfully put an extra slice of gammon into the sandwich and carefully fold it into the brown paper bag they carried so that the sandwiches didn't look like they were sandwiches.. Only the workers who dirtied their hands had that freedom. "Awfully nice of you, Isa," they would say, before the ritual "weather's terrible for this time of year".

David Russell always got an extra slice in the two sandwiches he got from her every morning. He was one of the nicest of the nice customers and got extra pleasantries as well as the extra slice. "And would you like a wee taste of mustard on them, Mr Russell?" She had worked at Duncan's Dairy more than eleven years and had known her Mr Russell most of that time. She had got to know a fair bit about him with her calculated questions, some subtle, some not so subtle, over the years. She knew he worked as a salesman, shirt and tie counter, in Forsyth's of Renfield Street, and it was nothing but toffs, real toffs, who went there and it was nothing but real gentlemen, and ladies too, who worked as assistants there. And she knew too he had nursed an ailing wife for years and that following her death Mr Russell seemed to take a new lease of life.

He was in his early fifties with an immaculately trimmed pencil moustache, wore a G. A. Dunn's guinea trilby, from the sides of which his wavy hair was attractively fringed grey, and he had what Isa would tell her girlfriends "a twinkle in his eye". David Russell lived in a room-and-kitchen in the Batson Street red sandstones near the corner of Calder Street in Govanhill. His wife, Alice, a Highland lady as he described her, had died from a stroke three years previously and their only child, a daughter, had married a civil servant who had been transferred to London where they lived. He was a man of most regular habits and every Friday night on his way home from work he would go via Victoria Road in the neighbouring suburb of Crosshill so that he could stop for a drink in the Victoria Bar, his own district being a dry area. His drink order was as regular as the time he arrived at the bar, four minutes past six o'clock. Two bottles of Whitbread, two whiskies. "Make them large ones, James," he would say to the owner, James Robertson who ran such a good shop, as they called it, that he even had his own-labelled whisky. Then he would return home and steambrush the trilby hat of which he was so proud, remembering being told by the salesman when he had bought it nine years previously that they only used the finest fur to make the felt for their hats, not mentioning, of course, that it was rabbit fur. After that he would tune in his new polished walnut Murphy "all waves" radio to the evening play on the Scottish National programme. A man of distinction and taste was David Russell . . . by comparison to so many others who lived around him, that is. He had a regular tradition on a Saturday night, too . . . one in which Isa Lawson was to be involved. He had paused outside the dairy one morning until the two customers who were inside had been served and left. "Good morning Isa," he said with a broad smile and even more of a twinkle in his eye than normal. He had, like many of the customers, called her Mrs Baird, but after his wife died it became Isa. "And what time will you finish here tonight then?" he asked when she served him his usual sandwich order.

"Oh, not till after four. Mr Duncan's missus comes down then to do a few hours till the shop shuts at seven."

"My goodness, you must be very tired after a long day like that!"

"Not at all . . . I'm still a very active person," she said, looking straight at him and laughing.

The twinkle, as Isa would have said, was there in David Russell's eyes.

"What about stepping out for a refreshment some evening then?"

"Aye . . . aye . . . that would be great. What night then?"

"Saturday . . . six o'clock at the bank corner of Allison Street and Victoria Road and I'll take you to my bar. The Victoria. Very select, you know. Don't forget then . . . Saturday at six."

"I'll be there, don't worry."

The bank corner in Victoria Road was just across from the Victoria Bar, but you never asked a lady to meet you outside a public house, even though it was select and the licensee sold his own-label whisky. Like most bars, the Victoria was mainly used by men although unlike many Gorbals pubs it didn't have the "no women admitted" sign neatly painted in white lettering above the entrance door. A small lounge, called the sitting-room, was set aside behind a partition with opaque glass where men could take their lady friends.

"My, what a lovely establishment," said Isa, pleased at her use of such a long word, when David returned from the bar with their order, a bottle of his customary Whitbread and a large whisky for himself, and a small whisky for his lady, topped up with water so that it was the same size as his unwatered double. They had two more rounds of the same drinks in the Victoria — built when the old queen, for whom it was named, still had eight years to reign — before David looked

straight into Isa's eyes and said meaningfully, "Shall we go?"
"Aye . . . fine then."

"Oh, what a posh close you have," Isa said as they entered the green
and cream tiled passageway which led to his flat on the first landing.
"Take a seat," he said pointing to the contemporary styled rexine
divan which was part of a three piece suite, then walking to a door at
the corner of the room. "My cocktail cabinet," he said, opening what
was in fact a foot-deep, seven-shelved press in which he stored bed
linen, piles of *London Illustrated* and various bric-a-brac, including one of
the new electric irons, keeping one shelf free for his drinks: a half-full
bottle of Dewars, flanked by four tall bottles of Whitbread, each with
Sam'l Whitbread's signature on the label, three half pint tumblers, and
half a dozen whisky glasses. "Dewars is my favourite," he said proudly
holding up the bottle. "Better even than Robertson's. They use more
malt in it you see." Isa smiled in agreement, although not
understanding what he meant about the malt. "You'll have another
refreshment?" And she smiled again.
They went to bed after another two drinks, Isa telling him she felt
"awful light headed".
David Russell didn't make love like Jamesie Nelson or her husband,
Henry Baird. They were rough and coarse, quick and uncaring,
pushing her from them like she was something unwanted when they
were finished. Nelson, who was strong, would repeat that process
several times in one night, taking her when he had the need,
discarding her when the need had been gratified. Baird, on the other
hand, was impotent and would push her away, cursing, before they
ever came fully together. There was never a lingering caress or a
sweet word from either of them.
But David Russell made love differently . . . slowly, softly, pulling
her even closer after he climaxed and making her feel for the very first
time that she had more to offer a man than those few seconds when
they quivered in their ecstasy. They lay together for more than an
hour after their love-making was over, gently stroking each other.
The pendulum wall clock through in the kitchen struck twelve and
Russell sat up sharply, reaching out for the clothes he had neatly folded
on the wicker chair by the bed. "Right, Mrs Baird," he said, "I'll be seeing
you down the road. I'll leave you at the Gushet at Dixon's. That be all
right?" The Gushet was the Y-junction by the ironworks which
marked the southern boundary of the Gorbals and David Russell had
no intention of going further than that. He was with another man's
wife and he had often read in the *Glasgow Herald*, the broadsheet he
referred to as "the quality paper", about the kind of things some men

got up to in the Gorbals — and so many of the stories which unfolded from the cases at the Sheriff Court seemed to be about disputes over women. He shuddered at the prospect of such violence for, although he was more manly at making love than any of the other men who had been with Isa Lawson, and she had what she said was "a good share", David Russell had never once been caught up in what he termed "fisticuffs". He had been called up in 1914 for service in the forces, a prospect which had terrified him, but he had been lucky enough to be sent to a clerks' battalion, with a posting to the War Office where he stayed until he was demobilised in 1919. Had he asked Isa Lawson to come and stay with him in Govanhill she would have done so in an instant.

That he was in fact a shallow and pretentious man meant nothing to her for she didn't see him like that. To her David Russell was posh . . . and all that meant; gentle, well behaved, nicely spoken. He lived up a close that didn't smell and in a house with more than one room, where you didn't have to sleep in a black and cramped cave in the wall. She would give anything to have a man like that. She would have had no compunction about leaving Baird. They were only together for the hours they shared their bed, Star hard by the wall because she was in first, Isa in the middle and Baird, stale ale and Woodbines, on the outside, his nightly fumbles quickly doused, his drunken staggers to the kitchen sink to relieve himself becoming more regular. It would have been good to get away from him and his foul habits, his uncaring ways and his love-making without love. Star was now twelve and it would have been good for her to escape from a stepfather for whom she cared little. But David Russell made it abundantly clear he was not for having a woman permanently about his house again. He had enjoyed being married and had grieved when his wife died. But her death had given him a new freedom, one he could never achieve when she was alive although he had tried. Because of illness she had been unable to make love for the last few years of her life; now the frustration of those days were in the past and he had vowed he would never be tied to one woman again. Women for him were the spice of his life. They were there to be had in a fashion which fitted into the strictly regulated pattern of his life. The routine never varied. He would have one, once a week. They would meet at the same bank corner of Allison Street, cross to the Victoria for his Robertson's and Whitbread and whatever the lady desired, then slowly walk to his flat.

Over the years he had formed a small circle of willing love partners, proof to the twinkle in his eye. There was Mamie McEwan, an usherette at the B.B. Cinerama Picture Hall, an attractive spinster in her late thirties who, ten years previously, had been jilted by her only love the day before they were to marry; Sadie Murray, a senior assistant in Hurry's, the busiest newsagent in Cathcart Road, a plump woman in her mid forties with enormous breasts, whose husband drove one of the ornately lettered Albions of the Glasgow Hiring Company on the Glasgow to London run; Marjorie McLeod, a soft-spoken mother of a grown-up family of four, who originally came from Stornoway and whose husband, Donald, was a greaser on the Clan Line's passenger service to New York. Marjorie was a slim, wiry woman whose sexual drive belied her appearance. She lived in the groundfloor flat immediately below his own house and would insist on staying with him until the next morning for, as she would say to him, she was as much a morning person as she was a night person. And now the latest was Isa Lawson. And she saw him, usually once a month, in rotation with the others. Their meetings and evenings of love were, despite their predictability and sameness, the highlight of her life. Mr Russell, as she called him when he collected his daily gammon sandwiches, was like no other man she had met. All he had to say, as he neatly folded his sandwich packet would be "Tomorrow night, Isa?", and she would nod with a smile. There was no need to say a time or place. It was always six o'clock. It was always at the Allison Street bank corner. And he always mentioned that Dewars was the best because of the malt in it.

Henry Baird had gone out the same night his wife Isa had one of her monthly trysts in Govanhill.

He had won £8 on a sixpenny treble he had placed with Sammy Wilson, son of old Jock Wilson the Florence Street bookie, that afternoon. He also had about £2 left from the wages he had collected the previous day. The word soon got round and the tappers were at him in the Moy. Little man was big man again, like he had been when they used to point him out for being the man who married Jamesie's expectant lover.

When the Moy bar closed at 9.30 he stood befuddled at the corner of Florence and Cumberland Streets, oblivious to the various groups of men arguing, some fighting, as they always did when they were ejected from the pubs on a Saturday night mid-way through an evening they would have wanted to continue until they and not somebody else said "no more". The cool night air helped him sober up enough to be aware that he had forgotten to buy more liquor from the Family Department, the carry-out section of the pub. A muskin of whisky and a couple of screwtops and a woman could put a new meaning to what there was of the night ahead. Oily Greig's and Red Nose Andrews, the local shebeens in Camden Street and Rutherglen Road, would be open, however. He went to them both and had more drink in the company of rowdy groups of gangrels, most of whom were the same walking paralytics he was, minds poached in an alcoholic swim, their words a blurred dementia. The only unaccompanied woman had been a shawled granny with a raucous laugh revealing vivid red gums with purply black indentations where there had once been teeth. But she would have done; she was female and he needed flesh, no matter what, flesh that he could press himself into to rid him of the urge he always had when the alcohol fuelled him to an uncontrollable intensity, an intensity that made an ugly and debauched granny desirable. He made a clumsy advance towards her, an awkward gropeclutch above her knee and she roared a fiery "dirty messin" at him.

From the shebeens he wandered to the Glasgow Green by the fetid River Clyde, the city's first parkland where a strolling Watt had got his inspiration about steam and where the Bonnie Prince had reviewed his troops before the long march north to disaster. It was a dangerous place for the innocent to wander at night. Other lonely and sex-hungry men like Henry Baird would go there for a partner of some kind whether it be a woman, and only the lowest of whores went there, or a boy or a craving man like himself. Often it would be either of the latter. Nobody went to the Green after dark for an innocent evening's constitutional. The meth drinkers would be there, purpled faces like the drink they mixed with cheap Spanish wine or the more potent fortified wine; if they could afford neither they would drink it straight like they did surgical spirits, tanner for a big bottle and a penny to the innocent boy they would ask to purchase it for them from a chemist. And groups of youths from both sides of the river would wander it on the hunt for mischief of some kind or other, mischief which invariably meant some kind of physical confrontation.

Baird didn't find the partner he sought, his frustration turning to desperation, hunter's eyes darting from one pathway to another, wildly seeking company of some kind to make his fantasies real. The alcohol began to dissipate and he could have done with more but even the shebeens were closing when he emerged from the dark and lonely park. He was just in time to get the last fish supper from Bridie Travis's chipshop at the bottom of Florence Street and he was still picking pieces from the thick, fleshy haddock when he noisily entered the house, wakening his stepdaughter, Star, asleep alone in her usual position by the wall of the bed recess.

When he kicked the door closed, he leaned back on it, savouring the hot vinegary fumes still rising from the grease-stained week-old newspaper in which his supper had been wrapped. He held it close to his face, slurping it loudly, cursing his luck at the same time by mumbling oaths over and over. When he finished he let out a loud, rasping belch, followed by another, then walked to the black jawbox sink to rid his bladder of the remnants of beer and whisky he still had in him. The fire in the small range had nearly died, but there was sufficient life in the darkening embers to cast a flickering glow over the small room. Star recoiled at the scene, the stench of the steaming urine and stale acidic aroma from his fingered meal reaching out to every corner of the little room that was their home. She turned round while he was still at the sink by the window and huddled as close to the wall as she possibly could.

"You sleepin', Mag'ret?" he roared, when he finished urinating, without flushing the remnants. He had always refused to call her Star, a name he hated as much as the name Nelson by which she was known. "Where's yer Maw, Mag'ret?" There was still no reply. "Aye, I know where she is. Away whoring again. That's where she is. Away kipping up wi' somebody. Bitch that she is. Whore that she is. Aye, that's what she is. Whore. Fuckin' whore."

He continued to speak, mainly in a mumble of curses and oaths as he slowly unbuttoned his trouser flies, then his shirt, fumbling at each button. He dropped the long grey woollen underpants he always wore then stood towards the heat of the dying embers, his hands outstretched on the mantelpiece, so that his slanting naked body could lean closer towards the diminishing heat.

The warmth aroused him and sparked the desires that had been temporarily diverted while he had been attending to other needs. Some embers slid through the grate to clank into the ashcan in a fountain of sparks and the burst of heat wafted over his body like a sensual caress.

He threw back the bedclothes so fiercely that the entire bed was uncovered, except for the portion of flannel sheet Star had been gripping tightly and fearfully under her chin. He advanced on her and pulled at the covering which she clutched even tighter.

"C'mon, Mag'ret, don't be feart. Yer Daddy just wants a wee cuddle... just like he used to when you were a wee lassie. C'mon, Mag'ret, come back a bit for a wee cuddle. Just a wee one."

"Leave me. Leave me alone," she pleaded, her voice pretending that she was still half asleep in the hope he would give up. But there was no stopping Henry Baird now. His unfulfilled drive had been rekindled. And before him was what he had desired and searched for since leaving the Moy three hours earlier.

Daughter, step-daughter, little girl, young girl, old woman, fat woman, ugly woman. Did it matter? He needed something. Anyway, she wasn't really his daughter so it wouldn't be as bad as some of the others had done; not that such rationalities mattered at that moment. She was Jamesie Nelson's daughter. Aye, Jamesie, hard man, idol of the Gorbals . . . he had shared one of his women and now here was his very own offspring. She represented all that was left on earth of Nelson. And he was going to have her.

Star recoiled with a startle at the stench of his greasy right hand as it passed over her face in what was supposed to be a gesture of tenderness, an emery palm coarsely rubbing the smooth skin of her cheeks. He had to prise the sheet from her fingers, one by one, before it came away from her and only the long flannelette nightgown covered her. She started punching and scratching and slapping at him, but Baird didn't feel a thing.

"My, but you're a strong wee wumman," he said, thrusting her arms behind her back, holding them tightly there by the wrists. The rest was easy, despite her sobs and pleas for him to go away. There was no going away. She was his, the body he had searched for to quench his uncontrollable lust, the lust that distorted and destroyed his meagre values so that a 12-year-old step-daughter was his desire. She sobbed even louder as he stretched himself over her and struggled more fiercely than she thought possible as he came at her, thrust himself between her and then, suddenly, recoiled in a convulsive shiver, emitting a loud sigh at the same time. It was only then that he let her go, rolling over on his back, eyes closed, his needs satisfied, the fire within him doused.

As he stilled, the girl leapt from the bed, crossed to the sink and washed the stickiness from her body with the net clout which always hung from the goose-necked faucet. When she had dried herself, she stood for some minutes by the sink, shaking with shock, and sobbing. Then she poured herself some water in the chipped enamel mug which always sat by the side of the sink. When she returned the mug again it knocked something which fell with a clatter into the metal sink. She put her hand into the sink to retrieve whatever it was, knowing instantly by the shape what it had been. It was her step-father's open razor, which always lay there on the bare pine wood, soft with wet rot, together with the enamel mug, toothbrushes, a cake of pink dentifrice and a potato peeling knife.

She held the long, smooth-handled razor in her hands, still trembling with shock and was just about to replace it when Baird began shouting again. "Where are ye Mag'ret? . . . c'mon back to bed. I'll no' hurt you this time. C'mon." He lay still for some more minutes before he started shouting again, this time at the pitch of his voice. "Mag'ret . . . Mag'ret. Dae as ye're telt." He sat up, the blue light from the gas standards in the street revealing Star by the sink. He jumped from the bed to walk the five paces towards her, angered at her refusal to do as she had been ordered. Star reached to her left and switched on the room's light, a single bare bulb and Baird, still naked, stopped stiffly when he saw what she was holding outstretched before her.

"Don't," she said sharply. "Don't you come near me. Anywhere near me."

"You wee bastard. Threaten me wi' that! Think you're yer auld fuckin' faither. I'll show you." And he advanced again.

There was no pain . . . yet . . . but he knew he had been marked and he sank to his knees as the girl darted round him, her right arm still upraised should he come at her again. The blood flowed from both his cheeks from ear to chin where he had been caught with the flashing blade, the first a downsweep, the second an upward swing. Baird screamed hysterically when he realised he had been cut for he had seen the Sheffield flail at him, blur-fast and he knew the result that would be in its wake.

Isa heard the screams as she entered the close mouth after having been left at the Gushet by David Russell. Neighbours too heard the screams, but sudden eruptions like that were commonplace. Just another family rammy, they thought. And no one interfered.

Henry Baird was crouched, naked and ball-like, his razored face buried in his hands, the blood oozing between his fingers and dripping on to the frayed linoleum which had once been a brown check he had carried home in a roll when they had bought it at the Kirkcaldy shop in the High Street. Isa screamed when she came into the house, Star running to her arms, sobbing out the briefest details of what had taken place. It wasn't difficult to assess what had happened. She had known about Baird's pursuits of young girls and old women but never suspected his lusts would extend to his own household. From beneath the bed recess where she kept an old suitcase full of linen she took a sheet which she tore in half and gave it to her husband to wrap round his face, helping him at the same time to dress.

"Right you," she said, leading him to the door. "Get yourself to the Royal . . . and tell the Busies nothing. Gie them a story. A gang got you in the Green . . . when you were whore hunting, dirty messin that you are." The blood from the deep furrows in his face quickly soaked the linen and she hurried him from the house, fearful he would pass out before getting treatment.

She took Star to her arms again when he left and she sobbed out more details of her experience. "Don't you worry about anything. The Busies will never know but, my God, everyone else will. Aye, their tongues will be going. Did you hear about Jamesie's daughter? Ripped her step-faither. They'll think it's great. I know . . . I used to think that way myself. And there's plenty of them that still glory in things like that. Well I don't want them glorying in what you did the night, Star." She hugged her tightly to her and they sobbed together. "Oh Christ, lassie, I wish there was some place you could go away from here."

4

THE WAR AND A SOLUTION

THE Gorbals, 1939, could be everything to every man, woman or child. It was street games, counting out rhymes and skipping choruses on the ram-finished, compressed rock asphalt streets which mirror-glistened in the rain. At the rainbow's end were the sweetie shops where swarms of children spent their farthings and ha'pennies and pennies, if they were lucky, on ogo-pogo eyes, conversation lozenges, cheugh jean candy, paradise fruits and jelly babies. Groups of men of all ages, called corner boys, talked the day away at street junctions; illegal street bookmakers openly plied their forbidden trade with their runners and other helpers, including the wife at the open window of the house by the close mouth ready to hide any evidence should the Busies arrive on the scene. Streets throbbed with noise and activity; gallus fruit hawkers and raucous fishwives; coalmen with colliers' faces like a Darkstedder chorus; knife sharpeners with their peculiar, single-wheeled barrow lathes; clothes hawkers with Santa Claus bags; tripe men with sloshing barrels of their offal delicacies; briquette sellers shouting like coalmen as they plied their steaming goods in yesteryear suits; swarthy Gizzi and the other Italian icecream men who needed no cries, for the children always announced when they were there; the firelighter sellers they called the stick men, like Darkie Marshall and his boys from Surrey Lane, with their neatly stringed bundles, tinder dry and ready to spark the morning fire; sooty sweeps and their mates enmeshed in ropes and weighted brushes, blacker even than the coalmen; trundling meter collectors called the gasmen, lopsided under the weight of their shouldered Gladstones crammed with coppers; and the bugle calls of the scrap and second-hand men scouring for the jetsam that gave them a living.

The Gorbals was public houses, more of them than any other area in all Scotland with names that intrigued . . . The Bible Class and the Pig 'n Whistle, The Grapes and The Lion, The Glue Pot and The Why Not and sufficient others for a man to use a different one each week and not go into the same one twice for more than two years; restaurants like Knotts with ham ribs dripping with the sweet, red pigmeat and dumpling, nugget brown and preserved fruit shiny with a taste that even Granny found it hard to match; dance halls like the Lochwood and The Parlour where if you were under five feet, and because of the deprivation many were, you could enter the bantam dance contests, and if you weren't that small there was a night of fun quickstepping and foxtrotting and novelty dancing the Boomps-a-Daisy and the Black Bottom hoping that by the end of the evening you would have a lumber . . . a walk home partner.

Summer nights were arms folded on cushions across the sill of an open window to watch the world go by, or as they termed it, have a "hing". It would be light till eleven o'clock and many of the children would be at their day-long games even then, darting from one side of the seventy-foot wide streets to the other in pursuit of another set of winners and losers. More would come to their windows for a hing when they heard the buskers and backcourt entertainers were on their rounds, particularly if they were the best of them, like O'Leary, Tracy and O'Leary, street slapstick at its finest, or Larry McGriskin giving his partner Eddie Gauchan the best of Benny Goodman so that he could do the best of Fred Astaire. They were all well worth the coppers they would throw down to them in screws of newspaper.

Winter nights were for the Coliseum and Bedford, the Eglinton Electric and the Wellington Palace for William Powell and Myrna Loy, Paul Muni and, of course, Jimmy Cagney, whom they liked better than anyone else for, with his up-a-close face he could have been one of them. There was the Royal Princess's for the raucous Tommy Morgan, and wasn't he the funniest man in all the world, Big Beanie himself with his rasping clarion call of "Clairty, clairty," which the fans knew meant "I declare to you". Every time he said it they would convulse with laughter.

The Gorbals was jam factories and bakeries, dye works and a distillery, blacksmiths and furniture makers, traders and tradesmen, the most concentrated stockyard of humanity in all the land, crammed together in the smoke-fouled three-storey tenements in which only the fittest survived and those who didn't shared a lair in the only place in the district in which there wasn't a building . . . the Southern Necropolis.

And the Gorbals too was Star Nelson. Star was different from the other girls of Florence Street. "She's been here afore," the older wives would say because she didn't have the shyness of the others. She was a strong robust girl who stood out from the crowd, all attributes of her father, with the dark red hair and sensuousness of her mother. Jamesie Nelson had taken on a legendary status since his death, particularly among those of violent ways, and when the word got round about that Henry Baird and his injuries, the ones who gossiped were saying, just as Isa had said they would, "I told you so" and "Just like her father".

They kept Baird in the Royal Infirmary for some weeks as the deep marks of the slashes had severed some nerve ends and destroyed muscle tissue on his face. As well as being severely scarred the damage to muscle nerves had affected his mouth which was twisted in a permanent and pathetic snarl, altering his entire appearance. Isa considered several alternatives about where to send Star when Baird was discharged from hospital. She couldn't leave home with her daughter for houses were at a premium and there was little prospect of other accommodation, her mother, Old Maw Lawson, having died. But there was always a granny or auntie in the Gorbals, or somebody who would be willing to help out for the sake of a child or two, even though it meant adding to their own overcrowding problems. But an opportunity, the like of which Isa never imagined, was to present itself as an ideal solution. Sir Samuel Hoare, the trim and wiry Home Secretary, had given the details the previous year in an announcement to the House of Commons. A committee had been appointed, he said, to "study the problems of transferring people from one area to another in the event of war and the prospect of air attacks on the civil population". Throughout the country registration schemes were established, reception and billeting offices and various committees were appointed in the rural areas for the children in cities they thought most vulnerable to attack. Glasgow was one of those and on Friday, September 1, 1939, and the following two days, 120,000 children were removed, transported and settled into houses and homes in scores of country communities where they would be safe from what they feared the Luftwaffe would do, and eventually did, to their cities.

They called it the Evacuation. Those who went were called the Evacuees, shortened to the Vacs. Star Nelson was one of them.

"You'll love it, Star," Isa had assured her the night before as they packed her small case, bought specially by her mother at the Barrows market, along with all the other items stated on the official list each parent was given: change of clothing, night clothes, house shoes, spare stockings, warm coat or mackintosh, tin cup or mug, packet of food sufficient for one day, toothbrush, towel and face cloth, comb, handkerchiefs and, if over twelve years of age, blanket and gas mask.

They cried that night in houses in the Gorbals and throughout Glasgow as mothers and fathers prepared to be separated from their children for the first time in their lives. But there were no tears at 188

Florence Street in the single-end house registered in the name of Henry Baird, hospital patient. Not that Isa and her daughter were without sadness at the prospect of being parted. But it was Star's personality which prevailed . . . sensible and calm, asking her mother the appropriate questions a girl of twelve should know about looking after herself.

"My, but you never cease to amaze me, Star," said Isa. "You've a head on you that's twice the age. I'll have no worries about you being away in the country. You'll just love it anyway. It's all fields you know. I was there once . . . at my cousin Bessie's wedding. She had this job in a big house. Wore a lovely uniform and everything. And we all went on a day excursion trip wi' the LMS. D'ye know, I never knew there were so many fields? Just one after another. You'll really love it."

Kids from Camden Street School and some of the other schools round about were to go to Sanquhar, Kirkconnel and the little hamlets that surrounded them in Upper Nithsdale, Dumfriesshire. Isa, like most of the mothers, had never heard of Sanquhar, the principal town of the area. "It's in Dumfriesshire," explained Miss Kennedy, one of the head teachers, adding, "That's in the south of Scotland you know. It's a lovely place. The River Nith flows through it." But none of them had heard of that either.

The big steam engine, the kind the train buffs called a 4-6-0, clanked slowly and noisily along the long single platform of the Sanquhar station as Willie Waugh, the porter, or head porter as he told everyone, as well as deputy stationmaster, roared the name of the station at the arriving train. "Song...cherrr, Song...cherrr." This was the Lallans way of saying Sanquhar, although Willie made the last part sound as though he was clearing his tubes for a bronchial expectoration. Mrs Jane Fordyce, wife of Colonel Mitchell Fordyce, ex-Ayrshire and Dumfriesshire Yeomanry, venerated local gentleman and veteran of the World War and before that the Boer War, was there on the platform, rosy-cheeked and excited at what she called her "big day". She had been preparing for weeks. It was the culmination of the biggest operation they had in the area, bigger even than the committee work of the annual Riding of the Marches, of which she had twice been president. Mrs Fordyce, whom they fondly called Lady Jane, had been appointed by Town Clerk William Ker, one 'r' being the Sanquhar spelling, as the Billeting Officer for the area. Town Clerk Ker, a paid Local Government servant, was technically in charge of the operation as the official Reception Officer. But if he was the Commanding Officer it was Lady Jane who was the officer . . . in command.

As she told everyone, her job was fully spelled out in the Government's new emergency regulations. "Part VIII actually," she would say with great pride, "of the Civil Defence Act of 1939 and authorised under the regulations passed under the Emergency Powers (Defence) Act." And in these trying days, as she had told Mrs Robert Dalgleish of the former colliery-owning family who now had their own estate at Mennock, it was indeed a very responsible role. She knew the regulations off by heart. "The persons selected as billeting officers were to be as far as possible persons known to the householders in the district and possessing an intimate knowledge of the district." And, as she emphasised to Mrs Dalgleish over afternoon tea at the Temperance Hotel, "Well, they certainly had people like myself in mind when they wrote out this Act. I'm known in every house, from the smallest of cottages to the ones of our dimensions, from Thornhill up to the Ayrshire march." She went on to detail the statutory provisions of the reception and billeting officers' roles, a litany she had repeated daily to ensure that, in fact, they had done everything to make their big day a great success:

"That the station and its approaches were cleared; that first aid staff and equipment were available; that persons were to be present to take groups to the billeting officers and to assist in carrying luggage and to aid young or sick children; that schools and halls should be used to shelter the evacuees until billets were settled; that evacuated children were supplied on arrival with hot food or drink and that voluntary agencies were enrolled to undertake the work; that the appropriate number of persons was sent to each billeting district; that the 48-hour emergency rations forwarded by the Government to each detraining station were distributed to evacuees".

The Red Cross Voluntary Aid, the Women's Voluntary Service, the special action committees of eight churches, the Boy Scouts and Girl Guides, scrubbed and crisp, were on the platform and in the school hall was the Women's Rural Institute, with Desperate Dan teapots, hillocks of shrimp paste sandwiches and proud sponge cakes that only country wives could make, all set out on trestle tables they had kept out from the church league's badminton dance the night before. And at the head of all her troops was Lady Jane. She held out her hand to the first party of teachers to detrain with a "Welcome to the Royal Burgh of Sanquhar. We're so pleased to have you and to be such a vital part of our country's war effort."

"Carry your case?" laughed the Scouts and Guides, friendly-like, and their young guests gripped their luggage tighter and closer to them for Mammy had said they weren't to leave hold of them and, anyway, they would probably run off with them if they handed them over. They would in the Gorbals.

After tea and Sharp's locally-made lemonade, the evacuees were divided alphabetically for distribution throughout the town, some to the council scheme off the Dumfries Road, some to the handsome villas and sandstone terraces on the Glasgow Road and in Queen's Drive, with their own names in gold letters on the fanlight window above the vestibule door. One group was directed to Johnny Beith's Fordson bus, the same one he used for the service up the steep hills to Wanlockhead and Leadhills: if too many were on board, half would get out and walk the steepest stretches or else the old bus wouldn't make it. The bus party of evacuees were destined for the farms and country houses that had applied to take them.

The first of them were dropped off at the dairy farms that dotted the gentle slopes of the Nith with sheltered pastures and dark grass which swelled the big bags of the high-horned Ayrshires. After that the old bus climbed to the higher meadows of the mixed arable farms where nicky-tam men walked deliberate steps behind sweating Clydesdales that furrowed and harrowed and patterned fields which yielded Arran Pilots and Golden Wonders and bronzed oats. The last group went to the furthest farms, high on the hills where whaups soared and only the mottle-nosed Blackfaces grazed.

Glenmulloch was at the furthest end of the parish in the shade of the high and dominating Corsincon Hill, the most northerly part of the long and broad dale. It was one of the five farms on the Lydeburn Estate, owned by Colonel Fordyce. They were High Mulloch, lonely and isolated, reached by a grassy track called the Old Lime Road, where they reared 2000 Blackface ewes which they crossed with the aloof Border Leicesters for a yearly crop of fat lambs; Glenmulloch, on the shoulder of Neviston Hill; Laigh Mulloch, by the river; High Shiel, on the other side of the valley, and the Home Farm, which saw to it that Lydeburn House got all the provisions required for people of their station in life, great friends that they were of the Duke and Duchess and once even having the Prince himself, the one from London, as a house guest. That's how important the Fordyces were.

Mrs Annie Cameron, the wife of the Glenmulloch's tenant farmer, Wullie Cameron, stood at the entrance to the farmyard, her white hair thin and willowy, flying in the breeze, her fresh apron flapping. "So you're our vac," she said to Star when Jenny Milligan, one of the assisting billeting officers, led her from the bus, requesting Annie to sign the official form which would ensure she got the stipulated ten shillings and sixpence a week allotted to the ten to fourteen year olds for their maintenance.

"Do they call you Maggie or Meg?" the farm wife asked when she looked at the name on the big label pinned to the girl's coat.

"No . . . it's Star," she replied smiling.

"Oh, michty me," said Mrs Cameron. "I didn't read the label properly. Margaret Star Nelson. Goodness, that's a right fancy name you have. But you're a braw lassie just the same. And how did you get your, name?"

"Well, you see it was supposed to be Margaret but my father said he liked Star. I was just a baby when he died so they started calling me by my middle name . . . Star."

"And you're twelve, Star? You're a fine big lassie for your age. You'll get plenty to do about here for there's always work to be done on a farm, you know. That'll put some colour on your face. You can always tell the Glasgow folk. A' white faces. Must be awful bad air they have up there."

She led Star into the house, past a scullery and a walk-in pantry to the big kitchen, stone-floored and warmed by a long range on top of which sat a shiny black kettle with a long spout trailing two feet of steam. Star had never been in such a large room and looked round in wonderment at its dimensions. Mrs Cameron showed her the rest of the house, a door from the kitchen leading to a long hall, off which there was a bedroom, and two public rooms and a bathroom with a bath that was even longer than the ones they had in the public bathhouse in the Main Street, Gorbals, and with taps that surely must have been made for a giant. A generous staircase with a half-way landing over which there was a stained-glass window led to the four bedrooms and second bathroom and boxroom which occupied the top half of the house. "Aye, it's a big house, Star. O'er big for Wullie and me and Wull the grieve who lives in the bothy at the back of the house. But it's what comes with a place like Glenmulloch and you just have to put up with it. What's your house like in Glasgow?"

"Well," she paused thinking of an appropriate answer. "Well, it's just a wee house Missus. Nothing like this."

They sat by the kitchen range and gossiped, finding out about each other. About an hour later the loud grating of tackets on stone heralded the arrival of someone. Star looked up with a startle when the latch of the kitchen door lifted with a crack and a big man filled the doorway, his enormous boots grinding on the stone floor. He had a horned shepherd's crook in one hand and at his feet was a fussing collie looking up at him with affectionate eyes. She didn't know what to make of the scene for, at first appearance, he looked like the tramps she would regularly see in Glasgow, the skip of his dirty cloth cap unfastened and pulled low over his eyes, his old waterproof coat torn and grease-stained down the front and tied with hairy, coarse string, one end of which hung loose. Above his boots, which had peculiar upturned toes, he wore canvas gaiters which, like his trousers and the bottom of his coat, were soaking wet. He was a tall, gaunt man with a three day growth of grey grizzle and when he took off his cap the white of his forehead contrasted with the deep tan and windburn of his face. Star Nelson had never seen a working hill farmer before.

"Well, mistress," he said, "what do we have here? A lassie be God. They might have sent us a laddie. Plenty of work about here for a boy." Then his mood of mock seriousness broke and he let out a loud guffaw of infectious laughter and in an instant Star felt relaxed and somehow, strange though it seemed to her, at home. Mrs Cameron introduced them. "Star!" roared the big farmer when he heard her name. "Oh tae dang . . . I've never heard the like." Mrs Cameron chastened him for his gibe. "Well lass," he said. "ye'll be something special wi' a name like that."

Wullie Cameron was a man of the hills. His father had been a small farmer from Sorn in Ayrshire and had come to be the tenant at Glenmulloch when Wullie was a schoolboy. And when the father died, Wullie had taken over the tenancy, marrying Annie Eadie, the daughter of a neighbouring farmer. That had been twenty-five years ago and in that time they had never left Glenmulloch, except for trips to Ayr, Kilmarnock and Thornhill, their market towns.

Joking about his rheumatics, Wullie Cameron eased himself into a battered wooden armchair by the fire, stripping off his dripping gaiters and heavy boots to change his socks. Normally he spoke in the broadest Lallans, more broad than even his wife could understand at times. But he modified his speech for the new member of the household. "So ye're from Glasgow, lass. They tell me it's a big place. But I couldn't be doing with it. I'd get lost. Have you ever been on a farm before, Star?" When she said she hadn't he laughed in mock disbelief saying, with impish wonderment, "Imagine that. Oh well, you'll find plenty to interest you here lass. We might look a' nice and peaceful from the road end, but I'm telling you we never stand still. D'ye ken how tae make tea? Right then, make Wullie here a big mug o' it. And watch you don't scald yoursel'." He roared with his infectious laughter again after making a joke about his house being full of women and, as they shared the joke with him, Star felt she was in the company of a couple she had known a long time. She was going to enjoy her stay here at Glenmulloch.

Star had learned in her talk with Mrs Cameron before her husband had come in from the hill, that they had had a daughter whom they had also christened Margaret but she had died at the age of five with meningitis, despite the heroic efforts of Wull, their worker, who had run the five miles down the railway track to Kirkconnel for the doctor. Margaret had been their only child.

Sanquhar and Kirkconnel and all the other rural areas had never known the presence of so many children during those first few days of evacuation. But it was not to be that way for long. Within days they were streaming home to Glasgow again, Hitler and his bombers or no.

And before Christmas of the year war was declared more than thee-quarters of all the evacuees were back in their cities. The best laid plans of the Government had gone very astray, merely because they had overlooked one human element. It was called homesickness. They returned for a variety of reasons, from the imagined to the unimagined. They said the country boys had picked on them because their accent was different, which was true in some cases. They said they didn't like the strange food, even though it was more wholesome, served up by their temporary foster parents. Others missed the teeming streets and the games of the city suburbs. And one wee girl, sent to one of the farms, became terrified of the country at night time . . . for never had she experienced darkness like that before: black, black dark so that when she opened her eyes in bed it seemed even darker than it was when her eyes were tightly shut. It was never like that in the Gorbals with its all-night street-lamps and Dixon's as their permanent beacon to light and brighten up their long nights. Anyway, home is home even though it was up an uninviting and smelly close and you slept three, sometimes more, to a bed in a hole in the wall.

Life on the farm fascinated Star, despite the rigours of that first winter and the long walk she had down the farm track, past a creaking giant of a sycamore they called the beggars' bush, a glen with a burn that roared and where eerie owls hunted, to the road end and transport for school. Their way of life and methods of farming hadn't changed very much since Burns's time. The houses were lit by oil and fuelled by windfall wood and coal and they depended on horse power for ploughing and planting, harrowing and harvest, carting and carrying and for getting the huge woolsacks from the year's clip to the rail terminal and back, the best part of a day's ride.

Before breakfast in the spring and summer months she would go to the high meadow, in the middle of which was the spring that supplied them with water, to catch the horses for their day's work. With her she would take a rope halter and a small bucket with some oats. The horses were Nell and Bell, a pair of Clydesdale mares with contrasting personalities. Nell was gentle and always willing to work and would always come first to her for the bucket of oats, even though she knew that the halter would be put over her head and she would be led back to the farm for the day's work. Bell, a bigger horse, was obstinate and aggressive and would shy from the oats-bucket for fear of being haltered. However, if Nell was led away, the other horse would meekly follow, for even pulling the Bamford reaper was better than a day in the high meadow without the company of her companion. Wull Andrews, the grieve, had taught her most of the duties in the stables and she would dress Nell, her favourite. She knew the appropriate harness, whether for shaft or trace, and would stand on a stool to lift on the heavy saddle for the ridge ties which took the weight of the shafts, then throw over the back and loin straps, the bellyband and the leather halter with the split bit, leaving only the collar for Wull to put on, an awkward job as it had to be turned upside down and pushed high over the horse's head, turning it the right way round by the tips of the hames.

Spring was different in the country. In the Gorbals she had never remembered seasons; the children of the tenements, where no grass grew, no flowers bloomed, only remembered their summers for that was the time they didn't go to school. Spring at Glenmulloch was a great physical experience, the green returning to the grass, the birds breaking their long hibernal silence, the sombre greyness of the preceding months giving way to a magnificence of colour at every turn, highlighting the great beauty around them.

It signalled an end to her first winter there. It had been one of the harshest in Upper Nithsdale for years, the cold being of an intensity which she had never known before and which had been tempered only by the presence of snow and the new appearance it gave to the countryside around them, transforming Corsincon to a magical Alpine slope and the triangular Kirkland Hill to a miniature Matterhorn. The snow storms of January had been so fierce that when they opened the back door to the cobbled yard one morning there was such a solid wall of snow the men couldn't clear it . . . so Wull Andrews tunnelled through it to get to the byres and the rest of the steading. The first of the lambs, from the sheep that grazed in the low-lying pastures near the river, came not long after the end of these great snow storms.

At that time of the year Wullie Cameron spent every minute of his waking day with his flock till the last lamb had been delivered, often staying the entire day on the hill, returning home in the gloaming, man and dog stiff and soaked with the cold and rain. Star attended her first birth of a lamb in the field they called the park, immediately next to the steading and reserved for animals likely to require attention. It was a gimmer and it was common for them, being their first-born, to have complications, needing the shepherd as midwife. Wullie had caught the ewe gently by the neck with his crook, keeping Major, his dog, well back. "Right Star," he said, "you can haud her by the han'les . . . the horns, lassie, that is unless you feel sick for if you haven't seen this afore that's just what you might be." But she wasn't. Instead she seemed to feel a communion between herself and the dignified suffering of the ewe whose head she cradled between her knees as Wullie Cameron pulled the messy bundle from the sheep. They looked at each other and laughed as the spluttering lamb caught its first breath in the sharp air, letting out a squeaky bleat. Later she was able to deliver the occasional one by herself and to help in the byre when the first cows calved that year.

At the weekends and school holidays she would willingly join in the rest of their labours, learning each one in turn: hoeing turnips, kneeling behind the drill plough at the potato harvest, driving Nell from the wide metal seat of the hay rake, getting the long lines of gathered hay as straight as she could, building the ricks, treading the rucks, tying corn sheaves, stooking them, milking, separating, making butter in the end-over-end churn, getting the Wyandottes and Leghorns to come running to her biddy-bad-bad and not being scared to thrust her hand beneath menacing cloakers for their eggs.

But the best days of all were in the late spring and summer when they were out tending the sheep on the heights of Glenmulloch Hill. The peewee and whaup chicks would have stopped their comical scurrying from before their feet and would be on the wing with their parents, the one flapping frenetically, as was their way, the other gracefully soaring and sounding the loud haunting call, a music that was the very spirit of those high and lonely moors. It was a hard slog, climbing more than 1200 feet from the farm to the summit of the hill, broken only by rests when Wullie Cameron stopped to give instructions to his dog, Major, strange words of command which Star herself was to learn: "Kim-meer-'way-bawk oota-that." "Que-hey-tae-me-hurr." "Stawn. Stawnstill." "Kim-min-tae-me." "Kim-meer-'way-oot." "Kim-in-by."

But Major wasn't a brilliant sheepdog and between commands there would be lots of swear words as well, which was unusual for he wasn't a swearing man. He only cursed at the animals and when he did it was, it seemed, excusable, for he did it with great relish and enthusiasm, uncaring who might be there to hear him. "They're no' the worse for a guid sweerin," he would say to Star. "Aye," he would add, " and a guid stick across their backs as well." He disdained the shepherds who used whistles, mainly because when he had tried one himself it had only confused Major, and that led to an extra swearing for running the sheep the wrong way.

Star wore wellingtons and waterproof trousers for these long patrols and used to lament that she didn't have a pair of Johnny Souter boots with the upturned toes that the farmer wore, made specially for the high moorland men as an aid to their long and arduous uphill marches. From the summit of Glenmulloch they could look north-east over a vast empty moor which went all the way to Muirkirk and the

Moss where the Covenanters slew Richard Cameron, the man from whom the Cameronians took their name and who, said Wullie when he told Star the story, was a distant relative of his. To convince her that it wasn't one of his more fanciful tales he added by way of proof, "Now that's a fact, lass, for the auld faither," meaning his dad, "telt me his sel'." They wouldn't wait long at the summit of the hill, only going that far to check the fences and that none of the flock had wandered or stravaigled as Wullie would say. They would then descend the steepest part of the hill to the Old Lime Road, a rugged track carved out of the hillside more than a century before by the lime quarriers and now just a sheep trail. There was a trough there where the big farmer had his customary rest when "at the hill". There he would light one of his Gold Flake and contemplate the beauty of the gracious valley of the Upper Nith he loved so much.

"D'ye know, Star, I've never been to Glasgow and from what they tell me I've nae notion. I've never been to Edinburgh or Carlisle. The markets at Kilmarnock and Ayr and that's the furthest I've been. But d'ye see everything afore ye? Well I ken and am kenned in every house as far as the eye can see in a' directions." And he would rhyme off the farms of the valley going down the Eastern ridge, pointing his long ash crook till she knew exactly the spot to which he was referring. "Knowehead, Hillhead, Neviston, Samiston, but the Lethans and the Clocklowie are out of sight behind that hill, then there's Laigh Cairn and the Cairn Smiddy down there by the river, and further on Nether Cairn, Nethertoun, the Rigg, the Lagrae, Kirkland, the Vennel and ahint the trees by Kirkconnel is the Tower and coming back the other way you have Corserig, but out of sight, Crockroy wi' the Deil's Dyke running by it and it's that auld naebody knows who built it, High Cairn, Marchburn, and Overburn, then Burnton and the three Polquhirters and they last ones are all in Ayrshire. They're different up there in Ayrshire. One year one of them had snow on top of his hay rucks! Just imagine that?"

Often the morning mist would still be lying over the twisting Nith, a long string of cotton wool waiting for the first zephyr of the day to disperse it, and the scene took on an almost ethereal proportion. It was a beauty the like of which Star Nelson had never seen before and never knew existed. She would gaze on it fondly and lovingly till Wullie Cameron took the last deep pull of his cigarette, nipping the butt and putting the remnants in his waistcoat pocket for a minute smoke sometime later. "C'mon lass, there's a lot to be done back at Glenmulloch." They had tasted their beauty, but it was not for the feasting.

5

LIFE IN THE HILLS

AFTER three years the tiny number of evacuees who had stayed on in Upper Nithsdale had become so much a part of the local community they were consumed by it and hardly anyone thought of them as "vacs". The three years at Glenmulloch had changed Star. She had arrived from Glasgow aged twelve and a half, with the same wan face and tight suspicious mouth as the others in the party. Now she was nearly sixteen. Life on the moors around Glenmulloch had quickly dispersed the pale complexion, her cheeks had a highly flushed sparkle like those of the other country girls, her skin smooth and golden-tanned. The drawn mouth had vanished and in its place a wide smile from a generous and attractive mouth, retaining only some of the gamin influence of the Gorbals. She was big for her age and the hard physical work in which she had so eagerly participated had given her a strong, upright physique, her femininity displaying a shapely figure, her ample and firm breasts giving her the appearance of a girl much older.

She had grown to love the Camerons as much as she did the country and thought of Mrs Cameron as a second mother. In fact, she wished her own mother could have been like that. Isa could be as coarse as the coarsest in the Gorbals She loved what she called her "wee refreshment" and she even smoked, uncaringly, in the street, and Star heard what they said about women who did that. Her mother would speak often nostalgically about the "good old days" when she was young and the envy of all the young men, the fighting young men, at the Tripe and the Parlour and the Lochwood dance halls, and how she had always been dressed in the height of fashion, even though, in fact, her style had been a cheap and gaudy mockery of what the real fashion was. Other than that, her conversation would be limited to gossip related to her work at Duncan's Dairy. And when it came to tea time it was only rarely that anything was prepared and anyway, she would say, a plate of Knotts pigs trotters and cabbage was better for you than any wife on the street could make.

Mrs Cameron, on the other hand, was homely and gentle and her recollections were of the happy times when they had their own baby daughter and of the great days they had at Glenmulloch in the past when gangs of men would come for the shearing and the hay time and the corn harvest and what great characters some of them had been. Although it had all been hard work with long hours on such occasions, they were what made her happy memories, and as a housewife and cook she would display all the pride that had won her prizes at the Ayr, Thornhill and Castle Douglas shows. Despite the fact that she had lived on lonely farms all her life Annie Cameron could speak to Star about a wide variety of subjects. She was an avid radio listener, their pitch battery and glass accumulator set invariably tuned into the Home Service, and she never missed a line from the two newspapers, the *Dumfries and Galloway Standard* and the Saturday edition of the *Glasgow Herald* which postman Sam Grieve brought with the mail and the gossip on his heavy-framed Post Office Coventry just when he knew the tea for the break was being poured.

"What did you think we would be like in the country, Star?" Mrs Cameron asked her one day, "I bet you thought we would be an auld bunch o' loons."

"You know, I didn't know what to expect. The only thing I can remember thinking about the country before I left was that it had grass and fields and cows because they were all in our primary picture books and we would draw them and the best of them would be pinned on the classroom walls. It was a real mystery to me and after three years I'm still learning. What I did find out right at the start is how much more the young people know about life, the real life that is, about nature and the things that are really important. In Glasgow it's other things we're concerned with, things that don't really seem to matter once you're away from them . . . it seems to be always about other people, about who is a bad one in your class or up your street, about the devilment someone is up to, about rammies up the stair or who is wenching who . . . "

"Rammies and wenching!"

"Aye, you know, a rammy is when they're having a big squabble and wenching . . . Mrs Cameron, you must know about couples wenching . . ."

"You mean courting?"

"Aye. You see, we even have different words for things. I'll never forget the time when I first came and you asked me if I was starvin' and I said no, that I wasn't hungry and you laughed for you meant was

I cold. Aye, as I was saying, it's always people we seem to talk about and things they're getting up to."

"I suppose you miss all the picture halls and dance halls they have in Glasgow."

"I used to miss the pictures, but not any more . . . I'm getting like you, I like the plays on the wireless. But I never went to the dancing . . . I was only twelve-and-a-half remember?"

"So you were. But you would be going now."

"No."

"What way?"

Star's face flushed and she took a seat at the kitchen's big dining table which had just been given its daily scrub. Mrs Cameron looked at Star anxiously. "Are you all right lass? . . . My, you look as if you've had a turn. Is it your . . . ?"

She had never spoken about her stepfather to the Camerons. When she had first come to Glenmulloch and Mrs Cameron asked about her parents she would avoid him by concentrating on her mother and how she worked in a dairy and that was great for she brought home big bags of broken biscuits which she would take to school with her to share with her friends. When Mrs Cameron had been more specific once and asked about her stepfather she answered briefly, "He's no' well." The three words spoke volumes and Mrs Cameron understood there was something in the background which she didn't want to discuss. Being the understanding woman she was, she never asked again. There were other occasions too when an innocent question rekindled the memory of that dreadful night over three years ago. There were invitations from boys at school and on nearby farms to go walking together, one of their ways of initial courting in the long light of the spring and summer nights. She would have loved to accept such invites, even the one from Tommy Walker of Tamsmiddy, gossip that he was. But the prospect of being alone with a young man, lads that they were, terrified her. She had wanted to tell Mrs Cameron but there had never been the appropriate opportunity to take her into confidence; at least she kept telling herself that because of her reluctance to speak about the most terrible moments of her life. Now there was that chance again, the tension of the occasion was almost too much for her. Mrs Cameron's comforting arm around her gave her the assurance she needed and in an instant she became composed again.

"Well Star, is it your . . .?" Mrs Cameron repeated.

"No. No . . . nothing like that. I'm sorry. I just felt a little faint, that's all. It happens any time I think about it and when you mentioned about me going to the dancing it all came back again. Forgive me. I know it must all sound so terribly mysterious. But it was something which happened to me before I became an evacuee. It's to do with my stepfather."

She went over the story . . . slowly . . . calmly . . . not missing any of the detail, even the things that previously she would have been terrified to think about, let alone discuss. "You know, I've never been able to do this before, not even to my mother . . . she gathered what had happened because she arrived home when she did, but we never spoke about it afterwards. I've so much wanted to tell someone, not just anyone but someone I could trust . . . like yourself. You've no idea what this has meant being able to tell you everything. All of a sudden I feel different, as though I've lost the most worrying thing in my life . . . as though I've been . . . " She paused, trying to find the appropriate word. "As though I've been . . . purified. Would that be the right kind of expression?"

"No my dearest . . . there's nothing about you needing purified. But I know what you mean. You feel cleansed of the whole nasty business. Star lass, I've never heard such a story, especially from someone as young and good as yourself. The world has a queer way of working and if the good of the earth got what they deserved — and the bad ones as well — then it would be a much better place. But that's no' the way it works and it does make it difficult to keep accepting what they tell us on a Sunday. Anyway, you've your life to live. The past is the past and you've dwelt on it long enough. I'm sure what you've told me today will lighten your burden. You've a wise head on you and I know you'll no' be letting it affect you like it has anymore."

The latch on the kitchen door gave a loud crack, startling the two women whose minds had been diverted from the normal activities of the farm. Major, the collie, burst through, as he always did, followed closely by his master. Mr Cameron was soaked to the thighs as usual from the wet marsh grass on the hill and his heavy nailed boots scraped noisily on the stone floor of the kitchen. He was in his normal jovial mood and laughed loudly when his wife scolded him for his appearance. "Wullie Cameron, you're an awful sight. You havenae shaved this week and it's Friday."

"Dae ye think the yowes would ken?" he laughed back. At that moment a fiddle music programme came on the radio and he deftly turned up the volume. "Come on mistress. Let's show the lassie how good you are at the Gay Gordon." Mrs Cameron and Star shrieked with laughter as he spun his wife into the impromptu reel, the sparks flying from his Herd Laddie's tackets. "Never mind mistress," he said, "I'll have a shave the night so that even Lady Jane would think me the most handsome farmer in Nithsdale."

Star Nelson had never returned to the Gorbals during those three years, although her mother faithfully came to visit her every second month, bringing little parcels of clothing she had bought at Paddy's Market or the Barrows Market where you could get second hand dresses for a few pennies. She would relate all the local gossip about schoolmates and relations, but never mentioned her stepfather, Henry Baird, except to say they were still trying to get him into Hawkhead Hospital which everyone in Glasgow knew was for mental defectives. There were lots of wounded Servicemen arriving back home, however, and they were being given preference for all hospital places.

Baird was now a pitiful character. The deep scars on his face were as viciously raw as the day he received them and so terrible was the sight he presented that if he spoke to children they would run screaming. He spent his days walking the streets, talking incessantly to himself and would often go to the Green to seek the company of the derelicts and to drink whatever concoctions they might be having, more often that not fortified wine mixed with surgical or methylated spirits. The alcohol and the beatings he had received over the years as a result of thwarted sexual depravities had scattered his brain and although he was barely forty, he had the appearance of a man twenty years older, his mind having reverted to that of a child. But for better or worse he had been betrothed to Isa Lawson and she did what she could for him, living in the hope that they would finally admit him to an institution. She had tried to raise the subject on her latest visit to her daughter at Kirkconnel. They had met, as usual, at the station and gone across the road to the Commercial Hotel for tea and scones, there not being enough time to travel to Glenmulloch and back. She mentioned the difficulty over the institution, adding, "But when we do get him in you can come back to live in your own home again." Star looked away, too embarrassed to reveal her thoughts on the prospect of that. She was due to leave school later that year and was on course to gain her Leaving Certificate for two Higher and two Lower subjects. Star changed the subject quickly to speak about her schooling. "My goodness," said her mother, "imagine you staying on a' these years at school" and once more reminding her that she had left at thirteen.

"You know," Star suggested, "I could get a job about here if I wanted. There's plenty of work on the farms . . . all sorts of jobs like being a dairy maid, or working in one of the houses. It's great fun working with the dogs and the horses. And Mrs Cameron has been teaching me how to cook and bake."

She had been going to say that she didn't want to return to the Gorbals and Glasgow to live, but changed her mind for the sake of her mother's feelings.

"Well, we can talk about what you're going to do some other time," said Isa. "There's no hurry for that. But just you mind. Your hame is your hame. And hame's the best they aye say."

One night, the week after her mother's visit, Mrs Cameron announced that she should look out one of her better dresses for they were wanted at Lydeburn to help with the harvest. There had never been a harvest in the big paddocks and parklands around the estate house before, but the Ministry of Agriculture, as part of the grow more food campaign, had ordered that fields which had never been touched by the plough before should be planted. Mr Cameron was ordered to put a crop of oats on a high meadow that bordered on his hill pasture and had laughed at the idea of growing corn at such a level. But it had worked, despite the job they had trekking up there with reaping equipment and having to haul the harvest down to the steading. It was the same with the fields around Lydeburn. They had been merely decorative until now, grazing leggy riding ponies. One of the parks featured the Colonel's favourite Highland cattle, long horned and shaggy and something of a joke with the local farmers, whose fields were for the practical, not the pretty.

"You never know," said Mrs Cameron, "You might even get seeing some of the big house. They used to have tea parties there every year before the war and we were all invited. Even the Duke and the Duchess would be there. Awfy nice people, you know. Just like the Colonel and Mrs Fordyce. Gracious, you could call them."

It was traditional at hay and harvest time, as well as the sheep shearing season, for the local farmers to pool their labour in order to get through the big tasks which demanded so many hands. This was Lydeburn's first harvest and each of the tenant farmers sent men along to help. Wullie Cameron had gone along with his Clydesdales for four of them were needed to pull the big Massey Harris binder, on loan from the Home Farm. Wullie Cameron had only seen the big, red-painted binder from the distance before and was clearly overawed by its presence. "Michty me, what a creation. Cutting, sheafing and tying a' at once. What will they be coming up wi' next?"

They laboured all that day behind the high revolving sails of the machine, gently combing the bronzed crop towards it, cruising steadily up and down the fields, a schooner upon a golden sea. The hands were needed to stook the tied sheafs, tied tighter than even Wull Andrews, Glenmulloch's hardy strongman, could tie them, eight sheafs to the stook. It was "Lady Jane" Fordyce herself who brought the basket of food for the traditional three o'clock break and they all sat together, master and servant, landowner's wife and tenants, the labourers, the lads and the lassies from the Lydeburn farms, and although they never thought of it as such, it seemed like a happy family picnic to Star Nelson.

They had what they called beggars' tea, a quantity of dry tea placed in each cup, pouring hot water into it from the big urn carried down to the field by two of the maids from the house. Wullie Cameron, as always, was the life and soul of such gatherings. He would speak in his broadest Lallans, knowing only Wull Andrews and some of the grieves from the other farms would understand him, until eventually Mrs Fordyce, who knew Lallans, but not at its broadest, would ask him to translate some of what he was saying.

"I was only speiring them if they took their drummock in the morn, mistress."

"Drummock, Mr Cameron . . . I don't know that one."

"The auld faither used to have it in the summertime afore he went to the hill. It's raw meal and cauld water. He said a man didnae need to eat more than that. 'Pit a nieve-fu o' drummock in yer pechan and ye'll no' luck ahint ye a' day' he would say."

"Oh, Mr Cameron."

"S'true, mistress. Aye, an' say what ye like but the auld yin was right. As boys we used to leave Glenmulloch at night in the summertime. I had my fiddle, the brother Geordie had a buttonbox and the other brother Tam had the bagpipes and we'd go out o'er the hill there, up o'er the Old Lime Road, aye, an richt out o'er the tap to the herd's house at Ellergoffe . . . that's a guid six miles, six hard miles at that. Jimmy Pringle was the herd there at the time . . . big, wild-looking man that ran six dugs and the only time they ever saw him in toun was when he went yince a year to Erchie McMath in Sanquhar to get new soles and tackets in his Herd Laddie bits. A pig and a braxy ewe and a kist fu' o' oatmeal and another o' flour and a garden o' tatties an' neeps and his coo and Jimmy Pringle depended on nae other man nor beast from one year's end to the next.

"But there were herds further out than him, yin at the Benault and others way over towards the Kyle, and ye cannae get further away than that and the only fowk they ever saw was each other when they met at their marches or when they went looking for stravaigling yowes. We'd meet them a' at the nights we had thegether at Jimmy Pringle's. A bottle of John Barleycorn atween us and we'd play and sing the night awa'. Pringle knew a' the tunes o' the great Lowlands fiddlers, John Riddell from Ayr, Captain Robert Riddell o' Friars Carse, John Bruce the Doonhamer and John McGill, the Girvan man. Some grand numbers there were, *Merry Lads o' Ayr*, *Whistle o'er the lave o't*, *Toluch Gorum*, *A Mile To Ride*, *The Cadgers o' The Canongate*, och an' scores o' others. We'd play and sing till after four when we had to come back o'er the hill again.

"Auld faither would be up when we got back and would gie us a' a

swearin'. Could swear something terrible at man an' beast could the
auld yin. And he wouldnae let us eat when we come back. 'You've nae
time for that,' he would say. 'Put some drummock in ye and get on wi'
yer work.' And that's what we did . . . I'd get the dog and be off to the
hill, Tam was the pleughman so he had the horse to get, and Geordie
was the byreman wi' sixty to milk, a' by hand, then mucking out and
carting the milk tae the road end. Aye, it's no' like it is the day mistress.
See a' they young yins . . . they don't ken the hard life," throwing back
his head in loud laughter as if to emphasise he wasn't to be taken too
seriously.

"Oh, Mr Cameron" said Mrs Fordyce, "You do tell some fanciful
stories."

"Not a bit o' it mistress. They've been having nights like I was telling
you there in these parts since Rabbie Burns himsel' was riding up and
down past the road end there on his way from Mauchline to Ellisland.
He used to stop down there about Nethercairn after coming up
through a' they twists and hills on the road between Kirkconnel and
the Rigg. And when he got to Nethercairn he would gie his horse a
breather and a bite to eat by the roadside and take in a' that beauty we
can see afore us this very minute.

"But wi' him being the poet an' that it used to affect him a lot more
than it did you and me. It was from down there he got the inspiration
for "Parnassus Hill":

But Nith Maun be my Muses' well.
My Muse maun be thy bonie sel,
On Corsincon I'll glowr and spell,
And write how dear I love thee.

There you are . . . that's what he thought of our ain Corsincon. Loved
it that much it gave him the inspiration to write. By gees, though, he
must hae passed it on the days when it had its hat off. And there's no'
been many of them this past year, I'm telling ye."

"Just how do you know all these stories, Mr Cameron?" asked Mrs
Fordyce, a keen Burns scholar.

"About Rabbie, ye mean?"

"Yes."

"What ye've tae realise, mistress, is that his presence is still about us
here. There's fowk about here that had a distant touch o' the man. You
take auld Jake Douglas from High Rigg. Auld Jake's ninety, born in
the year 1852. Now his auld faither, and I mind o' him when I was a
boy for they used to call him Auld Cackers because o' the steel-rimmed
clogs he wore, well he was born about the year 1820 and he used to tell
the story that his grandfather, and he was a Jake as well, had worked
in Whigham's Inn at Sanquhar and Rabbie used to go in there and the
two o' them used to get fou' thegether. And then there's auld Jessie

Hunter, 95 last Martinmas Day. She's a Doonhamer and her mither was a cronie o' auld Jean Armour hersel'. Now that's her ain mither that had a hand's touch tae Rabbie himsel' a' be it through his mistress and there she is, still hale and hearty wi' the story to tell. And there's others like them. So you see, mistress, Rabbie is a lot closer to us than you think."

He downed the last of the tea in the big mug, looking over to the hill on the main road about a mile away and which they called the Smiddy Brae. "There's the twenty past three," he said nodding towards the red, single-decker bus slowing to first gear on the steep climb on the road south after it crossed the Polhole Burn. The red buses, one going north, the other going south, always met at that point at twenty past every hour throughout the day and served as a visible timepiece for the day's activities. The twenty past eleven was the signal that their morning break was over, the twenty past twelve meant time to be heading for the house for dinner, the twenty past two was when the wives would start preparing the baskets for the three o'clock tea break, the twenty past that hour telling them it was time to be working again as it was at that moment. "Well, that's enough o' the blethering. We'll want to get as much cut and stookit afore the weather changes," said Wullie Cameron, squeezing the life out of half a cigarette, blowing the last of the exhaled smoke at its black end before slipping it beside the others in his waistcoat pockets.

Star helped Mrs Fordyce fold the big, red check teacloth she had spread for the plates of scones, pancakes and meal biscuits she had brought to the field for the break. "Goodness girl, how you have grown. Star Nelson—I don't believe it. Life at Glenmulloch with the Camerons must be suiting you fine." Star smiled and nodded in reply. "Come and give me a hand back to the house with the tea stuff. I'm sure Mr Cameron will excuse you stooking for a little while . . . anyway there's plenty of hands in the field."

The tall, panelled oak door to the big library was open as they passed and Mrs Fordyce could see Star visibly gape at the sight of the shelves from floor to ceiling packed tightly with books, more books in the one place than she had ever seen before, more even it seemed there were in the Norfolk Street Library in the Gorbals.

"Oh, the Colonel must be back," said Mrs Fordyce.

"Are you there, dear . . . oh, I see you. Everything go well at the War Effort meeting?"

He rose from the high, leather Winchester club chair in which he had been sitting. He was a handsome man, much older than Mrs Fordyce with a crisp, distinguished appearance, his ruddy complexion highlighting his silver military moustache.

"Splendid, my dear. We've just raised enough to buy our third

Lancaster bomber and now we're going for a major effort to buy two more of them. Show those damned Jerries a thing or two they will. And who's this lovely girl you have with you? Ah, the Glenmulloch evacuee. Yes, I remember you telling me about her. From Glasgow eh? Great port is Glasgow. Sailed from there you know on the old *Carthaginian* when we went to South Africa. She was one of the Allan Line's ships. Beautiful vessel. Got to Cape Town in one month exactly with just one stopover at Las Palmas where they bunkered and brought on fresh meat and things like that. Left Glasgow on Friday, February 23, in 1900. Aye, you never forget the important dates in your life, and the first job we had to put the men to was to clear the decks of snow. And there we were a month later in South Africa in the middle of their summer. But there was no time for enjoying ourselves or anything like that. We had to ride off to the north to fight the Boers . . ."

Mrs Fordyce cut in at that point. "Now I'm sure our young visitor isn't interested in your adventures in the Yeomanry . . . " But the Colonel had an audience and he wasn't so easily put off when there was a new ear at hand.

"Here girl . . . come and have a look at this photograph. There, that's the Scottish Yeomanry . . . our platoon of them that is."

It was a large sepia photograph mounted on a handsome gilt frame by the fireplace of the library of an earnest group of uniformed horsemen, each with a leather bandolier slung round one shoulder. The words, in neat scroll, beneath it read: "C. Platoon, D. Company, Scottish Yeomanry, Camp Maitland, Cape Town, South Africa, April 1900."

"Aren't they Australians?" Star asked.

"No, no girl. It's the hats that make us look like the blessed Australians. All the Yeomanry wore hats like that, probably before the damned Australians made them popular. But, my, what a lovely spot of the world that was. Camp Maitland was our first camp. It was on the lower slopes of Green Point and Sea Point on Table Bay and all around us this lovely semi-tropical country dotted with beautiful villas. Mrs Fordyce and I were going to go there for a visit three years ago . . . then this Mr Hitler started all his funny tricks. War doesn't look so bad when you see a photograph like that, all the chaps fresh in their new uniforms, the horses all wonderfully groomed. But I look at that photograph in a different light for I know that only half those chaps came back and all up and down Nithsdale there were sad houses where the women wept for months on end." And at that point he fell silent, standing before the picture, staring at it. Mrs Fordyce and Star left him with his thoughts as they wandered round the library, stopping every now and then to lift out and speak about a different book.

They had ridden out, those boys from Ayrshire and Dumfries,
together with the others from Glasgow and the Lothians, Lanarkshire
and Fife who made up the Scottish Yeomanry, for the long trek that
took them from the beauty of Table Bay and its lush surroundings,
north across the great rivers and the lonely and hot veldt in pursuit of
the Boer commando, the hardy settlers who would not bow to the
greatest empire on the face of the earth and who were to fight for
their farms and settlements and way of life with a tenacity which
astounded the Canadians and New Zealanders, the Australians and all
the British regiments that had gone there in huge convoys of ships.
    They left Camp Maitland in April, two days after the photograph
had been taken, and by that July they had ridden more than 800 miles
on their Argentinian ponies from the southern tip of the vast
continent through Stellenbosch, Camp Wellington, Camp Worcester,
Kimberley, and across the Orange to the battlefields of Belmont and
Graspan and Enslin then over the Modder to Bechuanaland and the
very heartland of these resilient Dutch Boers, to Potchefstroom
and Kalkspruit, Lichtenburg and Krugersdorp, Frankfort and
Johannesburg. Lord Roberts was there and so too was General
Hunter and they addressed the survivors of that long and dangerous
trek. They told them how well they had done, how bravely they had
fought and how fortunate they had been to have come so far without
having suffered too many casualties. And they bade them well for the
tough times that lay ahead of them.
    It was hard rations after Johannesburg, three ounces of tea or coffee
and sugar per man per day and meat they said had been fresh at one
time and which the men called trek ox but chewed nevertheless, for it
gave them the energy they needed. With their trek ox they had
compressed vegetables every few days to prevent scurvy, a tablespoon
of jam once a week and on Saturday night every man, from General to
Bugler, had half a wine glass of rum, dark and overproof. If you
managed also to get the ration of your mate who didn't drink you
could forget about the boredom of the trek for the rest of the night. It
was at a town strangely called Bethlehem that the bullets from the
Boer mausers zip, zip, zipped through the air in numbers they had
never known before and the horses fell from beneath them in their
scores.
    There they met up with the Camerons and the Highland Light
Infantry, the Seaforths and the Black Watch and it had seemed at
times that it was Scotland itself that was fighting the Boer War.
General Hector Macdonald, Fighting Mac himself, was there. They

rode with him into Harrismith and they stood at the salute as the Union Flag was raised over what they called their rightful territory once more. Then they rode the hundreds of miles south to Camp Maitland again, the war in the sun and the heat over. Behind them the gallant troopers of the Scottish Yeomanry had left every tenth man dead in a grave in the veldt. Of those who did make it back, every third man was wounded and most of them were never to be right again.

"Our friend can come back another time Mitchell," said Mrs Fordyce as they made to leave the library, the Colonel still standing by the big photograph.

"Yes . . . yes . . . of course. I'm afraid I was day-dreaming there. Yes . . . yes . . . do come back. Here, make her take a book. What are you reading?" Before she could answer he picked a volume from the table in front of him. "You'll love this. Just finished reading it again. *Rob Roy.*"

Star smiled. "I've read *Ivanhoe* and *The Fair Maid of Perth* in preparation for my leaving certificate."

"Then you're reading well. You'll like *Rob Roy* even better. I wish our sons would read, tykes that they are. You know, I've told them time and time again that life is like taking a stroll down a street in which there are many doorways. And from each doorway there is on offer all the fine things of life. From one the best music, Beethoven and Bach and Mozart. From the next a display of the finest works of art, Cellini and Michaelangelo, Canaletto and Gauguin. And so on, each doorway offering the finest in literature and the arts and all the great things in life which make life a happy experience. Now supposing you appreciate none of these things. What a dull walk you are going to have down that street. But, ah, what about the person who has an appreciation of all of them! That same walk down that same street will be a totally different experience for them; a truly wonderful experience they'll have. Now a girl like you is just at the start of that walk down that street . . . make sure you don't pass one single door in it without appreciating and enjoying all it has to offer. Anyway, do come back my dear when *Rob Roy* is finished. Books like these are not just for decorating the shelves. They're there to be read and enjoyed. I keep telling Robbie and Andrew that but I might as well talk to the wall over there, the scalliwags."

Star had taken an instant liking to the Colonel for he had shown a genuine interest in her and he wasn't at all like the kind of person she had imagined to live in a house as huge as Lydeburn and own so much land. She had thought somehow that he would be like the house factors in the Gorbals. And no one had a good word to say about them.

6

THE LAIRD AND HIS SONS

BECAUSE of his wounds in the Boer War, Mitchell Fordyce had not been called for active duty in the First World War, the Great War, the war that was to end all wars. Instead, he had served with the recruiting staff of the Highland Light Infantry, stationed at their Regimental HQ, Maryhill Barracks, in Glasgow, grim and ancient and surrounded by an unclimbable granite-block wall which gave it the same appearance as two other fortress-like institutions in the city: Duke Street and Barlinnie, the two prisons. He was nearly forty when he was finally demobilised in the rank of colonel in 1919, returning home to Lydeburn to inherit the estate as the only son of Mitchell Fordyce Senior who had died that year. He planned to carry on his inheritance in the same honourable and respected fashion which had made the family one of the most popular in that part of the country.

The following year he met his wife-to-be, Jane. She was from Ryecroft, a small farm at Kirkmahoe in the south near Dumfries. The house, a cottage, lime-white and picture-postcard trim, with fragrant roses dotting a wooden archway at the front door which was reached by a crazy path up a long front garden containing a burn and a stone bridge. Jane's brothers had taught her how to guddle for brown trout in the burn on the days when it was lazy, and adventure for them would be to climb and explore the earth mounds which had once been Roman forts, and to pretend they were Caesar's very own legionnaires. Jane had been bright at school, obtaining her Higher Day School certificate at Dumfries Academy, qualifying for a place at the Teachers' College in Edinburgh.

They sent fresh young teachers to the small schools which were part of every rural community. After a year at Auldgirth, near her home, Jane was posted to be the dominie at the one-classroom school they called Cairn Smiddy at the junction of the farm roads which led to the Lydeburn Estate properties and the main Kilmarnock to Dumfries Road, five miles north of the village of Kirkconnel. They had met at the first garden party which Mitchell Fordyce had given after inheriting the estate and a fortnight later, after only one outing, that being a Sunday drive in his big Wolseley to the Buccleuch and Queensberry at Thornhill for a genteel Sunday lunch, he proposed and she said yes. They married in the June of 1922 and their honeymoon was to the exotic and fashionable Ostende, their hotel on the splendid Promenade Albert I, all befitting a gentleman and his lady from Scotland who wanted nothing but the best. The twins, their only children, were born three years later, and they rarely left home after that, dedicating themselves to the estate and the community.

Lydeburn House was one of the surviving fortified houses, as they were known, of Dumfriesshire. Once there had been 130 of them, created by a new land class 400 years ago when the vast church lands were being apportioned out. Only about a score of them now remained: places like the castellated Amisfield Tower; Closeburn Castle, oblong and massive and going back to the fourteenth century; Maxwelton House, graceful and modernised and the home of Annie Laurie herself; Westerhall, the mansion that grew from a fortalice; and Lydeburn, two-storeyed and garreted with a steeply pitched roof and crow-stepped gables and originally one of the houses of the great Douglas family.

Mitchell Fordyce of Lydeburn was a pillar of the church and the Estate Owners' Association and Jane threw her energies into every activity which time spared her. She had been President of the Women's Rural Institute for Dumfriesshire, a Vice President of the County Branch of the Red Cross, had held all the senior posts in the Sanquhar Riding of the Marches, the ancient territorial custom around which was an annual gala and festival, worked tirelessly raising funds for the mission the church had adopted in Nyasaland, was one of the best players in the church's badminton league and was known with respect throughout Nithsdale, from Dalswinton to Durisdeer, Kirkconnel to Kirkmahoe, in the tiny pennies-a-week cottages amidst the bings of the old lead mines up in high Wanlockhead, and in the big estate houses, grand and permanent, of Moniaive and Thornhill and even in the grandest house of them all, Drumlanrig, home of the Buccleuchs for three hundred years and one-time resting place of Bonnie Prince Charles himself.

Nothing had been good enough for their twin sons, Robert, whom they called Robbie, and Andrew. They would one day become the masters of Lydeburn, and be part of the permanence which the Fordyces had established in Upper Nithsdale. A nurse had stayed with them for the first few months of their lives and afterwards they had a nanny, Dora Murdoch, who had previously been with one of the big estate houses bordering on Balmoral whose family, as they proudly told everyone, were friends of the King himself. The boys had doted on their Mrs Dora, as they called her, as she had on them. The saddest time of their lives had been in 1935 when they had to leave for the boarding school that had been chosen for them, Glenhazel College in Perthshire, their father's old school.

The trauma of that parting had been such that it had taken the boys more than a year to cope with their new life without the doting Dora. It was easier for her. She could share her love, as she did, with another child from another big house. For the boys there was only each other and they became closer, much closer than even twins normally were; so much so that they thought and acted as one and could not bear the prospect of being out of each other's sight, even for a few minutes. They protected each other with an uncanny awareness throughout their years at Glenhazel, coming close to expulsion on more than one occasion, once for being drunk, an offence of which they were able to plead innocence by maintaining they had been duped by others who had given them whisky in a Tizer bottle. The truth was that the spirit was 105-proof cask-strength whisky from the nearby Glenturret distillery and they had bought it from men in the village who sold it in lemonade bottles. They in turn re-sold it to other boys at threepence a swig, from which they had made sufficient funds to buy boxes of Passing Cloud and Balkan Sobranie cigarettes and brandy for the Saturday midnight parties they regularly conducted. They were to encounter similar trouble in the Halls of Residence at St Andrews University, into which they only just managed to enter by dint of six months' cramming with special tutors.

Star had seen the twins twice before that day she called at Lydeburn to return the *Rob Roy* book the Colonel had loaned her. The first time had been at St Conal's Church, where she went every Sunday with Mrs Cameron, Wullie always finding an excuse, like going to the hill, not to accompany them. The Fordyces had their own pew on the main aisle of the little church and just by the big brass plaque which listed the 86 Kirkconnel men who hadn't returned from the Great War. She remembered the occasion for they had started giggling and nudging each other during the singing of Hymn 100, *Jesus, friend of little children,* and she thought how rude they had been. They had passed her another time when she was working at the hay and they had looked at her disdainfully.

She had thought then how in the country there were many orders of life, much more than they had in the Gorbals where order, when it did manifest itself, was treated with open contempt. That was a freedom which most workers and their families didn't have in the rural communities, depending as they did on their masters for their living. Farm workers were of the lowest order, as low as that of miners, although miners were more free of the class system, being confined to their own communities, anonymous blackened men to whom no one gave a second thought. The maids and house servants were the lowest of the caste, followed by those who did the various forms of work on the farms, the grieves, byremen and general labourers, dairy and byremaids. The more skilled men, like the ploughmen and dairymen, were higher up the scale by virtue of their expertise, the shepherds higher still for they were separate men, living out their lonely lives on the distant hills with their flocks. The farm managers were above them all, except, that is, head gamekeepers and tenant farmers who were at the top of the working order. Above them were a few farmers who owned their own properties and were called their ain-lairds. But none of them were on the same plain as the estate owners, the lords and masters of them all, whose own order was measured in acreage and in whether or not they had a title. An estate owner's son, like Robbie or Andrew Fordyce, was many times removed from someone who lived on a tenant's farm and who was seen labouring in the fields like an ordinary worker. Someone like that was a distant person.

But they were different that night she returned with the book. The Colonel and his wife had gone to Ardlui by Loch Lomond to visit cousins who had an estate, much bigger than theirs, and who were great friends of the revered dukes and clan leaders that were their neighbours. As it was Martinmas the house staff had been given their term leave and the boys looked after the house on a week's study leave from University before their final exams.

On the Saturday night they had sneaked two dairy maids they had met in Kilmarnock back with them to Lydeburn. Although they were the Laird's sons, they had to take every precaution not to be seen with the girls, for very little happened in the country without it being observed. There was always someone watching at Tamsmiddy, the busy blacksmiths, at the Lydeburn road end and not a car or van or person on foot left the main road for the single track that led to Lydeburn, as well as the Home Farm and Glenmulloch and some of the outlying cottages, without being seen and noted. The blacksmith's was run by Geordie Walker and his three sons, one of whom was always standing by the wide door of the forge which overlooked the junction. When buses came at twenty past the hour, there would be other faces there to see who was coming or going or what parcels were being dropped off for collection. Robbie and Andrew had taken girls to

Lydeburn before when their parents had been away and they had had some wild parties there too. Such had been their cunning at getting people in and out of the big house unnoticed, not even the Walkers, guardians of the road end, had seen them, although they got to know later from the staff at the house — and when the Walkers knew then Upper Nithsdale knew. But this time the staff were away, apart from Tam McGinlay, the gardener, and Hugh McKechnie, the stableman, who each had a tiny room in the cottage beneath the stable hayloft.

The two girls were rough, hard-working lassies who had spent their days pulling and stripping the milk from big horned Ayrshires around the farm dairies of Kyle and Cunningham. They were willing partners for a night of revelry followed by a good bedding from two of the wildest lads in the county, each swapping his for the other in the morning. Then they were smuggled beneath tartan rugs in the rear seat of the Hillman for the drive to Cumnock where they were given their busfares, and some to spare, as a reward for their company.

With another free night before their parents returned the Fordyce boys had tried to repeat their previous evening's lark and coax another two girls back with them from the square round the ancient Mercat Cross at Cumnock where the Sunday night strollers would meet. When that proved unsuccessful they tried again in New Cumnock, although they had to be more circumspect there for more people knew who they were in the little Ayrshire town that was nearest to Lydeburn.

"Well, there's nothing for it Robbie," said Andrew, the wilder of the two, "but to go home and finish off that Smith's Glenlivet we started on. I'm blowed if I'm going to put my nose between the books tonight."

"I know where you would rather be putting your nose . . . where you had it last night. Must look out for them again some time."

They were into their third glass of the smooth twelve-year-old when Star walked into the courtyard, the handsome book in a paper parcel under her arm. Andrew, standing drinking by the window, was the first to see her. "Robbie, quick. Come and see what we have here. A fine, comely wench, as they say. And what a lovely shape, Robbie. God, look at the breasts."

Robbie joined him at the window. "It's the Glenmulloch girl. My, she has grown, hasn't she?"

"Is that who she is? She's the Glasgow one. I've heard them say she can work as good as any of the men in the fields. But look at her, all upright and full of confidence. Almost arrogant as though she's not one of them."

"Never mind the analysis, Dr Andrew. Let's get her in for a drink. She might be fun."

Andrew went to the door after she had pulled the brass handle, the rods activating pulleys which rang the big brass bell in the hall as well as a smaller one in the servants' quarters, where there was no one to hear. He pulled the heavy panelled door towards him and smiled at the surprised look on the girl's face.

"Is Colonel Fordyce at home?" she asked, returning Andrew's smile.

"Come in. You're the Glenmulloch girl . . . what is it they call you again?"

"Star."

"Star, indeed. What an unusual name. Do come in."

"I've come to return the book the Colonel kindly loaned me." Then she added, almost nervously as though she felt she had to keep speaking, "It's *Rob Roy*. Scott's *Rob Roy*."

"*Rob Roy* eh? Should I be saying then, a hearty welcome to Osbaldistone Hall?"

At that Robbie appeared with a drink in his hand. "Whence and what art thou?" There was a pause before he added, "The quotation from Milton my dears, in the chapter where Frank Osbaldistone is at the point he thinks he should immediately repair to London. Remember? And who have we here, Andrew?"

"We have a Star, so we have."

"A star?"

"It's her name old boy."

"Really! Well do come in Star. Come into the library."

"Where are the Colonel and Mrs Fordyce?" asked Star, more out of curiosity than apprehension.

"Oh, they're somewhere around," said Andrew quickly. "Probably with Mr McKechnie at the stables. Yes, one of the mares is in foal. Due tonight I heard them saying."

Beside him on an ornately carved camphor table was a three-bottle tantalus, its lock collar open and one of the heavy crystal decanters placed on the table beside it with its stopper removed. They had got the keys for it the night before, having discovered many years previously their father's formula for hiding them: fourth shelf from the left behind a book, and each week the key was moved behind the book immediately to the right; when it reached the end of the long shelf, which took more than two years, it went back along the shelf again. Yet, oddly, despite his precautions with the keys, the boys had known that their father never checked the contents of the bottles. They could take what they wanted without it ever being noticed.

"Here Star, have this," said Andrew, proffering a big crystal glass towards her. She smelled the contents and shook her head vigorously as the pungent fumes sharply nipped her senses. In disgust she exclaimed, "That's whisky."

"What a clever girl we have, Robbie. Reads Sir Walter and knows whisky at a sniff. My, my, haven't you come on since Glasgow. Or should I say Glesca?"

The boys laughed together at that and, in an instant, Star felt alone and frightened. "Is the Colonel here . . . and Mrs Fordyce?" she asked again, nervously this time.

"No, actually, they're not. But we are. Robbie and Andrew Fordyce. Can we do anything to help you?"

Andrew was still grinning as he lifted the heavy glass to his mouth. "Lovely stuff this, sweetie. You don't know what you're missing. Whisky, you know, the stuff that makes the boys frisky? And the girls?"

At that she quickly put the book on the table, turning abruptly for the door . . . and stopped sharply in her tracks. Robbie had moved there when Andrew had been speaking. He gave it a loud click as he pushed it closed. "Don't be in a hurry, dear girl. We're the Fordyce boys, the friendly and hospitable Fordyces of Lydeburn, the finest run estate in all Dumfriesshire . . . well, after the Buccleuchs that is. Family motto: "Never Dishonour". Does your family have a motto darling?"

"Never Disown Her," said Andrew quickly, chuckling loudly at his *bon mot*.

"Aren't you inspired today, Andrew," said Robbie. "Must be that Glenlivet. Pour me another glass . . . and one for our little Star."

She ran for the door when Robbie walked towards the fireplace and the decanters. He casually ignored her panic. "Sorry dear, it's locked. Anyway, why should a nice girl like you want to get away from two very nice boys like us? Stay and make the best of it. Here, relax yourself and have some of this. I'll water it for you if you think it's a bit strong. I thought all you Glasgow people did nothing but drink anyway. It certainly seems that way when we're changing stations for St Andrews. I walked around the houses at the back of Queen Street Station one Friday night and there were drunks everywhere. The women were fighting as much as the men. What a place!"

Star turned from the locked door, fearstruck, remembering another place, another time, and the same fear: the same pain in her chest as her heart countered the panic by pumping the blood faster and faster and oh God, dear God, she pleaded in her mind, don't let this time be like the other time! Surely it's just a game they're playing. Not the Fordyce boys. No, not them. They would never do anything like that. Would they? And her mind spun, almost out of control, racing from logic and trying to figure out how to escape, to terror and panic and confusion.

They raised their glasses towards her in a toast.

"You really should have a drink, you know," said Andrew. "Makes everything more pleasant. What was it our Robbie, the other Robbie, said: "Will make a man forget his woe, will heighten all his joy . . ."

Robbie intervened to finish the verse: "Will make the widow's heart to sing, tho' the tear were in her eye."

"Well done, Robbie. But the lass isn't a widow. Are you dear? You're a bonnie young lass. A veritable Star indeed. Who's your boyfriend then?"

"Bet it's one of the Walker boys from the Smiddy. The eyes and ears of the country. They lech at all the womenfolk when they pass, coarse oafs that they are."

"Please . . . please. It's getting dark and I want to get home."

"To Glasgow or Glenmulloch?" laughed Andrew, Robbie joining him in the joke.

"You're right about the dark. Let's get the lamps lit."

"No," said Andrew. "There's plenty of light from the fire. Time for another log anyway."

A tidy pile of them, each neatly cut in eighteen-inch lengths, had been stacked by the side of the hearth earlier in the day by Tam McGinlay, the gardener one of whose jobs was collecting windfall timber from the three glens which slashed the side of the Glenmulloch Hill. Andrew fumbled as he picked up the log from the top of the pile, knocking some of the others down with a clatter. They rolled across the broad slate hearth of the big, wide stone fireplace. "Oops. Must be the John Barleycorn. Robbie, let's have another glass. And give one to our Star," he said, throwing the heavy log in the middle of the fire which burst forth a fountain of brilliant sparks.

"No," she replied, the panic in her voice turning to anger. "Open that door and let me go . . . or else!"

"Oh, hear that, Robbie? Or else she says. Is that your Glasgow talk girl? Threatening us eh? Right Robbie, let's have some fun with this little Star that's dropped in on us."

She made to run but there was nowhere to go. The anger vanished, replaced by panic again, nightmare panic, unbelievable nightmare panic, for this couldn't be happening to her, not again. The room became a kaleidoscope whirl, vivid pink, frightening orange and brilliant yellow. They came at her, like they were in slow motion, their faces, handsome faces, distorted, ugly and gloating and shouting at her, words that came like barks through hideous equine teeth. "Still . . . wider . . . now Robbie." All around the air was hot and sweaty and that smell, that same horrible, hellish stale whisky smell, enveloped her in a cloying fog from which there was no escape. The pain of them between her, man, stupefied and primitive man, into woman, was the only sense of reality of what was happening.

Wull Andrews ran the five miles down to Kirkconnel just like the
night he had when the Camerons' bairn had taken meningitis, the
only light to guide him being from the occasional vehicle on the distant
main road. He scrambled and slithered down the steep ridge alongside
the Glenmulloch Glen, hunting houlets flapping in the black of the
night, till he reached the tunnel that took the burn's gushing waters
under the railway and on to the Nith. Through the taut wire fence and
up the steep embankment, brambles tearing at his legs, to the up-line
of the railway track, leaping over the long water trough from which
the London expresses scooped supplies at high speed as they
thundered south. It was easy after that, the red and green lights
of the semaphores pointing the way along the track and the only
noise the thud, thud, thudding of Souter boots on the creosoted
sleepers.

Big Sam Niven, the senior of the two Kirkconnel policemen,
cadaverous faced and ungainly tall, was in the red-bricked police
house on the west side of the main street when Wull hammered at the
door. It was his custom every night to spit and polish the black leather
gaiters he wore with his breeches, layering the polish with spit till it
took on a veneer like patent leather, a custom he had learned as a
regular in the Scots Guards where they had to gloss the toecaps of
their ammunition boots in a similar fashion. "That's a serious
allegation you're making, Wull Andrews," he said, a long cloth dotted
with polish stains dangling from one hand, a gaiter through the arm of
his other hand. "I'd better get dressed. I take it the doctor will pick me
up? I only have my bicycle."

Dr Hyslop, Tommy Hyslop to his closest friends, the best bridge and
whist player from the Ayrshire march to Thornhill, so they said, came
down from the upstairs bedroom, from which he had asked the
Camerons and Constable Niven to leave in order to make his
examination. They were waiting for him at the foot of the stairs and
Mrs Cameron went towards him anxiously. "Doctor?"

"The lass will be all right, Mrs Cameron. I've given her a sleeping
draught . . . a right powerful one. She needs sedation. You'll no' hear
from her till the best part of the morn. She's badly shocked and there's
some bruising, but apart from that there will be nothing permanent,
except, of course, how her mind copes with it. I've also given her a
douche but we won't know what will be until her time of the month.
Well, Mr Niven, you'll be wanting me to make a statement?"

"I've come across nothing like this in the seven years I've been in
Kirkconnel," said the constable as he wrote down the details from the
doctor. "It's not just the nature of the allegations, doctor. It's the fact
they're involving the Fordyces. I mean people like that don't get in this
sort of trouble. Do they?"

Dr Hyslop looked over the top of his gold-rimmed spectacles at the policeman. "Mr Niven, drink and the de'il walk hand in hand and when they're thegether they'll knock on anybody's door. Aye, even the Fordyces. That apart, the lassie has had a bad time. A very bad time. It's enough when this is done to them by one . . . but by two. Terrible, Mr Niven. Just terrible."

The following day, the Monday, Colonel and Mrs Fordyce returned from their weekend. A sleek, black Humber, its mudguard tips rimmed in the white stipulated by blackout regulations, was in the courtyard and that puzzled them for they knew all the cars belonging to their friends and the various people who called on them. "Ministry of Agriculture, I bet," said the Colonel. "They'll be wanting us to put potatoes in the stallion's paddock next or else wondering if corn ever grew on the top of Glenmulloch Hill." He chuckled to himself at the prospect of that.

Constable Niven was with the two tall men with serious faces and sombre suits, each holding a soft hat in one hand. The local policeman coughed nervously and gave a semblance of a salute as the Colonel approached. Then he introduced the two men. " This is Detective Sergeant Edgar and Detective Constable Park from Dumfries, sir. They would like to have a word with you."

The Colonel ushered them into the small study off the library which he used for administrative work. He cleared the desk of papers he had left there the previous Friday and when the men were all seated he sat down himself in his leather swivel chair. "Well, gentlemen, how can I help you?"

Delivering bad news was no new experience for the three policemen, but rarely had they remembered anyone so shocked as Colonel Mitchell Fordyce when they unfolded the story to him. The sergeant, a big, square-jawed man with thin lips and piercing eyes, did all of the talking, detailing what they knew of the events that had occurred that Sunday evening. "We have seen the lads about the alleged offence and, as a result of our enquiries and statements they have made to us, they were taken to Dumfries, where they are being held in custody. We have also interviewed a number of other witnesses, including Dr Hyslop of Kirkconnel, Mr and Mrs Cameron of Glenmulloch and your gardener, Mr McGinlay who heard the screams and found the girl on the track outside your house. She was in a terrible state after the . . ." and at that he paused to find a suitable word, continuing, "the . . . ordeal. But I won't say any more about that at this point. I'll have to ask you and Mrs Fordyce to make a statement about your whereabouts."

The Colonel sat silent and unblinking, staring with unseeing eyes at
a point which was nowhere and a vision which was nothing. The
uniformed constable coughed nervously once more after a few
minutes and the Colonel's eyes closed momentarily. Then, after a few
seconds they began blinking normally again. "Yes, Sergeant," he said.
"Yes, it's a terrible shock. We've never had dishonour before in the
family and we go back a long time. A long, long time. 'Dishonour
Never'. That's our family motto, you know? And we've lived by it. You
want to speak to Mrs Fordyce too, you say? Then I'll have a word with
her first of all, if you don't mind. We must be at our most considerate
with the ladies at a time like this. I don't know how she'll take the
news. Sergeant, I don't suppose? No. What I mean is . . . Sergeant, do
you have any doubts about it at all . . . that it was someone else maybe?
That the girl might not be telling the truth?"
The detective made no comment, simply indicating by shaking his
head. "I would like to have a word with Mrs Fordyce now, sir, as I
would like to take a statement."

The police were back at Lydeburn again the following day. Sergeant
Edgar and Constable Niven were there and so was Inspector George
Black, a uniformed man, from Thornhill. They were led by Tam
McGinlay and Hugh McKechnie, the stable man, to a seat by a gazebo
in the highest part of the side garden which had a vantage point
looking south towards the Lowthers and to the high moors west of
Sanquhar which formed the graceful sweep of that part of Nithsdale.
The Colonel would often sit there in the long summer nights,
listening to the soaring swallows squealing as they fed on the wing. A
shiny black labrador was on the ground by the seat, lying
outstretched, its nose resting between its front paws. It only casually
looked up at the approaching men.
    "I found him," said McGinlay, his voice shaking with emotion. "I
was going to spend the day working in this part of the garden. And
there he was lying still on the seat there. The dog was whimpering and
I didn't realise anything was wrong till I looked at him and saw his
head. The poor man. The poor, poor man."
    The Inspector bent down to retrieve the shotgun which lay beside
the long rustic seat. "Have you touched anything, Mr McGinlay?" he
asked.
    "No sir, I touched nothing — all I did was run to the house and fetch
the sheet which I put over him. Mrs Fordyce left this morning for
Dumfries to visit the lads and I knew the Colonel had said he felt
unwell and wouldn't be going for the Mistress had told Davie Burns,
ye ken, the driver?, and we were talking about it when he came back

from the station. She had also said how worried she was about the whole affair and that most of her worry had been about the Colonel. Apparently he had gone into some kind of trance last night and was unable to talk to anyone. Davie . . . Davie Burns that is . . . said that he couldn't even bid the Mistress farewell this morning. He just stood there looking at her wi' not a word coming out of his mouth. Right shocked he must have been. And look at him now. A gentleman he was. A proper gentleman . . . and saddled wi' these two buggers o' boys."

The funeral was at the family vault in the little churchyard of St Conal's Church of Scotland, at the head of the village by the tumbling Polbower Burn. The Church was named after St Conal, the man who brought Christianity to the district, and the best known sons of the area were laid there: Alexander Anderson, the railway poet, whose monument looks over the Nith and the western ridge of the valley, with William Laing, the Guildhall poet, nearby; James Bryden too, the shepherd whose gravestone records, "He kept his fleecy charge below, And sank beneath the drifted snow"; all the distinctive names known in that area for centuries, the McCrones and the Crons; the Milligans and Muncies; the Hyslops and Howats; the McCrirircs and McCrindles. It was the biggest funeral in living memory in Kirkconnel and such was the respect for the man that the mourners were from all walks of life.

There were miners in ill-fitting dark blue suits and Sunday caps; shepherds from the high hills in the coarse black suits which they only wore once a year for the Autumn sheep sales, or if there was a wedding or funeral; estate workers and tenant farmers; ain-laird farmers and estate owners from as far away as Carlisle; and every shop owner in Kirkconnel and Sanquhar. They filed past the graveside after the service in final respect, looking up at the tall obelisk which bore the family name. Beneath it in the same bold lettering were two words on which their eyes lingered knowingly. "Never Dishonour."

7

BLACK MARKET SAMMY

SAMMY Nelson had no regular work after being dismissed from Myer's for the second time in 1927. It had been pointless trying the other warehouses and stores for they had known about his activities in the Myer strike and for that they had labelled him "Communist", "troublemaker", "bolshevik", "anarchist", "trade unionist" — none of which he really was. Despite the lack of full-time employment, Sammy was rarely idle or without income of some sort to supplement Peggy's wages and allow them to stay on in Govanhill. He earned money at a variety of jobs — as bookie's runner, making and selling briquettes, helping in a scrap merchant's yard. Occasionally he would work as a turnstyle man at Ibrox football stadium, a job which always saw him dressed in his heavy overcoat, even on the warmest days, because its pockets held the "skin" he made by letting fans crush through the one man style two at a time . . . for the price of one and a half. On the days he wasn't working, he would walk to the Gorbals to be with his old mates, the corner boys, standing at one of the regular meeting points in Florence Street. The habit wasn't practised on the same scale in Govanhill. Anyway, it was different there. Govanhill might have been a nicer place in which to live, but the district where he was born was the very well of his existence and he returned there as often and as regularly as he could.

He loved the banter and chat of the street corner men as much as he liked airing his own views on life to them. "See in Russia," he would say, always repeating his introduction. "See in Russia, they're all equal. Got rid of all their royalty and nobs. For you know what they are? Parasites. Aye, parasites. They feed off everybody else and dae nothing themselves. It's them that's ruined the country, so it is." The others would nod in agreement and there would be even more vitriolic attacks on the nobility until someone asked if they had heard the result of the three o'clock race.

Sammy was thirty-eight years of age when war broke out and despite the opinions he often expressed, he was one of the first volunteers for the army. "Jamesie would have liked a war," he joked with Peggy the night before he went for his medical. "Aye, imagine getting into a fight that was legal . . . and getting paid for it. Daft when you think about it, though."

"How long have you been bothered with your chest?" asked the doctor when it came to his turn in the long queue of volunteers and conscripts at the prefabricated medical centre in Dumbarton Road.

"Doesnae bother me that much, doctor" he replied. "Cough and spit a bit, like, you know. No more than anybody else."

They marked his papers "4F" and told him to report to his own doctor for treatment. When he did he was told he was a bronchitic "but there's a lot worse than you". He was also told to give up smoking cigarettes but continued to smoke Capstan Full Strength when he could afford them, Woodbines when he couldn't. When he could afford neither he would mix the cigarette ends he kept in a tobacco tin with some fresh shag, rolling it thinly in a Rizla for a hot smoke that made him splutter and cough.

Having been out of full-time work for so long, Sammy Nelson had little inclination to labour for a master again when jobs became plentiful because of the war. People who hadn't worked for years jammed the buses and tramcars for the factories which had to be in production day and night to meet the orders pouring in on them. The worker was wanted again and there were jobs with unlimited overtime. Many hadn't worked since their country last needed them in 1918. Others, like Sammy's wife, Peggy, changed jobs to one of the war effort factories where women were being rewarded with the same status they had a quarter of a century earlier: acceptance as capable enough to work alongside the men on the factory floor.

The war was to be good to the Nelsons. Peggy could earn up to £10 a week in one of the munitions plants at Hillington and, coupled with the earnings from Sammy's various small time enterprises, they were able to move to a better house in Govanhill, a room-and-kitchen in Allison Street with the ultimate in modern conveniences — its own toilet. "And," Peggy would emphasise to their friends, "it's in a red sandstone building."

Although he couldn't have tackled an assault course, Sammy's bad chest had no effect on his movements. Being short of breath and coughing was commonplace and, after the initial disappointment, he considered himself most fortunate in being rejected by the services for such an ordinary ailment. Now that he knew there would be no uniform for him, Sammy decided to make some advantage out of the war. Others were, so why not him? As long as it didn't mean working for a boss, Sammy decided he would try anything.

There were shortages of all description: food and clothing, drink and anything that had been considered a luxury. He couldn't even get his Capstan Full Strength, an annoyance now that he was able to afford them. But, as he was to learn, there were ways of getting almost anything and there were people who specialised in getting things and, in turn, selling them. And didn't they do well, flash clothes and never short of a penny? Just like the bookies. Sammy decided he would become one of them. One of the best of them.

"Fuck it," he said one day when he returned to stand at the street corner in the Gorbals with the "old chinas"—the ones that were left, that is, for even they were getting scarce what with the call up and all the work that was about. "You run with the hard men and you end up getting what my brother got. Some get it sooner, some get it later but they all get it one way or another when you play that game. Work for a gaffer and what do you get? Hee haw. That's what you get. Knock your melt in all your days and you'll still be up one of these closes, with Rothesay once a year. If you're lucky that is. Or else you can take your chance in life. Know what I mean like? Naw, no tea-leaving or anything like that. Taking your chance. A bit of the old enterprise. That's what the real wide boys do. Ones like auld Nat Myer. Came to this country wi' nothing and look at him now. House like a castle in the 'Shields. And all for buying and selling. Buy for sweeties, add on your whack, make your fortune and what do people think about you? Dead respectable. Wear a three piece Benson and a Crombie, drive a fancy car and live in St Andrew's Drive, and that's you respectable. And all the time they're bigger bandits than my brother Jamesie. So as I said — fuck it. I'm going to be up to the same tricks as them. One-man business, that'll be me. A little bit of enterprise here, a little bit of enterprise there. See, with this war there's never been so much scope. For them that's clever that is. And I'm gonnie be one of them."

Lord Woolton, the Minister of Food, announced the new food rations on January 8th, 1940 and the nation was justifiably shocked. His civil servants had counted the stocks, figured out what could still be brought in by running the U-boat gauntlets, divided it all up by fifty million, and the answer they came up with meant a strict and sparse ration on which it seemed, at first, impossible to live. But make do was a good master, and there was always what could be obtained with the help of the new style entrepreneurs like Sammy Nelson.

It didn't take long for Sammy to get involved. The nation might have been shocked at the paucity of their rations, but for many in the Gorbals, and the various other areas of Glasgow which equated with them, four ounces of this and eight ounces of that was a big improvement on their existing diet kept on the shelf in the press: a loaf of black-crusted plain bread, a pat of butter and a jar of jam. The better off might have had some eggs, a piece of cheese and a tin of corned beef, supplemented occasionally by visits to places like the Deep Sea fish-and-chip shop or Knotts Restaurant.

To buy food, customers had to register with specific grocers, making it difficult to trade in food coupons from the ration books which were issued together with an Identity Card. Coupons for clothing and sweets, however, could be used anywhere and were easily transferable. Sammy was quick to learn that and became the first coupon trader in the Gorbals, keeping them in a big morocco wallet in the inside pocket of the imitation belted Crombie he wore. He paid £2 for a book of clothing coupons and sold them for £4 or, if his customer looked well heeled enough, £5. Trade blossomed and soon he had a variety of agents bringing him coupons from all over the city where they were buying them for less than £2.

He gave them commission based on the number of books they brought him. "It's incentive," he called it. For every ten books he obtained he would give them another £2, plus the £2 per book. And they, in turn, made further profit by buying the books as cheaply as possible, usually making between five and ten shillings per book on the deal. But the trade in coupons was just to be a start for Sammy. The more he traded and moved around, the more he saw the great opportunities there were to branch out and make himself what he called "an honest penny or two".

Thousands of American troops were constantly passing through the city and establishing camps in various places, one of them at Cowglen, an open space near the big housing scheme Glasgow Corporation had built at Pollok. From what he had heard about Americans, there would be a few Sammy Nelsons among them and if there were, what a wonderful idea to team up with one or more of them. In a commercial sense, that is. Do a turn for them, disperse some of their wonderful luxuries among the hard-pressed people of Glasgow and, of course, boost the Nelson enterprise a little. But how could a civilian like him get into an American camp? Give them a service would be one way. But what? No one was better fed or clothed or had more availability of the pleasures of life than the US servicemen stationed in Britain. So what service could be offered they didn't have already?

It was Hughie "Plug" Connor who worked in the despatch department of Outrams, the newspaper publishers, in Mitchell Lane

who unwittingly put him up to the idea. The men in the machine room
at Outram's had nicknamed him "Plug" from one of his first
enterprises as a younger man. He used to collect all the wooden plugs
from the centres of the big reels of newsprint used at the works and
take them home in parcels every night. Then at weekends he would
chop them up and sell them as firewood around the Gorbals. But he
was soon to discover there were more lucrative ways of making
money.

Connor was, as Sammy would have said, a man just like himself. A
man of enterprise. Much of his time at work was spent conducting his
business in the men's locker room. He dealt in coupons, shirts, nylon
stockings and most kinds of foodstuffs, although he didn't like
perishables. "Stink the place out," he would say. Nelson and Connor
used to meet regularly in the Seaforth Bar close by the Princess's
Theatre in Main Street, Gorbals, Connor being a Sandyfaulds Street
man. They would deal with each other just as any kind of business
man negotiating might, each finding out from the other what
particular commodity might be in short supply and what kind of prices
were currently ruling. Nat Myer and the other Argyle Street
warehousemen did exactly the same thing, Sammy often said to
himself. If one had a shortage of a particular item or had a big order to
meet, the other would help out, if the price was right that is.

"Can get you ten quire of the evening paper every day, half price
and delivered where you want them," said Hughie that day they met
in Seaforth.

"Ten quire of the *Times!* Are you fuckin' joking, Hughie? Me . . . a
vendor! Get your *Times, News, Citi* . . . *zen.* No' my style Hughie."

"I know, ya mug. But you could sell them to somebody else."

"No' enough in it for me, Hughie. I'm doing well with the coupons
and the other stuff."

"Aye, but the papers could do you a wee extra turn. And see on a
Saturday you can take them to the games and just walk in wi' a nod
and a bundle under your arm. If you think the gateman's a greedy
bugger, and you know the fiddles they get up to, just gie him a couple
of papers. And a nod. There's one o' the boys gets into the dancing wi'
them. 'Get your war latest' he says, then he gets a couple of dances
and if he's lucky a lumber. And a' his papers sold as well."

"Oh, Christ, aye, Hughie, I can just imagine it. Me with the good
suedes and Crombie . . . "

"That's no' a Crombie."

"Awright, the imitation Crombie. Me with the suedes and the
imitation Crombie humping the papers into the Plaza for a rumba."

"You never know, Sammy. You might get a lumber as well. A rumba
then a lumber. No' bad eh?"

Sammy ordered another two pints. When he returned he said, "Right, be serious. You said you could deliver them anywhere?"

"Anywhere. In Glasgow that is. But don't say you want them in Dunoon."

"No. Not Dunoon. Cowglen."

"What?"

"Cowglen."

"Where the fuck's that?"

"Fields . . . just past Pollokshaws Toll."

"Whit . . . gonnie sell them tae the coos?"

"Naw . . . sheep. Cut the capers. I've got an idea. There's a camp in the fields. Yanks. And I want to get into the camp and get hold of some of their stuff. Loaded so they are. Lucky Strikes and Camels. All the whisky they can drink. And have you seen their smart gear? See they officers' pants. Pure gaberdine so they are. Would love a pair masel'. And have you seen the new coats they're wearing, the officers that is? Like a cross between a Crombie, and nane of your fuckin' imitation stuff, a Crombie and camel hair. Nothing but the best. Get hold of a few of them and I'm telling you. Quids in, so I'll be."

"Right, then. So you want your deliveries to your Cowglen. It's ten quire for ten bob and you can sell them for twice that."

Hughie ordered another two pints and the deal was struck after he reminded Sammy he needed the money in advance.

"Just one thing, Hughie," said Sammy as they parted. "What's a quire?"

"What do you think . . . a sing song? It's two dozen and you've got ten of them. You get them for a ha'penny each and sell them for a penny each. A hundred per cent profit. No' bad eh? Cowglen, right!"

Sammy smiled. "Aye. Cowglen . . . right."

"And . . . Sammy. Give the driver a bung."

The following day Sammy took a No. 14 Corporation bus bound for Househillwood which went past the entrance to the sprawling camp of Americans.

"Hello there boys," he said, a wide grin on his face, to the two Snowdrops, the regimental policemen guarding the gate. At the side a large sign proclaimed "316th Station Hospital, United States Army Medical Department". They looked at him with expressionless faces as he gave them his spiel. "I'm Sammy. Sammy Nelson the newspaperman. You boys could be doing with a good guide to what's doing in Glasgow. Well, I've got it and can deliver it to you every night. Tells you what's on at all the pictures. The movies you know. And what bands are playing at the dancing . . . Locarno, Green's Playhouse, the West End Ballroom, Albert, and that. And I'm starting deliveries next Monday. Tuppence each. Two pennies you know. That be all right boys?"

They were totally unimpressed. "You better see the Captain, bud," said one of them stiffly.

"Aye, fine boys. The Captain then."

After about twenty minutes an officer appeared at the gate and Sammy gazed enviously at his dark olive shirt and light tie.

"Hi, there," said the officer politely. "I'm Captain Ed Ridgman, the public affairs officer. Is there something I can do to help you?"

Sammy gave him the story, embellishing it a bit more. "It's not only the information you've to think of. It would be a great help for morale. And I know all about morale. Was at Dunkirk, you know. One of the last off the beaches. And do you know how we kept our spirits up? We sat there reading papers and magazines the welfare officers had brought us."

"Well how about that! You a Dunkirk man?"

"That's right sir. Had to be invalided out when we got back to Blighty . . . that's what we called Britain in the army. Shellshock, you know. Oh, I'm all right now except for the terrible headaches. That's why I don't work in the munitions factories. I would love to be in one of them turning out the stuff for our boys, and your boys, too, Captain. But you know how it is. So I just do light work, like the newspapers. Spreading the word around, you know. All the very latest about the big campaigns. I feel it's my own little war effort. Know what I mean, Captain?"

"Been a pleasure speaking to you, Sam. I don't see too many problems. We don't let traders into the camp of course. But I hardly interpret your activities as trading."

"Of course not, Captain."

It was easy after that. His hunch was right and he discovered more than one Sammy Nelson among the eager buyers for the evening paper he sold by proclaiming: "Get your Glasgow Guide, all the latest about the movies and the dancing." The fact that it was called something else made little difference. And no one even bothered about being charged tuppence for a newspaper whose marked price was a penny.

The American camp at Cowglen and what it provided for him was to become Sammy Nelson's biggest single enterprise. After a while he didn't even care whether or not he sold his newspapers; they were his passport to better things, and because of that he began giving them away to the troops, first of all to the regimental police at the gate because he knew they were to him the most important men in the camp, then to the officers, then to the NCOs, until eventually everyone was getting their copy free, the money and cigarettes they gave him in tips more than covering his costs. But it was what he got out of the camp that made Sammy real money. Wartime Glasgow was one vast and incredible market place of eager buyers who collectively found themselves in the paradoxical position of having more money than at any time in their lives, but with precious few luxuries on which to spend it. Good cigarettes became scarce, whisky had all but disappeared, except for coarse, bulk supplies, and the man who could produce a pair of nylon stockings was a hero to every woman in sight. With every commodity scarce, everyone, it seemed, had become a willing buyer of anything that put a little cheer into their hard-pressed lives. And Sammy was there to help with that cheer. His trade in clothing coupons had become firmly established — "Pays the rent and buys the rations" he would say. His trading with the Americans was to provide a lot more.

He started quietly buying small amounts of nylon stockings, spirits and cigarettes from the US servicemen, his ploy being to wait until he had completely won the confidence of the Regimental Police, men he considered were like Busies anywhere — to be treated with great caution.

They laughed at him the first day he turned up at the camp with a big suitcase, struggling as he walked through the gate with the weight of its contents. "You coming here for a holiday?" joked one of the guards.

"Like my case, boys? Thought you would. I ruined two dozen of my newspapers last week with the rain . . . but Sammy boy has found the answer. They're in the case." And so Sammy and his case became something of a fixture around the camp. He made a great display of it at various points around the base. It became so much a part of him and his appearance at the camp every day, they would have asked questions had they seen him without it.

They would have asked a lot more questions had they seen what was inside it when he left the camp pretending, as he did, that it was only a fraction of the weight he had carried into the post. The various customers — Sammy preferred to call them his "agents" — with whom he dealt among the Servicemen were willing to sell him anything they could obtain. Some days it was shirts and shoes, other days trousers, cartons of cigarettes, whisky and brandy; on a good day he could get two of the officers' greatcoats which made him spectacular profits, and on other days he did his food-run special — cheese, coffee and butter — although there wasn't so much profit in them when the weight ratio was considered. But for a man like Sammy there was a way round everything and he got round that one too by coming to an arrangement with the van driver who delivered his papers, a packet of Camels keeping him more than happy for returning to the camp to pick up Sammy and his case at the gates.

They were good days for Sammy and Peggy Nelson. They never had so much money. Between his coupons, his evening papers and what he called "the importing side" of his business, he could average £30 a week. Sometimes he could make as much as £50, six or seven times more than the average wage of a well-paid munitions worker. And his money was all tax free.

Although he could have afforded to buy a real Crombie now instead of the imitation one he wore, Sammy kept his dress fairly humble. "Bang goes your price if you start going about like the real toff," he explained to Peggy one night. "You know, it's amazing this money stuff," he went on. "When you've got a wee bit, it changes everything . . . the way you think, the way people think about you. I mean, there's me, for instance. Had nothing and meant nothing to anybody . . . except you, hen, all my days. Now I can bung a driver a packet of Yankee fags and he thinks I'm big time and he'll go out of his way for me. I go into the pub and they give me the nod and the smile, no' because I've done anything for them or that they even know me . . . to talk to like. They do it for they've heard about me and they talk about me. They say to each other, 'See him, he's doing all right that yin.' They look at me for I represent a wee bit of money and material wealth to them. And that means power to them . . . for none of them has anything. They know they're going to be up a close all their lives. And all of a sudden I'm their pal.

"Some of them talk to me like they've known me all their lives. It's Sammy this and Sammy that. Crack a rotten joke and they think it's great. You know, the same way it is wi' the bookies. The bookies are aye everybody's pal. And you get these punters going about boasting that they're a big china of so-and-so the bookie and that's supposed to impress you. What they're really telling you is that they, like everyone else, don't have a tosser to their name, but they're that wee bit different for they *know* somebody that does have a few shekels. They used to look at Jamesie the way they're looking at me now. Jamesie had power . . . by Christ he did. One had a white ivory handle. The other was black. But it was the same kind of treatment he got . . . laughing at his patter in the pubs, shouting 'How's it gaun', Jamesie,' one trying to shout it louder than the next, hoping he'd even remember their names. Christ, see if Jamesie knew your name . . . you were in, so you were. I never thought that would happen to me, Peggy. At least I knew it would never happen to me because I was a hard man. For I'm no'. Sure, I used to have the odd scrap as a young fellow in some of Jamesie's stramashes before he took to the serious stuff with the weapons and that, and I thought nothing of being the only sticker to

help him out when the Holden gang went for him. But that was all.
They can keep the hard nonsense. It's really weird, though, when you
think about it, me ending up getting the same treatment as my
brother but for different reasons. I mean . . . inside I'm still the same old
me. I still think we should all be equal an' that. And you would never
get me looking up to someone because he's what they call a big shot.
That's no' me Peggy. And never will be."

"I know it's not, Sammy. That's how you're that bit special. The
others are not like that. Gie them money and it goes straight to their
heads. Just like that Harry Brannigan. Mind when he used to sell
briquettes and sticks?"

"Aye, and smell to high doh."

"God, he was a right scruff. Then he starts lifting lines and look at
him now, a bookie wi' three pitches and he stands there in Ballater
Street and looks down his nose at you when you pass."

"Aye, and he still doesnae wash."

"I met his wee wife, Ettie, the other day in the Beehive. She was all
apologies for being seen there. 'Oh I usually do all my shopping in
Buchanan Street,' she says. 'We've an account, you know.' And there
she was trying to talk all posh and no' making it. God, wee Ettie
Brannigan . . . and she still walks like a wee bachle."

"Aye, and she doesnae wash either."

When they finished laughing at that. Peggy said, "Sammy, we'll not
let money change us. We'll get on in life with it though, and we'll enjoy
it, but we'll never be like the Brannigans and them."

"No fear, hen. That's another reason why I'm not cutting about in
the flash clothes. Don't want them thinking I'm some kind of spiv. I
would detest that. Some of them get ideas, you know, just because
you're into a bit of buying and selling and showing enterprise. If I'm a
spiv, what does that make Myer and Woolworths and Lewis's and
Bremner and Goldberg . . . highway robbers? They're just at the same
game as me really. In fact, you could say I'm doing it even better for I'm
getting the stuff none of them can get. I'm the specialist, the one that's
making them all happy."

By the end of that year the Nelsons were able to move from the
tenement in Allison Street, Govanhill, to what Peggy called her dream
home, a semi-detached villa in Stamperland, a new garden suburb in
the vicinity of Clarkston, five miles south of the Gorbals. When they
had first married, Peggy used to love the walk with Sammy to
Eglinton Toll where, just across from the Plaza Ballroom, MacTaggart
and Mickel the builders had a showhouse bungalow. The big sign
outside it proclaimed: "Only £25 down and 21 shillings a week covers
all outlays . . . free removal provided." And Stamperland was one of
the areas where the bungalows and houses of other designs were

being built. "Oh, do you think we'll ever see the day when we'll be able to afford a house like that?" she would say. Always the optimist he would reply "Aye, hen. We'll get one even better."

Allison Street had the ultimate in modern living . . . an inside toilet. But in Randolph Drive, Stamperland, the semi-villa, although not quite as grand as the Eglinton Toll showhouse, offered them a new dimension in their ultimate. Not only did they have their own inside toilet, they also had a bath, a front and rear garden, and doors leading to both. They were in dreamland.

"Changed days," said Peggy when they moved in.

"Aye, you're right, hen. Changed bloody days."

8

THE END OF AN ERA

ROBBIE and Andrew Fordyce were released two weeks later on bail of £50 each from Jessiefield Prison in Dumfries. They returned home to Lydeburn on the Glasgow bus and when the Walker boys at the blacksmiths saw them, the word went round the district. The reality of what they had done had a profound effect upon them, and neither could lift his head as they walked, unspeaking, from the road end along the winding track that eventually opened up to the graceful drive which led up to their imposing residence. They went straight to their rooms, Robbie collapsing on his bed, weeping bitterly and repeating over and over to himself, "Dad . . . dad . . . dad." Andrew stood by his window which looked north towards Corsincon, the tears streaming from his unblinking eyes, blurring the long ridge of the small mountain. His throat pained as he forced himself from openly crying. A little over an hour after arriving home, there was a knock at their bedroom doors and Ginty Burns, the housekeeper and the wife of Davie, the driver, brought each of them tea and scones on trays in a trolley and the message that when they were finished, Mrs Fordyce wanted to see them. "In the library", said Ginty, icily and without looking directly at either of them, her instructions being addressed to the nearest wall.

"Take a seat, boys," said their mother, totally composed and revealing a strength of character they didn't realise she possessed. The Victorian cameo brooch which her late husband had presented her after the birth of the twins was pinned to the neck of her black dress, her plainness taking on a quality of beauty. There was no emotion, no hostility in her voice as she spoke to her sons.

"Your father is dead and the fact that he is will be something for you and your consciences to live with. Nevertheless, you are my children, my beloved children, as much a part of me as you were your father and his forebears. Why you have behaved as you did is beyond my comprehension, but then mankind is full of uncomprehending things. What you deserve for what you did to that lovely girl is not for me to judge. As your mother it is understanding that I have to try to give, not judgment. Others will give their judgment on you, including the law. Now, and in the future, you will have to show from what you are made. The past cannot be undone . . . oh that it could! Your father was the first man I loved, the only man I ever loved. I am still a young woman but I will love no other man. And if you dedicate the rest of your lives in a fashion that in any way approaches that of your father, you will have gone some way towards amending what has happened this past fortnight. But whatever . . . I am your mother and nothing will alter my love and affection for you both."

Within a week, Robbie and Andrew Fordyce each had received a letter from the Crown Office in Edinburgh telling them that it had been decided not to proceed with the charges against them. Both of them then wrote to the Principal of St Andrews University informing him that they would not be returning "until after the hostilities". Then they left for Glasgow and the Army Recruiting Office where, as volunteers, they were told they would be able to nominate the regiment in which they wished to serve, although it didn't necessarily mean the request would be granted. In their case it was, for the one they chose needed as many men as they could get . . . the Highland Light Infantry.

The scandal of that mid-November day was the only topic of conversation in the farms and cottages, the little hamlets and villages and the towns of Upper Nithsdale for months afterwards. All the comings and goings to Lydeburn were noted with more interest than normally by a community whose daily interest in each other's lives was, by virtue of their rural existence, detailed and intense. They would look around the other farms, cottages and houses first thing in the morning to see who was up and who wasn't, knowing all the tell-tale signs that carried such facts, the dim light of paraffin lamps from bedroom and kitchen windows, the yellow smoke from a new day's fire. They would note who was first to start their harvest and who had finished theirs last. And what they couldn't see they would find out from the provision roundsmen and the postmen who called on them and were great sources for exchanging gossip and information. They noted that Mrs Fordyce had never left the house, although the whispers from the staff were that she was composed and living normally. They saw that the boys had returned and they knew that they had left again, probably for Glasgow for it was the through bus, as they called it, that the Walker boys had seen them get at the road end "wi' cases as big as trunks, coats an a'". They knew too when the

word had come up from Dumfries that there were to be no charges
against the Fordyce boys. Sam Niven had blethered about that "just
atween you and me" in the back shop of Wull Moffat's, the Kirkconnel
cobbler's where certain favoured men would meet for a smoke and a
gossip around a cosy fire that never slept.

Willie Gibb, an oversman at the Lady Ann Colliery, Tam Anderson,
the station porter and Jimmy Purdie, the Merkland milkman had all
been there. They were regulars in Moffat's back shop, sitting on small
stools round the walls of the room to avoid the rows of J-toed herds '
boots, steel capped miners' ones, sturdy brown market brogues, a
handsome pair of Veldtschoen, a few pairs of Church's, the women's
walking out shoes, flimsy by comparison, and a variety of lasts, all on
the floor which was the cobbler's workbench. The cobbler would
speak about the owners of the footwear, often criticising them for the
character they revealed through their soles and heels.

But there was no chat about the footwear's owners that day.
Constable Niven had told them about the news he had had from his
headquarters in Dumfries. "Ah kent fine they would be dropped," said
Willie Gibb the miner, a raw stony-faced man who had spent his
lifetime hewing coal from the Lady Ann Colliery's seams. "It's because
the Duke kens them."

"Nothing of the kind," countered the policeman. "The Fiscal says
they've suffered enough with the death of the Colonel and that a guid
lawyer might have got them off and anyway, the doctor says they
havenae bairn'd the lassie."

Normally it was only at Christmas that they killed a fowl at
Glenmulloch. But on Mrs Cameron's instructions, Wull Andrews
chose the plumpest and healthiest bird he could find, a big heavy-
chested Wyandotte, and despatched it, ready for the pot. "She'll be
needing all the strength she can get," said the farmer's wife.

Star had refused food and any desire to communicate on her first
day in bed, sleeping most of the time. Mrs Cameron brought her a big
mug of the chicken tea, strong and oily, which she had made from the
heavy, yellow-skinned fowl. "My mother gave me this the first time I
had flu and I had it as well after our wee Margaret arrived and my, it
fairly puts you on your feet," she said when she brought the steaming
broth to the girl she loved as if she were her own. On her third day in
bed she looked a lot brighter when Mrs Cameron came into the room
with more of the strong chicken tea. She had been up and bathed and
her hair was shining again. She even managed a smile when Mrs
Cameron, who she now called Aunt Anne, came into the room.

"What did I tell you," she said. "You cannae beat the auld fashioned
remedies," and she told her how Wull Andrews had gone to great
lengths to choose the biggest and healthiest of the poultry for it had to

be nothing but the best for "our Star". She was touched at the way she had said "our" and felt closer to the Camerons and Wull Andrews and Glenmulloch than at any time since she arrived.

"You've had a time of it, lass," said Mrs Cameron. "One person doesn't deserve all you've been through. Now that your stepfather is in the hospital, you'll be thinking about going home and I wouldn't blame you if you wanted to leave us the morn. To think of all the things you must have heard them talk about your Glasgow and the keelies and we've got even worse ones here, and right among us. It doesn't bear thinking about."

"No, Aunt Anne, you're wrong. I know what they think about Glasgow, all right. I got plenty of that from the other lassies at school when I first came here. But I haven't thought about going home . . . and I wouldn't just because of . . . you know. Oh Aunt Anne, I'm so confused. I love Glenmulloch and everything about here and you and Uncle Wullie and Wull. I never had a family around me before, just my Ma and my Maw Lawson but Ma was always working or out somewhere and I was never sure who would be looking after me from one day to the next. Here it's been so different, so permanent. That's what has made it so difficult for me to decide about going home." She held Mrs Cameron's hand tightly and tears welled in her eyes. "Will I be all right do you think? I'm not . . . am I?"

"Don't you be worrying, dear, for you'll be fine. And if anything does happen, we'll look after you here."

Three mornings later she got up and dressed, putting on the overalls she wore at weekends and other occasions when she worked on the farm. Wullie Cameron was sitting in the kitchen by the big range, one of his legs resting on a stool. "It's my turn lass, to be no' well," he laughed. "The rheumatics, by gees, they're giving the auld yin gyp. Do you want to go to the hill, Star?"

She smiled at the suggestion for working with the sheep was what she liked best. "I'll be ready when you are," she said.

"No . . . on your own I mean."

She had always wanted to do that and work the dog on her own and the old farmer knew she would love the chance to do it. Her eyes widened at the suggestion. Before she could say anything further, he began rhyming off the various locations where he wanted the sheep counted. "And mind that dug doesnae run them too fast once you're up by the Auld Lime Road. He's an auld bugger for that . . . just you gie him a swearing if he does."

"Wullie!" Mrs. Cameron chided. "It's the lassie you're talking to — no' Wull Andrews."

"Oh, tuts, woman."

"And Star," he went on, "don't be hunting for that auld one-eyed yowe that's always in that bit at the top of the glen, or that yin that gave us triplets the last two years, and Coupie, as you used to call her, the one you saved twice when she had coupit, and Blackie the one that grazed up at the Hillhead march . . . they're all away. Went away on Monday with the other draft yowes for the Ayr sale."

The smile left Star's face and she turned her back on the Camerons in order not to show her feelings, fussily tidying the newspapers and magazines that always littered the big settee by the window and which served as seats for the dining table. She had cried the very first time the sheep had gone to market, particularly the lambs, for it was Wull Andrews who told her when she had asked, that the other farmers would buy them in order to fatten them and the next man to buy them would be the butcher. "And if you stop and think o'er much about that then there's no place for you in the country," he had said. And she had taken his advice, or tried to, yet it still hurt when she heard that some of her favourite old ewes were gone.

She turned round after having tidied the papers and the smile was on her face again. "I'll away to the hill."

When she had left with Major the collie, reluctant at first because he knew his master wasn't going, Mrs Cameron asked her husband why he had let her go to the hill on her own. "And it's not just your rheumatism, I know that."

"She loves it up there, Annie. And the feeling you can get up there can blaw away the worst of bad times. And she's needing that, by God she is."

It was a long trek to the hill, but Star knew the road well. Wullie Cameron had taught her his regular route, using the same tracks and paths his father had used before him and other generations of sheepmen before them . . . straight up the middle of the horses' meadow, rising steeply to the well by a solitary rowan tree, then veering right by the side of the steep glen, till you reached the five-bar gate on the Old Lime Road that marked the southern march of Glenmulloch with its neighbour Samsiston. The old road was a rough metalled cart track with tall grass growing between the tracks. It ran from south to north across the entire property, rising high on Glenmulloch Hill and ending on the slopes of Corsincon itself at another five-bar gate which was the northern march of the farm.

It was more than an hour before she reached there, her cheeks burnished red with the chill winter wind. She climbed up and sat atop the stout gatepost, looking south down Nithsdale, the collie's long tongue greedily lapping water from the gushing burn by the roadside. The noisy curlews and frenetic peewits and the shrilling snipes had all gone back to the estuaries with their young and the sheep were silent, the lambs all having gone, except the two score of purebred Blackfaces kept for breeding stock. The silence was only broken by the occasional caw of a flapping hoodie and the burn whose home was destined to be the Nith and then the sea. She reflected on her conversation with Wull Andrews when she passed with Major that morning. It was the first time he had seen her since he had run to Kirkconnel for the doctor. Mrs Cameron had told her about his gallant run and how the doctor had been back at the farm just over an hour after Wull had left. She had said, "Thanks Wull," to him when she passed and he had looked embarrassed, the embarrassment not so much for himself but for her and how she must feel facing the world and people, some who would understand, some who would misunderstand.

He had made no mention of it at first and spoke to her as he would every morning, about the weather and what his prediction was for that day, then telling her that he had felt like giving big Bell the Clydesdale a whipping earlier that morning for refusing to take the halter, and that two of the Khaki Campbell ducks had disappeared, either to the fox or nesting up the glen. It was just as she made to walk away that he had said "Star . . . how are you feeling?" When she assured him she was all right he smiled fondly at her saying how pleased he was to see her looking so well. "You know lass, you've no' to be building any fences around yoursel' because of anything that might have happened. Mind of that time that I told you about the lambs and bullocks and what happened to them after they left here? Think too much about that and you would get yourself in an awfy state. It's just the way of it. Farming goes on. Life goes on. The same when somebody dies. You cannae die with them or build a fence around yoursel'. They built a stretch o' high deer fence where I used to work at Moniaive and d'ye know what happened? The rabbits got under it. Never shut life out, no matter what. You be yoursel' lass and don't be letting last Saturday be having any further effect on you. It's by and done wi'. And we a' love you here." He looked away at that for he was not a man of words or open emotion and she was most surprised at what he had said for he had never spoken in any great depth to her before.

As she feasted on the idyllic view down the long wide valley, she reflected on how nice it had been of Wull to say what he had and how brave he had been for saying it for he was such a quiet man. And she wondered what it would have been like if the events of the previous Saturday had occurred in the Gorbals. Would there have been the love, the understanding and the affection that had been shown to her at Glenmulloch? The more she thought about it the more reluctant she was to reach a conclusion. Ther' certainly wouldn't have been the

solace of being among the most beautiful scenery in all of Scotland . . .
well that's what Wullie Cameron had told her it was the very first day
they had climbed to his favourite spot on the hill, the trough by the
spring on the Old Lime Road.

The following week they got word that Mrs Fordyce wanted to see
Star at Lydeburn. It was a mild and sunny day for being so late in the
year and she dressed in her best frock, one that Mrs Cameron had
made for her from one of her own old dresses, and set off alone for the
mile and a half walk to the big estate house. The Walkers had seen her
from the Tamsmiddy and knew by her bright dress that she must have
been going somewhere and because she didn't pass the smithy that
she must have gone to Lydeburn. That much they knew, but they
were never to know what went on between Mrs Fordyce and Star
Nelson that day.

Ginty Burns brought them afternoon tea in the big lounge which
had french doors leading to the front garden, at the side of which was
the gazebo and the rustic seat where they had found the Colonel.
They gossiped about the mild weather and the magnificent view of the
dale from the window as Mrs Burns set out the hand painted delf
plates on a big drum table by which there was a set of Louis XV chairs.

When the housekeeper had left the room, Mrs Fordyce looked at
Star and outstretched a hand towards her. She spoke softly and with
great feeling. "How are you my dear? It's been a terrible experience . . .
for both of us. But you're a strong person. I can tell. And you'll get
over all this . . . and I will live through it all too, although life will never
be the same again. We think, sometimes, that life is going to go on for
ever as we know it. Then something happens, sometimes an eventful
thing, other times an uneventful thing, but yet it changes life for you
completely. We studied Napoleon for our French history at college and
his letters fascinated me. In one he wrote, "Our hour is marked and no
one can claim a moment in life beyond what fate has predestined". I
never forgot those words. Every turn in my own life seems to have
been predestined . . . becoming a teacher, being sent to Auldgirth then
to Cairn Smiddy School. Another young teacher had wanted to go
there, you know, because it was near her home, but they said no
because they didn't think her ready for a one-teacher school. What if
she had? Would she be sitting with you here now? We do seem all
linked in some unfathomable fashion, I'm convinced of that. Who
knows what would have happened if I had not come here. But had I not
I would have missed all those wonderful years at Lydeburn. Likewise,
had it not been for the war you would not have come to Glenmulloch
and been, in turn, so intertwined with our lives . . . and we in yours."

She stopped at that point, as though to compose herself by pouring out a fresh cup of tea from the handsome Georgian pot. "Well Star, I have come to a decision about my future. Whether or not it will effect you I don't know. The Colonel left the estate to me... and I'm going to sell it. I could never stay on here at Lydeburn. The memories are too sweet. I'm afraid the years ahead may make them another way. And I would dread that. I've bought a place in Maxwelton at Dumfries. Back to where I came from as it were. You are the first person I've told here. What changes it will bring about I don't know. I've asked that the two tenant farmers be given the chance to buy their properties. The others, which are run by managers, will be sold together with Lydeburn House. I've discussed it with the boys and they understand. They could never live here and be happy for what happened on that terrible day will always be remembered and be spoken about all over Upper Nithsdale. People in the country are like that, and I don't mean that as a criticism for they are dear, dear people. Nevertheless, that is their way."

They walked together to the end of the elm and sycamore-lined drive-way where two massive granite pillars marked the entrance to the policies of the house, some thirty acres of gardens and parkland, a big red cock pheasant scurrying into the field beyond the gate before fussily taking to flight. They stopped by the entrance and held hands and Star spoke. "I've never thought about life before like that, like the way you told me today. It's helped me see things a lot more clearly...a lot more differently. I may return to Glasgow. My mother wants me home, although she doesn't know about ... you know. And she's not going to know either. But perhaps it may be good for me to go there... for a spell anyway. As you can see, I'm not terribly sure. But something keeps telling me I should go."

"Your whole life is ahead of you, Star. Don't think about these terrible weeks. I had a long talk with the boys about everything and they say they'll carry the shame of what they did to you to their graves. They said there were no words they could find to express their sorrow to you. Don't have any bitterness in your heart for them, my dear. That would only hurt you, not them."

The tears welled in both their eyes as they embraced and said goodbye. And they waved to each other till Star reached the bend in the track as it descended towards the river. She walked down the hill out of sight of Mrs Fordyce and Lydeburn House.

The ramifications of that mad Martinmas night had an untold effect on the lives of more than one family in Upper Nithsdale, changing their way of life as well as that of the character of the community.

The church and the Red Cross, the Women's Rural Institute and the Riding of the Marches, among a variety of other welfare and charitable organisations were not only saddened but deprived of the energy and stimulus that had been given them over the years by the Fordyces. Glenmulloch had been one of the two tenanted farms but Wullie Cameron didn't take up the opportunity of buying it. He was in his mid-fifties and a lifetime of working in the high moors, waist high in wet grass every day for months on end on his treks through the tall marsh grass of the hill while tending his Blackfaces, had made him arthritic and he dreaded the prospect of another lambing season. Glenmulloch was therefore included with the estate in the sale, the purchasers being the Howiesons of Cumnock, a wealthy Ayrshire family with a chain of farms, who jumped at the chance of getting the prestigious Lydeburn Estate and at the same time providing themselves with a seat which they considered befitted their expanding enterprise.

The Howiesons were a rough and ready collection of brothers, self-made men, and the feel of the community meant little to them. Tam, the eldest of the brothers, came to see them at Glenmulloch when the sale was being negotiated. Wullie Cameron had met him several times before, mainly at Craig's Market in Ayr, and he was always the first to ask for the luckpenny, the backhander many would ask from the buyer after selling their livestock. It wasn't so much that he always insisted on the money, it was the grasping way he did it that made him so unpopular with the other farmers. He was a big, uncompromising man with a florid face, whose sole measurement of people was how hard they were prepared to work. And that judgment had even more critical standards if he was making it about people who worked for him. Coupled with that he had the reputation of being the hardest taskmaster in his county. He always spoke through clenched teeth and man and beast were addressed in the same stentorian fashion.

It was in that way he addressed them as he stood in the middle of the big kitchen at Glenmulloch. "That's a fine lassie you have there Mr Cameron . . . big, strong girl. She'll dae a turn o' work, I'll be thinking." Star didn't stop to look at him and, instead, continued to help Mrs Cameron clear away the dinnertime dishes. "An' they tell me that yer man Wull Andrews is the hardest working man in these parts. I'll take the pair of them aff yer hands then," he said without a further look in Star's direction. Wullie Cameron looked towards her but before he could speak she stopped on her way to the scullery and snapped at the big Ayrshireman.

"I'm no' for the taking, as you call it, Mr Howieson. I've got other plans."

Howieson was shocked at the retort for workers never spoke to him like that, or else they would be sent packing. "Ye've a quick tongue in yer heid, lass," he came back, showing more of his clenched teeth than normal. "Ah well, Mr Cameron, I wouldnae be wanting yin like that about my bit."

Wull Andrews too told him he had other plans when Howieson asked him to stay at Glenmulloch as his grieve. That really disappointed big Tam Howieson, for getting a man like Wull Andrews to work for you was like a prize; somebody that could ruck a hayfield quicker than any man in the valley, who could turn over more acreage with a swing plough than any other horseman between Thornhill and New Cumnock, who could scythe a storm-flattened cornfield like the old-timers who had worked that way before the turn of the century, and who, if he was asked, could do a turn as a smith or a herd — someone like that was a gem of a prize to have on your farm. But as the farmers knew the calibre of the men who worked the land, so did the workers know them. And Wull Andrews knew all about Big Tam. He inpersonated his high rasping voice to Star, spitting the words out through closed teeth and making her laugh so much that tears of mirth rolled down her cheeks.

"Naw, says I to Big Tam, I'll no' be working for you, sir," the sir being perfunctory, not complimentary. "Double my wages and I would not work even as your gardener," and the pair of them laughed together as he once more impersonated big Tam's high voice.

"So what are you going to do, Wull?"

"Oh, that's me finished with the farms. I left school when I was thirteen and the next day I was filling bogies down Knockshinnoch pit at New Cumnock. Five years of that and then I was into the forestry. The same hard grind but it was grand being in the open. And from there to the farms, the last fifteen years here wi' Wullie Cameron. After working for him so long I couldn't be doing with a different farmer for a boss. He left me alone to get on wi' it for he knew what I was doing and never interfered. They're no' all like that. The likes o' Big Tam, aye and others, they're never off yer back. And I couldn't be doing wi' that. I'm 43 now and for thirty years I've laboured from morning to night. I think I'm due something else now. I've a pal on the railways and he said he can get me the next vacancy as a surfaceman. Better hours and conditions than anything I've ever had before, aye, and they even give you a free ticket to go anywhere you like for your holidays. Holidays!" he exclaimed. "Never been away for a holiday in my life, except the time one June when I had a week at the fishing down by Sanquhar. Aye, and as well as the train for your holidays you get a railway house as well. God, I'll feel like a millionaire, Star. But I'll be in Kirkconnel so you'll aye come and see me won't you Star?"

"Don't you worry about that, Wull. I'll always be having some contact with here. That's a promise."

The Camerons had to make plans too. There was a smallholding near Guildhall in the north side of Kirkconnel. There were twelve acres, enough for a cow, some poultry and pigs and, having been thrifty with their savings from Glenmulloch, they had enough to buy it.

"You'll be coming with us, of course," said Annie to Star.

There was a long pause before she answered. "No Aunt Anne, my mother wants me back with her in Glasgow. And seeing as we're leaving Glenmulloch, then it's as good a time as any to be going home. I couldn't make up my mind before, but with everything changing as it is, it has helped me decide."

She stayed with them that last winter at Glenmulloch, celebrating her sixteenth birthday at a memorable Burns Night the Camerons held in one of the big front rooms of the farmhouse, the one that was completely bare of furniture, the floor covered with a brown patterned linoleum. They put a long trestle table in it for the occasion "for the drink and the puddin'," said Mr Cameron.

They came from all the Lydeburn farms and cottages and Wullie Cameron's old boyhood friends, the ones in the lonely herds'cottages beyond their hill on the edge of the vast moors that went all the way to Southern Lanarkshire, came too, to relive their adolescent days with fiddle, and buttonbox, pipes and all, with some "auld Scotch sangs". Mrs Cameron had made a haggis which was so big they had to boil it in the washhouse copper and that had taken the best part of six hours and when Wullie Cameron addressed it he said "There ne'er was a chieftain like it in a' the puddin' race." When he plunged a big butcher's slicing knife into its heart, it gasped an enormous cloud of steam into the room which made them all burst into spontaneous applause at the achievement. Beside the haggis on the trestle table there was a bottle of whisky and one of brandy and a crate of screwtop Coulson's beer to be shared between the 55 guests who sang and danced, recited and revelled the night away.

They had thought that she might take work locally, but Star's mind was firm on returning and on the day she left there was the same kind of silent hush about the house, sparse conversations conducted in whispers, like there is in the hours before a funeral.

"You've been a good lassie wi' us," said Mrs Cameron. "You've become like our very own daughter. We would have been proud had our wee Margaret turned out like you, Star."

Wullie Cameron never showed his emotions and wasn't for showing them on this sad day, barely a month since the Burns Night that had been the heartiest night Glenmulloch had known. He hid his feelings by issuing commands, like he would when they worked together in the fields and byres. "Better hurry yoursel' lassie or you'll be missing that through bus." Or: "You come back and see us, mind . . . d'ye hear?"

The bus was a few minutes late. Because of the emotion that choked them it seemed an eternity, and they stood silent, speaking only when the bus came into sight and began the long descent down Smiddy Brae. Mrs Cameron pulled Star to her and wept openly. "Look after yourself darling. Write to us, mind. It's been three happy years with you about the place."

Star wanted to cry too but forced her tears back. "I never thought I would be so sad at going home . . . but I have to, don't I? It's not the last you'll be seeing of me. That's a promise. You never know, I might be back to stay one day somewhere about here."

The bus climbed the high winding road that rose on the western slope of the high moorland which terminates the northern end of Nithsdale and, as she looked back, she could see the Nith ribboning in sculpted curves then Lydeburn House and all its farms slowly disappeared from view.

"Single or return?" said the conductress in an aggressive Glasgow accent which sounded strange to Star for, apart from her mother's visits, it was the first she had heard in more than three years.

"A single. And would you let me know when we get to the stop at the corner of Eglinton Street and Cumberland Street."

"In the Gorbals you mean?"

"Aye. The Gorbals."

9

MICKIE'S POTENT DROPS

THE war and all it brought with it continued. They were fighting
and dying in various fronts in Europe, the Russians were on the
offensive and the Japanese were being bombed, bayonetted and
burned out of the Pacific Islands, one by one, in a particularly brutal
slaughter of young men from both sides. They were dying for
freedom and democracy and to make the world a better place. And the
soldiers of both sides, wherever they fought, did what they did for
their homeland for these ideals, or some kind of interpretation of
them. In other places, away from the battlefronts, they starved and
slaved. Disposal factories were built to get rid of others because, it
was taught, they were not native to the Fatherland and were a curse to
them. The most fearful atrocities were committed. They were days of
tears.

But as the world writhed in suffering, it was the nature of things
that, just as some men killed, other men prospered. Sammy Nelson
would speak about them. "You listen to me," he would say. "My
conscience is clear about what I'm doing. I'm in the happiness
business. Every one of my customers leaves happy. They've got
coupons for a new suit, a packet of Luckies, toasted flavour and all, a
new shirt, a pair of nylons — and you know what you can get with
them, a tin of coffee or some extra tea? No' forgetting my Glasgow
Guide for the Yanks. Every one a happy customer. I'll no' be jumping
about in a big Rolls like a lot of them will when this lot is over. That's
your war effort boys, piling up fortunes from clapped out factories wi'
workers they treated like donkeys wi' peanuts for a wage until the war
came. It's the ones in the death trade that's making the real fortunes.
Everything they're making ends up with somebody copping it. No' me
pal. Christ, I'm keeping half the Gorbals from starving. It's the fuckin'
George Cross I should be getting, I'm telling you."

They were drinking in the Seaforth one day in early 1944, Sammy and his pal, Hughie "Plug" Connor. "How's the papers doing, Sammy? Could you take another few quire?"

Sammy was wearing his American officer's greatcoat, the latest *café-au-lait* model, as deep piled as an Aberdeen Crombie with a red silk hankie in the breast pocket and a vivid yellow Paisley harnish scarf, which hid the fact that he was wearing a shirt minus its detached collar and no tie. He had the flat bone buttons of the coat replaced with tan leather ones which matched his light tan shoes. His thoughts on dress hadn't changed and he didn't mean to look so affluent or too different from the others in case his customers got other ideas, but he had so many good clothes now it was difficult for him to look otherwise.

"Cracker of a coat, Sammy," said Connor.

"Aye, got it at the camp. Mind, I don't wear it when I'm out there wi' the papers. Can you imagine it! Me walking about wi' a pile o' my Guides under the oxter and looking like a fucking general. Christ, they would end up saluting me. No, I still play it easy out there. Don't want to kill the golden goose, as they say. And you've got to watch their regimental polis. Some of them are surly bastards and would turn you in quick as a nod if they thought you were up to something. But that's polis everywhere, isn't it? Christ, if they could see inside my case some days when I'm humping it out. Got half of their quartermaster's stores in it, so I have. And me walking out, all nonchalant and that, making out it's empty. Straining every muscle in my body, so I am. See this war! Hard fuckin' work so it is. Needing any coffee? I've got some of that new stuff in. Nescafé they call it. Doing a bomb wi' it wi' a' them that's on munitions. Saves them time, they say. No need for a percolator. Just make it like a cup of the old Bourn Vita. Trust the Yanks. Think of everything so they do."

"What do you want to drink?" said Connor.

"Half and a half."

"Nae whisky. They've got the signs up."

"Christ, and there's me wi' a couple of bottles of Johnnie Walker in the house as well. Naw, I don't want any of the mammy mine. See that stuff, last time I had it I ended up walking about like a ghost for a week. I'll stick to the heavy."

Hughie put the nuggety bubbling ale on the cast-legged table after taking a long draught that half-emptied the glass and complained about the lack of whisky. "I can get the odd half bottle in the work, Red Hackle usually," he said with disgust. "Think they make it wi' thistles. Don't like it one bit. Gets you right here," indicating his Adam's apple. "Terrible, so it is that we cannae get whisky . . . unless you're a docker, that is. That's where it's all going. Down to the docks and then out to

America to pay for the war. But half the crates are getting dropped and by the time the Inspectors get to them there's not a fuckin' bottle left. That's what you want to be doing, Sammy. Get yourself a few docker contacts and get a regular supply of the stuff. That's where the real money is."

"Not on your Nellie," replied Sammy earnestly. "I'm not into the off-the-back-of-a-lorry game. I'm legit, Hughie. Christ, you should know that. Don't touch knocked stuff."

"What about the papers?"

"Ach, but that's different. I mean, you said it yourself that thousands get sent back to your work every day and end up as waste. I'm saving some of that waste, you could say. It's no' real stealing, know what I mean like? But what the dockers do is. That's real tea-leaving."

"Anyway," said Hughie. "Whatever you say, getting the booze is the way to make the real money. Look at them all. They're going round the pubs wi' empty bottles and wee funnels and buying a "half" at a time and putting it in the bottle and ending up paying two quid for a thirteen-and-a-tanner half bottle. They'll only give it to you in the licensed grocers if they know your face. The one in Main Street there has no proprietary stuff, just bulk at three bob a gill and he warns you no' to come in more than once a week. Bastard. One of my chinas lives down in Clydebank and they'll only give you half a gill a week and you've to take your ain bottle wi' a label on it and they stamp the date and you don't get any more till you bring back the same bottle wi' the stamp on it. And d'ye know what big Tommy Robertson is doing at the Killarney in Cumberland Street? He's mixing bulk whisky wi' rum . . . and he hasnae had one complaint for the bulk is that rotten that the rum is improving it. Anyway, let's face it. We don't really give a fuck what it's like as long as it makes us bevvied. Isn't that right? See if you could get your hands on a good supply of whisky, or something like it. Make yourself a fortune. A fuckin' fortune, Sammy."

"You're right, Hughie. My business needs variety, That was auld Nat Myer's philosophy. If you're down in one department, ma boy, you've got to be up in the other, he would say. Know their stuff, the Jewboys. Got to hand it to them. Aye, that's a good idea, Hughie. Whisky. I'll need to get into whisky."

Old Mickie Doyle and his wife Bridie lived in Kidston Street at the far end of Florence Street facing directly on to Dixon's Blazes. The houses never knew darkness or peace because of the lights and the furnace flares of the ironworks which groaned its unearthly dins day and night and belched noxious fumes at will. The Kidston Street houses suffered most from them.

The Doyles had been in the Gorbals forever, it seemed, because everyone and their father knew them. Yet their accents and their ways were from Ireland. They had migrated before the First World War: Mickie was from Cookstown in County Tyrone and Bridie was a Cork woman. Mickie had worked most of his days as a navvy and you could hear Bridie before you saw her for she worked in Cumming's fish shop in Crown Street where the women, like all fish shop women, wore steel-rimmed clogs. The difference was that Bridie wore hers all the time. They were the only shoes she owned and even above the din of Dixon's she could be heard clip-clopping up and down the tenement stairs, honed knife-edged with wear. Like many of the wives she wore a dark brown plaid shawl, over the long black dress that had been in style when she left Ireland as a young woman.

Mickie and Bridie Doyle were a friendly and popular couple, the highlight of Mickie's week being to get drunk on a Friday night and having enough left over for what he called "a wee quiet drink" on the Saturday. Bridie was always on the move, always working at something, whether it be in Cumming's filleting, or as a cleaner in some of the bigger houses in Abbotsford Place with their wide sweeping turreted staircases, or part-time in Dambrosio's chip shop, the three jobs making up for the wages which were never handed over by her husband. Older wives, particularly Irish ones, would often call in at Kidston Street for Bridie's help. She was steeped in many of the old ways of County Cork and they said she had a cure, whether it worked or not, for everything, and you could bring your dog or horse too for she also knew how to treat them. The merest mention of an ailment to her in the fish and chip shop and she would be suggesting a cure. She made a cough mixture the original recipe of which required the yolk of a new-laid egg, but because of the war-time shortage of fresh eggs she substituted dried egg powder which she made into a thin paste, resembling a yolk, mixing it with rose water, sugar and other things which she said were best kept to herself. She sold it for a shilling a bottle and they swore it was the best cough cure in Glasgow. Even Billy Brough, the coalman with the loudest shout in the Gorbals, was convinced there was something of the magician about her after she cured his big mare, Daisy, of the strangles with a concoction she made with warm salt.

Mickie was a loner, except when he joined the other men in McNee's pub, at the corner of Naburn and Kidston Streets for games of dominoes. He considered himself an upright and law-abiding citizen, law-abiding particularly because of the one experience in Barlinnie which he had found to be a salutary lesson in life. It happened just after the Great War when the Doyles and the Nelsons had been neighbours in Rose Street, Mickie being one of Old James Nelson's drinking cronies in the Moy. Sammy, just a young man at the time, had always remembered the incident for it was the talk of the street and his father spoke about nothing else for weeks. "Trust the bloody Irish," he used to say. "Imagine making your ain whisky in your ain house and thinking you can get off with it. Christ, the smell was worse than Dixon's Blazes."

Like Bridie and her cures, Michael Doyle had come from Ireland with many of the old ways and the one which he knew best of all had been making poteen which he coloured and sold as whisky, except to his fellow countrymen who liked it the way it was for it was good stuff, him coming from Cookstown and all, and from a family that had been renowned as one of the finest poteen makers in Tyrone. But Mickie's shebeen was shortlived for when his customers left there were more fights in the street outside his close than outside most pubs. Every night was like a Friday. They gave him six months in Barlinnie and ordered all his equipment to be confiscated and destroyed. That had been the end of his poteen-making and he had been a law abiding man ever since.

The smell from Mickie and Bridie's single-end house hit Sammy Nelson when the dark-stained door opened. It was worse than any of the other houses he had known, and some had been bad, for they would shut themselves in, windows and doors closed tight, unwashed bodies exuding a sweaty odour which mixed with the heavy aroma of the cold grease from the ever-present frying pan and the cloying staleness of dissipated Virginia tobacco smoke. Blended together with the rancid stench of damp plaster and rotting wood from neglected tenements, the smell was so powerful that even momentary contact was sufficient for it to cling to clothes and flesh like some evil fixing agent. The Doyles' little apartment had all these smells . . . and more. For they were laced with the odours Bridie brought back from her work at Cumming's fish shop and Dambrosio's chip shop and together they made an odoriferous broth the like of which he had never experienced before. Sammy spluttered and apologised for not stepping into the house after identifying himself at the door.

"Auld James Nelson's boy . . . min' o' him fine," said Mickie . . . "But come in will ye?"

"I'm sorry," said Sammy. "It's the phobia. You know, cannae stand being in a wee room. Doctor says they're bad for my asthma as well."

"Why, my Bridie will have a cure for that."

"No, it's alright. Anyway, I've got a better cure. Fancy a wee half? C'mon, I'll stand ye a drink." Mickie reached for his bonnet and

Sammy took another deep breath from the sweet air of the close mouth, feeling it would purify him of what his lungs had experienced at the door of Mickie's house. "We'll go to Tommy Milligan's . . . he's got whisky in the day. Just bulk stuff but it's better than nothing."

The bar was quiet and they were able to get a table in the corner of the sitting room where Sammy outlined his proposals. "It's like this," he started. "The wife Peggy, she's one of the McGormans of Sandyfaulds Street."

"Know them fine,"said Mickie.

"Well, she's got herself a wee fruit shop in Cathcart Road at the corner of Carfin Street. We used to live there and she likes the area. Good customers you know. And she boils her own beets. Got a rare big cellar and at night after she closes she fills a big copper with the beets and cooks them. Stinks the place out, so it does. Can smell it all over Cathcart Road and Carfin Street when the steam pours up through the grating on the pavement. But nobody bothers."

"I know fine," said Mickie. "There's two or three in Cumberland Street, and Crown Street as well, do the same thing. Fine auld smell and all. Right fine whisky, that," he said. holding the small upturned glass to his mouth so that not a drop would be missed. "Good enough to have come out of a bottle."

The barman gave Sammy a slow, knowing nod and set up another two whiskies with the next two pints. He was one of Sammy's customers for American shirts and coffee.

"As I was saying, Mick, there's all this steam and smell and activity in all these wee fruit shop cellars at night and nobody bothers. Now supposing somebody was to start boiling other stuff besides the beets . . . or instead of the beets. Would anybody know the difference? You know, good stuff? Stuff that came out of a bottle. Know what I'm talking about Mickie?"

Doyle drew the tall pint glass towards him and half of it disappeared and all the time he kept staring at Sammy Nelson, emerging from the glass with a wry smile on his face. "Christ, Sammy, you're a bit of a lad are you not! You're right. Nobody would smell a thing. I know the smell of the stuff. Different like. But then, so's boiling the beets."

"Could you do it then?" asked Sammy eagerly.

"Oh, I could do it all right. You never lose the art, as it were. But I'm not for getting mixed up in any more shebeens. That Barlinnie place nearly killed me. Six months you know."

"But I'm not thinking of a shebeen, Mick. There'll be no selling it at the fruit shop. All you do is make it. I've got agents that do me a turn in my business . . . "

"You're in business then, Sammy? What's your line?"

"This and that, you might say. General trading, you know . . . "

"Aye."

"And my agents will be selling it. So there's no chance of the Busies nabbing you for being a shebeener is there?"

"No, Sammy. I couldn't be gripped again. One gripping is enough for me."

"Now calm yourself. Mickie. You'll no' be nabbed or gripped as you say. This is different. Guaranteed foolproof. And, anyway, it's like you doing your war effort. Keeping morale up, an' that. It's getting people down no' being able to get a good dram when they want it. You'd be doing them a good turn. And into the bargain there would be a few quid in it for yourself. Tax free at that."

"What kind of stuff do you have in mind, Sammy. Aythur or poteen?"

"What the fuck's aythur?"

"Aythur. Ach, ye make it with the first run, mix it with acid and give it another wee run. Like the stuff they give you in the hospitals."

"Jesus Christ. You mean ether! Ye cannae drink that."

"Can you not! Sammy, when I was a little boy in Cookstown they were drinking it all the time. Why, at the market which I used to go to with me Dad you couldn't smell the pigs or the men smoking their pipes for the smell of the aythur."

"But it would knock you on your back."

"Oh it would. That's why they had to hold their noses when they drank it. A wee tumblerful at a time, quick like, and you were drunk before you knew it. Nicely drunk, mind you. None of this fighting stuff they all do when they've been at the whisky. And after half an hour or so you would be sober again without so much as a hangover. Then you could have another wee dram o' it and get drunk all over again. Sure, there were men and their wives taking it thegether and sitting about all day with big smiles on their faces and all for a few pennies. Mind you, they had to be careful not to belch near the fire or be lighting their pipes. They say a man in Draperstown let out a big rift just as he was putting a taper to his pipe and he blew a flame six foot long and it burned down his house. Just terrible, so it was."

"Wait a minute, Mickie. I'm no' thinking about your ether. Jesus, we're bams enough here without getting into that. Its your other stuff."

"Poteen?"

"Aye, poteen. Whisky, isn't it?"

"Well it's like that. Lovely drink . . . but it's a different colour. Clear, like gin."

"But I want stuff that looks like whisky."

"Och, no bother. Bit of cold tea will soon do that. Me dad used to use the gravy browning."

"Jesus Christ!"

"T'was all right, Sammy. Swore that made the finest whisky of them all."

"Well, are you game then? Can you get the equipment to get started?"

"Well, I need some big copper pots, a worm, that's a curly piece of copper tubing, a big milk can, one of those big ten-gallon fellahs that you see down at the Co-op dairy, and a fire or a gas ring."

"What about the stuff to make it with?"

"Well now. Everyone had their own recipe. I was making it with oranges and carrots the last time for there was plenty of them. But if you can get me potatoes, malt and yeast then we're in business. Or beet pulp, treacle, barley, hops . . . "

"Beets. You can put beets in it! And spuds! No problems there, Mickie. But we cannae do you wi' the oranges. There's a war on. There's treacle about, though. And barley."

"I'm still worried about getting gripped, Sammy."

"Listen, don't you worry, Mickie. If the worst came to the worst it would only be a fine and I'll stump up. That make you feel better?"

"Could I have another half then?"

"No bother."

Another nod at the barman and the glasses were refilled. When they were gone there was another two and Mickie was humming to himself and tapping his feet and raring to get into song, which he did on the way home along Crown Street.

"When I was young I danced and sung and drank good whisky too;
Each shebeen shop that sold a drop of the real old mountain dew;
With the poteen still on every hill the peelers had no call;
Round sweet Stradone I am well known, round Lavey and Grouse Hall."

"Make poteen!" he laughed. "There's not another man in all the Gorbals that can make a finer drop than Mickie Doyle."

"Aye, fine Mickie. But we'll need to be quiet about it, eh?" Sammy cautioned. "Keep the voice down."

"Aye, quiet. You're right, Sam me boy. I'll keep it quiet, don't you worry. I won't even breathe a word, not even to my dear auld Bridie. She'll be after me for the money anyway, for when you're into the whisky making you're into the money, I'm telling you that, Sammy Nelson."

And that was good news.

Less than a month later the steam which emerged from the little fruitshop's pavement grille had the aroma of something other than beets. But no one knew or even suspected the change in the night time activities of Sammy Nelson's latest enterprise. The bottles had been easy to get, his "agents" merely lifting them from the rear doors of hotels and pubs where they had been left for the Corporation Cleansing Department men. And when it was ready for bottling, perfectly coloured in the traditional way of Mickie's forebears — with Bisto — it looked the real McCoy. To Sammy Nelson's great delight it also tasted like it. Because of the method of collecting the bottles it came in a variety of disguises . . . Black Label Johnnie Walker, Dewars, Haig's Dimple, Langs, Black and White and Red Hackle, as well as rum and brandy bottles.

"Finer stuff\ than all of them," said Mickie with pride at his achievement. And he had every right to be proud of his poteen. He had nursed it through all the initial stages from the mash he made of malt, potatoes and beet through the first-run singlings — "Put some of that on your chest and you'll have no more asthma, Sammy" — to the doubling when he knew he had got the taste right and on to the third run, pure and as strong as could be made.

Sammy had stayed with him during all the various stages of that first distillation, fascinated at the conversion of the unsightly wash to the clear third-run bottle of spirit he held before him. "Watch this," said Mickie. He shook the bottle of the finished product and a collection of bubbles rose to the top of the spirit and stayed there. "Ah, you little darlings," he said. "That's the podgereen. And when you see them there like that then you know you've got yourself a fine poteen. It's your very rale poitin."

The profits from Sammy Nelson's new business venture were way beyond anything he had ever imagined. It took them just over a month to get into full production which gave them a three-run spirit that was 90% alcohol, or 150 proof. That was then watered to double its bulk, reducing the proof to 75, making it five more than the normal brand of whisky. Mickie had said they could stretch it even further if they reduced it to 70 proof like other whiskies, but Sammy's theory was that they would get a readier market if they kept it stronger at 75 proof. Whisky, when it could be bought, was retailing at 25 shillings and ninepence a bottle but because they said their product was special and because of the scarcity value, Sammy and his agents had little difficulty getting thirty shillings a bottle, although publicans, being publicans, bought it in bulk from them at the normal rates.

"I don't believe it. I just don't believe it," said Sammy to his wife the night he did his first accountancy on the victualling project. "It's costing us two bob a bottle to make. That's basic mind. None of your rent, rates, wages and heating added on, like Myer and the Argyle Street mob do when they're figuring mark ups. That's just our actual cost per bottle. And we get thirty bob for it. D'ye know what that means? That's a profit of 1500 per cent. One thousand and five hundred percent. Nat Myer never got that in his life."

"Does Mickie Doyle know that?" asked his wife.

"Christ, no. He's got it up to peak production now and I took in £100 last week. He's quite happy sitting there wi' all the bevvy he can take. And I'm paying him a tenner a week . . . tax free. And you can bet your boots he's knocking me for a few bottles a week to sell himself. Anyway, he doesn't want any more money than that. Start flashing it around McNee's and he'll either get done or somebody will nark the Busies. And he knows that. He cannae take it home wi' him or else auld Bridie will get her mitts on it . . . although he could always hide it beneath her soap," and he laughed out loud at his joke.

No one did Mickie for his money, however, and no one informed the police and for the following year the steam merrily rose from the pavement grille of "Peggy's Orchard" fruitshop and the nocturnal activity of the cellar went unnoticed. Sometimes the steam would be coming from the big copper in which she boiled the beets that had given the little shop a reputation for their freshness and ready availability. At other times it was Mickie's mix, as they used to call it: a brew of various constituents, depending on supplies which gave him the first wash for the start of the distillation process. Between the income from the fruitshop, the clothing coupons, the newspapers, the coffee and cigarettes, nylons and Nescafé, and the whisky, the Nelsons amassed a small fortune that year, sufficient for them to buy outright a spendid home in St Andrew's Drive, Pollokshields.

It was a handsome red sandstone Victorian villa with six bedrooms, three public rooms, three bathrooms, a conservatory, a third floor billiard room, with its own toilet, and two concrete lions in repose guarding the front door. They named it Sammar, that being the combination of their Christian names, Peggy having been originally christened Margaret. The neighbours were "the best kind of people", Peggy would say. There was Mr Gordon Dykes, the head surgeon at the Victoria Infirmary, Mr Hector McIlwraith, the senior partner of McIlwraith, Bailie and McIlwraith, one of the leading establishment lawyers in the city, and Nat Myer lived five houses away in another red sandstone villa, although his was a much bigger one with half an acre of garden round it, big enough to have its own cottage for the man who tended the grounds. But they were the kind of neighbours who kept to themselves and no one asked any questions about the colourfully dressed new couple they had in their midst, the general assumption being that another bookmaker had joined the ranks of the *nouveau riche* who were infiltrating this most select district of Glasgow.

They had been living in Sammar for about a year when there was a phonecall from the Southern Police Station in Cragie Street one evening asking for "Mrs Margaret Nelson".

"Are you the keyholder of the fruitshop in Cathcart Road at Carfin Street?" said the voice, identifying himself as Superintendent Black. "Well, Mrs Nelson, you had better come immediately. There's been a dreadful explosion at your premises."

The Air Raid Wardens and three units of the Auxiliary Fire Brigade were there as well as a unit of the Royal Engineers bomb disposal squad. ARP men with street cleaners' brooms were everywhere, sweeping up glass from the hundreds of broken windows in the street.

"We though it was a bomb at first," said the police sergeant who met them in Cathcart Road. "The firemen have been in the shop, Missus. Very bad news. There's not a thing left. Everything's just blown to smithereens. The Salvage Corps man says he's never seen anything like it. They were puzzled by the smell at first. Said it was like chloroform and fruit all mixed together. But I told them you cooked beets there all the time and kept big supplies of them in the cellar. One of them says maybe the heat had made them ferment and that there had been some kind of spontaneous combustion. Aye, apparently that can happen. Biggest bang they've heard in Govanhill since the bomb fell in Boyd Street at the start of the war. I'm telling you, if we hadn't the Jerries on the run they would have thought that was them back. I'd better take a wee statement from you."

"Anyone injured, Sergeant?"

"No, Mister Nelson. Miracle so it is . . . as you can see. All the glass and that. One wife says she was nearly scalped when her bedroom window flew across the room, but there's been no hospital cases."

"Was there anyone in the shop?"

"Mister, if there was they'd be in fragments. But why do you ask? Did you think someone might have been in?"

"Oh, no, no. I was thinking maybe a burglar or something. We've been done twice, you know . . . petty cash and that."

After the sergeant took some details from them they left, Peggy to go home to the 'Shields, Sammy to the Gorbals.

It was a "whisky off" day at McNee's and there was only a handful of drinkers there caressing their pints. In the sitting room there was just one man on a chair by a table in the corner, the remains of a pint splashing from the glass in his hand which was keeping time with the tune he was humming. When he saw Sammy approaching he broke into song.

"What's the news, what's the news,

O my bold Shelmalier . . . led by Kelly the boy from Killanne."

"I'll fucking what's the news you, Mickie Doyle," said Sammy Nelson. "You bastard . . . you've been into that fucking ether. You're stinking to high doh wi' it. Christ, don't light up or you'll blow up this fucking place an a'."

Mickie's smile grew wider. *"Glory O to Mount Leinster's own darling and pride."*

"Ether Mickie. Were you making that fucking ether?"

He grinned even more as he carried on with his song . . . *"Dauntless Kelly, the boy from Killanne."*

At that point the barman burst into the sitting room. "You, Mickie Doyle. You should know fucking better. Nae singing in here. It's against the law."

Mickie just grinned even more and kept tapping his foot to the song that had now vanished from his lips and had become an orchestra in his mind which outplayed any dialogue that was being directed at him. Anyway, when you felt the way Mickie Doyle felt at that moment in a blissful ethereal high in which the most pleasant thing and place in the world was the joy of the here and now, and *"Glory O to Mount Leinster's own darling and pride, Dauntless Kelly the boy from Killanne"*, the law was a matter of little consequence.

It wasn't till the next day when Sammy Nelson got Mickie Doyle sober that he was able to piece the story together. The job of making the poteen had involved long and tedious hours in the Orchard's cellars. He had avoided the temptation of drinking the poteen, he said, as that would have made him incapable for the rest of the day. Instead he had decided to experiment by making some ether as a by-product so that he could get "a little drunk" and then sober up quickly again to concentrate on the job of distilling. Making the ether had been easy. He had added some sulphuric acid to some of the singlings then distilled the combination in a small retort he had made. "Sure, and I was only making about a pint a day and it was keeping me happy and every time I sobered up I could do a little bit of the work." He couldn't remember leaving the shop that night, however. "Well, it was like this. The aythur had made me feel that nice I decided to have a right good jar of it before leaving . . . you know, to see me right for the walk down to the Gorbals and McNee's bar, for I knew it was a whisky off day and I wanted to be right set up, like, to help me along with the beer. So, I had this right big swig. And, d'ye know, the next thing I'm knowing is you there shouting at me and all, but I wasn't caring, was I?"

What he couldn't remember was whether or not he had turned the heat off the brew that had been distilling. "And if I didn't, well, Sammy, I'm afraid the results might have been fearful."

"Aye you're right, Mickie. Fearful. That's what they were. Fucking fearful."

The following day Mickie returned to Carfin Street to see for himself the damage his ether drinking and forgetfulness had caused.

"Oh be jassus," he murmured as he looked at the gaping hole, now boarded up, where Peggy's fruitshop had once been. Up the incline of the street he could see the dozens of tenement windows which were also boarded up, having been blown out in the explosion. Peggy was also there. She was standing outside the shop with two men in soft hats who were making notes. Mickie took them to be policemen and, trying not to be seen, he stood across the road in the doorway of the Italian warehouseman's, its big plate glass windows also having suffered in the huge blast.

The men left after a while and Mickie called on Peggy. She was surprised to see him and he was relieved when she smiled at him. "I wanted to see you Peggy. Was all my fault you know. That's all your wee shop away just because stupid auld Mickie Doyle had too much to drink. Makes me want to go teetotal, so it does. Will you ever forgive me?"

"My goodness Mickie, we haven't been worried about it. As long as no one was killed. A few got cut with the flying glass, that was all. Although they say it would have been worse had the people in the houses not had all their windows taped to stop them splintering in the air raids. That was the insurance man I was talking to there. My policy is all paid up and everything and they say their company will see me all right."

"Sammy must be real angry wi' me though. I wasnae right sober when he came back to see me yesterday you know. And I like your Sammy. Good gaffer so he was when I had the little still going. I wouldn't like to think that he thought bad of me. You tell him for me Peggy, that I'm sorry like."

"Think bad of you Mickie? My Sammy's not like that. We were speaking about it last night and he said 'Well that's that. What's for you won't go by you' and that he would need to find some other kind of business. He's not the sort of man that bears grudges, Mickie. Not my Sammy. He's not one to be crossed, mind you, but as for thinking bad about you, or anybody else for that matter! No. No' my Sammy. I'll tell him though that you came by the day. He'll be pleased to hear that."

Mickie looked relieved at what she had said and as he turned to walk back to the Gorbals Peggy caught his arm. "And Mickie," she said, " no need to turn teetotal."

He laughed aloud. "You're a fine woman Peggy Nelson. A fine, fine woman."

The authorities never did find out the source of the explosion and in the official report by the Salvage Department, the "cause" column had two words entered in it: "Not known". The insurance company paid out and Peggy was able to have her little "Orchard" rebuilt. But that was the end of it as a distillery. The big copper boiled up the beets — and beets only — for sale in the shop. They were taking no more chances.

The loss of the whisky income meant a big drop in the Nelsons' income. But with their house in the 'Shields being fully paid for, they could still have a good living from the other enterprises. There was more bad news, however. With the war in Europe drawing to a close, the Americans were packing up at the Cowglen. They were being sent to the Pacific for what was left of the war there. Happier and more plentiful days were on the horizon and, although the Government warned there would be shortages for a long time to come, they could see the day that wasn't all that far off, when people wouldn't require coupons and ration cards . . . or men like Sammy Nelson. They discussed it together one night and Sammy's conclusion was, "Well, Peggy, I'll just have to get into something else. Move with the times, you know."

10

HOME SWEET HOME

FOR Star's return to the Gorbals, Isa had a party. Well, that was her
description of it. When the guests arrived for the big "gay and
hearty" that they had all been talking about and looking forward to
the week before, Star, it seemed was the least important person in the
room. She didn't know any of her mother's invited friends, a
rumbustious, coarse and noisy group for whom the war had been the
best thing that ever happened. Most of them, the women as well as the
men, were working for the first time in their lives and getting wages
far beyond anything they had ever expected to earn.

They had all obviously been drinking before the party and each of
them carried more liquor into the room. The men carried pairs of
screwtop bottles of beer in their jacket pockets, some had half bottles
of fortified wine, their whisky substitute, and some even had real
whisky. Each of the women produced smaller bottles from their
handbags; two had rum, one had gin and one had a clear white
fortified wine which one of the men joked was flame-thrower fuel. Isa
laughed loudly when two of the men thrust tumblers of the rich, red
fortified wine at Star: "C'mon hen, drap o' the El D . . . Mystic City an'
that". Another proffered cigarettes, with a shiny brass lighter at the
ready: "Made twenty of them this week and got three bob a time for
them in the pub," he boasted. "Aye, that was his war effort for the
week," said his pal. "You'll need to start sometime hen," they said
when Star refused them.

She had expected her mother to be shocked at such gestures but she
had merely thrown back her head in raucous laughter each time at
what she interpreted as a humorous situation. After initial nods in her
direction as they entered the house — none offering a hand or a
welcome home greeting, except two of the women who made remarks
about "hame's hame" and "hame's best" — the twenty or so guests got

down to their party, ignoring Star, who was the reason they were supposed to be there. Anyone who did not smoke or drink or appeared to be part of their noisy company was not to be considered one of them, it seemed.

Isa sat in one of the two old armchairs which had once been cut moquette. The pattern had faded long ago, the fabric worn smooth, and because its springs had expired it seemed to envelop her as she leaned back, a tumbler of ruby in one hand, a cigarette in the other. Four of the women were given the courtesy of the four wooden dining chairs which time and usage had stripped of varnish and stain and everyone else sat on the lino'd floor round the walls of the little room, which was about the size of the scullery or pantry at Glenmulloch. When she thought about that, Star remembered the welcome and homely smells of that little room off the big kitchen, the sharp tang of the bramble jam and jelly, the hooked hams, the muslin-wrapped cheese, the kist of meal, the rows of homemade chutney and rhubarb and ginger jam, nutmeg and cloves and the black puddings from the last pig.

The noise of the assembly quickly snapped her from her daydream. The object, it seemed, was to see who could talk the loudest and the coarsest for it was he, or she, who got the attention of the others.

The talk at first was mainly about their various social activities that week. The men started off with the football they had seen.

"Rare crowd at Firhill the day," said one. "Must have been about 20,000 there."

"What do you expect? The 'Gers were there." retorted another. "Playing great so they were. See that Gillick! Stoating player so he is. Scored a right bobby-dazzler in the first half. Venters got the other one. Two-nothing. Good result."

"I went to the Scotland-England Army International at Hampden," said another. "Wish I hadnae. Seven-nothing. Make ye greet. See that big Swift! They couldnae get a ba' by him. Need to shoot the swine tae have scored, so they would."

"Celtic were great," enthused another. "Beat Albion Rovers four-nothing. Delaney got a hat-trick an' a'. Some player, so he is."

From football it quickly passed onto the pictures and the dancing.

"We were at the Bedford last night," said the man who had spoken about the Rangers. "Right laugh, so it was. Joe. E. Brown and Judy Canova. She's got as big a mouth as him. But they're a right riot, so they are."

"Not as funny as Abbott and Costello," said the one who had gone to Hampden and wished he hadn't. "Did ye see them in *Who Done It?* Nearly peed masel' so I did."

"Helluva uncomfortable," said his pal.

"What?"

"Peeing yersel' in the pictures." He roared with laughter at his own remark.

"We went to the Playhouse last Saturday. See that Lew Stone! Some band, so he has. You want to hear his saxes. And can they swing it! Real Tommy Dorsey stuff. Had the place jumping, so he did."

"What were they charging?"

"A dollar."

"Wouldnae gie them it. West End's just as good for three-and-a-tanner. And see the talent!"

He turned to the man nearest him and whispered something. Loud guffaws of suggestive laughter followed.

"Order up, you two," shouted one of the women.

Although Star's mother hadn't told her, she gathered that they had regular nights like this in their various houses or at the Moy, the pub at the corner, for most of their conversation was about a prior night's drinking, each recounting their intoxication, each in turn relating how they had been, in fact, in a worse state than anyone else. "See ma heid the next day," said one of the men, a glass in either hand, one leading the other chasing. "Full of thunder and lightning, so it was. Every time I shut my eyes I thought I was going up in a blue light and when I opened them . . . Jesus Christ! Was like the Clydebank blitz, so it was. An' a' inside ma heid." When they laughed he elaborated: "An' see ma fuckin' mouth . . . smelled like Dirty Sarah's knickers so it did."

Big Bernie, one of the women, shouted in mock anger, "Hey you, mind the ham sandwich. There's a wean in the house . . . you'll be giving Star a bad impression of us."

"Christ," he retorted. "How could she get a good impression of us?" That filled the tiny room with even more laughter.

Star didn't know their names for there were no introductions, other than the nod as they came into the house in a burst of guffaws and loud laughter, although some of the women did ask her how she liked being home with her mother again. As the night wore on, however, she gathered some of their names as they noisily addressed each other, their shouts getting louder with the night. Some of the men had nicknames. There was Pug and Fingers, a Francie and a Bertie. Of the women there was Big Bernie, who was big and loud and smoked incessantly and had a voice like a man, Ina, Fanny, Meg and Mae, a Wee Jean and a Big Jean, the latter being mocked by the others for not drinking the wine and whisky. "I've got the bile," she shouted in her defence. "Green bile. Somebody had rotten whisky at Harry's party last Saturday and I've had the bile ever since."

"I had some as well," said the man called Fingers, a pale, thin man. Because of his name Star had automatically looked closely at his hands, the fingers of which were deeply scarred, some of them twisted grotesquely. "It's like the stuff we use at Beardmore's for taking the rust off metal."

"It'll be anti-freeze," said the one they called Pug, whose nose was spreadeagled half across his face. "There's a lot of them into it . . . mixing it wi' the wine and El D and anything they can get their mitts on. They're knocking it out of the army trucks, so they are. That was it they were drinking at that party in Townhead last month. Remember it . . . five of them lying deid in the morning. It wisnae strong enough for them mixed wi' Tizer, so they started drinking it straight wi' the screwtops. Ach well, they wouldnae feel anything."

"Aye, an' they'll no' freeze up on the road to see St Peter, eh Pug?" joked Fingers, his crooked hands struggling to grip the big beer bottle he was holding. That comment won the laugh of the night.

It was Wee Jean who started the singing. "See a' youse," she said. "Too much bloody talking, so youse are. Get the bottle Isa."

One of the empty screwtops was placed in the middle of the room. Isa spun it. Star looked on fascinated, wondering what was going to happen next. It was her first Glasgow party, for her mother had never had any when her stepfather had been at home and, although she had heard other children talking about them when she was younger, it was an aspect of the tenement culture which she had missed in her varied upbringing. The bottle spun wildly on the smooth linoleum floor and Isa had to pick it up again to give it another spin, a proper one this time. When it stopped it was pointing in the direction of the man they called Francie, a big, bony fellow with bad eczema and a huge knot in his tie, so big that the broad part of it only hung down about four inches below the knot — apparently the latest fashion with the men.

Some shouted that it was pointing to Wee Jean, the others saying it was Francie but there was no disputing their anxiety to take the floor and Francie, being polite, acceded to the woman's eagerness. In an ostentatious display of being a gentleman as well he leapt to his feet to give Wee Jean a hand, although in doing so he stumbled and she fell back exposing the flesh of her enormous thighs above her lisle stockings. The men on the other side of the room yelled "Wehh . . . helll . . . Knick. . . kerrs," and applauded enthusiastically as she struggled to cover up her bared areas. They were smartly brought to order when she stood in the middle of the floor and went straight into her song. They knew, of course, what it was going to be, just as they knew what the others were more than likely to sing, but they always acted surprised and pleased that she was singing "her" song.

"Where the heather bells are blooming, just outside Granny's door." That brought the first of the interjections.

"Aye. Gaun' yersel' Wee Jean."

"Where as lassies there we played in days of long ago . . ."

"Yer singing great hen."

"Neath the shadow of Ben Bhragie and Golspie's lordly stane . . ."

"Knew her granny fine."

"How I wished that I could see my Granny's Hielan' hame . . ."

"Aye, she was a Murray from Golspie. Lovely wee wumman."

"I can see Old Granny, a smile on her face, As sweet as the heather dew when she kissed me goodbye . . ."

"Hey, out of order youse."

"With a tear in her eye and said lassie, may God Bless You . . ."

That line brought the last of the interruptions. "Heh, one singer, one song." Then they all joined in when she repeated the first verse as a chorus.

They cheered when Wee Jean sat down again, protesting as she did so at the amount of talking they had done in the early part of her song, but the enthusiasm of the clapping and cheering helped assuage her feelings. The bottle was only spun another twice after that, for with each song there was more enthusiasm to participate and it only needed one or two of them to call another's name and a song would pour out. After their usual Scottish selection, they quickly moved on to the hit tunes their favourite bands like Carl Barriteau or the Squadronnaires, or local ones like Benny Loban at the Plaza and Eddie Shaw at the Locarno, were playing . . . *"Bewitched bothered and bewildered . . . he can laugh but what of it for the laugh's on me . . . Amapla . . . my pretty litt . . . telll pupp . . . peee" . . . "You are my Sunshine" . . . "Marta, rambling rose of the wild wood" . . .* and *"Let them begin the beguine"* which always got them singing like Hutch impersonators . . . *"Oh, yes, yes, yes, let them begin the beguine . . . till you whisper to me once more 'Darling I love you'. "* Each singer was given great encouragement. "Aye . . . that's his best wan" . . . "Oh, she does this awfy well" . . . "Sang it last week at Freddie's . . . best turn of the night."

The singing stopped abruptly when Big Jean announced that her bile had returned and had to make a dash for the sink where a long spout of watery sick flew from her mouth. "Oh Christ," she said, shaking her head in nausea before retching once more into the little jawbox sink by the window. "Knew I shouldnae had that Eldorado there. That's what done it." There was little sympathy for her obvious suffering. The women laughed and the men shouted "Get it up hen." Star recoiled in revulsion into the corner of the room where she desperately wanted to hide herself. Big Jean looked ghastly when she returned, the colour having been drained from her face, her hair hanging damp and limp. "See me," she exclaimed, "that's me finished wi' the Mammy Mine." Then she gave a laugh and ordered someone to bring her a glass of beer. "It might take that rotten taste out of my mouth."

Star was curled asleep when the last of the wine and most of the beer had been consumed and the songs had gone from Scots to popular to maudlin to spectacular, the latter being their *Bill Bailey*, at which each of them took a turn before all joining in for a lusty rousing encore rendition which not only filled the tenement with the loud enthusiastic beat of the jazz favourite they all loved so much, but drifted out into Florence Street and could be heard at the Cumberland Street corner. The Wallaces who lived in the house immediately below them began knocking up, using the end of a brush handle, as they always did, and the Reillys, who lived above them, knocked down, using the father's mason's hammer, as they always did. There were shouts too from other houses, angry and loud and profane, and when Bailey finally did go home the din mellowed again to some sweeter and softer songs. Bernadette, the woman who had come with Francie and whom they called Big Bernie, gave them her very own favourite of that variety, although for reasons she knew too well, she didn't always sing it at parties, not mixed parties anyway like Isa Lawson's was that night. "*Oh Danny Boy, the pipes the pipes are calling,*" spinning the last word out like "*caa . . . haul . . . leeeng.*" She had only got to the end of the first verse — "*Tis you must go and I must hide*" when there was an interjection from Fingers who had been muttering to himself as soon as he heard the words of the illustrious Irish boy, "Fuckin' fenian song."

"You be quiet," shouted one of the women. "Danny was her Da from Donegal, God bless his soul." And Bernie continued, unhearing and uncaring of the first ripples of disorder.

"Still a fuckin' Fenian song," replied Fingers, more loudly this time.

But still Bernie persevered, looking at a distant space and putting more fervour and feeling into her beloved ballad. It was the last line of the second verse that was too much for Fingers, and Bernie, ever-sensitive, put even more passion into her words. "*Oh Danny Boy, oh Danny Boy, I love you so.*"

"Fenian bastards," he said, looking up for the first time from the spot he had been staring at on the floor between his feet. He nodded his head then repeated the words.

"I heard that," said Francie, Bernie's man.

"Need to be deef no' tae hear it," a voice said.

"You're the bastard," said Francie. "A fuckin' bastard an' a'."

He got to his feet with the words and leapt across the room to tackle Fingers before he could rise, getting two vicious kicks in at him while Bernie launched into action by picking up one of the empty screwtop bottles. Before anyone could stop her she brought it down so hard on the head of the rising Fingers that it smashed with a loud explosion, showering everyone with fragments of glass and dregs. That was enough for Big Jean who, despite her girth and her bile was quick on her feet and together with Wee Jean, blue knickers and pink blancmange thighs bared in her undignified dive into the fray, she went for Bernie.

Star wakened with a startle. The entire room was a mass of struggling, punching, kicking, screaming, cursing bodies in an unbelievable mêlée that only minutes before had been a happy-go-lucky sing-song party. Some were fighting each other and some were fighting even harder trying to separate those who were head on in combat. Fingers lay crumpled on the floor unconscious, a woman kneeling by him and screaming hysterically that he had been murdered, and another man was angled on the wall, dazed with blood pouring from a big gash above his eye. Francie staggered drunkenly towards the door, supported by Bernie, screaming abuse at everyone with a variety of epithets but mainly "Orange bastards". A bottle flew through the air and crashed into the wall, cascading its mahogany fortified contents on the distempered plaster as it smashed into a hail of splinters.

There were only two of them left when the police arrived with drawn batons . . . Fingers slowly coming to on the floor and being cared for by Ina, the woman who had been screaming earlier. The constables left almost immediately, however, being assured by Isa that it had only been a party and that nothing had happened, despite the broken glass, the upturned table, the blood and the long trail of wine stains on the wall. It was an old story unworthy of follow-up action and the neighbours who had gathered on the stairhead to witness what conclusions there might be dispersed back to their houses in a mutter of "Terrible, so it is."

These were confusing days for Star Nelson. She had never realised her Gorbals could be so mean. She had lived most of her life in it, but was not to see it as it really was until her return from the country. She had never smelled the dank, horrid stench of the closes before, handy and available urinals for men and animals; hideaway rendezvous for lovers. She had never felt the claustrophobic dimensions of the tiny dwellings which reeked with decay; unkempt humans and unkempt buildings. She had never known the coarseness of the people, so coarse and rough and hard, it seemed, that it had become a culture of its own in which each inhabitant tried to be more coarse, more rough, more hard than the next one to win respect; and so they had become imprisoned in a lifestyle they partly created, adding yet another barrier against their escape from it. She had never experienced the hatred that could be so instantly generated at the slightest provocation and which would be expressed nightly in the litany of beatings and brutalities, stabbings and slashings, a sort of permanent street war that could erupt anywhere at any time. She had lived with all of these things before but had never known them, as they had not known them; for they were the environment and the environment was them, and with the progress of time, the one that made the other did so with an unrelenting regression on people and place. It was only those who had escaped and then returned who saw their Gorbals in a different light. Some of the returned soldiers knew. Most of them had gone off to a hell somewhere, but many had seen other things and when they had come home they had seen another Gorbals. And now Star Nelson for the first time in her life was seeing it as well. Of course there was still the camaraderie and neighbourliness born of people caught together in a common struggle, theirs being poverty and deprivation, but now she could see all the other faces of the suburb that was a town, a town that had suffered all the blight of progress labelled as the industrial revolution.

She knew and felt it in a contrast that penetrated and pained, that shocked and saddened: a sadness for them and their ways, a sadness for herself and a life that seemed to be over before it had begun. For now that she was back in the Gorbals she feared that she would become a part of them and their ways, that their unquestioned ways would become her ways again and that she would become trapped, as they were trapped, in the community whose gods were the rough and the gruff, where hardman was hero and fighter was fêted and those who thought otherwise were to be despised.

Only the love of a daughter dispelled any new feelings she might have had about her mother. Before the evacuation she had known and loved her as child to mother but now she also saw her as woman to woman: and the woman she now knew had all the scars of a lifetime in the Gorbals. While that grieved her, it didn't make her feel any less for her mother. What concerned her more was that she too would become like her . . . like them. She was clever and mature enough to know that could be her fate. She was wise and intelligent enough to know that there was only one way for her to avoid that fate. Star Nelson would have to escape from the Gorbals. But that was to prove easier said than done.

Isa lay in bed most of that Sunday after the party. The long lie, as they called it, was a feature of many houses on the Sabbath, there being little other stimulus to do anything else, except mass for the Catholics and morning service for the Protestants. Other than that everything was closed, the pubs, the shops, the places of entertainment; even in the swingparks, the children's playgrounds, the swings were chained so that they couldn't be used, the roundabouts firmly padlocked in order to deny the children their amusement.

The Lord had said the day was for resting and in a country where Calvin held his sway, that was to be the way of it. It was after three o'clock when Isa stirred. Star had been up since nine o'clock and had spent most of the day trying to restore some order to the little single-roomed house, gathering all the broken glass and the other litter from the night before for the pail, the chipped enamel bucket in which they kept the household refuse. She did five trips to the midden in the backcourt with the remains of the party, mostly bottles of all shapes and sizes, dark ones and clear ones and ones that gave off the stale and foul smell of what had been the desire of thirsty palates the night before. Isa had set out soup bowls for ash trays and the ones which hadn't been spilled were half-filled. Star was amazed at the mounds of cigarette ends they contained, many with the ugly red stain of lipstick, contrasting with the others as if they had died bleeding when they had been crumpled.

"Make me a cup of tea, hen," said Isa hoarsely from the bed as she drowsily roused before asking what time it was. There was no surprise when she was told it was mid-afternoon.

"Been up long dear?"

"Aye, since about nine."

"My God, what were you doing up at that time? It's Sunday. D'ye no' like a long lie?"

"Now and again, but nine o'clock is a long lie for me now."

"It's a long lie for your mother as well. Mind, I'm up at the scratch of dawn all week. But after a wee party, it's good to get a decent long lie. Did you enjoy yersel' last night then?"

She paused before answering and when she did it was to pose the same question she had been asked. "Enjoy myself?"

"What . . . did it get a wee bit too rowdy do you think?"

"Aye Ma, rowdy is the word. How long have you known them?"

"Who?"

"Them . . . the crowd that was here last night. I didn't know you knew people like that."

"Like what, Star?"

"Well, they don't seem to be exactly your type, Ma."

"And what's my type?"

"Well, I was surprised that was your type. It's not the way I think of you. I mean, you go out to work every day all respectable and that and work in a respectable place among respectable people, yet you mix with people like that."

"What are you saying, Star? That there's something wrong wi' my friends? I've known all of them for a long while now. All the time you were away in the country and obviously enjoying yourself. And I've had lots of good nights and laughs with good sing-songs with them. It's no' all like it was last night. Maybe it did get a wee bit out of order. But that's nothing unusual, not about here anyway. You should know that."

"I know I should . . . but I'd forgotten what it can be like here. I'd forgotten a lot of things about here. I was away a long time you know."

"Aye, a long, long time, Star. And I had to look after that man o' mine till they took him into Hawkhead. He gave me a helluva time, you know. Every week he would get worse, talking to himsel', to the walls, blethering about nothing, slabbering at the mouth and even having to be fed and washed like a wean. I nearly ended up in there wi' him. That's how bad it was. There'd be nights I'd come home and have to go out on the streets to look for him. And there were nights when he took his turns . . . fits you know. Between working from morning till night at Duncan's then coming home and having to work wi' him meant I never had a minute tae masel'. And when he went away I needed laughs. I needed laughs and company. You've no idea how much I needed them. So when he went, that's what I looked for. The crowd that was here last night took me in wi' them and they stood by me. If I was ever short, it made no difference to them, I could go out wi' them for the night and not have to pay a penny. Hearts of gold, so they have. I know what you're thinking, Star. That they're rough an' that. Maybe they are, but they cannae help that. They're no' always at each other's throats like they were last night. There's been lots of nights when we've sung one another's songs like that. Something just happened last night. So! These things happen. We can't help the way we are. Can we?"

Star had wanted to say that was the very point which worried her: that she would get to the stage where she couldn't help the way she was. And that terrified her. But she thought she had said enough. Of course her mother had the right to the friends of her own choice, just as she had that right. And she knew too that she had scratched the surface of her emotions on the subject, for the party crowd were obviously near and dear to her . . . epithets, fisticuffs, bottles through the air and all.

"Ma . . . you've not to misunderstand me. Your friends are your business. All I meant was, it was a bit of a surprise to me. It wasn't as I had imagined. But I understand a lot better now. C'mon, that cup of tea is ready."

11

AT WAR WITH THE GLASGOW HIGHLANDERS

THE war they thought would be over in months with the boys hanging out the washing on the Siegfried Line was not to be. Chased from Europe, thrashed in the desert, humiliated in the jungles, bombed and deprived on the mainland, it was years before a turning point arrived. Those who had begun the war as schoolchildren grew old enough to become the new servicemen who were to march, fly and sail to fight and be killed.

The Fordyce twins were fourteen years of age and pupils at Glenhazel in Perthshire when the war was declared. The end of November, 1942, just after their release from custody in Dumfries, marked their eighteenth birthdays. A week later they were at Maryhill Barracks in Glasgow, serving their basic training with the Highland Light Infantry. From there they travelled to a "Wosbie", a War Office Selection Board, conducted in a commandeered mansion house at Penrith in Cumberland where they underwent a series of tests to determine whether they were material for an OCTU, an Officer Cadet Training Unit.

While they had their moments of depravity, the Fordyces of Kirkconnel proved to be outstanding examples of the kind of man who could lead, inspire and command other men . . . harder men than they had ever known. They went through their Wosbie and their OCTU with flying colours, returning to Maryhill as Second Lieutenants at the end of Spring, 1943, and ready for posting to one of the battalions in full-scale training for that great day that everyone awaited — D-Day and the return to Europe.

The HLI was famous to some, infamous to others, for its hard core of Glasgow fighting men. They had been part of the division the Germans had labelled the "Ladies from Hell" in the First World War, although they were one of the few Scottish regiments which did not wear the kilt, that distinction having been taken from them with great consternation more than 130 years previously when they had become the 71st regiment of the British Line and, as a light infantry, had to change their dress and weapons. They wore tartan trousers instead to demonstrate they were still Scottish.

The twins were two of the youngest lieutenants in the regiment when they graduated from OCTU. From Maryhill they were first of all posted to the 1st Battalion and then transferred on detachment to the 2nd Battalion, the Glasgow Highlanders, the regiment's territorial battalion. The Highlanders had been on the move to various camps in England, including Felixstowe in Suffolk where they had been practising beach landings for a role they had all been anticipating — the Invasion. The Fordyce boys joined them at Bingley in Yorkshire for the big exercises codenamed Blackcock and Eagle. Both distinguished themselves for their leadership and enterprise, particularly Andrew, the first born and more adventurous of the two. He was to further demonstrate that by winning the middleweight boxing title and coming third in the cross country race when the Scottish Brigade, stationed in the area, held their sports championships.

"You're best sticking with your books," he joked with Robbie who had been unplaced in all the events he had contested. Indeed, much to his own surprise, Andrew had taken to Army life right from the day they joined. "I was sure I was going to detest all this bloody discipline. Instead I'm enjoying it. I don't resent it at all when it comes from people who are better than me, and some of the majors really know their stuff. And, of course, I don't object to giving it. God, you wouldn't get a more well-scrubbed lot than what we have and most of them had never seen a bath before. That's what discipline does, Robbie."

By mid-May, 1944, the war games were over. They were posted to the South of England and told that the big day was imminent: the invasion fleet sailed on June 6th. The 2nd Battalion's first companies landed eleven days later, the last of them seven days after that.

They had been warned to expect it hard right from the start and that was the way of it even before they landed on the beach at Vienne en Bessin in Normandy. Their initial objective was to capture Cheux, which the men christened Chooks. It was the first time in action for most of the men and opposing them was the cream of the German forces in that part of France, the 12th Panzers. It was everything they had been told about during the long months of preparation in England. The officers had lectured them that they would be meeting the most efficient army the world had known and they would have to show that they were something better if they wanted to beat them.

And there was no question, said the officers, of them *not* doing that. They were going to win, for they were in the right. Those who thought about such things questioned themselves as to what the German officers might be telling their men, but it was wise not to think about that too much — not before a battle.

Again, as he had done at OCTU and in the sports championships, Andrew demonstrated that he was the fighter of the Fordyces. Robbie was quietly efficient when he led his sections into their first encounters. Andrew, bold Andrew, did it with flair and much more enthusiasm, obviously enjoying every minute of leadership and relishing the excitement of the real fight after all the war games back in England. There were two other regiments with them on that first attack: the Cameronians were on the left, the Royal Scots on the right. The Highlanders were given the task of facing the Panzers head-on. Because of the size and strength of the Scottish attack, German reinforcements, men from the 2nd Battalion Der Fuehrer Regiment of the 2nd S.S. Panzer Division, were rushed to the battle. Their machine-gun posts and their *nebelwerfers*, the multi-barrelled mortars the Scots called "moaning minnies", stopped the advance. Forward patrols were despatched to take on the machine-gun nests and the most forward of these was led by Lieutenant Andrew Fordyce who, with a corporal, went ahead to tackle a concentration of the Panzer gunners whose murderous firepower had threatened the entire advance. Between them they wiped out six of the posts, returning to their lines with six prisoners. They got their Chooks all right, but the Battalion had lost its first men of the war — three officers and nineteen men killed, 178 seriously wounded, many of whom were to die later. The Battalion Padre, who had been with them for five years and had counselled and consoled, advised and inspired hundreds of the men with his understanding, wisdom and gentleness, was killed when his truck received a direct hit. Each man felt as though he had lost his own brother.

Unknown to Andrew, Robbie had been to talk with the Padre regularly. He had told him all about the rape at Lydeburn and about their father's suicide because of the shame it had brought. He pleaded to be given some kind of explanation for a deed which had a profound effect on him and which time wasn't diminishing. They had been having a continuing dialogue about it and for the first time in the three years since his father had blasted his life away, Robbie Fordyce was beginning to come to an understanding with himself. "It's not something that will happen overnight," the Padre had told him. "It's something you must work at." It was something, he had said, that he could never run away from.

On that last evening they had met, sitting in his small tent on either side of a table covered with the flag of Saint Andrew, he had spoken at some length about it to the troubled officer. His theme had been again about running away from the past. "Would we ever win this war if we ran away from it? All humanity would lose if we did that. Just like you are losing by seeking some kind of escape rather than facing up to those against whom you sinned, even though that may be an entire community which you let down by your deeds. You have permitted your mind to shut out the past. You must lift that barrier and learn to live with the past so that you can come to terms with it in reality when you go home after the war. Remember, there is no hiding place except in the Lord. Jesus was understanding of the sinner. He told his disciples that the things which make people sin are bound to happen. You are suffering from the shame of defeat . . . the defeat of your conscience. You imagine that your enemies are those you ran away from and that they are gloating over you. Only when you have the courage to face them will you discover there is no malice in their hearts for you. Try if you can, Robbie, to remember the words of Paul in his letter to the Colossians . . . 'He rescued us from the power of darkness and brought us safe into the Kingdom of His dear Son by whom we are set free, that is . . . our sins are forgiven'." As a final message he had added, "Have courage, my son." There were no doubts in Robbie's mind after that last visit and he was happier within himself than at any time for years. If he survived the war, he knew there was a future which wasn't so full of the gloom that he had imagined and lived with for so long.

The exploits of Lieutenant Andrew Fordyce became something of a legend in the Battalion. For his work at Cheux he was awarded the Military Cross, the Corporal who had accompanied him the MM. Cheux had been a more fearsome battle than those seeing action for the first time imagined. They had to fight every inch of the way and the crack German troops had thrown everything at them. But there was worse to come. War Command treated them as one of their best fighting units and as such they were used for the next year in one bloody battle after another, new faces constantly appearing among them, a reminder of the fallen comrades they were replacing. From Cheux they went on to fight at Eterville, Esquay, Ghent, Best, Lensel Wood, Blerick, Groosebeck, Moyland Wood, Bucholt, Hegemannskath, Stadensen and Uelzen. They were with the Canadians at Caen and they crossed the Seine, the Albert Canal, the Rhine and into Germany itself. The men from the slums of Glasgow fought in the once placid countryside of Normandy and in the wide open fields of Belgium.

They shot it out in the dense woods, they winkled out the snipers in house to house fighting in countless towns and villages. In Ghent they fought among the horrors of crazed civilians running among them, away from the murderous guns that were everywhere. They lost ten men there, 56 wounded. The Battle of Best claimed 138 casualties, including 50 missing — usually a euphemism for being blown to pieces. At Lensel Wood they were rushed in on TCVs and tracked carriers to help out the exhausted Americans who had suffered fearful casualties from an enemy force which couldn't be dislodged from the cover of the trees. They went out at night together with the Royal Scots, their only targets being the occasional gunflash or the odd noise in the dark. Robbie had joked with his men that it was just like going out with the gamekeeper at home looking for poachers and his men laughed for if any of them had lived in the country they would have been the poachers. They took the woods that had stopped the Americans and another fifty of the Glasgow Highlanders were casualties. They fought through that summer and autumn and on into a bitter winter when they stood up to German 88M and mortar fire at point blank range during the battle for a single farm at Hegemannskath.

When winter was over, those who had been with them for a full year were changed men in many ways. As fighting men they were more ruthless than they had been at Cheux where they had been blooded. As ordinary men there were new values forged within them; the preciousness of comradeship, the futility of materialism, and a greater love of those they had left behind in Scotland. And with their being in Germany, the homeland of the enemy, there was also a new spirit of optimism among them that the war would soon be over.

But even in their dying throes, the men they had come to fight were still to provide some of the bloodiest battles of the war. When the Germans knew that the Scots were in Stadensen they rushed the newly formed and equipped Panzer Division Clausewitz, specially prepared for the last offensive, to challenge them. The confrontation resulted in the most vicious street fighting of all their battles, and they lost more than fifty men, including a Captain and a Lieutenant. Once again it was Andrew who distinguished himself, using hand grenades against the snipers hiding in houses. Although they didn't know it, the next battle after that, on April 10th at Uelzen, was to be their last major engagement. Because of the viciousness of Stadensen, the Glasgow Highlanders gave no quarter at Uelzen and the platoons led by Andrew Fordyce fought like men possessed, sparing nothing or no one for the sake of a quick victory. They got it. And the Germans went into full retreat, badly shaken at the mauling these new "Ladies from Hell", the ones with trousers, had given them.

Because their companies had been separated for some weeks, it wasn't till the night after they had won the battle for Uelzen that

Robbie and Andrew met up again. Robbie had felt like throwing his arms around his brother in relief at seeing him well and unhurt again. And so had Andrew. But they were officers and gentlemen and had met with their platoons beside what remained of a *bierkeller* at the most easterly end of the little town. Each left their men to walk towards the other coming smartly to attention and saluting as they met.

"Lieutenant Andrew," said Robbie.

"Lieutenant Robbie," said Andrew grinning widely and thrusting one hand forward, then another to hold his brother fondly by the hand and the arm. "Great to see you young one. No cuts or bruises?"

"No. I've been lucky. Yourself?"

"I've been luckier. Jerry even sent a special squad to try and get me at Stadensen . . . and my men got every one of them."

"How did you get on there?"

"Stadensen! I never want to hear that name again. I was in a building that got hit by so much 88M stuff it just disintegrated and vanished around us. And not one of us got a scratch."

"Uelzen?"

"Frightening, wasn't it? I didn't know the lads could be so ruthless. It was like a gang fight with 303s, Brens and mortars. The Gorbals and Brigton boys were in their glory."

"I bet you were too, Andrew."

One of Andrew's sergeants, helping himself, like the others, to some war reparations, found some brandy in the cellar along with two unbroken balloon glasses, thought immediately about his favourite officer and came straight to him with the find. "Had a feeling it might meet with your approval, sir," he said. There were no other senior officers around and with their picquets posted for the night the two brothers sat down for a rare chat together.

"I've heard from HQ we'll be here for a few days to rest up," said Andrew. "It'll be a job for the mobile boys now . . . they certainly got out of here as fast as they could. Wonder if we'll see much more of them? Anyway, Robbie, we've come this far together. Do you think we'll make the whole show?"

"After Stadensen I think we'll make anything, Andrew. And, God, I for one will be glad when it's all over. I've never seen men so vicious as they were getting those last few days. They were just mowing them down. You just had to turn your back on them at times."

"But that's war Robbie. War is not about mercy. It's about killing . . . and winning. You can't go around feeling sorry for the people you're against. The plain fact is that we were sent here to kill and I've done my bloody share of it, I can tell you. Did I tell you I am thinking of signing on?"

"Don't do that, Andrew."

"Why not? Miss your big brother will you? We've got to part some time. We would be anyway when it's all over. I mean, we've got to be getting into something. And I rather fancy the Army. I've enjoyed the life in the regiment."

"Is it not the war rather than the HLI you enjoy?"

"Maybe it is. You know, when a battle is over, I feel like I do after a few drinks. You know, all high."

"I do too but it's not enjoyment. It's bloody nerves with me."

"But seriously Robbie. I do feel like that. No tension or anything. Some people are cut out to be soldiers I suppose. And I'm probably one of them. There's talk of short service commissions. I could take one of them and if I'm still in the same frame of mind after that then I could sign on again."

"There won't always be wars for you, though. Can you imagine being a peacetime soldier? It's not you Andrew. Parades and exercises and the bull. You hated OCTU enough."

"Actually you're wrong. I would like it in peacetime too, although I know I would miss the excitement of what we've had this last year."

"They say you've been very brave. Saw it for myself that time you got the MC at Chooks."

"They've recommended a bar to it for Lensel Wood."

"Congratulations. God, that really is something, Andrew."

"Yes, I am rather pleased. But you mentioned being brave. What is being brave? You see, I don't feel I'm being brave or that I actually was brave. I just enjoy a fight. It's like a bloody big game to me. The big adventure . . . you know like it used to be when we were wee boys climbing up Neviston Glen, all dark and eerie and wondering if we were going to be attacked by wild cats or big eagles or Red Indians. I used to love that. It's the same here. I'm in my element when we go into action. But is that being brave? A lot of people might call it something else. And it's the same with the Jocks. Some of the Gorbals ones I've got in the platoon! You've got to hold the buggers back at times. Wouldn't like to meet any of them in the street. The Jerries must think they've got the savages coming at them. But then there are others who are not like them. I've watched them. You can literally see the fear in them . . . real stark terror coming out of their eyes. Trembling like they were going to take a fit. Then you bark an order and in they go. And they would do it again and again when they were ordered to. Now to me Robbie, they are the really brave ones. they have to overcome their fear. They have to live with it night and day. But not me. I don't have to overcome anything. Perhaps if I had I wouldn't be able to do it. I might be a coward. Who can tell? Why don't you fancy signing on too, Robbie?"

"You know, I actually thought about it . . . then I put it out of my mind again. I was going to do it for the wrong reasons. That's why I changed my mind. Anyway, I've got other things to do when I get back."

"Like what?"

"To face them in Kirkconnel."

"To what?"

"I'm going straight back to Kirkconnel. I want to confront everyone. I want to show them the sinner . . . and that I'm not scared to face them again and seek their forgiveness and show them that there really is honour in our family. And that includes the girl. She went back to Glasgow but I want to find her and seek the same forgiveness from her as the others."

"Forgiveness! Forgiveness for what? We did nothing to them at Kirkconnel."

"Yes we did, Andrew. We let them down. The people on the estate looked up to us. They had respect for us and our family. And so did all the neighbouring farms and their workers. They had faith and trust in us and our family. We broke that trust. We ruined that respect. We destroyed that faith. I want to restore it. I must do it . . . even if it's just for the peace of my mind."

"You're mad, Robbie Fordyce. That's all in the past. All right, we were a couple of wild bastards. Maybe I was the worst."

"Maybe!"

"You know what I mean. But it's in the past. Done with. You've got to look forward. Even that's been a bit difficult this past year when we were just lucky to get through one day at a time."

"But surely you must think about it, Andrew. About the girl . . . and everybody?"

"The girl!" Andrew smiled. "Yes, she was rather good wasn't she?"

"Don't be so bloody flippant, Andrew."

"Why are you so serious?"

"Well it is serious. She's haunted me ever since."

"Good God, Robbie. I thought Caen and Lensel Wood and Stadensen and what we saw there would haunt you more than a young lassie back in Kirkconnel."

"Oh aye, they did. They did. But every night when I thought that's it, I've made another day, she would be on my mind again and everything we did and what happened would come back."

"Oh Christ, Robbie . . . we didn't beat her or anything like that. We're not bloody sadists are we? You'd be surprised at what's gone on in haylofts around Kirkconnel without there being all that police fuss."

"Being bad like being brave comes in degrees, I suppose. There are those who are bad and don't know they are being bad. And then there

are those who know it . . . and are still bad. Who's worse? I know what
we did was bad. And it has worried me like hell. I think of her and what
became of her. We could have ruined her life, you know. And for all we
know, maybe we did."

"Robbie, she was a bloody servant lass . . . a dairy maid or
something."

"She was the Camerons' evacuee from Glasgow. But what
difference is that supposed to make? Is there a difference between her
being a servant girl and a laird's lass? Are you saying that it would only
have been terrible if she had come, say, from Drumlanrig? People are
people no matter what they are or where they come from."

"My, my . . . you're sounding like some of those in the Socialist Club
at St Andrews or a Christian or something. You've been reading too
much again, Robbie. I told you to stop it after Glenhazel. Can do your
mind damage you know. Get you thinking all sorts of unnatural
things."

"Andrew, can you never be serious, even for a moment? I had been
seeing the Padre regularly about what happened . . . until that terrible
day at Cheux. We got on well together and I was shattered when he
went. We had discussed everything. How she haunted me. How I felt
about everyone back in Kirkconnel. You can't keep running, he told
me. And he was right. We joined the Army to get away. We were
running. That's why I had felt so bad, because I was using the Army
and the war as an escape. Do you know I longed to be killed until the
Padre helped me? I thought that if I'd been killed it would have
expunged everything. Wiped the slate clean. And then they would
have forgiven me . . . mother, the girl, everyone at Kirkconnel. You've
no idea of the chances I was taking in the very first actions."

"Touch of the ironies about that, is there not? There's you taking
chances because you want yourself killed and me taking them because
I'm enjoying them. Robbie Fordyce, I should be worried about you.
Trying to get yourself bloody-well killed!"

"Andrew, do bear with me. Please. That's why I went to the Padre
for I knew I could never discuss it with you . . . and get any help that is.
But now that I see things differently I want you to understand how I
feel. Do try, Andrew."

"It's difficult, little brother. I do know what you are talking about.
I'm not that bad am I? But I still think it's a lot of nonsense. Look . . .
examine what we did. We were crazy seventeen-year-olds. All right, I
was worse than you. She was a lovely ripe piece of fruit there for the
picking and probably enjoyed every minute of it. So I'll admit it was
disgraceful. Not the way of two proper young gentlemen. Downright
bloody disgraceful if you want. And then with father and that. Well
Robbie, you just can't legislate for things like that in life. If anything

was ever to haunt me it was that. It shattered me more than you'll ever realise for I worshipped the old boy. But I had to come to some terms with myself too and there was nothing I could do which would bring dear old Dad back. Nor could I ever make sufficient amends to help Mother. What's done is done and thinking your way will mean you having to carry a cross for your conscience for the rest of your life. I know what we did all right. But that's it. There's nothing you or I can do about it."

"Not even seek forgiveness, Andrew? You're hiding just like I was. There is no hiding place . . . except in the Lord."

"Oh my God Robbie . . . you *are* becoming a Christian! Is that why you haven't poured me a drink in the last half hour? C'mon, little brother. Let's have some more. The Hun's on the run for the night so we can leave it all to those wallahs in their little tanks and armoured cars. Fill your own glass too. Might make you forget all that rubbish you've been talking. Robbie . . . promise me something. Don't become the kind of Christian that won't sit and have a drink with your big brother."

"Andrew, that could never happen. Never."

"Good. God, it'll be great to get back to France. This non-fraternisation rule with the Jerry frauleins is a bit much. Imagine putting it on orders! They're just dying to be shagged you know. Hitler indoctrinated them. Make love to the soldiers. Give yourselves to the brave men in uniform, he said. And he's got them so well trained they'll give it to anyone in a bloody uniform. Oh well, we'll wait till we get back to France. Orders are orders."

"Andrew, you'll never change."

There was no more action for the Battalion the rest of that April. On 2nd May the Glasgow Highlanders were called in to clear the vast Sachsenwald Forest where hundreds of Germans were hiding. There was little opposition, most of the Germans surrendering with great relief when they saw it was the British who had come for them and not the dreaded Russians. Some snipers, however, put up a rearguard action and had to be rooted out at the cost of another two men from the 2nd Battalion. They were among the last casualties suffered in the war. Three days later an urgent radio message reached the Battalion HQ. The German Army had surrendered.

12

LIFE AT THE TOP

THE Gorbals was a magnet whose field of force would not free Sammy Nelson. He lived in the beautiful Pollokshields with its Victorian splendour: leafy and luxurious, sophisticated and spacious and paradoxically just a mile away from the Gorbals — heaven on hell's doorstep. Every day he would return to the suburb that spawned him to spend some time with old corner-boy friends.

Peggy had managed to acquire some of the veneer of Pollokshields. It had been her ambition which had taken them to Govanhill and then on to the great adventure of moving to Stamperland and a house with a mortgage which was, to their traditional way of thinking, a thing to be deprecated. During the war years when Sammy had his great boomtime with money pouring in from his various ventures, particularly from his incredible year with the whisky, it was Peggy again who insisted that they invest in a bigger and better house. She knew precisely where that house should be — her coveted St Andrew's Drive, the finest street in Glasgow south of the River Clyde . . . and with few challengers north of it. Every dwelling there was grand enough to have been an estate house in some rich county. She had worked hard at getting to St Andrew's Drive and she worked hard at being part of it, acquiring the local accent, intently devoid of the glottal stop, the Glasgow caste mark, although those who knew could tell that her speech was a gloss which struggled hard to hide its tenemental origins. She could hide more with her dress, being able to afford the very best stores up town, Pettigrew's and Copland's, Kirsop's and Karter's and, of course, an account in Forsyth's. Son John also became a part of her new image. He was sent to the best school money could buy south of the Clyde, Hutchesons' Grammar, whose old buildings ironically were in Crown Street in the very heart of the Gorbals. But John was only to know the Gorbals as the grim place which surrounded his school. It was never mentioned to him, even now when he was ready for Glasgow University and aiming to be a lawyer, that his parents had come from there and that his Uncle James had been the most notorious character the district had ever produced.

For Sammy there was no such cutting of the umbilical to the Gorbals. He needed it. He needed its characters, its chat, its flavour, the patter, the patois; he was of it as much as it was of him. With the war and his days of active street hustling behind him, he could now be less discreet about showing his wealth and he dressed in a genuine Crombie — the American officer's coat long since discarded . . . for a price that is. His shoes were the very best Saxone suedes. Despite that the appearance was always flash: loud ties and even louder mufflers, usually a vivid Paisley harnish; Gorbals wide man made good, like the bookies and the big-time scrapmen who were making fortunes from the precious metals like lead and copper, much of it stripped by night from the flashing of churches, factories and houses, occupied or not. Sammy had fancied the scrap trade as he needed a new business to secure his future. The Americans had all gone and although food and clothes rationing was still imposed, everyone it seemed had got into the coupon rackets and the amount he dealt with now barely gave him what he called his "fag money" — although it was still in excess of the average working man's wage. He had made enquiries about the scrap metal business and word had got to some of the principal dealers in the district. The whisper came back that there "may be difficulties" as there were enough trading in it already and it might be unwise to have any more. You listened to whispers like that in the Gorbals. Sammy Nelson did. He knew their violent ways and how the big men, in whatever activity they were engaged, had followers who would willingly do their dirty deeds for them.

Then one day, when he was drinking with his old friend Hughie "Plug" Connor in the Seaforth, Sammy got the idea about the kind of business that might just be the ideal substitute for his "import-export" dealings with the Americans. An old face they hadn't seen for years came into the pub.

"I know that yin," said Sammy. "Can't put a name to him, but does he not come from Eglinton Street?"

"That's Danny Byrne . . . it was Bedford Street he came from."

"Aye, I remember . ·. the Parlour dance hall close, next one to where auld Maw Lawson stayed, you know . . . the mother of our Jamesie's old flame Isa? Danny Byrne eh? Got five years for the Stockwell jeweller's reset."

"Same man."

"Looking old and decrepit, isn't he? What's he up to now?"

"Gets a few bob for his man-of-straw bit."

He had to ask Hughie to explain that one.

"Man-of-straw. It's a new racket. You buy some occupied tenements, right. Old ones you can get for a song, but with plenty of rent money coming in from them. Then you get the titles of them transferred to some old geyser like Danny. Somebody without a tosser. Any of the crookit lawyers up town will do the work for you. And when the officials look up their books for the owner to chase him up for repairs or anything, they find some useless old fucker like Danny Byrne. And they cannae do a thing. It's his name that's on the titles and the law says you can't take blood from a stone. And the smart alec keeps collecting the rents. It was Danny McGrory who telt me about him. He took him home one night he was drunk. Lives in the Cumberland Lane now. Couldnae get into the house for the smell. He'd been given a fiver that day for putting his name to a bit of paper that made him the owner of five closes in Portugal Street. Is it no your turn for the drink? Get us a Red Hackle. Bad enough as it is its better than bulk pish. And better than that stuff you used to peddle. Christ, used to hit you like a V2."

When Sammy brought over the fresh drinks, Connor returned to an earlier point in the conversation. "You mentioned Isa Lawson there. D'ye know she's got a daughter?"

"Aye, to that plasterer she married? Baird . . . him that was the bam?"

"No. The father was your Jamesie."

"What?"

"I'm telling you. The lassie's called Star Nelson. Works beside the sister-in-law as a machinist in Gordon's, you know the big factory over the Suspension Bridge."

"And she's Jamesie's girl . . . our Jamesie?"

"Christ, did you no' know?"

"Aye, I knew Isa Lawson had a wean but we thought it was to that daft man o' hers."

"He's in Hawkhead, you know? Went real mental."

"Aye, we heard that. Does she still live in Florence Street?"

"That's right. Two closes from the Moy."

"And what did you say they call the girl?"

"Star."

"Star Nelson . . . eh?"

They didn't mention the subject of the property racket again. But Sammy thought plenty of it. For his income was fast drying up and he needed a new line of business . . . a new line that was legal for there was no prospect of him trying anything that wasn't, with his dread of

imprisonment. Their house in St Andrew's Drive was paid for . . .
£4000 it had cost him including lawyer's fees, virtually their entire
savings. But the rates were crippling and there was the outlay for the
education of son John, now at University. They had sold the fruitshop
in Govanhill, mainly because Peggy had wanted to have the lifestyle
which befitted a lady from Pollokshields — there would have been no
time for coffee mornings with the other local ladies if she had
continued to be a fruitshop wife. Being a property owner in
conjunction with some man-of-straw like Danny Bryne seemed like a
good idea. It didn't even matter whether he smelled or not for there
would be just the one transaction, his signature for accepting the
property. Once it was his on paper there would be no further dealings,
unless he wanted to add more properties, and Sammy, or somebody
acting for him, could go ahead and collect all the rents. He dismissed
the prospect of Danny Bryne as his man-of-straw. There were better
people to deal with. People he could trust . . . like Mickie Doyle.

Mickie couldn't understand the scheme when it was outlined for
him by Sammy the following week. So it was simplified for him. "All I
want, Mickie, is your signature for some houses I'm buying . . . and
there's a fiver in it every time for you. You can trust me, Mickie. We've
known each other long enough and I'm not up to any tricks that will
get you into trouble."

"And I get a fiver . . . just for giving you my signature?"

"That's right, Mickie."

"Sure, and you've got me completely puzzled, Sammy Nelson."

"Mickie, I'll explain it again. There's these tenements and I want to
buy them to get the rents for them. But if the authorities start chasing
me up for repairs and that, I'll end up making nothing from them. So
we put your name on the valuation rolls and the title deeds and if they
come to ask you to do the repairs you just tell them you don't have any
money. Not a penny to your name."

"But that's the truth, Sammy."

"That's right. That's the truth. You'll no' be telling them any lies.
Except that you won't say how you got the houses or anything about
me. Just say they were left to you by an aunt in Ireland. They'll believe
that."

"And I still get the fiver?"

"Right Mickie. A nice crisp fiver."

"Are you sure you wouldn't be wanting me to make some of that
lovely whisky instead?"

"Not on your nellie, Mickie. Christ, you blew up as much of
Govanhill as the Jerries did."

"I still wish me old Bridie hadn't died on me for she could have
explained all this to me much better. But I'll do as you ask me for

you're a good man, Sammy, and I know you wouldn't do anything that would be getting me into trouble or anything like that."

"Mickie, you don't need to understand. I'm telling you there'll be no problems. C'mon, let's have another dram."

Ronnie McLaren worked in one of the warren of offices called the Waterloo Chambers in Waterloo Street in the city centre. His desk was an absurdity of untidiness, piled on one side with a four-foot stack of books and ledgers and on the other with an alp of papers and documents and a variety of mail, leaving him one fragment of bare desk on which to lay the particular document he was working on at the time. He was a little man of about thirty years of age with big glasses and an owlish, schoolboy face which had the air of every class's little stinker. He loved the pomposity of the legal profession, always knowing better than the client who sat opposite him, correcting them at every turn if they used a word which wasn't appropriate and constantly reminding them of what the law said on that matter. Sammy Nelson had known him for years. His firm, Dunstan, Dalrymple and McLaren, had a considerable clientèle from the Gorbals. Harold Dunstan was one of the best criminal lawyers in the city, while Roger Dalrymple and Ronald McLaren did all the routine office duties like deeds, trusts, divorces and conveyancing, the latter being McLaren's speciality. He had done the work for the Nelson's three houses and they used to meet from time to time in the art deco lounge bar of the "One-O-One", round the corner from his office in Hope Street.

"You'll realise," he said, going all pompous as he always did when he gave out advice, "that what you are doing is quite immoral, Mr Nelson?"

"Cut the patter out wee man," said Sammy, one of the few people who could speak to him that way. "You know lawyers do fuck all for fuck all. There's a big fat fee in what I'm suggesting. I just want to know can it be done? Legally, that is?"

"How good is your man-of-straw?"

"Brilliant. Hasnae even got a fuckin' piggy bank."

"How many houses do you want to start with?"

"You mean how much do I want tae spend? Lets talk about fifteen hundred. Including your fee. What can you get me for that? And you still haven't said if it's legal."

"Don't worry. It's legal all right. There's no law to prevent you from buying a house, whether it's a single one or a group of tenements. And there's no law to prevent you from selling, or even giving for that matter, your own property to someone else. What happens thereafter is not for me to say. The onus, of course, is on the legitimate owner to maintain and keep the rented property under the provisions of the Housing (Scotland) Act which, in effect, means that they must be wind and water tight and kept to a reasonable standard."

"You're joking. What houses do you know in the Gorbals that are in a reasonable standard?"

"I don't know any. I never go to the Gorbals."

"Reasonable standard! Christ! Is it worth my while putting them in somebody else's name? They're not even bothered to chase up the owners as it is to do repairs."

"The law, Mr Nelson, is about practicality. If they had to enforce all the sanitary regulations, for instance, I think you would find every eating establishment in your district would be closed. If they were to enforce the housing laws to the letter, the owners would be immediately bankrupt and you'd never get repairs done. Commonsense must be applied to our laws. However, in your case, it would still be a wise precaution to get somebody else involved. I can get you houses all right, but it might not be all that long before officials start asking questions about them. And that might prove . . . er . . . embarrassing for you. Would it not, Samuel?"

"Aye. Embarrassing. Right. How many houses can you get me for the money?"

"Well as it happens, Duncan McPhail, the factors in Caledonia Road . . ."

"We paid rent to them for years. Bastards all."

"Well, they are selling off a lot of their properties. the more mature ones, as Mr McPhail put it to me when he was in here the other day."

"You mean the worst ones."

"Mature is a nice word."

"Cut the crap."

"Anyway, as I was saying, they're selling off quite a number on behalf of a variety of clients."

"Oh aye, I know the clients. We were told about them when I was in the ILP. Every bastard has had his finger into the Gorbals for what he could get out of it. There were Swedes, Belgians, Indian Army officers, and the ones from your Home Counties . . . all with their money in their S-c-o-t-t-i-s-h investments. Sucked the place dry for years so they did and there was hardly anyone chased them up for repairs . . . and all their names and addresses were there on your valuation rolls. I'm better than them. At least I come from here. Now they're all getting out. The sinking ship and that."

"You mean some get off . . . some get on . . .?"

"Don't be smart, Ronnie. I'm no' going in there to do evil. But they did. They did it for years, no' bothering their arses to maintain the buildings, backed up by McPhail and the other factors. I'm just gonnie have a wee flutter at it, that's all. Anyway, why have I got to justify myself?"

"You don't . . . not to me anyway. That seems to be a matter between you and your conscience."

"Look, I'm not worrying about my conscience. It'll be clear. If I don't do what I'm gonnie do, some right bastard will get in there, jack the rents up and be a proper extortionist. I'll no' be like that."

He had worked hard at squaring his conscience, as he always did, for it was important to him, even though his conclusions were often doubtful. This had been a difficult one for any conscience to grapple with but Sammy could always find an avenue for escape. On this occasion he focused his mind on the harm the previous owners had done over the years, plundering the district of fortunes in rent money and putting so little back by way of maintenance so that the tenements, stoutly built by expert tradesmen and good enough to last several lifetimes, had decayed so much by the time they were sixty years old they had degenerated into grim, blackened monoliths, vermin-infested and diseased, ugly caves they called houses into which they crowded humans in a fashion unequalled in Britain. That was a fact the authorities themselves revealed. So was Sammy Nelson worse than any of the previous owners? Indeed he wasn't, he assured himself. He was one of the people, one of the Gorbals people. He wasn't starting the racket, like others had. He was merely providing an ownership and giving tenants more time to stay in their crumbling homes until the great new redevelopment schemes the Glasgow Corporation said were on the horizon were put into operation. In fact, Sammy Nelson was doing them a favour. He was convinced about that.

"So how much are McPhail's houses?"

"How long is a piece of string, Sammy? You can get them at all sorts of prices. For instance, there's three closes in Florence Street . . . 31 houses in all plus some premises. Shops, you know. You'll get the lot for about £1200 and they'll pay for themselves through the rents in under two years. Of course, you'll have to pay two lots of conveyancing . . . from McPhail to you and from you to your man-of-straw."

"You're a greedy wee bastard, Ronnie. Why two lots of conveyancing anyway? Why not do the sale direct from McPhail to my man?"

"What? Have my very good client McPhail and Sons selling directly to a man-of-straw? That would be highly improper, would it not? I mustn't be seen doing anything unethical, you know."

"But you're letting me, your other very good client, sell them to a man-of-straw."

"Yes, but that's proper. For you wish to do that and your man is in agreement. I doubt if Mr McPhail and his company would like to be subject to a deal of that nature."

"Christ, you've got all the answers, haven't you?"

"And another thing. What other lawyer do you know who would be giving you advice like this?"

"I don't know any. But I bet there's plenty. Who knows a poor lawyer? The only people in your trade that's poor are the clerks you've got out there that do all your conveyancing work. All you do is stick your wee signature on the papers."

"Correct, my friend. Lawyers' signatures do cost a lot of money. Conveyancing clerks' don't."

"Let's say I'm interested in the houses. Can you get me money to buy them?"

"You said you had fifteen hundred?"

"I said I wanted to spend fifteen hundred. I didn't say I had it. Can you get me money to buy them?"

"Sam, I can arrange anything. Anything that's legal that is. But there'll be a separate fee for the loan."

"Are you charging me for talking to you?"

"I could. That's perfectly permissible. But I'm not. You're a favoured customer."

Sammy Nelson was back in Ronnie McLaren's office six months later, full of enthusiasm about his new line of business. "Goes like clockwork, so it does. The money keeps coming in, nothing goes out, except to the rent collectors . . . don't want to be seen masel' knocking on doors. That would be . . . what do you call it?"

"Demeaning?"

"Aye, something like that. Anyway, I'm in the market for more houses. And another loan. Don't want to touch the old capital, you know. And, Ronnie . . . no need to give us the old routine this time. I know it's double conveyancing. And I know there's a fee for the loan. Why do you think I'm making my boy a lawyer?"

The property market turned out to be Sammy Nelson's most lucrative venture, even though he was in the dung heap end of the trade. Within a year and a half he had bought many more closes in various parts of the Gorbals, all of them entered in the City's valuation rolls as being owned by Mickie Doyle of Kidston Street. Mickie had got used to the regular visits by frustrated officials who could do nothing to enforce him to carry out the essential repairs required of so many of the properties. But they had many bigger problems with the chronic housing shortage and no action of any kind was ever taken against him. No one even queried the fact that a poor old man had become one of the biggest property-owners in the Gorbals . . . on paper that is.

Meanwhile, Sammy Nelson, the real landlord, would meet his two rent collectors — he preferred to call them agents — in what he jokingly termed his factor's office — the Old Judge Bar in Lawmoor Street. He chose the Old Judge because it was a pub where he was not known and it was in the vicinity of where he had bought most of the houses. There he collected the takings from his men, congratulating himself as he walked home on the simplicity and efficiency of the scheme he had adapted for himself. Peggy took a new lease of life at the return of the security which removed any prospect of them ever having to leave Sammar and the Pollokshields, and young John, the polite, well-behaved and well-mannered product of Hutchesons' Grammar was well on his way to even higher academic achievements at Glasgow University where he was studying the subject nearest and dearest to his father's heart — law.

"It's like this son," he would say to John. "you always go into a trade that's connected with something everybody always needs. And we're always needing the law, especially here in Glasgow. Every time I think of Ronnie McLaren, my lawyer, I think of you, son, and your future. For he just sits up there in his office raking in the money. Somebody presented him with a plaque and he showed me it once. Frightened to put it up on the wall so he keeps it in a drawer. It shows two farmers arguing over who owns a cow. One is pulling the horns, the other is pulling it by the tail. And who's milking it? You've got it. A lawyer. And that'll be you one day, son."

13

WEALTH FROM THE SLUMS

RAB Blair and Jimmy McLean were Sammy Nelson's two loyal assistants or agents as he called them. They had been with him since his early days "in the business" and he trusted them implicitly. They had sold his whisky, bought and sold his food and clothing coupons, and hawked the coats, shirts, nylons and other material he used to get at the American camp. Rab was a thin, slightly nervous man who had missed the war because of ulcers. Despite the regular agony they gave him he was always cheerful and was one of the most popular men in the Adelphi Street area of the Gorbals where he lived. Jimmy McLean, his partner, was tall and lantern-jawed with a foxy look about him. Some nicknamed him Eyes-in-the-back-o'-the-heid because of his perpetual shiftiness — a result of a wartime escapade which he was still living out — but most called him by his official nickname — Claney.

Claney was a deserter from the Army. He had been with the Royal Engineers in North Africa, and had specialised in mine-lifting. Every night, platoons of sappers would be sent into the desert probing and scouring for mines, working through the darkness till near dawn, interrupted only by the occasional explosion. In the morning when they got back to camp there would be a roll call before they bedded down to sleep . . . and it was only then that they would know which of their mates hadn't returned. Those unanswered names every morning began to have an effect on Claney, so much so that it was the roll call he feared more than the actual hazards of searching for the mines. "I could do the job all right for I was good at it and it was like a challenge to me every night — my skill against theirs," he would say on the rare occasions he told his story. "But it was those mornings. Those terrible, horrible fuckin' mornings. Some days it would be your mucker from the next bed, the guy you had shared your *Sunday Post* with the day before or who had brought you cocoa from the canteen that night. The first you knew you would never see him again was when he didn't answer his name in the morning parade. It might have been different had you seen him cop it. That would have been normal like . . . you know, maybe getting the chance to save him or something as it is in battle? But no . . . they just disappeared. You went out together at night and they just wouldn't be there in the morning. And you wondered if that would be you the next morning . . . a name that doesn't get an answer to it. And if it's not the next morning, would it be the one after that? One night there was a whole platoon of them who didn't come back."

He was on the verge of a nervous breakdown when he deserted and, incredibly, made it all the way back to Britain from North Africa, one of the few men, maybe the only one, who had been able to achieve the feat. His worst moments, he used to recall, were getting back to Scotland from the South of England where the ship on which he had stowed away docked. It was a restricted zone and everything and anything that moved was stopped and questioned. The sailors who had helped him had warned about the difficulty he would have in the area. He left the ship at night, loaded with provisions they gave him and, moving only during darkness, which he had been used to in the desert, he was able to beat the constant patrols of Military Police keeping watch for unauthorised personnel in the zone. It took him two nights to get clear of the area. Two days later he was back in Glasgow.

Because of his desertion Claney had come to live in the Gorbals. After his escape he had lived in Cranstonhill in Anderston, in one of the verandah tenements that looked like old army barracks. The military and civilian police kept raiding the house looking for him. The nearest they got was one night he had been in bed with flu and escaped by clambering up a rone to the roof, a feat which resulted in him catching pneumonia from which he nearly died. It was then he had gone to live in Rutherglen Road with two elderly aunts who nursed him back to health and he had stayed there undetected ever since.

Despite the loyalty Blair and Claney showed to Sammy Nelson, they weren't immune to considering it quite legitimate to cut themselves in on his dealings as a bit of extra income on top of the wage he gave them. In the coupons racket they always bought them for less money than Nelson thought they were paying and when it was the whisky they invariably charged more per bottle than their boss's "recommended price". There had been less scope for them to do some "marking up" in their new duties as rent collectors, but where there was a way, Claney would usually find it. It was he who put the suggestion to Rab Blair.

"We'll put the rents up . . . and no' tell Sammy. He'll never find out for he never meets any of the tenants. Anyway, it will only be a tanner or a shilling and no one will kick up. And with the number of houses we're doing, it will soon mount up and make a nice wee bit extra."

Rab was apprehensive. "Could be a bit of a problem in some of the Caledonia Road houses. There's a few rough ones have been moving into them and they'll no' fancy the extra bob."

"I've thought about that. No problem. D'ye know Tommy Sharkey?"

"Him wi' the big ugly dug in Naburn Street?"

"Aye. It's father was an Alsatian and he says the mother was a lion. I think it was King Kong masel'. Well he said we can have a loan of it any time . . . for half a dollar, that is. That'll sort out any problems with them that wants to argue about their rent. One look at that brute and they'd give us double if we asked."

The rent increase went off virtually unnoticed and it gave the collectors another £5 a week between them for their scheme. "Rab," said Claney when they counted out their extra profit after the first week, "it's not what you know at this game, it's what you don't know. And Sammy will never have a clue. Will he?"

It was a Glasgow monsoon year, the kind that often happened. The rains had come in the autumn, persisted through the winter and on into the spring. Even when it came to the summer and they flocked from the city for their Fair holidays, they got the rain again. And all during these months the seemingly never-ending rain pounded into the neglected tenements, glazing their matt black surfaces, streaming in torrents from broken rones and gutterings into backcourts which became quagmires of mud, debris and the scatter of sodden waste pulled from the refuse bins by the dogs and the cats and the scroungers they called midgie-rakers, anonymous hungry men who had lost all dignity and would sift through the fetid waste for something that would fill their need.

As the grey and dismal Glasgow days continued through the seasons, the badly maintained houses degenerated at an alarming rate. The worst of Nelson's houses were in the western end of Caledonia Road and they suffered badly from the rains. The previous owners, an English company, had allowed them to run down with hardly any repairs in the previous ten years, only fixing what they were forced to by the local authority. The lead thieves had been on the roofs and with the ridge and chimney flashings gone, and some skylights missing too, they were suffering water penetration from the top floor right down to the basement. The tenants had become rightly querulous about paying their rents and Tommy Sharkey's dog had to be borrowed regularly. It usually worked, although at some doors there were tenants as aggressive as the beast: they would merely shout "fuck off", then bang the door.

Because he never went near the buildings, Sammy Nelson's conscience was untroubled. His house in Pollokshields never leaked and he gave no thought to what some of his tenants might be enduring. It began to worry Claney, however, and after one collection day when there had been trouble from angry tenants he had mentioned it to his partner, Rab. "Christ, Rab, is that what we were lifting mines for in the desert? The state of some of those houses has been making me think."

"Claney, let's face it. You were lifting mines in the desert for fuck all. They'll tell you it was for freedom. Who do you know in the Gorbals that's got freedom? There's HLI, Gordons, Argylls, Kosbies, sailors, marines and airmen from two wars up all they closes. That was their reward for going to fight for freedom. Some nice wee medals . . . and a single-end or a room and kitchen, If you and me are no' doing this, it would be some right bastards. And I mean *right* bastards. We're no' like that, are we Claney? I mean, the dug is a bit of a joke. And when they tell us to fuck off we don't bother them."

"Aye, that's because you're like me, Rab . . . feart."

Sammy Nelson knew all the pitfalls of the Gorbals. He knew there were few secrets there. The suburb that was a town was a village and like the best of villages they knew each other's business. The word could get around with amazing speed, just like it did on the day all those years ago when his brother Jamesie had been released from Barlinnie and half the pubs in the Gorbals had the word within a few hours. That was why he exercised the utmost discretion. There were too many people who should not be aware what he was up to . . . the taxman, the Corporation and other authorities and the men who were the bad men in the Gorbals just being a few of them. It had been more difficult in the past to keep his affairs private, moving around as he did with coupons and the items he sold from the camp. Now it was easier for others were doing his business. Only Ronnie McLaren, the lawyer, knew the full details of the growing housing empire based on the man-of-straw. Mickie Doyle still didn't fully realise what it was all about, and didn't particularly care because of the regular bungs he got for his acquiescence. His two rent collectors were under strict instructions never to reveal the identity of the person for whom they worked. Apart from his regular meetings with the two in the small lounge in the Old Judge where the money was handed over surreptitiously, there was nothing to link Sammy Nelson with the houses he operated in the Gorbals. And that was the way he wanted it. When anyone did ask, and many did, what his business was they were merely told "a bit of this and that" and most assumed he was an uptown bookie.

Meanwhile, the houses in Caledonia Road continued to deteriorate. As well as flooding and damp, they were experiencing regular electrical failures and Blair and McLean did their diplomatic best with most of the unfortunate tenants, telling them they were only workers themselves — "We're just doing a job for a wage missus" — and that worked as well as anything. They would also tell them that they had reported the need for repairs to the factor but he couldn't get the good tradesmen he wanted — "And you know the price of lead and copper." That would work too. None of them ever got to know the name of the factor or the owner.

The tenants would often bemoan their ill fortune at having to live in such houses when they met in the Bellwood, the pub just along the street from them. "Love to get my hands on the bastards that own them," said one of them.

Tommy Farrell, a quiet little man who lived by himself and who rarely spoke, joined in the conversation. "I know who he is. He's a bookie. A' flash and that. Big coat, yellow scarf and suede shoes. I've seen him drinking with the rent men in the Old Judge down in Lawmoor Street. Seen them thegether twice, so I have."

One of the group, a short wiry man with a badly scarred face took particular interest in Farrell's news. "How d'ye know he's the gaffer then?"

"Och, ye can tell," said Farrell. "Both times was on a Friday after they'd been collecting and I saw them hand him something. Probably the rent money. Christ, ye cannae hide it when you're a bookie or up to something. Youse should know that."

"The Old Judge on a Friday, you said?"

"Aye, that's right. What are you gonnie do . . . ask for your rent money back?"

The man never answered.

It was nearly twenty years since Snakey Holden, with his brother Jakey and their gang, had killed Jamesie Nelson in that merciless attack in Crown Street. He wasn't aware at the time that Sammy was there defending his brother; there was just one man he had been looking for: the Jamesie one. But Sammy had been pointed out to him in the street afterwards and he knew him by sight. And the following Friday night when he went to the Old Judge and saw the three men emerge from the little sitting room to stand by the bar he immediately recognised Sammy Nelson. He had it confirmed when he whispered to the barman "Who's the one with the coat there?"

"Nelson," replied the barman, pausing before he spoke again. "Sammy Nelson. Brother used to be the razor man."

"What's he?"

"They say he's a bookie uptown. But I don't know. He's into something wi' money anyway by the style of him."

"Aye, looks lousy, the bastard."

The barman smiled in agreement.

By the rules of their society, Snakey Holden had become known as the hardest man in the Gorbals after he had killed Jamesie Nelson. The old king was dead. Long live the new king. But his reign was to be pitifully short-lived. A week after he had slashed Jamesie to death he himself had been viciously attacked by an unknown assailant near Gorbals Cross. That hadn't gone down well with the rest of his gang. Leaders didn't get done like that. The marks were still on his face — deep ugly scars, and there were others too on his arms and hands from other fights. Although he had been deserted by his gang, he had been continually in trouble of one kind or another because of his mean and vicious temper. Whenever he thought he could get the better of a weaker individual he would do so and had been a regular customer of Mr James Shortwood, the Stipendiary Magistrate at the Central Police Court.

Holden had been married, but his wife and their two children had fled after a series of beatings, the last one earning the comment from Mr Shortwood "Is there no end to your depravity?" But words like that had little effect on types such as Snakey Holden who, like Jamesie Nelson himself, was born to violence: they had known it all their lives; they had known it since they had been old enough to crawl from their tenement house to play in the street with the other children. The violent met the violently minded and they produced more violence, so much so, that violence became such a part of their lives they neither knew nor wanted to know any other way. And the slashings and bayonetings and jailings and the loss of wife and children and the warning words from the Stipendiary Magistrate were of no meaning to them. Snakey had also been to the war; he and his brother Jakey served in the illustrious Highland Division, Jakey being killed at Tobruk. Snakey had been a good and brave soldier when they were in action for he could be as mean and as vicious as he liked then. But he couldn't stop it when the action was over and was regularly in detention for fighting with other soldiers. He ended up being discharged with ignominy at the end of the war for having led a gang into Maryhill Barracks in order to beat up and razor slash the Provost Sergeant. And when he saw Sammy Nelson that night in the Old Judge the violence welled within him wanting to erupt. But for once he reasoned with himself. There was a better time. A better place. A

better way. He also wanted to find out more about the man Nelson
who was now as much involved with his life, it seemed, as another
man of the same surname.

A week later Snakey Holden was back in the Old Judge and the two
rent men and Sammy were there once more. They were on the loud
yins, the big yins, the ones they called "a large Scaatch" in the movies,
with pint chasers into the bargain, and there were few people who
drank in the Old Judge or the Bellwood or the Windsor or Teachers or
any of the other pubs locally that could afford to drink like that. The
only ones who ever did were the ones who had just had the best day of
their year at the bookies, or those who were "wetting" a baby's head.
And they were laughing too; obviously enjoying their world,
whatever it was. Snakey Holden resented that. There was little
enjoyment in his world. There never had been, it seemed, except that
exhilarating day he terminated Jamesie's life and for the short time
after it when he had been regarded as the hardest man in the hardest
part of the city. But the moment of glory had been brief. What had
those bastards at the other end of the bar got to laugh about anyway?
Were they laughing at the rent money they had collected that day?
Were they laughing because they could afford the double whiskies and
pints and fat Senior Service while the people they took the rent money
from considered themselves lucky if they could get the occasional half
and a half pint and a Willie Woodbine to themselves?
  The whisky warmed him and fired his aggression and he had to
restrain himself, repeating again in his mind that there had to be
another way of getting at them. He ordered another and as he slid the
change into the pocket of his old coat, it rattled against something. He
put his hand in and felt the long slim object. Its smoothness invited
him to grip it in the palm of his hand, then stroking it with his thumb.
It gave him a comforting feeling. He had forgotten his razor was there
and the aggression he had tried to restrain erupted again. He could
feel his face flush with the vicious anger that made him there and then
want to spoil the faces of the three men who had now become an
obsession with him. He hungered for violence and in some kind of way
he would have to satisfy that hunger. He had another whisky, but
didn't water it this time. It slid from the glass in two quick gulps, then
he turned quickly and walked from the bar.
  He went along Caledonia Road, towards Crown Street. It was the
time of night the drunks were at their most numerous, the happy ones
singing, the crazed ones fighting mad like the one on the corner of
Camden Street, his shirt opened to the waist as he shouted, "C'mon,
c'mon . . . I'll take youse all on!" Between there and the next corner one
of the more subtle challengers, as they thought of themselves, came at

him. It was the old shake-the-hand routine. Shake their hands and it showed you were a friend and not a foe: suffer the consequences if you didn't.

"Fuck off" said Holden to the man as he approached him, hand outstretched.

"Think you're a fuckin' wide-o pal!" said the drunk, using the hand to shove Holden away.

It was all over in seconds, so quickly that nobody saw it happen, or would have said they saw it happen. The razor cut the man on both cheeks, from ear to chin, then his nose had been smashed by a vicious butt from Holden's scarred forehead. He sank to his knees before crumpling forward on his face.

Snakey Holden was more than fifty yards away, one of the bustling night-time crowd, when he heard the loud shrieks and screams of women and the noisy commotion as a crowd gathered around the felled man whose head lay in a pool of blood still spurting from his face.

As he thumbed the smooth handle of the folded razor in his right-hand pocket, the trace of a smile lifted one corner of his mouth. His lust, an orgasm of violence, had been temporarily satisfied.

The following Friday he returned to the Old Judge. Nelson was there, as usual, with the two rent men. And just as before they looked happy, self-satisfied men, the kind who didn't worry where the money for the next whisky or beer would come from. Holden stood, taking his drink slowly, at the same spot where he had been before and again he could sense feelings growing in him towards the three men, but particularly Nelson: resentment and indignation, then anger and animosity, his passions finally fermenting into a rage-exasperated bitterness.

The bar was crowded and Snakey Holden was able to remain anonymous among the men as they stood with their beer and whisky. When Nelson and his two friends left the pub shortly after he saw them standing up the street at the corner of Caledonia Road and Florence Street. Then there were farewells, the rent collectors going down Florence Street towards the river, Nelson heading west along Caledonia Road. Holden followed about a hundred yards behind him, along to Crown Street where there was a tramcar to town but instead Sammy Nelson continued walking. At the Gushetfaulds junction, near the big coal rea where the horse-drawn lorries gathered every morning to collect supplies for their rounds, he turned left along Pollokshaws Road, past the big red-brick Corporation Printing Works, a quiet stretch of road on which there were only a few houses and Holden feared he would turn round and see him. But, then, who

was he to see? Sammy Nelson wouldn't know Snakey Holden, even if
Snakey Holden knew the Nelsons. He knew Jamesie. Now he knew
Sammy. And he knew . . . and suffered . . . because of the way their
lives had become intertwined.

At Eglinton Toll, the busiest junction in the South Side where the
red, yellow, green and blue trams all converged in a grinding thunder
and rattle as their metal bogeys crossed the various tracks of the hectic
intersection, Nelson stopped to wait for a respite in the heavy flow of
traffic, then sprinted across the tramlines towards Maxwell Road.
The junction marked the meeting of the boundaries between Gorbals,
Govanhill and Pollokshields. From one side of the street, which was
the most southerly part of the Gorbals, Nelson had gone over to the
beginning of Pollokshields, as different as night and day to the area he
had just left. It was now obvious that wherever he was heading he
would be walking all the way. That suited Holden.

He walked along streets of handsome apartment houses, the ones
they called posh tenements, spacious and well maintained with
ornately tiled entrances, bright and welcoming, unlike the dark slits
they called closes in the Gorbals. There were even roses and other
flowers in the buildings' front gardens. The Pollokshields tenements
were built around the eastern fringe of the suburb to "protect" the
more stately western part of the district. They had been clever these
planners for they had ringed much of the suburb with such tenement
buildings. The ones on the outer edge and nearest the Gorbals end
were more basic; the more you penetrated the suburb towards the
villas, the higher the amenities and standards of the tenements, until
you reached the streets which flanked the part with the big villas.
There the tenements were of the highest order, among the finest built
in the city with broad staircases and rooms that you could see from the
street were bigger than two entire Gorbals houses. In Snakey
Holden's case you could have put his miserable little single-end
dwelling into one of their sculleries. He thought about that and
muttered "bastards" to himself, for they had to be bastards that lived
in these kind of places, bastards that made money out of the kind of
people like him who lived in the Gorbals.

Sammy Nelson kept walking up Maxwell Road until it became
Maxwell Drive and the tenements gave way to the first of the villas,
huge, rambling buildings, the like of which Holden had never seen
before, some even as big as the public halls in which he used to go
dancing as a youth. When he could go no further in Maxwell Drive,
Sammy turned left into St Andrew's Drive and Snakey Holden was in
an area of Glasgow he never knew existed. The houses were even
bigger and grander than all the beautiful ones he had passed earlier.
They overwhelmed him so much that his attention from his mission

was momentarily diverted to gaze at the handsome mansions, each with their own high gate piers where the driveways met the pavement proclaiming nice names like "Lorne" and "Ardenlee", "Doralee" and "Kilbrandon", "Dalmeny" and "Cairnsmore". All were the best examples of the great architects of their day . . . Turnbull, Clifford, Rowan but especially Thomson — "Greek" Thomson whose shallow pitch roofs and great flair for the gracious and the Grecian had made the area so beautiful.

No two houses were alike. Some had stained-glass staircase windows, tall as a Gorbals chapel, others had sculpted Gothic windows. There were brass bell knobs as big as a Knotts dinner plate and observatories attached to some like a botanical garden's. There were marbled vestibules and there was ornamental ironwork around verandas that must have been made by tradesmen who were artists. All of them had gardens bigger than the wee swing park in which he used to play as a boy.

There were just the two of them in the street now and Holden had his chance. It was getting dark and the street lights had come on. Holden felt excited, more excited than he had been for some time. It wasn't like the kind of excitement he experienced the previous week when he had gone out to look for someone in order to satiate his anger, he knew then he would fell some unlikely and unfortunate victim who meant nothing to him, except as a means of fulfilling his evil need. This time it was different. The excitement which was mounting within him was like the old days when he used to go into battle with his gang, like the times he had supported Jamesie Nelson in his confrontations, like the time too when he had organised the team to go after and kill the Jamesie one.

His lapsed concentration on the man he had been following was abruptly jogged into reality when he saw Nelson halting . . . then, suddenly, turning round. He was about 75 yards in front of Holden who hesitated when he saw the prey now facing him. It was like that moment when the sportsman senses that the stag has been alerted to him and is about to dart off in a leaping sprint, giving him only the merest fraction of a second to pull the trigger for a kill . . . or let it flee. A moment that freezes time, an imprint in the memory, yet only the blur of a fraction of a second.

Nelson buried his head into the upturned collar of his Crombie and a puff of blue smoke emerged from the cigarette which he had stopped and turned his back to the wind in order to light. He sucked it hard, and the breeze quickly dispersed his exhalation as he turned again to walk along St Andrew's Drive. The pause for the cigarette had considerably reduced the distance between the two men. Holden thrust his hand into his coat pocket and there was almost a sensual feel about the smoothness of the slim metallic object he held tightly in his right hand. He breathed deeply in anticipation. He hadn't the same respect or feel for the object in his other coat pocket, a joiner's hammer, its shaft cut down to about six inches. It was ugly by comparison with the lethal beauty of the folded razor. There was only about twenty-five paces between the men now; a mere dash that even Snakey could complete in seconds.

Suddenly Sammy Nelson vanished as though he had been dissolved by some spirit. One moment he had been there, the next he was gone. One minute the street had contained two men, one walking behind the other, the next there was just one man, amazed and dismayed at what had happened. He kept walking. There was the sound of dogs, the high pitched yelps of little dogs as he passed the next big villa, one of the "Greek" Thomson's. A man was approaching the vestibule of the house at the end of a short drive bordered by gleaming white granite chips, and the two terriers were excitedly greeting the person who was obviously part of the household — the man he had been following, Sammy Nelson. Holden continued walking along the street, past the driveway which his prey had disappeared. He only gave the house the glances, but his eyes took in the whole scene, its dimensions and the gold lettering on the tall peaked palistrades which said SAMMAR. And he muttered "Bastard!"

A half hour later, Holden was back in the Gorbals, desperate for a drink. He went back to the Old Judge and, without asking, the barman said to him, "Mind you were asking me about the bloke I said was the uptown bookie? Well, I gave you bum information. He's no' a bookie at all. He's a property owner. A china knows one of the two blokes he's in here with every Friday and he was telling me. They say he owns more than a hundred closes. Might be an exaggeration that. But that's what the china says. A pint is it?"

"Half and a half . . . tell me, how would you find out who owns your house; I mean my ain house, like?"

"Sure, your factor would tell you,"

"Wouldnae ask the bastard."

"Well, you can get it on the valuation rolls. You know, the big books they keep in the City Chambers in John Street. Get the one for your district, look up your street and it's all there . . . your name and the owner's name. We had to do it when we were living in Nicholson Street. You know the state o' the fuckin' houses there! Well, the factor, the fly fucker so he was, had the ownership of the houses transferred to a dosser in the Portugal Street model so that the authorities couldn't chase him up for repairs. The owner in the eyes of the law is the name on the valuation roll and if he hasn't a penny they can't do anything about it."

"But the real owners, the ones that collect the money . . . they can be somebody else?"

"You've got it."

"Bastards".

"Aye, right. Bastards."

"Gie's another half."

The whisky and the beer didn't give Snakey Holden any bliss that night. His passions rose to a rage, a volcano that wanted to burst. Fortunately no one crossed him and he merely stood at the bar slowly drinking, his mind a confusion of anger and frustration, bitterness and hatred. When the harsh alarm bell sounded the 9.30 p.m. closing of the bar for the night, he walked out into the streets of the Gorbals and home to his cupboard of a home, two up left in a black wall in Caledonia Road, and contemplated the events of that day.

14

A MENACE FROM THE PAST

DETECTIVE Inspector Norman Struthers, an erect man with a stern West Highland face and piercing brown eyes, took the crisp white handkerchief from the top pocket of his plain navy suit and held it over his nose and mouth. "Somebody open a window . . . if it will open that is," he said in a commanding voice. A constable struggled with the rotted frame of the window but it wouldn't move. "Oh leave it, it probably hasn't opened for years." Then he leaned over the crumpled body of the man, his eyes taking in everything the mind of a sleuth takes in when he makes his first examination of a murdered person . . . position of the body, areas of injury, types of wounds, disturbance to the immediate area, signs of weapons, and the specific injury, if possible, which caused the death. He stayed beside the body for several minutes then rose quickly and left the room with the other tall detective.

When they reached the stair landing at the end of the dark lobby which led to the house he removed the handkerchief from his face and took a deep gulp of the purer air. "Powerful, isn't it?" he said to the detective he had with him, Sergeant David Ross. "Powerful, sir . . . bit of an understatement that! Smelt like a fish and chip shop that hasn't been cleaned for a year."

"What did you make of the body?" Then he continued to speak without waiting for a reply. "Mess isn't it? The throat wound did it obviously. From the ear to the throat, cut the windpipe as well. But it's quite a rare one. In fact, unique to me."

Ross asked why.

"Well, in my view it was done with a razor or else a knife that had been honed like one, you know, like a butcher's filleting knife. More like a razor though. Did you notice how clean the wound was? Just one long slit. Long, deep and clean. That's the mark of a razor. No tearing or bruising or raggedness. It's a bloody horrible weapon, I'm telling you. And anyway, had it been a knife he would probably have had a go at stabbing him as well. There are no other wounds as far as I can see, although Mr Inglis from the University might find more. He doesn't miss much. There's been no fight. No bruising or cuts on his hands. Obviously been someone younger and more powerful, although the victim appears to have been a fairly frail old boy. What do you say the name was?"

"Doyle. Michael Tone Doyle. Known locally as Mickie Doyle. Bit of a character, they say. Hasn't worked for years, seemingly, although he was always a regular in the local pubs. Maybe somebody thought he had some money."

"Doubt it. The place is like a tip but I think that's been Mr Doyle's doing, not an intruder. It doesn't appear to have been ransacked, although it's hard to tell. God, the way some of those people live. Talk about the pigs of Drogheda. Did he live alone?"

"Yes. His wife died some time ago."

"The wound puzzles me, though. The razor men keep their weapons for the street. I've never known one to use it in the house, except the O'Hara party. Remember that? Five of them got stuck into each other and you would have thought they had painted the house red. God, never seen so much blood! But this is different. Just one man against another. The lock's not broken so the old fellow must have let him in or come home with him. Whatever, he's been an evil bugger who used that weapon to kill. And he did it with one swipe. Has Mr Inglis been called?"

Snakey Holden knew everything he wanted to know about Sammy Nelson now. In those last few terror-stricken moments of Mickie Doyle's life, with Holden advancing on him, silver razor held high and menacing in the hand of his raised right arm, he had told everything he knew. He had done so in exchange for his life, with Holden threatening "Tell me, you old fucker, or you'll get this." And when he told what little he knew he thought he would be excused the menace of the glistening sliver of stainless steel held over his head. But there was no mercy in Snakey Holden's heart that night. Not even to the old man who pleaded that all he knew about the houses was that he signed the papers and if anyone asked he was to say he was penniless and to say no more. "And that's all I know mister. Nothing more. Honest to God, and may He have mercy on my soul if I'm telling you a lie." That was all that Holden wanted to know. And when he knew it, his arm scythed and Mickie Doyle gurgled to his convulsive death.

The murder caused a great shock in the Gorbals, for despite the violence and the violent men, there were few deaths like Mickie Doyle's and the story was big news in the morning and evening papers for several days. Despite appeals for witnesses, none came forward; not because of the normal reluctance to help the police or out of fear of reprisal, but for the simple reason there had been no witnesses. Holden had gone to inspect the valuation rolls and had learned Doyle's name and address from them. He had also seen how the name was peppered through the pages of neighbouring streets in the big register. He kept the information to himself, telling none of his neighbours, even when they were together and complaining about the owners. There was nothing to connect him with his visit to Kidston Street on the night Mickie Doyle had met his death and he intended to keep it that way.

Now that he knew everything about Nelson and his operation, Holden decided to make no immediate moves. Nelson could wait . . . and suffer. He was glad now he hadn't murdered him the night he followed him home. That would have been too quick. There would have been no suffering. And Nelson needed to suffer . . . oh, my God he had, thought Holden, for what he and his brother had done to his life. So he would be clever this time. He would wait. And do it right.

The murder of Mickie Doyle had a deep effect on Sammy and Peggy Nelson. She remembered him fondly as the character who used to share her fruitshop basement in Carfin Street, she boiling the beets and he making his mash and fiddling around with various pieces of tubes and bits of copper, cheerfully chatting away in his broad brogue, addressing his product as it dripped out on its third run as "me darling little jewels . . . every one a little gem, so dey are." And she would make cheese sandwiches, rough and thick, the way he liked them — "God's own bite, so they are Peggy" — and a big bowl of tea: "D'ye know, I've never drunk tay out of a cup in me life . . . and sure, does it not taste all the better out of a bowl anyway?" She cried for the thought of him brought back fond memories of happy days when they had been surrounded by the warmth and character that had been so special about the Gorbals, and Govanhill too, and which was now missing from her life, even though she had a house and a lifestyle that was beyond her wildest dreams as a young woman.

Sammy too was saddened and shocked for he had similar feelings about the Gorbals and the old days, one of the reasons why he retained his contact with the area. But within him there were other more sinister feelings which he sensed about the murder of Mickie Doyle. He had discussed them with Blair and McLean, the rent men, but never once mentioned his thoughts to his wife for fear of alarming her.

The three men talked quietly in the Old Judge on the first Friday after Mickie Doyle's murder and after he had been laid to rest beside his wife Bridie in the Western end of the Southern Necropolis.

"There's a lot of madmen about," said Sammy. "There always has been, hasn't there? But why old Mickie? There wouldn't be a more harmless man in the whole of the Gorbals. And nobody would be thinking he had any money. He had nothing and everybody knew he had nothing. I mean, even the ones that we all know have a few bob, they don't get touched, do they? I just can't get it off my mind and the only thing I can think is that it had something to do with the houses. Just what I don't know. But something. Maybe somebody at the Corporation leaked it to one of the tenants that Mickie was . . . oh I don't know. What could they say about him? Maybe he got drunk and blabbered something himself. But no, he wouldn't. Would he? What could he blabber about? He didn't know enough. I've just got this feeling that for some reason it has to do with us and the houses. But what? We'll never know. Will we?"

Rab Blair had his own theory. It was more sinister. "Maybe somebody got his name and address as the owner and did him in for that. You know some of the houses are getting in a bit of a mess, Sammy. See some of those closes in Cally Road! Like the bloody dark ages so they are. And some of them that's in the houses! Murder polis stuff, so they are."

"You might have something, Rab."

"Or else," said Claney, "they were right fly fuckers and knew what Mickie was up to and wanted him to tell who was collecting the money and who was getting the rents."

"I had given that a thought masel'," said Sammy. "Then I put the thought right out of my mind again. I mean, Christ, we're no' into extortion or going about screwing wives or anything like that. We're doing the bastards a service, so we are. I don't see anybody going bananas for something like that. No, it can't be that."

"But you don't know some of these gadgies we're getting rents from, Sammy. Talk about tuaregs! D'ye know we're taking Tommy Sharkey's big dug wi' us for the Cally Road closes Rab was talking about? S'got a face on it like a fuckin' werewolf, so it has, and even then they still look at you and say 'Fuck off'. If one of them found out... I'm telling you, I wouldn't like them to have my address. Tell you that for nothing."

Whatever the cause, whoever the person, their conclusion was that Mickie Doyle had met his end because he was linked with their housing operation and that from now on they would be more guarded about their business — if that was possible, that is, for it wasn't the kind of trade that they volunteered information about to anyone anyway.

The death of Mickie Doyle haunted Sammy Nelson. Could Rab Blair have been right that the old man had died merely because someone had discovered his name was listed as the owner of the houses or was it like Claney thought, that the killer was really after them or maybe just one of them — Sammy Nelson? He asked himself these same questions and others over and over again, day after day, night after night. But there were no answers.

The police were just as baffled by the murder. Not one clue had been found nor had one single word been passed to them from the usual coterie of informers they used in the district. The prospect that some maniac may now be after him gnawed at Sammy Nelson's mind so much it altered his views on the housing business. What he had thought had been one of his greatest enterprises, swelling his bank account, paying for John to go through University and for Peggy's vast new wardrobe, for the maintenance of their Sammar, had now gone sour and he could only think of it with distaste at the best, with a chill of fear at the worst. It worried him when he opened his eyes to a new day, knowing there was the prospect of the worry being with him throughout the day, and it worried him when he settled into the pillow at night. Even then there was no release, the darkness and the still of night accentuating his thoughts and fears, his mind conjuring up all sorts of weird circumstances which might eventuate as a result of the killer, or was it killers, who might be out to get him.

About three months later, after one such restless night, he wakened with a startle to the fearful shrieks and screams of his wife, Peggy. John came bursting into the big upstairs master bedroom which overlooked the rear gardens. "Oh, Dad . . . Dad . . . Dad," he sobbed. "You'll need to come quick." Peggy was lying on the floor of the dining room screaming uncontrollably, her eyes dilated, her body shaking violently in an emotional fit, one unnatural screech following upon the other. John, shocked speechless, indicated in the direction of the front door. At first Sammy couldn't believe the sight that met him when he went to the door. Its crudity was unreal, its appallingness incalculable, its horror hellish. All he could say was "Oh God . . . oh my God."

Dido and Fido were their pet Cairn terriers, fussy little dogs with chummy faces when they were romping around the house or being petted by the fire, but easily irritated and readily aggressive with a flash of their needle teeth at things which displeased them. There was a dog flap in the rear door for them and as soon as it was light in the morning they would go out in the spacious gardens to the rear, running round to the front to bark a challenge to the milk and paper boys or anyone who did not belong to Sammar, barking in unison until whoever displeased them was out of sight. They barked so often that no one paid any attention to them for they could always find something or someone to whom they could proclaim themselves. They had done the same that fateful morning, only this time the barks and the yelps they would have made were to be their last. There they were, or what was left of them, in front of him. Their heads had been severed and each was grotesquely perched on top of the wide necked milk bottles which were put out each night for the morning delivery. A pool of bright red blood was around the base of each bottle, one of the pools tailing off to drip down the stairs. Their heads had been placed such that they were looking towards the front door, each with its mouth twisted in a cruel death snarl, their tongues, short, pink ribbons, hanging limp, their skulls smashed and bloodied. Sammy Nelson stared at them in disbelief and then, in some kind of reflex action, ran past the gruesome scene to the front garden and into the street, still in his pyjamas.

The broad drive was eerie quiet, as it always was at that time in the morning, the still broken only by nesting blackbirds agitatedly proclaiming their territory. Then, as he walked slowly back towards the house, the shock of it all hit him and he bent over by the steps leading to the vestibule, the polished terrazzo steps spattered with blood, and retched.

The doctor had to attend Peggy every day for a week, such was the state of her shock. It was worse than a death to them. Not only had they lost their beloved pets in such a dastardly fashion but they also knew that someone evil, someone unimaginably wicked and evil, wanted revenge on them. Peggy and her son John had no idea what the reason might be for Sammy had never conveyed his fears to them: nor did they know about the complexities of the housing empire. But Sammy Nelson was convinced more than ever that one of the tenants, and there were two or three hundred of them now, was out to get him. Would one of the names in the rent books mean something to him? Even that was pointless for he knew that many of the tenancies had changed and Rab and Claney usually didn't bother to alter the names. Anyway, had there been a name which meant something, what would it have proved? How would he know what that person had discovered; how would he know that even if they had discovered something that took them to Mickie Doyle that it had been him or them who murdered the old man and then come to his house to commit the terrible atrocity to the pets? And if he ever did find out who that person was who had done these vile things, what could he do about it? Tell the police? Tell them that he was Mr S. Nelson, the faceless man who owned the worst houses in the Gorbals? That Mickie Doyle had been his man-of-straw and had been murdered because of his innocent involvement in a despicable slum racket? Was he to tell the police all that? Was he to lay bare his whole seedy empire? Proclaim it to the Gorbals . . . to Govanhill . . . to Pollokshields? He might have reasoned with his own conscience about his activities, but no one else would be convinced by that. Sammy Nelson was trapped in a web he had spun himself and it seemed there was no way out. Somebody was clearly after him, his friends and family. It could be Rab or Claney or even, God forbid he told himself, Peggy, his son John or himself who might be the next victim.

A strange sensation went through him at the prospect of that; an alarming experience, for he had never felt fear, not real fear, before. He was never afraid in the Gorbals for he was wise of it and its ways. He had never been scared either by the men of violence, the hard men, for they had never been a threat to him, except at the time when he went to the aid of his brother. He had done that without thinking of his own safety. But there was a lot more at stake now. He had a family and he had wealth. The wealth, he thought, had made him a free and independent man; free from the burdens of the daily grind that was so much a part of their lives over in the Gorbals. They said it was a free country, but it was a lot more free if you had the wealth which Sammy now had. That made him free of the squalor and the indignities of the black three-storeyed rows of aging and neglected tenements with their smell of wet brick, limp plaster and acrid coal fire smoke. He was free from that, but not of that for it was there that he had made his wealth and it was from there that he still found reason in his life; he was closer to them than to the more beautiful people of the Thomson villas.

The police were never told about the murder and mutilation of the Nelson pets, Peggy being convinced that was the wisest course to take. Sammy even thought at first his men, Rab and Claney, should not be told, but he had second thoughts about that for they would have to be extra cautious now themselves. He passed word to them to meet him urgently at the Devon Bar, one of a string of public houses in Eglinton Street on the western boundary of the Gorbals.

"You look in a right state, Sammy," said Rab Blair who arrived first.

"I'll wait until Claney comes, Rab, as I only want to tell this story once."

"Is it that bad?"

"It's worse."

Claney turned up about ten minutes later, cupping his hands, as he usually did, then rubbing them vigorously with his customary greeting "How's it gaun?" There was no answer.

"I haven't told Rab what the news is, Claney. I wanted you together. You're the only two I can tell ... and am going to tell." He lifted the half glass of neat whisky that was on the bar. "I'll need this first."

He told the story as it happened the morning before, recounting in as much detail as he could the horrifying events. "Murder is murder ... but this is worse. For there's a fuckin' monster on the loose and he's after me."

"Us," said Claney.

"Aye, you're right. Us. For if he knew about Mickie and knows about me, then he knows about you two as well. Who the fuckin' hell is he? What is he? Is it a team, d'ye think?"

"S'no' a team, Sammy," said Rab. "A team would act like a team. They would just move right in on us. Anyway, it didn't need a team to do in poor old Mickie. Or your dogs."

"What can we do then?"

"Chrisknows ... but I might have another think about the housing operation."

"What d'ye mean, Sammy?"

"Oh, I don't know. They've got something to do with it ... haven't they? It's got to be ... there's nothing else that links us."

"I think we're all jumping to conclusions," said Rab, always the optimist. "Look, Mickie could have been done by some screwball from up his street. He could have thought he had money ... him drunk nearly every night and that. And the dogs ... well Sammy, you know how dogs send some folk bananas. Mind Josie Turner? Used to feed a' the big dugs in the street wi' sausages stuffed wi' chopped-up glass, then laugh his heid aff when they were dying in agony. Dugs dae things like that tae some people. Maybe you've got some toff bam that lives near you that felt the same about yours. Did they bark a lot?"

"Christ, aye."

"There you go. It's been some neighbour that's sorted them out. D'ye know your neighbours?"

"No ... just to give a nod to, that's all."

"You know, Rab could be right," said Claney.

"Chrisknows," said Sammy. "Chrisknows. Get me another whisky, quick. A loud yin. I'll need tae go ... I don't want to be home late."

"Don't worry about it, Sammy."

"It's not me. It's Peggy. She's in a bit of a state."

When he returned home later that evening, his wife was sitting on her own in the big front lounge which looked down the neat lawn that sloped to the street. Normally she would have come to greet him in the high, glass-roofed vestibule or in the spacious hall with its elegant crystal chandelier and its broad, sweeping staircase. But she didn't even look up at first when he entered the lounge, only doing so when he approached her.

"How are you hen?" said Sammy softly. Her head turned towards him in a slow, strained movement. "Oh, I'm so glad you're home. The worry is driving me out of my mind."

He pulled over one of the large leather pouffés to sit beside her, holding her slender hand in his. "You feel freezing, love. Are you warm enough?"

She didn't answer the question. "Oh, Sammy, what's going to become of us? Is this what all our struggles have been for? Look at us. We've got everything. And it's all meaningless. St Andrew's Drive. John's education. Our house. All our lovely furniture. My clothes. Everything. It's all worthless. Oh God, it was terrible. I'll never get that sight out of my mind. Now all I can think about is what's going to happen next. Is it going to be you? Or John? I'm terrified out of my mind, Sammy."

She broke down and wept and he put his arms round her and felt her body trembling, slightly at first as though she was shivering, then growing steadily worse until her whole body seemed to be quivering violently as she sobbed uncontrollably. He held her tighter to him, comforting her till her crying had stopped and the shaking had slowed down and eventually finished. By that time she was fast asleep. It was the first she had slept in two days and he placed a pillow by her head as he eased her back in the soft cushions of the big easy chair in which she had been sitting.

He stood up and looked down at his sleeping wife and was shocked at how old and tired she looked. She appeared a completely different woman from a few days earlier. He spoke to her as though she was still awake. "Don't you worry, my dear. We'll get whoever it was. The bastard is going to pay for this."

15

GETTING A CONSCIENCE

THE Nelsons became increasingly nervous about the likelihood of some other kind of outrage being inflicted on them. Peggy changed dramatically, becoming introverted and a virtual recluse, frightened to leave the house because she imagined something would happen to her property and at the same time frightened when she was at home in case the monster who so brutally murdered their dogs would return. Because of that they hired the McDougalls, a professional housekeeper and her handyman husband, to live with them. There were plenty of spare rooms. The money continued to come in from the properties; it was vital to them for the upkeep of the house, John's education and living expenses. But it was being paid for dearly in the stress it caused them, Sammy still being firmly enmeshed in his own web. He had the rent books handed to him in order to study all the names in the hope that one of them might mean something to him. None did.

"Anyway," said Rab, "some of them keep doing moonlights, others come in and we don't bother with their names. Just so long as somebody in the house pays, it's all right."

"Right then, I'll come round with you this Friday and see the faces for myself. Maybe one of them might mean something . . . or else I'll mean something to them, more likely. We've got to find this bastard."

"Sammy, you're worrying yourself for nothing," said Rab. "It's all coincidence. You've been putting two and two thegether and getting five."

"I'm still coming round with you on Friday."

Rab and Claney looked at each other and said nothing. Before they met again that Friday, the two collectors had got together to discuss their own problem . . . being found out by Sammy for charging more than he knew for the rents. "Don't worry," said Claney. "We'll just tell him we do that to subsidise the ones who don't pay us so that he keeps getting the same money every week." As he thought, Nelson accepted the story.

It had been a while since Sammy had seen his properties. Some of them were the average decayed Gorbals tenement block. But the others were so rotted and worn that they were only standing because of the support given by the houses on either side of them. You could tell as soon as you entered the close, the smell being heavier and more foul than the others. In one the first landing toilet, a cubby hole shared by six families, had been blocked and was overflowing.

"Mind your feet," said Rab as they carefully negotiated the dark and winding staircase.

"How can we mind our feet when we cannae fuckin' see?" answered Claney.

Sammy knocked on all the doors so that he could see the tenant and the tenant could see him. All of them had remarked about "the new man", many with considerable hostility, demanding to know if he was the factor or the landlord. But there was no other reaction.

As always they left the Caledonia Road houses to the last. "Jesus Christ," said Sammy when they went into the first close. The skylight at the head of the stairwell was missing and there were long gouges and red staining down the high walls round the stairs where the rain had poured in. The smell of dampness was overpowering and when Rab saw the look on his face he said, "There's worse than this. Have you seen some of the ones in South Portland Street and Nicholson Street recently? And the landlords down there are taking more than us."

"Just the same, these are fuckin' diabolical," he replied.

Many of the tenants weren't at home, others could be heard moving around inside the houses but refused to come to the door. "See our problem?" said Claney.

"Aye," said Sammy. "I see your problem. I can hear somebody in this one. Who lives in there? It's McNeil in the book."

"There's been about ten since then, Sammy. No point in changing the names. Anyway, it's a crabbit bugger called Holden. We don't usually bother him."

"Holden?" queried Sammy. "Would it be Jackie . . . or Jakey . . . or Stevie that they sometimes call Snakey?"

"Don't know, it's mostly just their surnames we know and he's just Auld Holden to us. Cheeky bastard. Name mean something to you?"

"Not really. Just a name from the past, that's all. It's a common enough name."

The following week when they met Sammy said he didn't want the really bad houses collected from, "That one wi' the choked lavvy, the one with the two missing stairs and no banisters on the landings and the ones in Cally Road."

"Getting a conscience, Sammy?" said Claney.

Sammy's mood changed at that. "Listen pal," — he always said pal when he was angered — "I've always had a conscience. That's different from the bastards who have no conscience and there's plenty of them. I work at my conscience, believe it or not, all the time. I try and keep it right, make it happy. Aye, despite all the tricks I've got up to, I've never really done anything that affected the old conscience. When we were at the coupons and whisky and that the conscience had a right old song and dance to itself 'cos I really felt I was helping people. I was. Helping myself too. Sure, I admit that. But that's all right, isn't it? Wasn't putting the screws on anyone. None of your extortion or violence or anything like that. And the same with the houses. We're doing them a turn are we not. They've got to live somewhere and it's me that's providing a place for them. Orright, so some of them are a bit dodgy. The only people I'm really doing are the taxman, the Corporation and a few bye-laws. And nobody minds that, do they? No' my conscience anyway."

"What you're saying then, Sammy," said Rab, "is that it's still alright to take the rents from Cally Road. What's the difference there for your conscience to get worried about?"

"So the conscience is changing. It didn't worry about them before. Now it does. So no more rents from them and any others that's as bad as them."

"Well, Rab," said Claney, after Sammy had left to walk home. "Looks like you and I have just been given a nice wee rise by the gaffer. Don't take any more rent from the Cally Road houses! Who the fuck is he trying to kid? Christ, it's only a shower of gadgies that's living there. All that bilge about his conscience having changed. My conscience would change if I was living up in the 'Shields! Tell Tommy we'll be wanting the dug for Friday."

Snakey Holden wasn't in his house when they called that Friday for the rent. They were working harder now at collecting rents from the racalcitrants for the money was coming to them and the extra effort was worth it. They hammered at his door for some minutes, thinking he was in. A door down the dark passageway opened. It was old Kate Gallacher, another of the tenants.

"Stop your bloody hammering . . . he's away," she shouted.

"Keep your hair on, Missus," said Claney. "Where's Auld Holden away to?"

"Went wi' the jailers. They came for him last Sunday night when I came back from mass. They've caught him chasing the wummin again.

When are youse gonnie fix my roof? Half the ceiling's down."

"Missus, we've got your name down for repairs. No' our fault. The gaffer knows about it. He's getting the repairs done. Have you got your rent money?"

The story was always the same. They contemplated getting another tenant for Holden's house as it was a shame to be losing his money. "D'ye realise that's two halfs and two pints we're losing through no' getting his money?" said Claney.

"Christ, you're always one jump ahead of me," said Rab. "I've never figured it out that way." They decided, however, not to break into his house, for changing the locks and getting a new tenant was more trouble than it was worth. "We'll just screw the bastard for back money when he comes out of the nick," said Claney and Rab nodded in agreement.

There had been a number of rapes and attacks on women and young girls in the vicinity in the weeks before Holden had been arrested. They had come for him after an incident in which a drunk woman he had picked up had begun screaming when she realised he was about to have intercourse with her in a back close. Someone had recognised him running away from the close where he had taken her. He was remanded in custody on both the occasions he appeared before Mr Shortwood at the Central Police Court so that the police could make more enquiries. He was brought before the Stipendiary Magistrate for a third appearance when the Fiscal, to Holden's great surprise, announced that he was withdrawing the charges of attempted rape, recommending that he be released from custody. It was the first time he had ever appeared before the Magistrate and not ended up in Barlinnie and the significance of that made him give the bench a sneer, knowing better than to let him have the swearing he would have preferred for he had seen Shortwood bring prisoners back and double their sentence just for muttering "bastard" at him.

The men from the Lawmoor Police Station, responsible for that part of the Gorbals where Holden lived and where the attacks had been taking place, were furious when they heard the news for they were convinced he was the man involved in at least two of the incidents. They warned him in the cells below the courtroom when he returned to collect his property on release. "See you, Holden," said one of them. "We'll take you into Lawmoor Street and give you the biggest fucking kicking you've had in your life if we catch you at it again. Then we'll do you for anything we can find in the book." But warnings like that made little difference to the arrogant Holden, who met the threat with a contemptuous laugh. When he was leaving the station he turned to the policeman who had given him the warning. "You watch your face, copper. I know it . . . and I'll no' be forgetting it."

To their surprise Holden answered the door when they called the following week, again accompanied by the dog. He was as unmoved as ever, refusing to hand over the money despite a variety of threats from Blair and McLean about coming back with more men. "Knock this fuckin' door again wi' that beast and I'll take its fuckin' heid aff," he said with a chilling gruffness which left no confusion in their minds about the earnestnes of the threat. "And youse can tell that Nelson he'll get fuck all out of me again."

Blair and McLean were still shocked when they got to the Clachan, a pub they used in McNeil Street, at the farthest end of the district, if they didn't want to meet Sammy. "How did he know about Sammy?" said Rab. "Christ, that's sinister, so it is. Real sinister. Somebody's wagged. But who? Do you think he knows who Sammy is . . . or is it just a name he's heard?"

"You don't think," said Claney, always the more shrewd of the two, "that he knew Mickie?"

"You mean . . .?"

"Aye, you know what I'm thinking."

"But how would he get to know Mickie?"

"I don't know. I don't know."

"We should be telling Sammy, Claney."

"Aye, we should . . . but we're not. Want him to find out we're still getting rents from all these houses he thinks we've given up? Likely to put a team on us for that . . . wi' his conscience singing. No, Rab, we'll say nothing to nobody about it. We'll leave Holden alone and he'll be all right. Got it? We're saying nothing."

"Aye, maybe you're right Claney. Holden can have his miserable fuckin' single-end. Christ, he's a fierce looking bastard, isn't he? How about the scars and that? Got a face like the Eglinton Toll tramlines. Tell you what. Even the bloody dug was feart. I could feel it shaking through the lead. He really meant it about taking its heid aff."

"It's heid aff!" repeated Claney. "Christ . . . you know . . . Sammy's dugs and that!"

"Oh Christ. I never thought."

"Aye . . . and didn't Sammy ask what Holden's first name was?"

"You're right. Jesus. What do you think it is, Claney? What the bloody hell is going on? It is Holden . . . isn't it? But how did he know Mickie? And what's the connection wi' Sammy? Asking his first name, and that. How did he want to know his first name . . . what the hell is it anyway?"

"Fuck knows. It's just Holden that's down on the rentbook. Anyway, who gives a stuff about any of their first names. Och, maybe we're jumping to conclusions again, Rab. We both got a fright there. That's all that happened. We got a fright. If we leave him alone nothing else will happen. We don't want to get involved, do we? I mean, telling the Busies and things like that? You're not on Rab, no involvement."

"I suppose you're right, Claney. No involvement. Christ, get me a drink, quick."

As they agreed, they never went back to Holden's house, although they still continued to collect rent from the other houses nearby, some of them now woefully neglected and in a dangerous state, But from the rents they were collecting they were making more money in a week than they had ever made in their lives.

They had hoped that by not returning for the rent money Holden would forget. But he was not a man like that. He had become obsessed by the Nelsons, first by the hard man and then by the landlord. If he hadn't killed Jamesie and become the top hard man himself — although no one remembered him for that because his reign had been so brief — he would never had got the slashings, the marks of which he would carry to his grave. Being *the* Hard Man had only meant he was number one target of every knife and razor man in the South Side and he had never been a match for that sort of opposition. He was no Jamesie Nelson and he knew it and resented it bitterly. As though to put the boot in on his conscience, another one was to come along with his men to try to extract a few miserable shillings from him for his stinking hovel of a house. He resented that just as bitterly and even though he had exacted some revenge he wasn't satisfied. The name Nelson had become a poison in his mind and he wanted it cleansed from him.

Meanwhile, obsessed with the worry which hung over him and his family, Sammy Nelson was now more determined than ever to get rid of his housing empire in some way and at the same time find the person or persons who had wreaked such havoc on his family. Neither was to be easy, particularly his property business which seemed to cling to him like an unwanted disease. His houses should have been officially listed as having no owner with the death of Mickie Doyle, but no one informed the Glasgow Corporation of the fact and his name continued in the valuation rolls: not that the Corporation cared anyway. They had enough problems over the chronic housing shortage without the extra burden of having to take over more slums and be responsible to the tenants for the maintenance of their houses or their re-housing. The tenants themselves, apart from Snakey Holden, were quite unaware of such matters. The man who owned them, as far as they were concerned, was the rent collector: pay them once a week and their quarters, however dilapidated, were secure for another seven days. Who cared who the owner was? They were all bastards anyway; owners, factors and rent collectors.

1947 began bleakly. There were fierce snow blizzards blown in with the Arctic northerlies and when warmer Atlantic winds puffed in they brought seemingly endless banks of heavy rain clouds. There had been peace for nearly two years but it still seemed like wartime. There was a critical fuel shortage and the cutbacks in industry were so bad they had to reduce the sweet ration from four ounces to two ounces and food and clothing were still rationed, although there were some relaxations . . . you could get a pair of nylons for three coupons. Rab summed it up one day when the three of them met for a drink.

You can definitely tell the war's over boys," he said. "Read the papers this morning. The London dockers are out and so are the porters. The Glasgow binmen want £5 a week wages and the Corporation have said nae chance so they're on strike from the day. The Clyde yards are having token strikes for they want a forty-four hour week. All the men at Cardowan colliery have come out in dispute with their new bosses and the nurses at Robroyston have given notice that they'll be out in a week's time if their demands are no' met. Nurses on strike! Christ, what next? Aye, well seen it's peacetime. Just as well Claney and me don't form a wee union, Sammy. We'd be givin' you demands."

"Aye, that'll be right," laughed Sammy. "See you two . . . get more than a docker, a miner and a nurse put together. Forty-four hour week! Christ, youse wouldnae be doing that in a month."

"Aye, but there's a lot of stress, Sammy," said Claney. And they laughed together.

Apart from the strikes, people were now thinking ahead for the first time in more than six years. Although the present was still redolent of wartime grey and decay, there was now a new horizon and the politicians were speaking with hope about the future: but then they usually did, whether they were in power or not. They were thinking ahead for the boom years that the peace was to bring them for winning the war against the Axis. Plans were revealed for a whole new conception of living for thousands of Glasgow people. They were going to build a brand new town for them. Everything new, right from scratch. New houses and shops, theatres and pubs, and factories galore to produce for the great new era which they said was just around the corner. It was to be centred on the little agricultural village of East Kilbride, which nestled beneath the high moorlands to the south of Glasgow. But they were just plans and, if they were ever achieved, it would be many years off.

They were talking too about new attitudes in other aspects of living. Part of the great debate about the future was the revolution they said would come to the public houses of Glasgow. For years they had been drinking shops. The men who drank in them called them that. A good one was called a good shop. And there were more bad shops than good ones. It was an appropriate term. For, just like a shop, you went in, got your particular order and left again when your order had been fulfilled. There was little else on offer . . . no cheer, no frills, no accompanying music. It was even against the law to sing or play an instrument. The law didn't say you weren't to smile and be happy and hearty; but it meant it. That was why they didn't let the women in, except in ones with special sitting rooms to which they would furtively slink. Women weren't for public houses. They would have giggled and laughed; or worse, they might even have made merry. And they would have none of that. Drinking was a dour business. Even sitting was proscribed in many of them. Sitting! Sitting was relaxing; relaxing was enjoying. And drinking wasn't for enjoying. It was for doing. Like working. And so they stood there, the connoisseurs of the morose, as the poet said, standing by the bar, one foot on the brass rail, the other by the sawdust-filled trough which went round the bar and served as litter bin, ash tray and wall-to-wall spittoon. The drinkers were herded out at 9.30pm to the accompaniment of strident alarm bells. That was law and order's way of saying the drinking was over for the day and, often as not, some police would also be there to remind them that drinking was a business that was about law and order.

But the men who had gone to the war had found that in many of the countries where they had travelled men and women could drink together and could even be bold enough to sing and enjoy themselves while drinking. They dared not to ask such things before the war, but they were asking lots of things now. And they wanted answers too. One of the things they were asking was why couldn't they have civilised places in which to drink and relax? The municipal correspondents of the newspapers were urging sweeping changes to brighten the image of the city's cheerless drinking shops. They were also mentioning that with the vast redevelopment schemes being planned, there would be considerable relocation of pubs and redistribution of licences.

Sammy had followed all the reports in the papers with more than the normal interest for, as he told Peggy one night, he too was thinking about the future and the great years ahead they were all anticipating now that the war was over. "All the best businessmen plan for the future," he told her. "That was one of the first lessons I learned from old Myer. Shop for the summer in the winter and for the winter in the summer, he used to say. And the big future in this city is in building and in pubs. We don't have the capital for the building game; anyway I don't fancy it. But we could get into pubs. There's going to be a right boom in them . . . started already. You should see the women that's using them . . . putting lemonade in their whiskies, silly bitches. But they're there and it's all changing. Gees, Peg, when we were young it was only a whore that would go into a pub. Anyway, I'm thinking about trying to get one of these suspended licences that the Corporation has got. All you need is that one, Peggy, and that would be us in the drinks business."

"You mean everything above board?"

"Peggy . . . you know me."

"That's how I'm asking."

"Aye, everything above board. Total legit. That's me from now onwards. No cutting corners. An honest and upright citizen. Gees, my conscience will be doing handstands. But I'll need to get in quick. The licence will not be that easy to get for there's a lot of others like me thinking the same thing and they say you've got to have a lot of pull before you get one. Got to go before a special court, so you have. But it's the old story, love. Not what you know . . . Know what I mean, like?"

"Well, who do you know?"

"D'ye remember John English . . . the one that was always talking about John Maclean when I was in hardware at Myers? Got the sack before me for trying to get us all into a union. Well, I met him the other day. Hadn't seen him in all those years but we knew each other right away. Done all right has the boy. Dressed like a toff and he's a Bailie in the Corporation. Socialist like. And he says that if there was any help I needed, he's the boy. This could be the big chance I've been looking for, hen. It'll not happen overnight, like, but I've got to start working on something for the future and this is the best thing that's come up. Life's funny isn't it? Bump into a guy in a pub, get on the chat and the next thing you know your whole life could be changing."

16

A VISIT TO MISERY HALL

H E had been drinking one lunchtime in the Ingram, just off George
Square, one of the city's better bars, when he had met John
English. The bar had two sitting rooms, the Merchants' Room and the
Royal Exchange Room, and English was in the latter quietly enjoying
his drink with the *Glasgow Herald* behind one of the balustraded
divisions in the well-kept establishment.

They hadn't seen each other since before the war when they had
both been young lads at Myer's. Sammy Nelson had thought a lot
about his Socialist principles then and was always willing to speak
about them, even to lead the Myer's strike. But, by comparison,
English had been even more of an activist. He had been a staunch
member of the Independent Labour Party, getting himself sacked
from Myer's six months before the strike in which Nelson had been
involved. They caught English having regular lunchtime meetings
with the staff, teaching them about the theories of trade unionism and
workers in revolt against the bosses.

It was Nelson who noticed English first. "Jesus Christ, if it isn't . . .
how's the revolution?" Large ones were poured and memories flooded
back.

"Last time I saw you, John, you had your wee paint bucket and
brush, sneaking round our streets painting your ILP slogans at all
the street corners."

"I was the best signwriter they ever had. Did thirty street corners in
one night . . . VOTE ILP. They don't do it any more . . . d'ye notice
that? It's all posters now. Not as good as painting the streets."

It was changed days from the muffler and cloth cap for both of
them. English looked as prosperous as Nelson, although more
conservatively so in an expensive blue nap coat over a three-piece

business suit, contrasting with Nelson's bookie flash, a touch of daring yellow here, a bit of suede there, rounded off with an oversize signet ring ornately enscrolled with his initials.

"Gees, you look as though you've really knocked it off, Sammy."

"Look who's talking. You didn't pick that coat up in Burton's."

"Forsyth's actually."

"Aye, looks it."

"Where are you living then?"

"St Andrew's Drive."

"Pollokshields?"

"Aye."

"Christ, you cannae hide money."

"Yourself?"

"Kelvinside. Red sandstone villa."

"You should talk. What's your game?"

"Insurance."

"What? All the insurance men I know live up a close."

"Aye, but some do better than others."

"What about politics then?"

"Oh, I'm still into that. Never read about me? I'm the Labour member for the Northside Ward. Bailie John English, that's me."

"What about the revolution then?"

"Oh, I think that can wait, Sammy. If they knew what I was making off some of the policies I'm selling they'd have me up against the wall. How are you off for insurance anyway, Sammy?"

"Up to my neck . . . and not one of them's in paper. Got a bit of property . . . you know."

"Now that's real insurance, old pal. Not like the stuff I'm selling . . . but don't tell anybody that. Do you still vote Labour?"

"Christ, aye. I'm still a Socialist."

"A St Andrew's Drive Socialist!"

"Aye, just like you're a Kelvinside one."

Nelson could hold his drink much better than English who, after three large ones, revealed himself to be such a different person from the young John English Sammy had remembered, a man he had admired for his courage and effort in persuading others to the cause of Socialism. Now his conversation was peppered with material things, about the money his wife spent in the big Sauchiehall Street stores and last year's holiday to Jersey. And when he spoke of the car it was always "The Snipe . . . Super Snipe, actually". The problems of society, it seemed, were for others to talk and worry about, although no doubt he did plenty of that when he was taking part in debates in the City Chambers, just round the corner and across the bestatued George Square from the pub where they drank. He was as much a contradiction in terms as Sammy. With English it was material wealth versus his politics; with Sammy his actions versus his conscience.

"What's your game anyway, Sammy?" said English, apologising for having commandeered so much of the conversation. "No, don't tell me. You're either in scrap or a bookie . . . sorry, turf agent. Would have to be a turf agent with a coat like that."

"No, as I said . . . property. That's my full-time business, as well as my insurance. I own a few houses, and that. I collect a few rents, or at least my men do, and that. And make myself a few bob and that."

"Aye, that'll be right, Sammy. You're not in St Andrew's Drive through collecting a few rents, and that, as you say."

"Well . . . maybe it's more than a few houses. But c'mon! You're not in Kelvinside through flogging a few insurance policies."

"Don't kid yourself, Sammy. There's money in insurance all right."

"Aye, but that much? Humber Snipes, sorry, Super Snipes, holidays in the Channel Islands. Got something on the side have you?"

English laughed at the suggestion. But Sammy interpreted it as a knowing laugh, a laugh that spoke a lot of words, words that would have said, "You're right, Sam Nelson. I am into something on the side and you're not knowing about it." He didn't need to say any more.

"Sammy," he said. "Do you know what they call me in the City Chambers? Honest John English. That's me. Honest John English." And he laughed again. And it was the same laugh as before. And it told as many words. Maybe more.

When they parted English produced a business card. "Give us a call sometime, Sammy. Enjoyed that wee talk the day. And you never know, you might need advice about something. I can always do a friend a wee turn . . . insurance . . . money for a house . . . or maybe something I can do at the Chambers. Know what I mean, like?"

"Aye, John . . . know what you mean like."

About a fortnight later he met English, once again in the Ingram. When he outlined his ambitions to him, the councillor slowly looked round the bar and lifted his drink from the polished walnut counter. "Remember what they used to say during the war — careless talk costs lives: even the walls have ears. And they've got ears in this place. There's a lot of Corporation staff come here for a drink. C'mon, let's go to the corner over there where there's no one near."

With disarming bluntness, English went straight to the point. "So you want a public house licence? Well, the news is . . . it can be done. But not by me. I'm in housing. Want a nice ground floor one or two bedroom job, garden and that, in a high amenity area like Knightswood, for your wee auntie maybe . . . or a nice semi in

Mosspark, awfully nice address you know, then I'm your boy. But pubs, no. That's Alex Campbell. You should know him. Gorbals boy. He's a magistrate on the Licensing Committee. But it's a long story, Sammy. Let me explain. There's two or three of us at George Square, maybe more, I only know about the two or three and we . . . how shall I put it? . . do special favours for certain people. It's not what you would call corruption or anything like that. It would if we were all in collusion. But we're not. And how can you call it corruption if you're just doing someone a wee favour even though it's for a little consideration, as they say? I can do it in housing, as I was saying, for if certain applications come before me in the committee, I can make sure they're approved. The others don't know I'm up to any tricks. That's our job anyway as councillors, to help people. So who knows whether you're helping them for a consideration or without a consideration?"

"So that's how you got to Kelvinside?"

"Sammy . . . I'm surprised at you suggesting anything like that," he grinned. "No, it's the wife. She's got money."

"Aye, so's mine. I gave her it."

And they both grinned.

"So what if I want a house for my wee auntie?"

"Is she a genuine case?"

"£100 genuine."

"Sammy, she'd need to be more genuine than that. Now if she was £200 genuine I'd see her all right . . . Bellahouston or Knightswood."

"And supposing my wee auntie wants a pub?"

"As I said, that's Alex Campbell. And I don't know what he's calling deserving cases. It'll be a lot more than your wee auntie can afford, anyway. But seriously, he's the man to see. I know he does it, although he's never said to me and I've never said to him. But I know. And I know too about Bailie O'Sullivan. Bailie Patrick O'Sullivan. Aye, one of them. He's got a big photo up in his lawyer's office of him down on the old hot peas kissing your man's hand at the Vatican. But Christ, I'll bet his confession box rattles on a Friday night. He used to be up to his neck in it when he was in housing, but now he's on the Licensing Committee as well. Don't go to him. It's just *them* that goes to him, you know. And he's at it more than any of us. He gets it all ways for he insists on becoming your lawyer as well. Now, see me Sammy. I don't ask anyone what church they go to. I just ask them what bank they go to." He laughed out loud at the joke and Sammy smiled. "But seriously, though, the likes of O'Sullivan and the way they play it gets right up my nose. They work at the dead respectable game. You'll see him every time there's a home game at Parkhead sitting in the best seats surrounded by priests and hob-nobbing it wi' the directors. That's the place to really show you're important and respectable . . . wi' them that is."

"Aye, just like our lot do at Ibrox."

"You're no' a cynic are you, Sammy? Anyway, you go and see Alex Campbell. Nice wee fellow. Good Labour man and works like a Trojan for the Party. His mother has that fruitshop near Gorbals Cross. Spoiled him rotten when he was a boy, so she did. But he's all right. And he's got his Member's ticket at Ibrox."

"Sitting wi' the ministers and the directors on a Saturday . . . "

"You *are* a cynic. How's the wife? Betty isn't it?"

"No. Peggy."

The councillors normally met constituents in the city's town hall, in a big room appropriately nicknamed Misery Hall. The town hall was grandly called the City Chambers, a swaggeringly opulent building dominating George Square and built in the wake of the bank failure of the middle 1800s. They had been out to show that Glasgow had recovered from the crippling effects of the financial crisis and could afford one of the greatest palaces in the land. Just like any ordinary Glaswegian does when he comes into money, they wanted to do it in style. There's nothing subtle about Glasgow style. When they go about the paraffin, as Jamesie Nelson called it, it's the kind of style that's there to be seen . . . flash, obvious, apparent and deliberate so that nobody will miss the fact that they have, indeed, got what they think is style. Real style. And style it was to be for the enormous pile of honey and pink Polonaise and Dunmore stone that came to be erected in the heart of the city. When the final design was chosen it wasn't because it was the most tasteful. It was because it was the most grand. It was to flaunt every great architectural influence in the books . . . sumptuous Renaissance detail larded with the finest French and Venetian effect, Flemish being the dominating influence. Hardly a square inch of wall was left bare and unadorned. They wanted the greatest civic gesture that could be built and they got it. Then the Glasgow soot descended on it and the detail and all the granite opulence disappeared in a smothering of filth. What should have been the jewel of the city centre ended up looking for all the world like some monstrous black wedding cake.

When they walked through the imposing entrance in George Square, created to suggest the Grand Arch of Constantine in Rome, and into the hall they called the Loggia, it made the humble Glasgow folk feel even more humble, doffing their caps on entering and speaking in the same hushed tones they would had they been in a cathedral. The uniformed attendants would point them in the direction of the magnificent staircase, and if they weren't overwhelmed when they entered the Chambers, they would be by the time they ascended the vast stairway, a treasure of alabaster and Brescia marble, its richness impressing the visitor with a knowledge that this place was important and in the midst of people who were important: people who had authority and who liked to show that they had authority. In a place like the City Chambers, that was easy.

Councillor Alex Wallace Campbell loved every minute of his life as the Labour member for the Rose Ward of the Gorbals district. When he stepped through the big doors of the Chambers and was greeted by the liveried attendant with a "Good morning, Bailie Campbell", he became another man. No longer was he wee Alex Campbell, whose mother had one of the best tenement flats in Crown Street, and who as a child had suffered the taunts of the local boys as Crapper Campbell, the youngster who always ran at the first sight of trouble. And there was no shortage of that in the streets around his house. His fear of violence had been so great that he had eventually given up bribing boys with sweets so they wouldn't hit him and would run straight home after school to play with the toys his doting mother heaped on him. As a man he retained the puffy cheeks and spoiled boy's face of his childhood, but his hair had receded prematurely. What remained was a thin straggle which he used to try and camouflage his high forehead but which the slightest wind would blow astray again.

Alex Campbell loved respect and patronage. And there was no easier way of getting it than being a local city councillor, for if you were a Socialist you were one of the people; it meant you spoke their language and had their thoughts; you could tell them that the Progressives, the Council's Tory Party, were nothing but a bunch of money-grubbers and exploiters and that the Socialists had sorted them out since becoming really strong in the thirties. They liked hearing things like that for it meant you were all for them, the people. And even the boys who remembered him as Crapper Campbell thought of him in a new light now that he was a councillor and liable to be one all his life because of the size of the majority he was assured of in the district. "Alex's the boy," they would say when they read the reports of the fiery debates in the City Chambers in which he always made a point of starring, never being short of the kind of phrases that captured headlines and increased his popularity with his constituents. "It's the Progressive we have to blame for the ruination of Glasgow". . . "the Progressive created the slums for the workers". . . "Every time you see a Progressive you are looking at an enemy" . . . "Treat the Progressives like lepers and give them clappers so that we can know they are coming" . . . "The Progressives are the Retrogressives." "Aye, our Alex's the boy all right," they would say. "He'll be the Lord Provost one day."

Alex Campbell thought that too. For being the city's number one citizen was his greatest mission in life. Nothing else mattered except achieving that ambition. He had only got married because his mother had said he couldn't be the Lord Provost unless he had a Lady Provost by his side for the countless functions they held in the great banqueting hall of the Chambers, awesome in its Venetian splendour, or sitting beside him in the wide beige velour seat of GO, the Provost's Rolls Royce, huge and silent and spacious as the King's carriage itself. For these reasons he had married Sheila Williamson, a Victoria Road girl, and Victoria Road girls were nice girls, whose mother, Sarah, was one of his staunchest supporters and an enthusiastic party worker. They had moved to Victoria Road from the Gorbals through the profits she made from money lending and the menages she ran. With money from both their mothers plus what he had amassed himself through his extra-curricular activities within the Chambers, Alex and his Sheila were established in Langside Drive, Newlands, second only to St Andrew's Drive in the quality of homes which it displayed. The house was part of his great dream, for you had to have a house like the kind in Newlands to show off the ornate cast lamp posts which the city presented to its Lord Provosts to mark, in style, the place where they had stayed, a custom which they had been carrying out since 1825. And you couldn't put a pair of magnificent lamp posts like that outside a close. When he got his lamp posts it would make the house the most imposing in all Newlands and they would point to it, the important and the wealthy who lived roundabout, and they would say, "That's the house of our Lord Provost." Alex Campbell's dreams were made of such things but despite that he rarely spoke about his big house in Langside Drive and he made sure none of his constituents ever visited him. He was terrified of spoiling his image as a man of the people. For a man of the Gorbals people didn't live where he did.

That was why he had spent token hours working in Jessie's, his mother's busy fruit shop, chatting up the women customers with the hackneyed pleasantries they loved to hear ... "I could fair go for you, Annie, and you on the pension an' a'" ... "Ah, there's wee Mary, my ain wee honey pear, how's the gran'weans hen?" ... "There ye are, Betty, darlin', two extra totties in your bag for you're special" ... and "Don't forget girls, if you or your men have any problems don't hesitate to come and see me in the City Chambers" or if it was election time ... "It was Rob Roy started the Progressives, noo they're out to rob you." He had thousands like them.

Sammy met Alex Campbell across a bare wooden table in Misery Hall. Like the other constituents meeting their councillors, they sat on long wooden benches. The woman next to him and sharing the same bench and table was laying it off to her councillor about her great need for a house transfer. She lived in a slum clearance house, she told him, "and my doctor says if I don't get a transfer urgent like, then he'll no' be responsible for my health. Says I'm gonnie have a nervous breakdown unless I get a nice quiet place to masel' in Mosspark with an inside toilet, bathroom and its own garden."

"Well, my friend," said Campbell with a patronising smile when he took his seat at the table. "What can Bailie Alex Campbell do for you today?"

"A lot, I hope," said Nelson, "but it's very personal, like. Is there eh, someplace we could talk?" Campbell immediately rose and indicated to follow.

"They call this the Crush Corridor," he said when they reached a black and white marbled hallway and, smiling again, added "So you can now tell Alex Campbell all your secrets in total privacy."

The smile changed perceptibly when Sammy Nelson introduced himself, saying that he needed advice about the licensing trade and that a friend had suggested he may be able to help. Campbell's eyes took in everything they could in order to make a quick calculation of the man who had something so special to ask of him that it had to be private. His quick assessment was that Nelson was a wealthy, flash, fly, malleable, suspicious, shifty, shady, wheeler-dealer. In the same instant Nelson was making his own calculations . . . ingratiating, false, hypocritical, patronising, untrustworthy, sneaky, weak, styleless, shallow.

"The Licensing Trade . . . it's a big subject, my friend. The kind of subject which goes up many avenues, covers many areas. Are you a Gorbals man, Mr . . . I'm sorry?"

"Nelson."

"Of course. Are you a Gorbals man, Mr Nelson?"

"Born and bred. But have moved now. In the 'Shields."

"Lovely place. And you say a friend advised you to come and see me?"

"That's right."

"I know the friend, presumably?"

"That's right. But he said . . . just say a friend. Know what I mean?"

"Perhaps. Tell me, did your friend say I could help you in a specific kind of way, Mr Nelson?"

"Very specific."

"How specific?"

"Specific enough to know that I'll end up with a nod from the Licensing Court."

"That's very specific, isn't it? Your friend seems to know a fair bit about, what shall we say, what goes on."

"He knows enough."

"And did your friend say how I could persuade the Licensing Court to give you the nod as you say?"

"No, not really. He merely said you were a very clever man and a very good councillor and had helped people like me before."

"And what kind of people are people like you?"

"People like me are very grateful to people who help them."

"Oh, so your friend said that being able to help people, by way of guidance that is, is indeed a very great favour? The kind of favour which is very difficult to achieve and one in which I in turn have to seek the aid of other people and to do that requires — how shall I put it? — requires some energy and a lot of time. And energy and time are very hard to come by for a busy man like myself."

"Oh, I appreciate that, Mr Campbell. But my friend says and I agree with him, that energy and time are commodities which can be compensated for."

"And who would be doing the compensating?"

"Oh, I could see to that all right."

"Did your friend realise just how much compensation for the time and energy might be?"

"Like energy and time themselves, compensation can be a variable commodity . . . can it not?"

"Supposing I was willing to devote my time and energy in order to help you then, Mr Nelson. You would realise, of course, that such time and energy would be way beyond my normal duties as a councillor and that I would be doing it for someone who is a complete stranger to me, apart from the fact that there is a friend somewhere who knows my . . . capabilities and expertise. I am a very busy man and apart from being a councillor I do have to make myself a living. We're not paid for our devotion to the city and the people, you know? I mean, why should one just drop everything in order to help someone who, at the end of the day is going to do all right by himself as a result of the work of a councillor?"

"A very good point, Mr Campbell. My friend says one should expect to be rewarded for such great endeavours . . . and I totally agree with him."

"But perhaps there's more to life than rewards, Mr Nelson?"

"Oh yes, indeed. I think life should have its inducements as well as its rewards."

"Maybe there's even more to life than inducements *and* rewards, though?"

"There's no one more aware of that than me, Mr Campbell. We need our inducements, our rewards . . . and our incentives to keep us going."

"It would appear you speak the same language as me then, Mr

Nelson. So much so I think we can be much more specific."

"Fine by me. I'm told there are some suspended licences. I want one."

"How badly do you want it?"

"That bad I can meet any inducement, incentive and reward that's ever been made before."

"Supposing it takes even more time and energy than before?"

"Then I'll top anything that's been made before."

"That could be quite a considerable . . . " At this point he paused, groping for a suitable word which would maintain his unbroken equivocation, completely avoiding the mention of figures or finance. ". . . considerable involvement on your part."

"The . . . involvement . . . will not be any great problem. Just you tell me the extent of the involvement and I'll see you are duly compensated."

"Compensated, Mr Nelson? That sounds to me like a very mercenary sort of word."

"Aye, you're right. I should have said I'll pay you every fuckin' penny you want."

Campbell's wan smile vanished and he paled visibly.

"Right. Cut the patter," said Nelson. "I want a pub. I've got the loot. You've got the pull. You're at it and I know you're at it. So . . . we're all at it. That's the way . . . isn't it? They make the rules and them in the real high places get round them for they've got the kind of influence that counts and everything is dead respectable. And the ordinary punter like me gets nowhere unless he knows the ropes. And this one knows the ropes as well as you do. How much?"

"You're a very blunt man, Mr Nelson. You're taking a great chance, you know. I could report you for . . . "

"For what? Finding out about you?"

"What do you know?"

"Enough to be here with you and saving . . . how much?"

"There's no answer to that question. It depends. I've got to oil the works, as it were."

"You mean . . . inducement!"

Campbell smiled.

"What about fifty to start with?"

"Mr Nelson . . . I can't talk about money here."

"Well, just listen then. Is fifty what you're talking about?"

"It might get us on the road. But I don't want any more mention of money here. Here's my card. Phone me and we'll arrange a meeting away from here."

"Okay by me. You'll be interested in what I have to put to you."

"Well, Mr Nelson, we shall see."

17

THE TERROR RETURNS

THE spring gave way to summer. Campbell had told Sammy to be
patient for he knew there would be some licences coming before
the Court in the autumn. During these months Sammy Nelson had
devoted countless hours wandering around his old haunts in the
Gorbals, meeting former friends and acquaintances, some he hadn't
seen since his schooldays, hoping to pick up from someone,
somewhere, a clue about who might have it in for him. Usually when
there was a claim out on a person, others would know. But there was
nothing to show for his efforts, not even a whisper. Maybe it was, as
Rab had said, a remarkable coincidence: maybe there was a neighbour
who did not like dogs, barking dogs: maybe there was someone who
had thought Mickie Doyle had money and had ended his days for it.
And, as the months passed with nothing further happening and with
Peggy slowly recovering, but still living the life of a near recluse, the
more acceptable became the coincidence theory. His men, Rab and
Claney, had, as they agreed, not returned to Holden's house for rent
and that, as they had thought, had kept him quiet. Holden, in fact, had
forsaken the practice of keeping a close watch on the three men when
they met: it even appeared he had given up interest in them. But while
they might be forsaken, they were not forgotten. The long and light
nights of spring and summer were not to his liking for that kind of
task; and anyway, he had other things on his mind. There would be
another time, another place, for what he had to do. When the autumn
did arrive and people said, as they had always said, that "the nights are
fairly drawing in", the evil obsession, like the darkness, returned to
the mind of Steven Holden. Late in that season they had one of the
worst fogs for some years. Ochre and acrid, it descended on Glasgow
in a foul swirling stench. The combined smoke of housefires and
industry, unable to penetrate the freezing cold blanket of Arctic air

which lay motionless above the chilled city, tumbled back down on them: a sinister, evil effluent which choked the healthy and snuffed the life out of the unhealthy. Hundreds of bronchitics and emphysemics died in its onslaught. Sammy Nelson had gone into the Old Judge that Friday, his yellow Paisley harnish scarf wound round his mouth and nose to prevent gulping the noxious mist which had enveloped them to the extent that the only traffic moving was the tramcars, led at walking pace by their conductors with torches guiding them back to the depots.

Rab and Claney were waiting for him in the bar, having done their rent rounds for the week. They set up his usual loud yin, a double whisky, plus a pint, as he unwound the scarf from his face. "Christ, that really goes for my chest. I was 4F you know. My tubes have had it, said the quack at the recruiting office. And there's me smoking thirty Senior Service every day. But that fog is diabolical. See when I go to sleep the night, I'll sound like an old set of bagpipes." And they laughed out loud together when Rab cracked, "Aye, and you can get the wife to play your chanter."

Sammy finished the drink quickly, as he always did, settling down to consume the round he set up in a more relaxed fashion. "Well, lads," he announced. "I've got news for you. I'm selling the houses."

Claney thumped his glass on the table in surprise. "What . . . selling the houses? Christ, Sammy, that's a big blow. And selling them?" emphasising selling. "Who's the bam that's gonnie buy them?"

"You said it. A bam. And I'm no' saying who the bam is. But I'm making a deal. And don't youse two get upset. I'm doing it in bits and pieces so I'll need rents coming in for a while. And when I get fixed up in my new line there'll be a turn for you in that."

"What new line?"

"Buying a pub. Maybe two. Going legit. Total legit. I can afford it now. Funny, isn't it. I've had to wait all these years in order to get enough money just to go legit."

"You could have been legit years ago," said Rab.

"Aye, and I'd still be up a close."

They were anxious for details about the pub he was planning to get and he told them that there were no details and that he was still negotiating to get a licence.

"You mean greasing somebody's palm," said Claney.

"That would be graft," replied Sammy with a mock look of shock on his face.

"So then it takes money *and* graft before you can go legit, Sammy."

"Aye, I suppose you could put it that way." Then he set up another round. Loud ones again.

Snakey Holden couldn't take his eyes off them when they emerged from the little lounge where they sat first of all and handed Sammy over the envelopes with the money, under the table as usual. The fog had penetrated the pub, making it difficult to see across the room. But even had there been no fog it's doubtful if they would have spotted him, as he was an anonymous figure, like most of the other men who drank there, grey intent faces beneath their peaked cloth caps, earnestly devouring their big glasses of tasty ale.

His hatred had never diminished for them, even though they didn't come for his rent any more. He had heard them the day before shouting at one of the other tenants in the close, the mangy dog barking. He had longed for them to come to his door for he had a weapon ready for the dog and despite its fierceness he would have used it on the animal. That was what he felt like doing to them this very minute and he had to keep repeating to himself that he had to wait . . . wait and be rewarded. He watched them put their glasses down for a last time and leave the bar together and he hurriedly sank his own drink and left quickly after them.

The fog was swirling even thicker than it had been earlier and he was able to stand close to them as they made their farewells, two of them going to the left, one of them turning to the right. It was Rab who had gone on his own and his parting words to them were, "Watch and no' end up in someone else's bed, boys."

"Wish we had the luck," laughed back Claney.

Like everyone else, Rab buried the lower half of his face into his overcoat lapels to prevent breathing directly the horrid yellow fumes that filled the streets. The only light was the faint diffused glow from the occasional shop window and street lamp. He walked quickly along Cumberland Street, turning left at the Moy Bar to go down Florence Street, past Knotts restaurant, a waft of its homely kitchen smells, cabbage and ribs, hough and turnip, momentarily penetrating the eerie night, then suddenly vanished like everything else in the all-consuming cloud. After Knotts he crossed over Old Rutherglen Road, then Ballater Street, and continued all the way down Florence Street to Adelphi Street where it met the Clyde and where, incredibly, the fog was even thicker than it had been a quarter of a mile back when he had left the Old Judge. The yellow descending cloud had been met by the white mist rising from the morbid river, the two mixing into a noxious nimbus polluting everything it touched. Thick banks of the noisome mixture hugged the riverside like jaundiced cotton wool, eerily deadening the ordinary sounds of the night, only the occasional sharp crack of a door banging shut or the loud bark of a cough from someone passing nearby breaking the muffled stillness.

Holden, unseen, unheard, padded closely behind Rab Blair as he turned right to walk along lonely Adelphi Street, with its single row of tenement houses. The other side of the road was the steep, scruffy embankment of the lifeless river, guarded by a fence of cast iron railings, some bent, others missing. Those standing were topped by ornately vicious spikes. Holden got even closer to Blair, so close that the man he was following was no longer a vague shadow in the mist; he was a clearer and identifiable outline, an outline for which Holden had well-laid plans.

The night was a God-sent gift to those with malice and evil in their hearts. A night when they could do their treachery with every man and woman around blind to anything further than two yards away from them; a night when they could murder or maim and not even have to run away; a night when they could rob or violate, destroy or disfigure and no one would know that they had been there; a night when they were but sinister spectres that could come and go and perpetrate their foul deeds without an accusing finger ever being pointed.

Holden revelled in the fog. Others fumbled and stumbled, coughed and cursed in discomfiture, but he wallowed in the wrapping of anonymity it gave him; he relished the realisation that what he was about to do could be done with total immunity; he gloated in the sense of gratification he knew he would be achieving shortly when his mission had been completed. He got even closer to Rab Blair, so close that not even the muffled night could hide his presence. And Rab, wary of the stranger who, it seemed, was almost on top of him, turned around in alarm.

The fog cleared in the early hours of the morning and the city awoke in a begrimed hangover. The contaminated cloud had deposited thousands of tons of soot and grime, leaving a black slimy coating on the streets, streaking the windows, dirtying clothes, and layering buildings with yet another coating of its filthy wake, black upon black. It was Netta McLeod, the East Kilbride Daries milk roundswoman, who made the discovery. She had been out before daybreak, as she was every morning, pushing the tall shelved handcart with ponytrap wheels which carried enough milk to provide three young delivery boys with supplies for their rounds. She had thought at first that someone had left a coat hanging on the tall railings flanking the riverbank. She had gone over to look. Her three young helpers came running when they heard her shrieks. She turned round quickly when she heard them coming, her arms outstretched in an effort to herd them away from the horrendous sight which had confronted her.

"Oh, my God, oh, my God," she kept repeating.

Detective Inspector Struthers and Sergeant Ross, the men who had been called out for Mickie Doyle's murder, were again on duty that morning. "Christ . . . Jesus Christ!" said Struthers softly when he looked at what faced him, and that was something, for he rarely profaned. "I thought I had seen everything."

Rab Blair's body hung from the railings, his coat collar impaled on the spikes, his knees bent like a collapsed puppet. The railings were not tall enough to hold him fully upright, and the front of his coat was soaked in fresh blood so that from the distance it looked like he had a long vivid red table napkin dangling from his neck. The detective looked across the road to the tenements where every window was filled with eager faces taking in the grim sight. He ordered two of the uniformed men to stand with their backs in front of the dead man and for the canvas screens they used in such circumstances to be brought quickly.

It was not all that unusual to find a body in the street or in a back court in the morning, left where it had been battered lifeless the night before, sometimes the victim of a gang attack, other times the loser in a fist and boot duel, dumped like garbage for collecting in the new day. The final indignity. Invariably they looked much the same, beaten, bruised and brutalised from the kind of hammering in which the loser's only escape was death. But the man they were to identify that morning as Robert Maxwell Blair of 184 Adelphi Street, married with four young sons, had not died in that sort of fashion. There had been no duel in the way Rab Blair met his end. He had been left hanging to die like the sheep and the bullocks up at the Duke Street slaughterhouse.

"By gees, somebody didnae like this lad," said Struthers after two uniformed policemen lifted his blood-drenched corpse down from the spikes. "Wonder what his connection was with Mickie Doyle? Remember the old fellow we got in the single-end in Kidston Street? The smelly one."

"Will I ever forget," said Ross. "Because of the throat, you mean?"

"Aye. It's the same. Left ear to thrapple. Just one slit. Only the razor cuts that way; clean as a whistle; not another mark. I was 99 per cent sure it was a razor that was used on old Doyle. Now I'm 100 per cent sure. And it's been the same man that's done the two of them. Somebody that knows the razor as a weapon, knows how to hold it tight and hard and use it fast, the faster the better for it goes in deeper. Takes skin, fat, muscle . . . aye, and even some bones like a knife to butter. Oh well, this poor fellow would never have known. He's been put unconscious on the railings first, then had his throat cut. Had he not there would have been blood spluttering everywhere. When Dr Inglis goes over him he'll probably find a head injury or something that's knocked him out first before pegging him to the spike. Wouldn't have been all that difficult . . . just grabbed him by the coat lapels there, picked him up in front of him and his weight would easily have driven the spike through the coat collar. But he's a mean vicious man. Can you imagine it? Having felled him unconscious, he then takes his razor and does this to him. I wonder what the connection was, Ross? We'll need to get the Doyle file out again and get your men to find out every single detail they can about our Mr Blair here. When we get the connection we'll be a lot nearer our mad razor man."

They read about the murder that night in the evening papers bought from the vendors wandering the streets, their usual three-paper cries being replaced with "Big Gorbals Murrr . . . derrr!" Claney had phoned Sammy as soon as he read the early edition and they met later when the pubs reopened at five o'clock. They drank the first two rounds with hardly a word passing between them, just long sighs and occasional expressions.

"Poor Rab."

"Aye, never hurt a fuckin' fly."

"He's left four young boys too."

"Aye, and a good wife."

Sammy was the more shocked. He lived with the reality that someone, somewhere knew about him and his house and although he wanted to believe that it had all been a coincidence, he knew that he was deluding himself. Now there were no doubts. There really was that someone . . . somewhere. And Claney knew too.

"It's the Cally Road houses . . . I'm positive of that now. It's someone from there, so it is."

"But you stopped collecting from there, Claney," said Sammy, surprised.

Claney was silent. A long staring silence.

"I said . . . you've stopped collecting from there."

Claney continued to stare into his drink.

"You. bastard, McLean. You've been going back. Collecting for yourselves. Pocketing the money. Jesus Christ, I fucking told you."

"Aw, hold it, Sammy. Rab and I agreed . . . "

"Agreed what? To fuckin' do me . . . to screw those poor bastards up the stinking closes?"

"It wasnae to do you. We thought you were a mug to give them up. Remember, it was us that had to go and collect the bloody money. It was us that had to stand the abuse from the bloody gadgies that are living there. So we agreed that if you weren't going to take the money from them, then we might as well. Was no skin off your nose. We weren't doing you. It was you yourself that said it . . . if we didn't do it someone else would. So Rab and I did."

"Even at the risk that it might be somebody that had done Mickie and my dogs?"

"We'd stopped thinking that, Sammy."

"And what the bloody hell were you thinking?"

"That it was a coincidence."

"No, I don't mean that. I mean how come you keep saying that it's someone from the Cally Road houses?"

"Oh, I just had that feeling. You know we go to lots of houses but there's no place where they're such a bad lot. Particularly one close."

"The one that Holden lives up?"

"What makes you say that name, Sammy? He's the worst one. The one that would do something like this. What is it? Have you two a connection of some kind?"

"No. What I mean is I don't know. There were a couple of Holden brothers once, Stevie and Jackie. They used to call them Snakey and Jakey. Christ, I'm talking about before the war. And I was involved in a gang fight with them."

"You in a gang fight, Sammy!"

"Aye . . . me in a gang fight. My brother was Jamesie Nelson. Doesn't mean a thing now, except to some old ones. But it did then. And it was the Holdens that killed him. But, as I say, I'm going back years and years. And I've never come across them since. They might have copped it in the war, I don't know. But the name stuck in my mind that time I mentioned it when we were up at the houses. There's no other connection. Nothing for this to happen. Christ, wait till my Peggy hears. It'll be the death of her. She hasn't fully recovered from the time the dogs were done in. And she'll see it in the papers tonight. Oh Jesus . . . I better get home to her, Claney. Do you still think it's someone in Cally Road?"

"Aye, I'm sure of it.

Claney stood alone at the bar after Sammy left. There was just one thought in his mind. The man Holden. It was him. He knew it was him.

"Knock-this-fuckin'-door-again-wi'-that-beast-and-I'll-take-its fuckin'-heid-aff . . . I'll-take-its-fuckin'-heid-aff . . . take-its-fuckin'-heid-aff." Holden's threat to Rab and Claney the last time they had called kept coming back to him. He had really meant that. It had happened to the Nelsons' dogs, hadn't it? And he remembered too the night that Holden had come into the Old Judge when just he and Sammy were there. He hadn't thought anything about it at the time for the pub was near to where Holden stayed — one of his "locals". But he was sure he had been watching them, fly-man fashion, looking at them but not being seen to be looking at them. It had happened on another night too when the three of them had been there. But the others from the houses had also come into the bar and looked at them and he had thought nothing about that. Why should he think any more about Holden? But he did . . . there was something fearsome about *that* man.

When he left the bar he went to the phone boxes in Cumberland Street at Crown Street, cursing that the first two had their cords slashed by vandals. The third had its light smashed and had just been used by somebody as a urinal. "I'm not giving you my name," he said when the Lawmoor Street Police Station came on the line. "But see that Adelphi Street murder? The man Blair? Well, try Holden who lives at 27 Caledonia Road." He hung up quickly and walked away.

"That's funny," said the policeman who took the message. "That's the second call we've received about Holden tonight. "The other one said 'and ask him about Mickie Doyle'. It was from a private house and we kept him talking to trace the call but he hung up. All the operator could say was that it was from somewhere in the exchange that takes in Govanhill, Strathbungo and Pollokshields. I'll pass on all the gen to CID."

The detectives lifted Holden and another man they had received anonymous calls about at three o'clock the following morning, a favourite time for such arrests, when violent suspects are least likely to resist. Both of them, however, were released the next day, no link having been established between them and Rab Blair's death. When they had asked Holden about Mickie Doyle he had replied, "Who's he?" There had been an open razor in Holden's house but no great significance was placed on it for there were similar shaving razors in most houses. Tests on Holden's and the other man's razor proved to be negative.

The news of Rab Blair's death stunned Peggy Nelson. With the help of another pair of Cairns, she had been slowly recovering from the horrific deaths of her Dido and Fido, the shock of which had had more effect on her than either Sammy or she had realised. Rab's death brought it all back to her and she reverted to her life as a complete recluse, terrified even to leave her own bedroom where she sat by the window, petting the Cairns and looking out on the lonely streets of Pollokshields, so unlike the Gorbals and Govanhill with their hustle and bustle and activity of all kinds.

A fortnight after the murder Sammy contacted Alex Campbell and at Campbell's suggestion they met in the Arran lounge of the Central Hotel, the kind of place he considered befitted the status of his life with its gentleman's club atmosphere, chintz chesterfields and ormolu mirrors with attentive waiters and waitresses who knew their place in life and called you "sir" when they brought the drinks in handsome crystals on silver trays.

"I come here a lot," said Campbell, "sort of treat it like my private club. Good place to meet special clients. And the staff all give me special attention. It's nice when you get that, isn't it? So, what's on your mind, Mr Nelson?"

"The same as last time. I want a pub licence. What's new is that I'm in a better position to talk terms. Real terms. So what's the score? How much? And Alex, the name's Sammy."

The "how much" brought a pained look to Campbell's face. "You're obviously deadly serious about this, Mr . . . Sammy."

"How much?"

"Please stop saying that. You make it sound as though you're in a shop and I'm behind the counter. It's not really like that. But, anyway, the going rate is fifty down and fifty expenses and five ton when the deal is done."

"I want two then."

"For Christ's sake. One at a time is pushing it."

"I still want two."

"That's a lot of money."

"I said I'm here to talk terms."

"Then it's double."

"Across the board?"

"Across the board . . . a hundred down, a hundred expenses and, when the deal is done, a round thousand."

"I'll make you a deal . . . "

"No, my friend. No deals. That's the deal."

"You've still to hear my deal. I've got a proposal which will mean you end up with even more than a thousand. How would you like to become my business partner?"

"Explain."

"Here's the score. I've got a lot of property. But the game's not exciting enough for me. I like new challenges . . . know what I mean? I see my future in the drinks game. Building up a wee chain of places and that. So I need all my capital, right. Now look at this. That's a rent book for 120 houses. After all expenses, paying your collectors and that, you'll clear about thirty notes a week. That's about £1500 clear a year. You won't be up for repairs and there's no taxes. Be my partner and you'll have fifteen hundred in your bank in a year. And next year us two partners can sit down and talk about another couple of licences."

"Wait a minute, Sammy. You go a bit fast. That's too much to take in. I'm not in local government for nothing. I know the rules. The laws and that. And you can't just go about flogging houses like a load of scrap."

"I know the rules too. Better than anybody. So well that I know how to get round them." He explained the methods and how it had worked perfectly over the years, with the authorities unable to take any action.

"Christ, Nelson, you're the kind of bastard I shout about in the Chambers. It's totally against all Socialist principles and policy!"

"Aye, but fifteen hundred quid can do a lot for your principles."

Campbell didn't answer that question. "I would still want the fifty down and the fifty expenses, per licence, that is. That is if I went through with this crazy deal. How do I know it works anyway?"

"Easy. There're the rent books. Get yourself a couple of men and try it for a month. We'll meet then and you'll be a hundred and twenty up . . . plus a ton for expenses. Alex, I'm telling you it works. There's no harm in collecting a few rents. I was reading about one or two of your men in Westminster. See the houses they've got! One of them has a couple of farms in Sussex. What were they before they became Labour MPs? One was an insurance clerk and the other was a railway man. And they're no' the only ones. So how did they get the big houses? Not on your MP's wage. Not on your nelly. They got it for privilege . . . the privilege of being on the spot where you can do someone a turn. Just like you, Alex. It's not graft or corruption or anything like that. That's only when there's a gang of you at it together and really at it. But one man like you! That's privilege, Alex. And your privilege is that you'll have fifteen hundred little thankyous from your business partner by the end of the year. Here . . . the rent books are inside that envelope, plus a hundred in cash . . . I thought it would be about that. Down payment for two. See you in a month's time with the expenses. A deal?"

"I'm not sure what I'm letting myself in for," replied Campbell. He paused for a minute or two then added, "It's a deal." And a hovering waiter was summoned.

Sammy had a big smile on his face when he greeted Peggy that night. "Great news for you, hen. I've cut the link. That's me finished with the houses. There's no way anyone can get to us now. Claney knows and I've paid him off, although I'll probably use him as one of my managers when I get my pubs. He'd only fiddle me for so much. Others! . . . milk you rotten, so they would. But the main thing is we're free of the houses. Free from that bastard, whoever it was, that had something on us. Isn't that great, Peggy?"

She tried to smile but couldn't. She stroked the ear of the drowsy Cairn that was on her lap and nodded her head. "Yes, Sammy, it sounds like great news. But only time will tell whether or not we're really free of . . . him. I still won't be venturing out of this room. I don't even want to go outside any longer. I'm frightened, Sammy. Terrified of everybody. That's what it has done to me. Every night I'm haunted by what the morning will bring us. And I don't think for one moment that because you got rid of the houses that it's all over . . . although I pray to God that it is. But tell me, what have you done with the houses?"

"I've done a deal. I've sold them. They're somebody else's worry now, not ours. I've got a good chance of getting a couple of pub licences from the Corporation and Ronnie McLaren will be seeing that everything's legal and legit. Peggy, I don't even need to worry about my conscience any more for everything is above board. Can't believe it, neither I can."

"No, Sammy. Neither can I."

He left her and went downstairs to the front lounge where he poured his usual sizeable whisky nightcap, taking the stopper off the heavy crystal decanter a second time to put an extra measure in the glass.

John was in the room reading. "Dad, what is it that's wrong with Mother?"

"It's her nerves, son."

"But she's looking really bad. I got a fright when I saw her at the beginning of the week. And Mrs McDougall tells me she's not eating."

"Aye, I know, son. I was up there with her just now. Thought the news I had might cheer her up, but it hasn't made any difference. We'll need to get the doctor back."

Sammy Nelson knew that only one thing would make any difference to his wife . . . if the killer was caught. He had read that the two men the police were questioning about Blair's death had been released without charges. The papers hadn't given their names but he knew who one of them was . . . Holden. If the police couldn't find any evidence, how could he? And who was this Holden man anyway? Was he one of the same Holdens who killed Jamesie? And what made Claney suspect him?

Sammy Nelson would have to make his own enquiries.

18

IN THE RAG TRADE

E SCAPE from the Gorbals was never easy. Most accepted it as
their fate and enjoyed and appreciated what there was to enjoy
about life there, the neighbourliness and camaraderie which sprang
from the early days when they shared the same trials and tribulations
of a life of unending poverty when the only horizon was that day and
the only real issue whether or not they would survive it; if they did
there was always another day and they could worry about that when
it came. Their menfolk went off to the wars and thousands of them
didn't return and those of them who did were rewarded with the
bitterness of broken promises: the land they had fought for to make fit
for heroes was to be a land of workless heroes on every street corner.
Despite that they flocked back loyally when they were needed to be
heroes again for the war that followed the war that was to end all
wars. When they returned yet again it was to a Gorbals that was
decayed and dying; but the death was to be prolonged and agonised
and another generation would have to live it out in the squalor and
decline with which the area was beset — conditions which they had
been saying for years were the worst in all Europe, except for Naples.
No one argued with that assertion.

The days passed, and every one that did made the prospect of escape
more difficult for Star Nelson. For nearly a year all she had wanted to
do was stay in the house and read. She was apprehensive about
walking out. Once the Gorbals had been a friendly and homely place
for her. Now she felt like a stranger. When she had left it had been her
home and she had known nothing else: everything and everyone had
been familiar places and faces. Now, although it was basically the same
place, everything seemed different, just as her mother was different
and the people and the streets were different. Old girlfriends who
came round when they heard she was home seemed coarse and

flippant. None of them, it seemed, had ever read a book and their conversations were limited to what had happened at work that day, the pictures the night before and how they wished it was Saturday for their big night uptown at the Whitehall for a wee bevvy and then the Locarno, dreamland of the twinkle toes, and if they were lucky a lumber, their way of saying an escort to accompany them home. Slowly, she felt herself being sucked into their way of life, at the same time desperately trying to retain the standards she had gained in the country, where, despite the rough and hard life, there had been other appreciations, other values.

Ella Brady, a cheery girl who lived at the foot of Florence Street near the Clyde, delighted Star's mother by coaxing her out of the house to take a job. Ella and Star had played together as children in the street which was a bustling, throbbing funfair of juvenile endeavour when school was out, engaging themselves in the endless round of games which one generation of tenement children had passed on to the next. They had gone to Camden Street School together and they had cried together when Star went off to the evacuation and Ella stayed at home with her parents and four sisters in their room-and-kitchen house. And when she returned, Ella was her first regular visitor. Knowing and understanding her as she did, she put her reluctance to join her and the other friends at the dancing down to shyness, obviously a result of her staying in the country.

"You should get a job, Star," she said one night sitting in the house.

"I know. My mother keeps telling me that. I'm not frightened of working you know, Ella. It's just that I've been delaying it, thinking that I might be going away again. Have you ever been confused about life, Ella?"

Ella laughed. "No. Confused? What about? Everything seems straightforward to me. You work, you eat and you enjoy yourself. Then one day Mr Right will appear. A wee house. Some weans. What's confusing about that?"

"Then you'll find it difficult to appreciate how I feel. There's nothing straightforward for me since coming home. I won't go into details. I need something. I don't know what. I'm home and it doesn't feel like home any more. I loved the country, more passionately than I could ever describe. Yet I used to long to come home to be with Ma and some of the old pals. Then when I come home I find it's this", and she held her hands up, looking round the small room which she shared with her mother. "They had a party for me the first Saturday I was home. At least that's what they called it . . . a party. Ella, you should have seen them! I thought, God, is it me or is it them? They were all enjoying themselves. And for me it was like looking through a window on another age. I never realised people could be so rough. It was like they were half civilised. Oh, God, that's a terrible thing to say, I know. But that was how I felt. I was seeing my people for the very first time. I was seeing my mother in a way I had never seen her before. You're lucky, Ella. You're not confused. Well, I am. But I suppose you're right. I should go out and work. I feel very conscious about the fact I haven't earned any money since I came home."

"It will be good for you, Star. There's lots of work for girls. Gordon's, where I work, is always looking for new starts. And the money's good now. We're on piece work. I made four pounds ten last week. Is that no' fantastic? Some of them are so good on the machines they can make more. I'll ask the boss about a job for you."

Gordon's was one of the biggest clothing factories in that part of the city around Saltmarket and the Stockwell. The girls of the Gorbals would reach there every morning by going over the pedestrian Suspension Bridge at the foot of South Portland Street. The Gordons were a Jewish family, like most of the others in the clothing trade. They were honest and hard-working and Myron Gordon, son of the founder and now the company manager, was rated by his workers as being one of the best gaffers in the trade. He had told Ella to bring her friend in some morning for the possibility of a job.

They went that following Monday morning at eight o'clock, starting time for the factory. There were few formalities about Gordon's — the work was the all-important factor. "Hey, Myron," said Ella, "this is the pal I told you about. Her name is Star . . . Star Nelson."

"You didn't tell me she was such a stunner," said Gordon eyeing her. "We'll need to get a job for you then, won't we? Can you soap?" Without waiting for an answer he told her to follow him to one of the big stainless steel tables which interspersed the machinists, too intent on their work to look up at the stranger with the boss. He picked up a thick cake of industrial soap and rubbed it vigorously into the reverse side of the cuffs and collar of a newly-finished coat. "There you are, Star. That's soaping. We do that when the coats are finished and before they go through to the other room for the pressers. That gives them a nice finish, nice and stiff without being starchy. And the girls who do that work are called soapers. Want to start? We're short so you might as well get your coat off and begin right away. Oh . . . it's three pounds a week. Eight till five and an hour for your dinner piece. Mind and bring some tomorrow. And if you stick in you might get on to the machines one day. They're on piece work. Some of them are making more money than me. And . . . by the way, your name suits you."

She smiled in reply and when she showed her willingness to start right away, he led her to a table where there was a pile of finished coats ready for soaping. The machinists beside the table, he explained,

worked on the cut patterns which came from the cutters who were on
another floor. The juniors did the linings because they were easier to
work with, and the seniors assembled the coats, then stitched the
finished linings into the garment.

The soapers were mainly girls younger than Star. They usually
started in Gordon's and the other factories when they had finished
school at fourteen; their nine years of training for the big world ahead
ending with a piece of soap in their hand and rubbing as hard as they
could all day long. But few, if any, questioned the system. That was
the way of life. They could be worse off and not working, their parents
would tell them, like they had been in the bad old days. The new
generation were the lucky ones.

She was exhausted that first night after she walked home from
Gordon's with Ella, her hands in a cramp with rubbing the soap into
the appropriate sections of the coat, more especially after one of the
pressers had complained that some garments were coming to them
with insufficient soap to give a proper finish. Instead of diminishing,
the tall stack of coats beside her had piled even higher as the day went
on. The machinists were able to finish them at a faster pace than she
could, making the work seemingly never ending; she was a cog in the
machine and the machine never stopped, or even slowed, until the
loud hooter sounded at five o'clock. She remembered being even more
tired after some of the hard tasks she had taken on in the fields around
Glenmulloch, like hoeing, or shawing turnips or the fourteen and
sixteen hour days at harvest. But there had always been diversions
then, whether it was the banter of Willie Cameron or Wull Andrews
making observations about some aspect of nature or the wildlife that
surrounded them. There were no such diversions now. With piece
work, the machinists concentrated on their job. They could take as
long as they liked for their morning and afternoon tea breaks; they
had the freedom to start when they liked, finish when they liked; but
the wage packet was the best gaffer of them all and there were no
shirkers. The tea was hurried and the smokes were invariably half a
cigarette, the other half stubbed and blown and returned to the packet
or a Vulcan matchbox for the afternoon break. Only at the dinner
piece break would there be time for a whole cigarette.

Star shared Ella Brady's sandwiches on the first day at the midday
break they called dinnertime. The women gathered in various groups
in the areas where they worked, there being no other facilities for
them. It seemed to Star that the ones sitting round her and Ella must
have been one of the toughest groups in the factory. She had known
them to be vulgar in the Gorbals, but rarely had she known a group so
coarse, cursing and swearing about the various aspects of life — but
mainly their menfolk — and openly talking about their performances

abed. Two of the machinists who worked next to Star's soaping table
were among them, Jean Hamilton from Baltic Street in Bridgeton and
Mary Donnelly from the Gallowgate. Jean was a big buxom woman
with dyed blonde hair and a street corner voice. She came from the
heartland of Protestantism in the East End and let everybody know it.

"What's your other name, hen?" she asked when Star and Ella sat by
them, the other name always being a pointer towards religion.

"Nelson . . . Star Nelson. I was christened Margaret Star but my
mother has always called me Star."

"Oh, Christ, get her," said the big woman, whose normal speaking
voice seemed to be a shout. "We've got a toffee-nose wi' us. Where are
you from, hen . . . the Heilans? You didnae get an accent or a name like
that up a close. Star . . . be Christ! If it's Eastern Star you'll be all right
wi' me hen."

"I'm from Florence Street, not the Highlands."

"Oh, lah-de-dah-de-dah. I-am-from-Florence-Street." the woman
retorted mockingly.

Star flushed at being made a fool of but held her head high and
defiant. Showing her displeasure at the big woman she answered back
quickly. "As I said, I am from Florence Street but I lived in the country
for some years."

"Oh did ye, hen? Must have been awfy nice. And then you came
back to live in Florence Street. Right Tim Malloy Street, that. But oor
Billy Boys can see that lot off. They've been up your street a few times,
giving them a tanking. You're no' wan, are ye?"

"What?"

"Tim. Pape. Fenian . . . hen? Your name sounds right suspicious."

"I went to a Protestant school if that's what you mean."

"Wehhhhh . . . heyyy . . . heelllll," roared the blonde. "Another
Proddie dog to join the gang. D'ye eat fish on Fridays? Well if you don't
you should. Eat as much of it as you can get on a Friday, hen . . . it stops
them getting it," a joke she thought hilarious, laughing raucously at the
prospect of depriving the Catholics of their Friday fare. "Don't you
worry, my wee Eastern Star, we'll look after you. That's the trouble
with this place. Getting overrun wi' Papes, so is is. I blame that on
Myron Gordon. See they Jews. As long as you can work they don't
care if you're a Pape or a Proddie. They don't even ask you what school
you went to. Terrible, so it is. Now see if it was a Tim that was the
gaffer! The place would be full of them. I'm telling you. See over in
Jacob's shirt factory in the Stockwell. The gaffer's a woman from
Donegal and you've to show a bloody rosary to get by the door. An'
they're making better money than we are as well. Terrible that, so it is,
for half of it will end up in the pineapple. We should have a Proddie as
the gaffer here instead of Myron just letting anybody in. Just as long

as he disnae ever make you the gaffer, Mary!" She nodded in the
direction of Mary Donnelly, a small, dark-haired woman who had
become inured over the years at being the butt of Jean Hamilton's
bigotry. "That's oor wee Mary, Star. The only Tim in our group here.
Aren't you, Mary?"

The smaller woman turned her head with the disdainful look of
someone who had heard it all before.

"You're quiet the day, wee Mary. Oor wee Mary. Look at her. A
rosary in her purse, a crucifix round her neck, a wee prayer card in her
bag and dying to get a man so they can have twelve mair Catholics.
Send your priest away a happy man every time he comes knocking on
your door. See if wan came to ma door. I'd show him my knickers.
Talking about knickers, Star. You watch it in the lavvy. Danny the
auld mechanic is always hanging about there hoping to get some wee
lassie on her ain. He gropes a' the new lassies. Tried it wi' me when I
started and I hit him wi' my piece tin. Never came back. Of course, you
might know. Danny. Danny Reilly. Wan o' them."

There was little respite from the Glasgow which seemed to
confront Star Nelson on all sides: the Glasgow of deprivation. Her
mother was now in her mid-forties, but her lifestyle of regular
drinking parties and the long hours she spent in the Govanhill dairy
had taken their toll and it was difficult to imagine she had once been as
beautiful as Star now was, the most beautiful of all Jamesie Nelson's
women. David Russell, her fancyman, was dead. "He went awfy nice,"
she would say when she spoke about the greatest lover of her life.
"Had a heart attack in the Victoria Bar and was dead before they could
get him to the Infirmary. Imagine getting the chance to die happy like
that!"

But a lot of Isa had died with David Russell. The gentle company and
the nights of attention and the wonderful and caring way he made
love to her were just sweet memories. He had been the first gentle
man in her life. He was to be the last. Men like David Russell were few:
all the others seemed to want was the drink and love was something
that came afterwards, the hurried moments in which they craved to
be released from the desires the alcohol had inspired; hot kisses,
desperate hands, a quick pump and the surge of delight in someone
else's back close and which vanished in a trace and the night wasn't even a
memory. In contrast to the cherished and memorable nights with
David Russell, the highlights of her life were now the nights with her
group of drinking friends, the same group who had welcomed Star
home, and not infrequently their nights would conclude as they had
done that night.

It was easier now for women to go into pubs, one of the blessings of
the war, although many premises still carried their "no women

permitted" sign. Isa was a frequent visitor to the pubs round about the single end at 188 Florence Street — the Moy, at the nearby corner, the Havannah, Archibald's and Souter's. The months passed and the two women rarely met long enough for a conversation despite sharing the same single room. Isa still left the house at six o'clock every morning for her job in Duncan's in Govanhill and Star would leave an hour and a half later to meet Ella Brady at the Ballater Street corner so they could walk together to Gordon's. When she returned at night, her mother would usually have been home and gone out again, either to one of her friends or the pub, rarely returning before Star retired for the night. On Saturdays and Sundays she worked only for a few hours in the morning at the dairy. Saturday was always party night somewhere and on Sundays when she got back from the shop she would return to her bed for the traditional long lie, exhausted from the onslaught of alcohol and merrymaking of the previous night. It was months after Star had begun at Gordon's before they were together one evening, Isa, for a change, not having to go out for the night. It was a rare moment for Star, one for which she had been longing.

"You know, Ma, you've never told me about my father. I've heard stories, of course. Lots of them. And I don't know what to believe. What happened? Where are the rest of my family . . . do I have any uncles or aunties or cousins?"

Isa replied "You've got your Uncle Harry and Tommy and Auntie Susan and umpteen cousins, sure."

"I mean the Nelsons . . . relatives on the side of my father."

Isa softened at the second mention of him, although she still didn't answer the direct question about the family. She looked dreamily into the fire and lifted the poker from the hearth to rake some of the white ash from the bottom of the grate, an immediate glow reappearing from the dying embers.

"It's all a long time ago, hen. A long, long time ago. You're what now . . . going on eighteen. My goodness, you're back nearly two years. You were just a bundle in a white shawl when he died. And a right wee beauty too. He saw you only the once. He was in Barlinnie . . . you know, he had been in trouble again. Anyway, I took you up to show him what you looked like. Well! You should have seen the look that came over his face. He wasn't a man for words or being soft or gentle and that but when he saw you he seemed to melt. It was then that he said you were just like a "wee star" and no matter what name you were given he would call you that. Now that was something for him to say for he was a man that never showed his soft side. He just couldn't. It wasn't in him. But, then, you've got to understand what kind of days they were. Oh, my God lassie, they were different, different days.

Like another century, so they were . . . and yet it was just nineteen years ago. It's difficult for the likes of me to believe that we've come through so much in such a short time. It's like I've been through three lifetimes . . . the years afore the war, the terrible years of the war, and now.

"You've no idea how hard life was before the war. It hadn't changed really since I was a wee lassie. You know, I can mind of us all sitting watching our Da getting an egg for his tea and wondering what one of us would be lucky enough to get the top he'd cut from it. For, you see, we never got a whole egg to ourselves. Maw couldn't afford it. She was always running out of food before the next wage came in and if it wasn't for them next door giving us a few cupfuls of meal to make porridge we would have been in a right bad way. Then there were a' the gangs. I know there are still gangs going about, but they're no' like the gangs of the auld days. There were battles, Star, big battles, wi' hundreds of men . . . and women fighting as well. And your father was the best of them all. He was *the* hard man. I suppose there's not a lot to be proud about that and I know I'm no good at explaining these things. I never was. But your father must have had something in him to be like he was. D'ye know there was no one had more respect in this street and roundabout here than him? When he walked down the street they would point him out,'Look,' they would say, 'there goes Jamesie.' They didn't need to say Nelson or anything else for there was only one Jamesie. Wee boys used to follow him and run in front of him just to get a second look. And see the women! If he spoke to them they thought they were something special. And anybody that was his friend was treated like royalty as well.

"I was thrilled when word got round that he had been with me a few times. We had met at the Parlour . . . oh, it's away now. Closed it after the Razzle Dazzle murder. Great wee dance hall so it was . . . just beside where your granny, old Maw Lawson, used to live in Bedford Street. I know your Da was married at the time. But that was him . . . wasn't it. And that was me. We weren't perfect, Star. Anyway, he took me there two or three times. He had other lassies as well . . . oh, you might as well know the full story seeing as you were asking. One of them had a wean to him as well, but it died. And that left you, the only one, for he had none to his wife who died no' long after him. Nice woman, so she was, but she just went to pieces when Jamesie died. She knew he went wi' other lassies. But she knew too that was just him and she accepted it. I suppose you've got to pay some price if you go about wi' someone that's treated special the way he was.

"I'd love a wee drink Star. Would you go and get me a quarter bottle out of Tommy Crosgrove's? You'd better take an empty wi' you. They still cannae get the good stuff. Terrible, so it is. Are you going to have a wee drink with me, hen? You should."

Star smiled as she replied.   "Right, I will have a wee drink with you
. . . Orangeade. It's my favourite."

The whisky helped and more memories flooded back as they sat
together by the fire in a rare night of family. Isa began to recall details
of the other Nelsons, about whom Star had been so keen to learn.
"There was a younger brother. Sammy they called him. I don't know
where he lives, but it's no' about here. But he still comes about the
Gorbals for I've seen him the odd time. I think he must be a bookie or a
big shot at something by the way he dresses. He disnae mind o' me. We
met only the once but I mind o' him all right. I was on your Da's arm as
we walked along Rutherglen Road and we bumps into Sammy and his
wife . . . Peggy, I think it is. The pair o' them gave me dirty looks.
Didnae even say a word to me and a' they kept asking Jamesie was the
whereabouts of his Nell. You know what sister-in-laws can be like!"

Star pressed her to tell her more about her father. "Well, as I said, he
was something special. You see, below all that roughness there was . . .
something. I don't know how to describe it to you, Star. But supposing
he hadn't been the hard man, you would still have said there was
something different about the man. You felt it if he came into a house
or into company. And there was only one man had a walk like him.
You could spot him a mile away with his walk. Och, I know all these
flymen have their ain wee walks. You would think some of them had a
flute band going on inside their heids the way they walk. You know,
wee 'gaun yersel' men. No, your Da's walk was nothing like that.
There was nobody walked like Jamesie. Nobody. See from the back . . .
you could see the big shoulders and there was no padding like
the others used. He loved the paraffin . . . the paraffin ile . . . the style,
as he called it. He never had the money to afford the good clothes he
would have liked, but he was always neat and tidy . . . and I've never
known a man to wash and scrub himself the way he did. D'ye see, if he
had been born in some other parts . . . you know, England and the likes,
he would have been one of they champions at something. Instead of
that he was the champion of the street fighters. It was mad. All that
training he did so that he could fight better than any of them. And
what did he make out of it? Not a tosser. He never even thought of
using his power to make money. In the pictures a' the gangsters end
up wi' money before they get killed. But not Jamesie.

"What made him fight the way he did, you ask? I don't think he ever
knew himself. I think he was a throwback of some kind. For he just
couldn't help himself. But it was the way of it Star. We were raised
among fights and fighting men. And when they were old enough all
they wanted to do was get into tartan breeks or the kilts of one of the
regiments. That was the height of their ambition . . . a sojer in a

fighting regiment. See the sailors and the other men, they were the
quiet ones. But the boys that stood at the corner and wanted to show
they were something were a' in the Cameronians or the HLI and the
likes. Your Da missed the Great War but he would have been away
with them had he no' been in trouble again. He would have been the
best Lady from Hell of them all. He was some man, I'm telling you.
Nobody else had a reputation like him in the whole of the Gorbals . . .
in the whole of Glasgow. And nobody ever replaced him . . . just as
well, I suppose."

"He died in a fight, didn't he? Somebody got the better of him in the
end, then?"

"D'ye want the whole story?"

"Yes . . . everything."

"Well, it was these two brothers that organised it. Holdens they
called them. Stevie and Jackie . . . or Snakey and Jakey as they were
nicknamed. The Snakey one wanted the same reputation as your Da
and he thought that if he got him killed he could then walk the streets
with everyone pointing at him instead. So they got a gang thegether.
It took about twenty of them . . . twenty of them against your Da and
his brother Sammy who happened to be there at the time. And that
was it. He died in hospital. The polis never made one arrest. They
knew fine who had done it, but they weren't in the least interested.
And Holden's plan didn't do him much good . . . for it didn't work. No
one thought of him like they did of your Da. And no' all that long after
it somebody attacked him and left him with an awfy face. He's still
about but looks like an auld man . . . and they say he's a dirty auld yin as
well. Know what I mean like, hen?"

"Aye, I know what you mean like. But tell me about my Da's brother
. . . my Uncle Sammy. He went to help him, you say? Was he one of the
gang then?"

"Not a bit of it. He just happened to be there at the time. I don't
know why. He just was. But it was all the talk at the time . . . him going
to help your Da, the two of them wi' just their fists and feet against
this mob that had hammers and knives and a' types of weapons."

"He was very brave then, my Uncle Sammy. It would be nice to meet
him sometime."

"Aye, it would be nice. Is there any more of that whisky, hen?"

The quarter bottle of whisky was empty but Isa was showing no
visible sign of its effects and because she had enjoyed their rare night
so much, Star ran down the stairs for another one, this time to the
Family Department of the Moy, as the licensed grocers had closed.

"You know," said Isa on her return, "that's the first time I've spoken
about your father for years. I think of him a lot, mind, and how it could
have been. But that's life isn't it! What about yoursel', hen? You

haven't been mixing much since you got back. You don't even have a boy, at least no' that I know about. You should be going to the dancing like I used to and meeting other young ones like yoursel'. You're always in the house. What is it wi' you? You'll no' even have a wee drink wi' your mother. What makes you so different?"

"Different, Ma? How can we tell what makes us different? You tell me the man who fathered me was different . . . above all the others, even though it was in such a terrible way. But then they admired that way, didn't they? Is there some of him in me? I know I'm different, Ma. I don't mean superior or anything like that. Or that I want to fight with people. God, it's the very opposite. But I know I'm different. I know I'm trapped in the Gorbals. The others don't. They just accept it. None of them try to do anything about it, except to show each other that they're harder or tougher or can drink more than the next, for these seem to be the only things that get any respect."

"I hope you're no' criticising the Gorbals, Star. It's your hame."

"See what I mean, Ma? You don't even see it yourself. If anyone says anything against the place it's taken personally. The Gorbals is rotten . . . stinking . . . horrible. And it makes people like it is. That's why I'm different, Ma. I see it. You don't. And I'm terrified I get to the stage where I don't see it. For I don't want to be like it. Is there anything bad about that? And I want to get away from here before it gets to me too. I've got to get away. I don't know how yet. I would have gone back to the country but for . . . well, for reasons I don't want to talk about."

"Sounds like a man, Star."

"Mother, I'm trying to explain something to you. There are events in all our lives which we don't talk about and I don't want to talk about. I've lived with this one for nearly three years and I'm still confused about it all. I have a mind of my own and I will find my own conclusions and my own solutions one day. But one thing I do know is that being away from the Gorbals as I was and living in the country made me see the place in a different light. It's like I'm an outsider looking in on it all. And I'm looking in at a whole lot of people who know and have seen nothing better. I'll do something about myself when the time is right. Someone once told me about the fates and I believe in them completely. And I know my fate is not to be staying in the Gorbals for the rest of my life."

She went that next morning to the grave in the west end of the Southern Necropolis cemetery, hard by the wall, as her mother had said, by the one with the tall lettered column which marked the resting place of the Freemasons. A small but handsome grey granite stone marked the grave. There were four names on it . . . James Nelson

1865-1920. Mary Nelson (Née McNulty) 1866-1923. Helen (Nell) Nelson (née Dunning) 1900-1927. And, beneath the three names, but on its own and in bolder lettering as ordered by Sammy when he had erected the stone, the single name . . . JAMESIE 1899-1927.

She pulled the long couch grass growing round the base of the stone and laid the small bunch of daffodils she had brought nestling against it. The big untidy graveyard was empty, but not silent. Dixon's Blazes, the neighbour that gave no one peace, not even the dead, was throbbing with its usual activity, puggy trains in the wide siding just over the wall shunting long lines of tip wagons, their molten contents filling the air with the foulest of stenches. She stood up after gently placing the flowers and stared at the humble stone marking the grave. "Well, Jamesie Nelson, father of mine," she thought, "did it all start with you? The fates gave you something . . . they just did it at the wrong time, though. So the only way you could be great was the way you were. And when you did that they came and took you away again. That would be their wisdom, I suppose. But if only it had been another time, another place."

A shunting engine screamed its presence with a shrill blast from its steam whistle and the loud clatter of buffer meeting buffer rebounded down the long line of trucks like a barrage of cannon fire. Star's thoughts were back in the Gorbals.

19

THE FLYMAN'S CONVENTION

GETTING a licence for a public house was easy . . . if you knew the tricks of the trade. Bailie Alex Campbell knew them all. He had masterminded the clique of five Magistrates who would always be part of the quorum of nine sitting and making decisions on the Licensing Court.

The Court sat twice a year, May and October, in the St Andrew's Halls, near Charing Cross — the City Chambers did not have a hall big enough for the applicants, officials, lawyers, clerks and members of the public who attended. Before voting on whether or not an applicant should be granted a licence, the premises would be the subject of reports from the Fire Brigade, the Health and Welfare authorities, the Dean of Guild and the Police. That was the easy part for there were regulations laid down on the required hygiene and safety standards and it was a case of merely following these. The Police would only object if the applicant was known to them either for his previous convictions or if he was what they termed "a known associate of criminals". They would object too if they considered there were sufficient public houses in the locality, although commercial opposition usually decided that. Objections to new premises usually came from the churches and nearby tenement neighbours. A few bottles of whisky appropriately distributed, however, would usually convince the latter that the new publican wasn't such a bad lad after all and that it might just be convenient to have a pub near them. The churchmen were predictable. The priests would be all right because of the Catholic attitude towards drink and society and the understanding that there was a need to enjoy oneself, even on a Sunday. The views of the Church of Scotland ministers, on the other hand, depended on their nearness to Calvin and the Court could expect a haranguing if it was a United Free Church that was objecting.

But a good lawyer could usually convince the Court that what they had heard from the Reverend was to be expected because of his views on life and that public houses weren't really the dens of the Devil which they termed them to be.

The best guarantee of all, however, in ensuring that your application for a public house licence was granted was having Bailie Alexander Wallace Campbell on your side. The group of other Magistrates, senior councillors, he controlled, were to their constituents just as he was to his, the soul and voice of the working class. They had been active in Labour Party circles all their lives and had risen to the distinction of being members of the local government of their city, prominent members at that with the rank of Bailie. Only the senior men such as them sat on the Licensing Court.

The five regular members of Campbell's civic clan had never sampled life so good till they entered the Corporation. Two of them were railwaymen, one was an assistant in the Co-operative drapery, one a baker and the other an insurance agent, and life for them had been the same hard struggle it was for the working class constituencies they represented. But being a friend of Alex Campbell had brought them a taste of other things. It would begin with a case of whisky delivered to their homes. And the doors of selected restaurants in the city were always open to them and their wives or mistresses; a night on the house, champagne and good cigars, and the luxury of being treated like a king by the manager and staff. It was the good life they deserved, they thought, for all the work they did for the city. Selling their souls? Corruption? Such thoughts never entered their heads. Anyway, what was corruption?

Was it corruption when a constituent asked you for help and you gave it to him because the man and his family were known to you, but you refused another constituent who wasn't known to you? Was it corruption when you helped someone the priest had sent to get a better house because the priest and the constituent were of your flock, but when another from another flock had come you weren't able to give that help? Was it corruption when you put more effort into helping some than you did others for whatever the reason, whether it be whim or the practical? And was it corruption when a publican was so pleased with the effort you had gone to in order to help him get or retain his licence that he gave you a small something in return? Why, a mate would buy you a drink if you helped him in a small way. Was that corruption? Of course we are not corrupt, they would have answered if anyone had suggested it to them. Corruption was big-time, they would have said. Corruption was openly holding out your hand and being persuaded to make decisions that wouldn't have been made otherwise.

Alex Campbell, on the other hand, knew all about corruption. For he knew he was corrupted and that he had corrupted them and that life itself was about corruption. Life to him wasn't about being forthright and fearless, honest and honourable. He had thought it was when he was young but had failed miserably at trying to live by such tenets. And when he had abandoned them and become dishonest and dishonourable he had succeeded — succeeded beyond his wildest dreams. Being that way had brought him riches, his house in Langside Drive which one day would have the big lamp posts on the pavement outside his front gates, and his right of access to the city's Rolls Royce to drive him everywhere. He would have his own liveried attendant in the City Chambers who would carry the Corporation mace, the symbol of authority, before him. He would sit in the magnificent chair, presented to the council by Queen Victoria herself, the throne of the Lord Provost, the first citizen in all the city, and the cupids and the angels of innocence carved in the glorious Spanish mahogany panels of the room could stare and accuse as much as they liked, but Alexander Wallace Campbell was clever enough to know that if he wasn't the way he was he would be a nobody. That's what corruption meant to him.

It had another meaning for Superintendent Tom Graham of the Central Division's Criminal Investigation Department. Graham was an elder in the Tron Church and a devout Christian, as that word was interpreted by the Church of Scotland. He saw his role as a senior policeman as a sort of messenger of God, protecting the good from the bad, the weak from the strong, the pure from the impure. Corruption to him began with the thought and his duty was to act when it became the deed. It was one of the worst crimes, he considered, for not only did it break the Commandments, it was against all the ethics of the Christianity on which he based his life.

Graham was the antithesis of the usual senior detective. He was a slim, nondescript sort of man in a battered soft hat, wearing a belted gaberdine raincoat which was never buttoned and was as much a part of him as the shallow-bowled pipe in the centre of his mouth. His crusade against corruption would always ensure his presence somewhere in the vicinity of the St Andrew's Halls during the entire sittings of the Licensing Courts. He would move about from bar to bar making mental notes, observing the social mix of the varied crowd involved in the dealings of the Court. They jigsawed in his mind in patterns only he could see, only he could read. Joe "The Scratcher" Neeson, Townhead hard man, drinking with Bailie O'Sullivan, Francis Patrick O'Sullivan, and Bernie Reilly, the former Scottish football internationalist, and nearby them another group of four men, friends of Neeson. That was an easy one for Graham to read. Reilly owned a pub and was involved in moneylending. "The Scratcher" was the boss of his collecting team, his tally men, the group who stood apart from them as they drank, the other ranks separated from the officers. O'Sullivan was the most crooked of all the city councillors and Graham knew he would get him one day. Good Christian that he was, Graham despised the Catholics, and this particular clique was Catholic to a man. They weren't real Christians, he thought, although he never committed his thoughts to words; a real Christian never did that. He would watch them at Parkhead, where their Celtic football team played, the O'Sullivans hob-nobbing it with the priests, shaking their hands and enjoying the crack, and then off to some roguery. The bad Protestants would never do that, he would think. They would never mix with the ministers. They were just plain bad. He had checked the licence application lists and Reilly, the footballer, had his name on it. So the story as he saw it would be that O'Sullivan was there to guide Reilly's licence through the Court. "The Scratcher" was there with them, for the Court, like Parkhead or Ibrox, was an event; a place to be seen with the right people. And the tally men were there also, for Neeson never went single-handed.

In another bar was Larry Brown, the East End bank robber who had spent his war years in Barlinnie for doing the famous Great Western Road raid in which he got away with £10,000, none of which had been recovered. He was with Hughie Davidson, an East End publican. Then Bailie Willie Donald joined them for a short period, just long enough to down three whiskies, large ones, with half pint chasers. He never once attempted to buy a round, Brown paid for all of them. Donald was one of the Campbell faction. Not a brain in his head, thought Graham, smiling to himself at the story they told about Donald when he first became a councillor. The Diary Clerk at the City Chambers had asked him for his personal details for the small, green-covered Corporation Diary which listed the various committees, their meeting dates, the members' addresses and phone numbers. This was issued to each councillor with his or her name embossed in gold on the cover. "Any initials after your name?" the Clerk had asked. "What do you mean?" said Donald, a draper's assistant with the SCWS, the Scottish Co-operative Wholesale Society. The Clerk had handed him a diary opened at one of the pages listing the councillors. Every initial they could get, it would appear, was thrown in after their names. There was MacDonald, FSAO, FBOA, DCLP, which meant merely he was an optician; and there was Archer, JP, FRIBA, FRIAS, who was an architect; and Burns, JP, MBTKS, the cinema projectionist at the Wellington Palace. "Right," said Donald to the Clerk. "It's William Donald, JP, SCWS." And his name was entered that way in the diary.

It was easy for Graham to figure their particular meeting. Davidson, the publican, was applying for licences for two more pubs. He would be fronting for Brown, the bank robber, putting some of his cash to use. And Donald, JP, SCWS, would have tipped Campbell and the others to give them the nod when the applications went through the Court.

In the Avalon Bar in Kent Road he saw Campbell with Sammy Nelson and Ronnie McLaren, Nelson's lawyer. He couldn't figure the reason for this particular grouping so easily. Campbell he knew, for he had an impressive dossier on him in his office at the Central Police Division's headquarters in Turnbull Street near the Glasgow Cross. Much of it had been supplied by Bailie Jimmy Andrew, one of the Progressives and, like Graham, a fierce crusader against corruption in the Corporation. He even knew he was involved in some kind of housing racket in the Gorbals and was having two men, rent collectors, regularly followed to try and establish some kind of connection between them and Campbell. He knew McLaren as a lawyer, but Nelson was unknown to him, although he assessed him as being a bit spivvy and therefore up to no good.

Because of the types of characters who would gather in the vicinity of the Licensing Court and show up on the public benches, Graham referred to it as "the flyman's convention". And when he returned to the police station after a day's sitting of the Court he would be bad-tempered with the frustration of being witness to what he knew was flagrant corruption and yet was virtually powerless to act against it. For corruption, like fraud, was the most difficult of crimes to prove. The courts demanded proof that an accused had purposefully set out to corrupt or defraud and acquiring that evidence was a long and painstaking task. Once they had tried to shortcut the job by wiring up a witness with an American Army surplus tape recorder. The man had been having negotiations with a councillor for a house and the idea had been to get a recording of him actually asking for the money. Their meeting had been in a pub but when they played back the tape all that could be deciphered was a succession of drink orders.

Superintendent Graham saw the three men, Campbell, McLaren and Nelson, leave the bar and he was there in the Court to hear Nelson's application for a transfer of a public house licence being granted. He couldn't tell whether there had been any corruption or not but he had his thoughts. Irrespective of that, Sammy was now in the licensed trade.

He rushed home that night overjoyed and eager to share his good news with Peggy. She was, as usual, upstairs sitting by the window of the front bedroom with her little Cairns, named after their murdered predecessors, Dido and Fido. "Isn't it great Peg? I've got my first licence and this contact I have at the Corporation says there'll be no problem getting me another one at the next sitting of the Court in May."

She looked up at him with unseeing eyes, a vague look on her face as though she wondered who he was and why he was in the room with her. She appeared not to have heard or understood what he had been saying. Then she looked into the face of the little dog she had been holding and smiled. "That's Daddy come home, my wee pet darling." Then she turned away to look out of the window once more, still talking to the little dog. "But we'll need to keep watching the garden and up the street for this might be the day our other little friends will come back to see us again. You'll hear them barking up the drive when they come, the little darlings. They've been away such a long, long time."

Sammy turned quietly and left the room.

After tea with John and the McDougalls downstairs he announced he was going out again, which wasn't unusual for he often went out at night to the Gorbals to meet various friends and contacts. It was a Tuesday night and he went to the Seaforth in Main Street, knowing his old contact "Plug" Connor, would be there. Plug's merchandising capabilities never ceased to amaze Sammy. He was the man who could obtain anything.

"Supposing," said Sammy, after the usual preliminaries about drink, the weather, and about Connor's current roaring trade in proprietary whisky — "80 proof export stuff, straight from the bond" — "supposing I wanted a gun?"

Hughie turned and looked at him hard in the eyes before replying. "A shooter!"

"Aye, a shooter."

"What the fuck do you want wi' a shooter?"

"It's no' to pick my teeth, Hughie."

"To do somebody in?"

"Shooters are for shooting, aren't they!"

"Somebody messing about wi' the wife?"

"Let's say there is . . . and leave it at that. Can you get a shooter?"

"Sammy, you know me. I could get you a fuckin' Lancaster bomber if you wanted it . . . and I thought it was gonnie make me a good skin, that is. But have you really thought it out? Guns are bad news. If you want somebody seen to, why don't you get a heavy team? Christ, there's plenty of them about . . . see some of the mob that used to hang about the boxing booths in the Gallowgate and Greendyke Street! Christ, they made the ones that were in the ring look like wee boys. You've got a bob or two and there's plenty of them willing to do a job for you."

Nelson considered that prospect. He hadn't thought of getting someone else to do what he had in mind until Connor reminded him. It was the old story, he thought. Money and power. If he had no money, he would have no options. But money simplified everything. It brought you freedom. It brought you power. And now, he was being reminded, it could quite easily achieve violence . . . even have people eliminated. It could do all these things, but it would never make his wife Peggy well again . . . would it?

"No, Hughie . . . I want a gun. Just say it's for business that only I can do."

"Might cost you twenty or thirty notes . . . depends on the size and the quality. There's some big Military Police ones going about. Like big cannons, so they are. Used them for shooting across the Channel during the war. " He laughed out loudly at his own joke. "But they're the cheapest."

"I don't know anything about guns, Hughie. But I don't want any big Tom Mix jobs. You know, it's the wee ones you see Cagney and Bogie with."

"Aye, I know the type. There's a lot of them about . . . a lot of daft boys have been bringing them back from the Army. Christ, it's different on the streets now, Sammy. We've got trained commandoes, paratroopers, snipers, jungle fighters, a' going about in their demob suits. Tell somebody to fuck off nowadays and they come at you with their trained-to-kill stuff. Anyway, I'll see what I can do for you. Should have something in about a week. Gie's a note of your phone number again."

Sammy handed him a printed card.

"Oh Christ, how's the flash! Samuel Nelson Esq., 'SAMMAR' St Andrew's Drive, POL 9833. Oh la-di-dah, Sam-you-ell."

Connor accepted the order as if it were for any other commodity in which he traded, knowing there would be a percentage in it for him and, being an expensive item, it was a good percentage at that. "Needing any shirts, Sammy? You should see the new Yankee Navy ones I've got. Real nylon. Five quid in the shops. Three nicker to you."

Sammy smiled. "You never stop. Do you, Hughie?"

20

THE LURE OF THE SIREN

THE corner boys were tribal. You could stand with the ones who would flank the corner nearest to your house and usually no other. For you would be a stranger at another corner and they didn't like that. A friend could bring you along and if you were in his presence you would be accepted. They were like a family and strangers were always treated with reserve and suspicion. You would never consider standing at a strange corner unless you had some connection with the group that gathered there. They all understood that. Some men had two or three corners at which they were accepted, usually because they had stood there before they had left to live in another part of the Gorbals.

Snakey Holden had made it his habit to regularly stand at the various corners at which he had some kind of territorial claim. There were three principal ones where he was openly accepted. First was the Ferry Bar corner, where Adelphi Street curved round from the river to meet Old Rutherglen Road, because the first gang he had run with all lived about there. It was also in the Ferry Bar that Bum Beaton had come with the news the day Jamesie Nelson had been released from Barlinnie. His second corner was at the Windsor Bar at the junction of Cumberland Street and Naburn Street, for the group there had been from the first Cumbie gang of which he had been a founder member. His third corner was at the city end of the district at the intersection of Adelphi and Crown Streets, outside Walker's Bar. He was accepted there for he was friendly with Snap McLatchie who lived locally.

The Snap, as they called him, and Holden had been friends for years and regularly got together to operate a variety of small-time confidence tricks for drink money. One of the most common of these tricks was to work as street photographers, preying on the young and innocent. They would take up stances in streets they knew they were likely to get appropriate customers and where they could escape the attention of the police checking for street trader's licences. One of their favourite areas was in Carlton Place at the Suspension Bridge. Snap was the photographer, Holden his ticket man. The camera was an old Kodak bellows model, large and impressive looking but bought for five shillings at the Barrows Market and incapable of taking photographs. Holden would give each customer a ticket for their photographs, solemnly writing their name in print on the half which he retained, giving them the other half. "Shilling for black-and-white, two bob for colour," he would say, "and the colour's the best bargain. Seen the price Jerome's are charging?" Cameras were such a novelty and knowledge of them so rare among their customers that no one ever queried how one camera could produce the picture options they were offering. Each customer was told the photographs would be ready in a week's time. "Our studios are in St Enoch Square, right next door to the scissors shop." Everyone knew the scissors shop in St Enoch Square, but there was no photographers' next door or anywhere else in the Square. They could work a week at that together before customers would come back looking for them. But they had that carefully timed and would be at a new stance by that time.

Sometimes they would travel to other districts for their quick kills, usually the entrances to some of the city's parks in the summertime. This involved buying a roll of film which the Snap would put in his unworkable camera. Customers would be told they were doing the new instant photography. "Special film they've just brought back from America." After each customer had his picture taken, the Snap, with great fuss, would hold the camera beneath his coat and with a small pair of scissors, cut off a length of the film, backing paper and all. The film would then be placed between pieces of folded white paper and the customers warned not to look at it for two hours, for if they did it would spoil the photo. "And it's in colour as well, son," they would say. Because of the novelty they claimed for these photos they charged half-a-crown a time and eight customers was enough for a bottle of whisky and four pints of beer between them, with ample left over for a few cigarettes. On a good day and keeping on the move so that neither customer nor police would catch up with them, they could make six pounds between them, some of which would disappear in the lunchtime session at Walker's, the rest of it at night as they joked about the various mugs they had taken money from that day.

The Snap was a small, undernourished man who had never changed the middle-parting style of his hair since he started using it in the early thirties. He liked having Holden with him for he was terrified of violence and the prospect of having some younger customer returning with a father or a big brother. Snakey was his insurance policy for that. Like the rest of the confidence tricksters who proliferated, Snakey and The Snap were small-time and the prospect of anything that was involved or likely to have made them large sums of money was to be disdained. They had no aspirations other than to earn sufficient for their needs for that day, most of their needs being liquid. And tomorrow? Well, something else would turn up. Maybe one of the newspaper vendors would give them a turn selling copies around the pubs. There might be some blackmarket material on the go which would give them a quick turnover. Or else there might be some stolen property somebody would want them to sell ... but nothing big; no they didn't want that. Maybe some watches, some pens; that would be enough for the day's beer money. There was only one problem, one care in life for them. Today. And living on their wits the way they did, they usually found a way to solve that.

The girls from the clothing factories who lived on the south side of the river would stream over the Suspension Bridge at five o'clock each evening from the big works which huddled close to the city. The Tradeston and Plantation girls would turn right after crossing the pedestrian bridge, the Gorbals and Oatlands girls turning to the left. Star Nelson was in her third year at Gordon's and had gone from Soaper to Junior Machinist to Senior Machinist. She had become as trapped in the Gorbals as anybody else. Her time in the country was just a memory. She usually walked home with Ella Brady and a group of other girls who lived nearby and they would laugh at the men who chirped, whistled and shouted at them from various street corners as they passed. It was usually cheery banter; the kind of thing Glasgow men had been shouting at Glasgow girls for generations, mild ribaldry, the worst gibe usually being "Haw, Hairy", an insult from the days when status was in a hat and the poor girls who couldn't afford them exposed their poverty in uncovered hair.

    Star and the workmates she walked with usually went along the riverside Adelphi Street, turning right at Main Street and then into Ballater Street, breaking off at their own various streets. But there was a tea one night for a show of wedding presents in the house of one of the girls at the far end of Adelphi Street and because of that the group who normally walked together had gone straight along the riverfront street, passing Walker's Bar and the group of men standing at the corner. The usual crowd of them were there, mainly those who had been to the war or with the occupational forces, and a few older men, including The Snap and Snakey Holden. They greeted the factory girls with the customary banter as they passed: "Haw . . . howsitgaun darlin'?" . . . "Widnae mind a wee cuddle wi' you, blondie!"

. . . "Fancy the pictures the night, dearie?" . . . to the accompaniment of their usual whistles and chirps. Star walked behind the main group with her friend Ella and she got some special whistles because of her long dark red hair and stylish walk, in such contrast to the cheeky feet and hurried short steps which were a feature among many of the tenement girls. "Oh, haw, you're special, hen," one of the men shouted. "See you at the Palais, gorgeous," said another.

"Fancied that big thing at the back," one of the men said after the girls had passed.

"Aye, did ye see the tits on it? Stoaters, so they were."

It was Joe McNoon, a small First War veteran who knew everyone locally and never seemed to be short for an answer about anyone or anything, who said, "That's Isa Baird's daughter. I used to work beside her man when I was with MacTaggart and Mickel's. He was a right bam. In Hawkhead now. Went real mental. She's no' his wean, but. Jamesie Nelson was the father . . . remember, the hard man?"

The remark went virtually unnoticed, the name meaning nothing to most of them, and the conversation rapidly passed on, as it always did, to another subject. But one man continued to look after the girls, taking in every detail he could of one of the two who had walked together at the rear of the group. Snakey Holden said nothing. All he did was observe and think about that chance remark made by little Joe McNoon. The smile that had been there when they were joking at the girls had vanished. His mouth was tight, his appearance grim and hostile; the very name Nelson affected him like that and he stood motionless and brooding, unheeding of the patter that was all around him until they began to disperse to go into the bar.

"For a half?" said The Snap, quickly adding, "Christ, whit's up wi' you, Snakey? You look like you've seen a ghost."

"Nothing . . . I just need a half, that's all."

Holden made sure he was back at the corner at precisely the same time the following night for he wanted another look at this girl they said was Jamesie Nelson's daughter. But she didn't pass. Nor did she come the next night or the night after that. On the fourth night Holden didn't go to the corner. Instead he walked along Adelphi Street to Carlton Place suspecting she would be one of the girls from the factories on the other side of the river who crossed over at that time of night. He stood across the road from the bridge at the South Portland Street corner, by the handsome palace-fronted terraced building which had once contained fine town houses, so fine they had imported skilled Italian craftsmen to make the ornate and exquisite ceilings which decorated the principal rooms.

There was no mistaking her, the elegant walk so different from the others. She threw her long hair back with a sensual shake of her head. Like that night when he had first seen her outside Walker's pub, she walked at the rear of the group, arm-in-arm with another girl, her friend Ella. Holden followed at a distance, past Laurieston House, the pilastered centrepiece of the dignified terrace, to Main Street where they turned right to Gorbals Cross, then to the left into Ballater Street, the group getting smaller the further they walked as girls left to go off on their own or in pairs for their own street and close. At Florence Street, Star and Ella stopped for a few words, as they always did, before they went off to their respective houses, Ella turning left for the bottom end of the street, Star crossing Ballater Street to walk towards Cumberland Street.

Holden returned the following day at the same time and to the same place . . . five minutes after five o'clock on the southern side of the Suspension Bridge. And Star with her friend Ella, as they always did, walked behind the other girls from the factory, happy and relieved that another day's work was over. He did the same the next day and once more the routine was punctually repeated. After a week, he returned once more and there they were again and it amazed him that people could be such creatures of habit, walking with the same ones in the same groupings along the same route at precisely the same time every night of the week . . . week after week, month after month, and undoubtedly, one year after another.

Snakey Holden could never put up with a life like that. Not for him the ordered way. Their habits fascinated him. But more than the fascination he was obsessed with the fact that he had found another Nelson. Jamesie's very own daughter. He had never thought that such a person existed. And the more he thought, the more he wanted to return to his vigil in Carlton Place where he could see the girls, the factory army, their peaked headscarves fluttering gaily in the wind, contrasting so vividly with their drab slacks and overcoats. And when he saw her there among them, a surge of voyeur excitement went through him. He had no explanation for it; just the sight of her was enough for him to feel that way. The woman Nelson. Graceful, shapely and poised and so unlike the others. He remembered how the first hero he had ever worshipped had been her father. What a man he was, he thought. But Snakey Holden had got the better of him. Hadn't he? Even though he had to be twenty-handed, he did it. Snakey Holden put the last blade into him. Didn't he? Snakey was better than him. Snakey Holden was better than any Nelson. Wasn't he? And his splayed mind conjured and fantasised about the Nelsons and himself and what might have been had it not been for them. And now, it seemed, they had sent another one to him, to stimulate and excite him with her untouchable, unreachable beauty.

They were bastards those Nelsons to do this to Steve Holden. It was them . . . them . . . them that was doing this to him; they were sending her there every day to taunt and tease him. Yes, that was what they were doing to him. They had put some curse on him . . . yes, that's what they had done, all because he had killed their Jamesie. Now it was a woman they had sent to him; a beauty whose looks were a siren song and were overwhelming him.

21

THE MARCH OF THE BILLY BOYS

E LLA Brady, faithful friend Ella, more than anyone else wanted to help Star to become rehabilitated to the Gorbals way of life. She had helped her to get the job at Gordon's where she was now one of the best machinists, sometimes earning more, because of the piece work system, than many men did for their basic 44-hour week. But her reluctance to go out at night and enjoy herself the way the other girls did concerned Ella. With that in mind she called at her house one Saturday night.

"Right, Star Nelson, you're getting ready to go out tonight. And I don't care what you say. I ask you every week to come with us and you say you're too busy or you have a book to read or something. Well, not tonight. It's time you started to enjoy yourself. Don't you realise . . . you're nearly twenty years old and you've never been to the Locarno? That's terrible, so it is. Well, you're coming tonight. Marjorie, Ina and Lilian from the work are coming and they say if you don't turn up they're all coming here to drag you there. All right?"

She liked Ella, plain and plump with a happy round face and dying, as one of the girls at work had said, to be some wean's wee Mammy. Ella was in total contrast to Star. She liked the conventional, Star the unconventional. When Ella made herself up she threw herself at the make-up bag. Everything went on. Powder went on top of powder, mascara on top of mascara, rouge on top of rouge and the greasy lipstick she used emphasised her bow lips so that her mouth looked in a permanent pucker, ready for a kiss. Star, on the other hand, used only a mention of make-up to look natural without it being noticeable. Ella's fashion was bold and Barrowland, cling tight skirts that inhibited her walk and enhanced her cheeky gait; Star's was plain but feminine, elegantly simple, preferring the appropriate to the apparent. Star had her romantic thoughts, but it was Ella who spoke of hers. Ella was gauche and gallus, Star subtle and sophisticated. Ella was extrovert, Star was introvert. Ella brought cheese sandwiches one day, Spam the next. It never varied. Star experimented with salads and items she used to buy from Capaldi's, the big Italian warehouseman's in Renfrew Street, which had resumed importations of mortadellas and salamis as well as varied cheeses. But despite their differences, they had a liking for each other and their personalities met at the hearts, soft and kind. Where others had only the caustic and the critical to say and think about their friends and workmates, Star and Ella preferred to be more benign and objective in their view of others and of life itself.

The girls met at the Whitehall for Star's first night uptown to the dancing. It was a basement lounge of a bar complex in Renfield Street, one of a new breed of such places where young people could meet or take their friends and enjoy the new-found freedom of having a drink in premises vastly different from the old style public house Sitting Rooms, hidden behind opaque glass partitions so the men at the bar couldn't see there were women in the shop. She joined the girls in their favourite drink, whisky-and lemonade, a mix the women had made popular. Their talk didn't vary much from what it did at Gordon's except that, as they didn't share the same meal break companions, they were able to talk about each other's group at work.

The dancing was the great meeting place. The cynical said it was a cattle market with music, where the young could eye their fancy and where their fancy might say yes if she was asked for the last dance, the dance when they would ask if they could see the girl home . . . their lumber as they called it. Provided she had been danced two or three times by that partner during the night, she would usually agree to the request. And, in turn, that would be the first conversation at work on the Monday.

The city dance halls were a varied lot, just like the ones they had in the suburbs in scores of public, Co-operative, masonic and church halls. There was the Albert in Bath Street. The men carried their pumps to it in brown paper parcels and only the best dancers went there. The West End was for an older crowd, the Playhouse for the best bands, the Barrowland if you liked excitement with your dancing for there was always the chance of a good fight there, but it was the Locarno that had a magic ring about it. The Locarno was "the" place. When you told your pals in the suburbs that you had been to the Locarno on Saturday it meant you were adult; uptown adult; a graduate of the city; one who knew what they were about in life. The Locarno was bigtime with a balcony and seats at tables with soft lights like a movie set where you could take your soft drink and lace it with the miniature your girlfriend had smuggled in inside her handbag.

The Locarno was cosmopolitan, which meant the real gangsters from various parts of the city went there. The Locarno was adventurous for when they had fights there they were better than any of the rival dance halls' fights. You went to other dance halls for the dancing or the talent. You went to the Locarno for the dancing and the talent and to say you had been there on Saturday. The Plaza could have its Matt Moors and George Colborn, Bobby Jones could shine at the Berkeley which he did for years, Lauri Blandford could keep the hordes swinging at the cavernous Palais de Danse, and Eric Winstone or Oscar Rabin and the great star bands could make them jump at the Playhouse, but when Jack Stone and his Famous Band, together with Arthur Wallwork and his Eight Piece Band, were in form on a good Saturday night at the Locarno, it was seventh heaven itself.

Star enjoyed her first night at the Whitehall and the Locarno, but not exuberantly so. Nevertheless, she went with the girls again, deliberately making a point of not joining them every Saturday, still fighting her fear of the total trap of a way of life she found strange, even though she had been back living in the Gorbals for more than three years. To have made her entire social life like theirs would have been the final surrender to her becoming entirely like them, forgetting that there were other ways, other places and other possibilities still to come.

On the second Saturday they went to the Locarno together the famous riot occurred. Although most of the American camps around Glasgow had closed, there were still thousands of servicemen stationed at Prestwick Airport and on ships visiting the Clyde. The visitors weren't impressed with the reputation of the Glasgow hard man; many of them were hard men themselves. Invariably they were bigger and broader hard men. The Glasgow men had similar disrespect for the tall swarthy men with movie accents and actions, colourfully decorated with Chesterfields and Camels, bulging wallets and medal ribbons. The girls had other views. They swooned for the handsome strangers who had a lot more to say to them than they were used to from the locals . . . "Dancin' and that?" when they were asked to dance and "Come here often?" or "The floor's smashing" when they got up for the dance.

When an accidental bump in a hectic fox-trot could cause a fight between two locals, there were all the ingredients for a lot more than that with the Americans being around. Star was dancing with one of them when the disturbance erupted. He was a good-looking Marine from a ship in dry dock at Greenock and when the missiles began flying and the two sides got into clear battle order, the Glasgow men, aided by British Servicemen, versus the Americans, he had smartly saluted her and said, "Sorry Ma'am. But my country needs me." Ella, with one of the other girls from Gordon's, grabbed Star and the three of them ran from the hall together, Ella cursing her luck as she said she had a lumber, lined up to see her home. He had preferred to get into the fight rather than escort her to safety.

The following Monday at the dinnerbreak at Gordon's, Jean Hamilton, the Bridgeton blonde and bigot, told them how it had all begun. She had been there, although not in the company of Star, Ella and their friends. Jean liked a fight as well as some of the men and had stayed to cheer on some of her friends engaged in the battle. "D'ye know that's the first time the Billy Boys have helped out your lot, Mary?" she said to her Catholic workmate. "It was some Kent Star from the Calton that started it," she said, the Kent Star being a Catholic gang from that area. The Americans had been getting the better of them and some of the Billy Boys had gone to their rivals' aid. Anyway, they could fight each other any time, it wasn't always that they got the chance to go into action against the Americans. Jean said that she had been in the thick of it and claimed she had knocked one of the Americans out herself, butting him unconscious with her head.

"Hey Jean," said one of the girls, "did you have your curlers on? If you had you could have disfigured the Yank for life." Someone else joined the banter. "He'd have been the only man wi' the permanent wave face."

The conversation continued from the riot to the activities of the Billy Boys who, the day after, had paraded with their flute band up Norman Street to the chapel so that the people on their way to and from mass would know that the men who had been to Aughrim, the Boyne and had guarded Old Derry's walls nearly three hundred years earlier, had descendants who were similarly willed. With the loudest drums they could get and the most stirring of flute marches they could play they were there to demonstrate that they too would never surrender. "And Christ, did it no' end up like the Locarno the night before," said Big Jean. "The Norman Conks turned out and started throwing bricks at the band. Then they started flinging stuff from the windows of the houses as well. Know what someone in the third floor house did? Threw a pail of piss. Aye, that's your lot, Mary Donnelly. Dirty messins, so they are."

The Billy Boys, the Brigton Billy Boys, were to become as much a part of gang history as the razor men of the South Side. They were formed in 1924 when Billy Fullerton, a Bridgeton lad who became a local legend in his own lifetime, had the temerity to score a goal against the Kent Star football team in a kickabout game on the Glasgow Green. After the game a group of Catholics from the Calton took their revenge on Fullerton by attacking him with hammers and it was only through his own toughness and skill as a street fighter that he had been able to survive that incident. Later there was a meeting of thirty young men, including Fullerton, all of them from Bridgeton. The result was the formation of the Billy Boys. Billy for their King Billy, the man on the white charger who had led them to great victory at the Boyne and other places. And Billy for their own King Billy, Billy Fullerton, the man who was to lead them to great victories on the streets of the East End of Glasgow and other places.

Unlike most other gangs, the Billy Boys were not territorial, they were theological. And their word of God was Protestantism. Within months the thirty founders had swelled to 800 strong with supporters from the heavy-industry Lanarkshire towns of Airdrie, Coatbridge and Cambuslang, each with his own membership card, bought and duly inscribed like a union card, from an East End printer at a shilling per 300. The members paid tuppence a week for the privilege of being one of the Billy Boys, their affiliation requiring them to live up to the simple and basic rules printed on the card: "To uphold King, Country and Constitution — and to defend other Protestants". The latter was important. For young Protestants found themselves under threat and attack from young Roman Catholics as much as young Roman Catholics did from young Protestants. It was a constant vigil for each was as antagonistic as the other. The one's religion was the other's poison, to be hated and detested and to be fought for, if necessary. And such was that readiness that in another game of football in which Fullerton played, this time against Kinghorn, some of whom were Kent Star members, an open razor fell from the pocket of the centre's shorts when Fullerton and he had been scrambling for the ball. On another occasion Fullerton was at a wedding in the East End and because of threats received, the bride stood before the minister with a sword hidden in her dress. The best man carried a gun. Both were needed, for outside the hall there was a crowd from the Calton Entry gang, with whom Fullerton, now attending the wedding with a head wound that had required fifteen stitches, had been involved the previous night. It wasn't confetti the gang were waiting to throw at the wedding guests. The cry went up when the wedding party emerged from the church: "Get the Orange bastards". A hail of bottles flew at the bride, the groom and the guests, who had to take to their heels and run all the way to the Masonic Hall in Struthers Street for the reception . . . and for more reinforcements from the Billy Boys to subscribe to what was, perhaps, the most important of their club rules, certainly the most practised, "to defend other Protestants".

With World War II over, many of the gangs re-formed, the horrors of Coventry and Dresden, Hamburg and Hiroshima, not to mention the gas chambers, having failed to quench their lust for aggression and the perpetuation of the old myths, whether through rivalry or religion. Old cries and slogans were heard in various parts of the city as the gangs, some of them new, set out to recreate the ways of the Thirties . . . the San Toy and Sally Boys, Stickers and Sticket, Black Muffler and Black Diamond, Butny Boys and Cowboys, the Antique Mob and the Kellybow, Cheeky Forty and Romeo Boys, the Beehive and, of course, the Billy Boys.

Following the battle of the day before, recounted in such lurid detail by Jean Hamilton that Monday dinner-piece break, there had been a series of minor gang fights in various parts of the East End during the Sunday, culminating at night in a particularly vicious battle in which a youth had died as a result of stabbing wounds. Jean Hamilton hadn't known about this incident and it wasn't till someone brought in the afternoon papers that they learned the details. The story read: "Following the death of Brian Docherty, five young men and two eighteen-year-old girls were taken into custody this morning after raids by police of the Eastern Division at houses and city clothing factories. Docherty, seventeen, of Claythorn Street, was one of a group of youths who were attacked by a bigger crowd of young men and girls, some of whom were armed with bayonets, swords and bicycle chains in one of the worst gang fights seen in the city since before the war. Seven youths were rushed to the Royal Infirmary following the disturbance and Docherty died of bayonet wounds shortly after admission. Another boy is on the critical list and police are waiting to take statements from three others who were detained for treatment. The raids this morning included visits by police to two city centre clothing factories where members of the female staff were questioned, two of them being taken to Tobago Street Police Station with the other youths in order to help police with their enquiries. A detective police sergeant at the station said there could be further arrests."

Jean Hamilton took time out from her furious machining to read out the details to as many as she could get to listen to her above the noise of the hectic workshop. One girl, Sally Hall, who was the young soaper to Star and her partner and who came from the Calton, kept diligently at her work as Jean read out the story. No one thought anything of her indifference as there were others similarly disinterested; but none of them had the same reason as Sally Hall.

Only when they were cascading down the long broad stairway that descended for two storeys without a landing did Sally Hall reveal some of her secret. From the top of the long flight some of the broad pavement of Clyde Street could be seen. There were a number of uniformed policemen questioning some of the girls as they left work. Star had been walking on her own down the stairs, Ella Brady having gone on ahead of her to wait in the street. She felt her arm being tugged. "You'll have to help me." It was Sally Hall, a look of desperation on her face. "The polis . . . they'll stop me. Please take this. Put it up the sleeve of your coat. They'll never stop you, Star." Before she could even reply, she felt the hard metal object, warm from its previous hiding place in the girl's sleeve. "Thanks . . . I'll explain later." Then she ran ahead down the stairs and, as she had predicted, was stopped by the police who were questioning several girls.

Star's mind was in a whirl. Should she confess what had happened? Should she throw the object down the stairs before reaching the police? Should she run back up the stairs again? What would happen if she did walk past and was caught with it? Would they believe she had nothing to do with whatever they were wanting to find out? So that was why Sally Hall had been so strangely quiet when Jean Hamilton had read from the papers! Was she at the murder? Was this one of the weapons they had been using? Was this *the* one they had used on the boy Docherty? Suffering from deep bayonet wounds . . . yes, that was it, bayonet wounds. That was what Jean Hamilton had read loudly from the papers. This then would be a bayonet for it went from her wrist to her elbow and she had to clasp her hands before her so that it wouldn't fall free. Surely they would see she looked worried . . . frightened? For she was. In an instant she had gone from innocence to guilt because, like it or not, she had been implicated. And she knew her face was showing it.

"Hey you . . . aye, you!" said one of the policemen as she passed. And something within her made her keep walking; she didn't know what or why; perhaps a resentment at being addressed like that and wanting to show that she didn't like it either. Two girls who were walking beside her had turned their heads when the policeman said "Hey you" and were told "Aye, you and you. Come here." Star kept walking. A voice came from the crowd this time. It was more direct . . . "Star!" She breathed a sigh of relief. It was Ella Brady. "Let's wait and see what's going on," she said.

"No, Ella . . . I've got a lot to do tonight. I'll keep walking." Ella said she would wait and anyway she said she wanted to go home to Ina Johnstone's house. "It's her mother's menage night."

Star was over the worst of her panic by the time she reached the other side of the Suspension Bridge, being a bit more rational with her thoughts about the weapon she was carrying in her coat. She felt it with her other hand, the bulky base of its handle was at her wrist and the rest of it lay flat and deadly along her forearm. She reflected that if she had been stopped by the police it would have meant trouble of some kind for her, even though she was totally innocent. Wouldn't the papers and the gossips have loved that! Star Nelson, daughter of Jamesie, the one-time hard man of the Gorbals, caught carrying a foot-long bayonet? The prospect of how near she had been to that actually having happened seemed too incredible. She wondered too, as she continued her walk home alone, the fog swirling up from the river as though it was smoke from a fire and hiding the far end of the bridge from view, how her father must have felt when he carried his lethal weapons to battle. Star felt scared and strange. He must have felt bold and confident, she thought, as he headed for the great unknown of every conflict; would this be the one in which he was marked, or from which he would not return? There was even a tinge of comfort in the heavy piece of metal as the night and the fog folded round her, thick banks of yellow cloud enveloping the riverside streets.

The busy and bustling scene that had occurred just minutes ago as she left her work seemed a long way and a long time ago. She didn't like being on her own like this for she had been accosted before by strange men, strange lonely men, anxious and desperate for the contact life had never given them and who, in their despair, could be bold enough when they were alone and anonymous to overcome their inhibitions. But why should she feel comfort in the long and deadly weapon that lay against her arm? Was that another sign that she was beginning to accept the ways of those who had succumbed to the acceptance of violence? How could *she* ever contemplate such a thing? Feeling comfort by carrying a brutal weapon of war! And if there was some comfort and security in carrying such a thing, could that mean she could also contemplate using it? She quickly dismissed the thoughts and went from the subjective to the objective. What was she going to do with the bayonet? Throw it in the river? No, she was too late for that, having turned into Carlton Place. Get rid of it in someone's rubbish midden? There was a handy disposal point in the rear of every close. Take it home and think more about it? Or would Sally Hall tell the police that she had given the bayonet to a workmate? The fog thickened and her thoughts were diverted by the noise of the tramcars belling their way across the Victoria Bridge heading for the Gorbals.

Snakey Holden was amazed to see her alone. He had been waiting at the south side of the Suspension Bridge hoping to see the girl he couldn't rid from his mind. He had been going back once, sometimes twice a week to that same spot since the first time he had seen her about five weeks previously. Usually he stood across the road watching the girls crossing the bridge, but because of the fog he had stood by the iron bollard at the beginning of the bridge, the same spot where he used to stand with Snap McLatchie when they played the photographers' game. She passed so close to him he could have

touched her. How he wanted to do that! But the one who had been
Jamesie's daughter had been untouchable to him until now; only in his
mind had he been able to do that, to nightly fantasise about this
alluring creature that he wanted to have but couldn't, that he wanted
to be free from because she was there, a living reminder of the Nelson
family which had become such a curse to him.

She wasn't even aware of his presence, close behind her, closer than
he had ever been, so close he could see her shapely legs, her long, well-
brushed hair dancing on her coat. He imagined he could smell her
femininity. Snakey Holden was going to have Nelson's girl and rid the
world of her. He had to. That was the only solution his mind could
fathom for the Nelsons. He had been given this night to do it, like he
had been given that night to deal with Rab Blair, like he had been given
the cold misty morning when his hammer had quickly despatched the
little dogs without him being seen.

Gorbals Cross was bustling and bright as usual, the light from the
shop windows dispelling some of the gloom of the evening. Star
paused only momentarily in order to peer through the thick fog-cloud
for traffic before crossing from one side of Main Street to the other,
then going along Ballater Street. To reach her house from there
meant turning right into Florence Street for a stretch of about 150
yards, crossing Old Rutherglen Road at the pawnshop, then up the
main part of the street, past Knotts Restaurant and a little fruitshop,
after which there were only about three to four hundred yards of
tenement building, broken only by dark closes whose hissing gaslights
struggled to break the thick night, and a lonely cobbled pend which led
to some stables. The fog had chased the children from the street and
after the restaurant there was only the occasional passerby, hurrying,
muffled figures quickly seeking out the comfort and warmth of their
little houses. Then there was no one she could see or hear.

She hurried into the loneliness unaware of the sinister figure of
Holden who was hurrying even faster . . . so fast and so intent on his
prey he had stalked that he, in turn, was unaware of the other figure
who followed. Holden was just ten paces behind the woman he had so
desired to be his victim when he thrust his hands into his coat pocket
for the vicious weapon he carried. He knew the moment had come, a
unique moment in time which had been presented to him, which he
saw as an omen justifying what he felt in his heart and mind about the
woman who walked before him, and which justified what he was about
to do.

22

REVENGE

DETECTIVE Inspector Norman Struthers was the first plain-clothesman on the scene, this time accompanied by another Detective Sergeant, Donald MacLeod, a Harrisman they called "Big Red" MacLeod, to differentiate him from the many other Donald MacLeods in the division. The fog was even thicker and they could only find the murder locus after searching half a dozen closes in vain looking for the uniformed policeman who would be there. Eventually they found the close, number 166. A uniformed sergeant was by the body, two constables stood by the close-mouth and on the pavement there was a small group of people, their breaths condensing as they spoke, contributing their own little cloud to the foggy night.

"It was one of the wee lads that lives in the close who found the body, sir," said the sergeant when the two detectives arrived. "He had been on the way to the midden with the ashes when he stumbled over it. Got the fright of his life he did when he saw what was sticking out of it. The corpse was still quite warm when we arrived. But there was no trace of life."

"Obviously," cut in the Inspector. "A weapon that size puts a very quick end to anyone's life. Bayonets! Ugh! That's the war for you. They've been bringing them back for souvenirs to show the kids that's what they fought the Jerries with when they were in the 51st. I bet there's at least one in every close in this street. You don't stand much of a chance when they go into you. Look at this one . . . good God! Almost up to the hilt. He's been an angry one that's done this, hasn't he? Somebody's been out for revenge all right. Any identification Sergeant?"

"Aye. There was an Identity Card. Steven Alexander Holden."

"What! Good gracious, so it is. Snakey Holden. The old . . . Imagine me not recognising that face. That's what a bayonet and the pain of death can do to you. Are you new here, Sergeant?"

"About three months, sir. Transferred here from the Eastern Division when they made me up."

"Where's MacLeod?"

"He's at the front close."

"Tell him to come back here for a moment."

"Found something, sir?"

"Aye . . . we've found something all right. Snakey Holden. Imagine me not recognising that face."

"I wouldn't have known him either," said MacLeod. "But I always had the feeling we'd find him like this. It had to be a sticky end, didn't it?"

The Inspector turned to the uniformed man again. "Mr MacLeod and I and everyone else at Lawmoor Street and Turnbull Street know this man and have been trying to get him where he belongs for a couple of years now. Committed at least two rapes last year and a few attempted ones but when we had him in they threw out the charges against him. No corroboration. The old story. And I've a feeling he had something to do with the Adelphi Street murder . . . you know, the one where the fellow was left hanging from the railings with his throat cut? That was the kind of thing Holden here would get up to. A vicious, wicked man he is. Was, I mean. Put your torches on his face again. Look at that . . . like a butcher's chopping board, although I've seen worse. What else does the Identity Card say, Sergeant?"

"Born in the year 1906 and gives an address in Cumberland Street."

"That's an old address. He lived in the abandoned houses in Caledonia Road. And just forty-two, eh! Looks like a man in his fifties, or even older. Well, we'll have some job getting the man for this. There's a dozen I know have old scores they wanted to settle with this one. I'll bet you anything you like there's a celebration going on somewhere for having despatched him. We'll get a whisper from someone . . . wait and see." The Inspector took another long look at the body. "It's like the end of an era looking at him lying there. He's the last of a breed that were brought up in the old razor school of fighting. It was him and his gang of turncoats that did Jamesie Nelson. He was their big hero. Some hero! And now it's him. Caught up with at last. But that's the way of it for them, isn't it? Reared in hatred and going about with hate in their hearts all their days. Little wonder the English generals wanted their Jocks in the frontline for them. Holden was there with his brother. Two of the best fighting men in the regiment they said. The brother didn't come back but Snakey did and they couldn't stop him fighting . . . even went for one of his own sergeants. Aye, there's a funny streak in them that's hard to figure out."

"In *them*, Mr. Struthers?" said MacLeod.

"Them! Aye . . . I know what you're meaning, MacLeod. You're right. There's a funny streak in *us*. Better get the fingerprint people, Sergeant. And is Dr Inglis on his way?"

Sammy Nelson sounded drunk when he answered the phone. All he could say was, "Aye, but who is it?"
"It's Claney, Sammy."
"Aye." There was a long pause in which the phone seemed to have been dropped and picked up again. "Who?"
"It's Claney, Sammy."
There was another long silence. "Claney . . . Claney's no' here," said the voice.
"This *is* Claney, Sammy."
The phone was dropped again. A younger voice came on. "Hello, it's John Nelson . . . my dad isn't well."
"John," said Claney. "This is a friend of your Da. Claney. Tell him to meet me in the Old Judge tomorrow night . . . usual time . . . seven o'clock. And John. Tell him it's urgent. And . . . eh . . . I think it might be a good idea if you could get your Da to bed, son."
When John put the phone down he was surprised to see a small revolver on the table, its magazine extracted and eight bullets scattered around it. He picked it up, fascinated by its smoothness and streamlined appearance, so unlike the big ones the cowboys used in the pictures. "Where did you get this, Dad?" he asked. There was no reply. "I said where did you get the gun, Dad?" The loud snore from the man slumped in the big chair indicated that there would be no answer. He carefully returned the revolver to the table and left the room, switching off the lights.

It was half past seven when Sammy came through the door of the Old Judge. It had been several months since they had been there together, the need for his regular contact with Claney having ended with the death of Rab Blair and the deal with Campbell which severed his connection with the houses. He looked pale, his face drawn and his first words were . . . "I'll set them up" — his way of saying, "How's it going?"
"I had to see you, Sammy," said Claney. "Have you read the night's papers?"
"What about?"
"The murder."
"No. Haven't read a thing the day."
Claney handed him a copy of the *Evening Times*, saying: "That's it

there, on the front page."

He read the story eagerly, repeating some of it aloud:" . . . police have identified the victim as Steven Holden of 27 Caledonia Road, Gorbals. A spokesman at the Central CID said he thought the man's death was the result of a gang feud. Holden, an unemployed labourer, is understood to have died from a stabbing injury . . . police say they are following several leads . . . the body was found beside the rubbish bins in the back court of 166 Florence Street . . . police say it was a particularly brutal stabbing . . . "

"The bastard," said Nelson. "You'll never believe this. But do you know where I was last night?"

"Aye, getting drunk."

"No . . . afore that."

"No idea."

"I was looking for the swine. Seriously. I was taking your word for it, Claney, that it was him, especially since Rab . . . you know? And we had that connection from way back . . . remember I told you about my brother and that? So I got a gun. Aye, Christ, me, Sammy Nelson, man of peace, out on the streets with a Mauser, a wee, smooth beauty it was too. I don't know anything about guns, but the pal that got me it said you couldn't miss wi' one like that, the grip's pitched to make aiming instinctive, so he said, anyway. I had it for a couple of weeks but was waiting till I got a good foggy night. And you know what it was like last night."

"Aye . . . I know."

"So I was gonnie get the bastard. I decided it was definitely him that had done the dogs and Mickie and Rab. I had racked my brains for months about it. There was nobody, nobody that could have been after me . . . or us . . . except Holden. He was the only one it could have been. All right, I had no evidence and your men with their wigs and gowns wouldn't have listened to a word of it had it been presented to them in Court. But I knew, Claney. You knew, didn't you? So I went up to his house in Cally Road, the wee shooter loaded wi' eight in it. But he wasn't there. Then I tried all the pubs in his street, starting at the Bellwood then the Service, Grant's, McLaren's, Elder's, Eadie's, the Windsor, Rosie's, Moir's and finally I came here. But not a sign of him. So I walked up and down outside his close after the pubs shut. Mind you, I had a few halfs in me by that time but it didn't have any effect on me, what with the cold and the nerves. When he didn't show up I just went home and polished off a half bottle of Black Label. Then young John told me this morning that you had phoned last night."

"Sammy, you could have won the coupons last night and you wouldn't have remembered."

"Aye, I know. And I'm feeling it the day. But I needed it, Claney.

Christ, I really did. I was sick with frustration for I really wanted to get him last night. You've no idea how much I wanted him."

He fell silent at that. Claney ordered some drink. "C'mon, Sammy, before you say any more, lift your drink and we'll go through to the wee room. There's nobody there and I've something to tell you." They sat in a corner of the little room, their faces only a few inches apart so that if anyone did come in, they couldn't overhear what Claney had to say. "Sammy," said Claney softly. "Sammy . . . it was me. I got him last night. I'd been waiting months for him, getting to know a' his habits, his whereabouts, where he drank . . . everything. I'm no' into the God business. But it was God that sent last night to me. It was just like He pulled down the curtains for me so that I could do him in right there in the middle of a busy street . . . and not a soul could see what was going on."

Sammy looked startled as Claney's story unfolded, taking in every word, shaking his head from time to time as he expressed a mixture of amazement and incredulity. Claney explained how he had set out to discover what he could about the evil Holden shortly after Rab Blair's death. He had carefully studied his movements for some weeks and had got to know the corners at which he stood, the bars in which he drank and when he usually used them. But it was in the Bellwood Bar, his local at the corner of Caledonia Road and Thistle Street, that he found the vital clue. The drinkers had been four deep at the bar and the elderly men were sitting by small tables round the wall, some of them playing dominoes. A group of them had got up and left, leaving one old man behind, a small, thin man, a big pint glass dwarfing his face when he raised it slowly for another sip. Claney sat beside him. "For a game, auld yin?" he said, putting the pieces face down on the board and rotating them clockwise before starting.

It had been easy after that. Claney bought him a whisky and a pint and as they played a second game he got him talking about the various characters that used the pub. He spoke about how some of them were confidence men who got up to various tricks up town, chuckling roguishly as he recounted some of their various enterprises, like selling "groanies", fake engagement rings, to unsuspecting couples. "Get a' types coming about here," he said. "Tappers, tricksters, tally men . . . them all." Then he mentioned that there were two or three of the old gang-fighters came in as well and, quite voluntarily, brought up the name of Holden. "Aye, we've even got the old razor man, Stevie Holden, who comes about the place. He was the one that did in Jamesie Nelson. They were the big names, so they were, back in the wild old days."

"Did you know Nelson?" asked Claney.

"Know him!" exclaimed the old man. "Ah knew his faither." Which was the Glasgow way of playing down someone's importance and achievements in life.

"And Holden?"

"Aye . . . knew his faither as well."

"Is he still a hard man?"·

"Christ, aye," he replied, nodding as he lifted the whisky he had just been bought. "Still has the razors, you know? Came in here one night drunk and tapped a drink off me. We were sitting just over there. And does he no' take out this black handled one to show me. 'See that,' he says. 'That's done in a few . . . and it did one the night, bastard that he was.' "

"When was that?"

"Oh Christ, I don't know. A few weeks ago. Hey, you're no' a nark are you?"

"You must be joking, auld yin. But I'm chapping."

And the subject quickly changed when the old man turned over a few more pieces saying . . . "The game's mine, son."

He now knew all he wanted to know about Holden: his connection with the Nelsons, his tenancy of Sammy's slum, his visits to the Old Judge, the threat about the dog, and what the old man had said about him. Snakey Holden was the man all right.

Claney had brought the bayonet with him from North Africa. It wasn't one of the new spike types they called the No. 4 Mark 11, short and with its tapered screwdriver point. They were no good for digging out detected mines in the desert. You needed the old model for that. A big P13, the kind they went over the top with in the First World War, seventeen inches long, patterned with a slim single-edged blade and a semi-spear point, sandblasted to eliminate reflection, and with two deep grooves on the wooden grip which showed it was the last model they had made. Claney had carried it with him for protection on his long hitch-hike back to Scotland from the Middle East. It was an old and trusty friend. And now he was going to use it one last time to avenge the death of his closest friend, Rab Blair. After being positive in his own mind following his visit to the Bellwood and the talk with the old man, he had started shadowing Holden and getting to know his regular movements, always taking the greatest care not to be seen by him as he would have been recognised. And always with the bayonet, safe in its scabbard, beneath his coat.

He even followed Holden on several occasions when he made his regular trips to Carlton Place to watch the factory girls stream across the Suspension Bridge, then trailing the one particular group of girls. But he couldn't figure out these strange pilgrimages, except to observe that they had the same pattern . . . standing vigil by the bridge then leaving to walk behind the same party of girls. He had remembered when Holden was involved in the suspected rape charge and assumed that he was seeking out another victim among the girls whom he followed with such diligence.

On the third consecutive Monday that Claney had watched Holden there the fog had descended. He could see his outline like a yellow apparition keeping his vigil by the iron bollards. They stood there for some minutes, two men with murder in their hearts; one because his narrow and corrupted mind blamed the name Nelson for the misery that life had brought him, the other to avenge the death of his friend. Claney watched the hazy form of Holden move off when a single girl passed, which was unusual for it had always been a noisy party of them, laughing and talking loudly, that he chose to follow. Claney set off behind him. Their minds were in a paradoxical parallel as they walked that last unseeing mile, each carefully crossing the busy thoroughfares with their long lines of fog-bound traffic, inching from and towards the city; each of them weighing the various alternatives to their individual plans for the attack and kill, neither of them knowing of the other and the frightened girl, Nelson, unaware of either of them. The only plan they had in common was that they would strike at a point in some street when it was at its quietest . . . and they were as close as they could get to their prey. Neither of them had realised that morning that the events of the day would fall into place as they had done. But each knew that the moment they longed for had come.

Holden, his mind focused on the shadowy figure of the girl in front of him, sometimes hidden by the eddying fog-cloud, sometimes visible, sometimes merely a shadowy shape, was taken completely unaware by the attack. Claney had chosen his moment, then run at him, sprinting with all the strength and speed he could muster, his hands raised above his head holding the long bayonet so that it would drive into him like some powered projectile. It hit him just below the base of the neck and he crumpled, without even a cry, on to the soot-slimed flagstones of the pavement. Claney stood over him, then looked around and listened to see if he had been seen or heard. He wasn't finished yet. He had another mission for Holden and, with his two hands beneath his armpits, he dragged him through the close to the back court. There he had expected to find the spiked railings which separated the rear courts of most properties; instead a brick wall divided them and he was unable to leave him like his friend Rab had been left, draped like some unwanted object on the palings. Claney cursed his luck. Then he addressed Holden's corpse. "Right, you bastard." He dragged it to the refuse shelter, a brick housing for the galvanised containers which held the residents' waste, and laid him on top of a small heap of overflow garbage spilling from piled bins.

"There . . . that's where you fuckin' well deserve to be, Snakey Holden . . . in the midden." He looked up quickly again with the clattering of pots and pans coming from a nearby kitchen window. Another window went up and someone threw rubbish down on the back court. But no one saw anything. No one could see anything. Only the night itself was visible, an ochred candyfloss cloud which smothered everything. He walked smartly through the close again into Florence Street, stopped and looked around him once more, then headed to the Old Judge for a drink and to use the telephone to contact Sammy.

"Can you imagine how I felt? Getting revenge for Rab and Mickie and your wee dugs? Sammy, don't you realise? That's you and your wife free of all your worry. The curse you've been living under is over. The bastard got what he was due for all he's done. He's away now, though. Gone. Finished. Peggy and you can start enjoying yourselves again. And me as well. Christ, he had me worried stiff as well, for I knew he'd be after me sooner or later. But no more, Sammy. No more."

"Aye," said Sammy, staring straight ahead, his face expressionless.

"What's up wi' you? Christ, you don't look like you've just heard the best news in years. What is it?"

"Claney!" He said the word slowly and there was a long gap before he said his next words.

"Claney. It's too late. They came and took Peggy away last Tuesday there. She went over the top. Flipped it. It was terrible, Claney. She began thinking she was a wee wean again and talking to her dogs like they were real people and telling them to keep looking out of the window for the other dogs coming back. Then she started talking about her wee dolls and wanting out to play on the pavement. Oh Christ, Claney, it was terrible. I never knew that's the way a mind could go. I don't know how I didn't flip as well, just watching her being destroyed right there in front of me. And every day she got worse . . . she even started screaming at me for not letting her go to school. So I decided to do something myself. I got a gun and was gonnie get the bastard Holden And Jesus, do you no' beat me to it?"

At that he got up, lifting the empty glasses, the tears running from his eyes. He went to the bar for more drink. When he returned he lifted his own glass and stared intently at the swirling whisky in it. "Christ, Claney. What would we do without it?"

23

WHAT'S HAPPENED TO US?

THE murder of "Snakey" Holden was the big news in the Gorbals that Saturday. The three local evening newspapers ran it on their front pages although none used it as the main story. It was obvious it had been a revenge killing, one thug doing away with another, a common enough tale; no intrigue; no mystery; just the law of the jungle emerging once again.

Star had hidden the bayonet she carried home that night. She put it in the small suitcase she kept beneath the bed recess, the same case her mother had bought her for the evacuation and which she had carried back again after four years at Glenmulloch. Now she used it to store some mementoes of her time in the country. She would take them out and look at them from time to time, each one triggering sweet memories . . . a Sanquhar Academy school jotter in the centre of which she had pressed a sprig of heather and a bog asphodel which she had picked on a walk to the summit of Blackcraig; a piece of bluestone flecked with quartz found in the short scree runs of the steep southern face of Corsincon when she had gone with Mr. Cameron searching for a stray ewe with twin lambs; a tuft of wool from her first pet lamb, Susie, who used to wander into the big farm kitchen and nudge the check that locked the dresser hunting for sweetmeats; a copy of the *Scottish Farmer* with a report about Glenmulloch's good prices for its Border Leicester cross lambs at the Thornhill sales and full of all the flavours of rural life with its advertisments for Cooper's dairy ointment, Karswood's pig powders, fly dip and bloom dip, and Country Wear boots by John Lees of Maybole.

Later that night Star made up her mind about the bayonet. She thought how offensive it was to let it share the same place as her sentimental reminders of her days in the country and she pulled the case out again to retrieve the long blade. She parcelled it in a thick wrapping of newspapers, took a bucket of ashes from the fireplace, then ran unnoticed in the lingering fog to the close by the dairy across the road from her own tenement. If Sally Hall did tell the police that she had the weapon and if they did come, she would deny it. They would search for it, of course, and would go to the middens looking for it but there was a limit to how far they would go. They certainly wouldn't start looking in the back courts across the street. After wedging the bayonet deep down the side of the waste bin, she poured the ashes on top to hide it. The bins were full, as always, but the collection squads, the midden men, would be round later with their big wicker creels to load the Garrets, the ugly electric refuse vehicles. Then it would be gone to the Kilbirnie Street incinerator and out of her mind forever.

Because of the fog, her mother had stayed with a friend in Bridgeton that night and it wasn't until the following night at a quarter to ten that she arrived home. That was always an ominous hour for it would mean, as it usually did, that she would have been in the Moy, or one of her other favourite pubs, until closing time at 9.30 p.m. Star's assumption was right. Her mother's first words when she came in told her that. "Your Mammy's no' well, hen," she said, which always meant that she had taken too much and a cup of tea should be poured. The kettle, as always, was just off the boil on the little range. Star made her mother a thick jam sandwich to accompany the cup of tea she was readying, her mother, as always, reminding her, "Mind and put the milk in first", to which Star gave a condescending smile and awaited the comment which always followed: "It tastes much nicer that way." Star put some extra sugar in the tea for they said that it helped the sobering process and together with the sandwich, whether the theory was right or not, her mother's condition changed noticeably.

"Did you read the papers the day?" she asked when she had finished the tea and bread. Star flushed, her conscience immediately linking the question to the events of the day before when she was leaving work. She was relieved when her mother continued to speak without waiting on a reply and that she wasn't referring to the East End murder. Star had read about the Florence Street murder but had quickly passed over it to read about the gang fight that had ended in the death of the Docherty boy and the detention of several youths for police enquiries. "Imagine them doing that to him right here in our street," said Isa. "You know who he was, of course."

Star shook her head.

"He was the one I told you about . . . Steven Holden, the one they called Snakey, the one that killed your father when they attacked him in Crown Street. There'll be a few rejoicing at what he got last night,

I'm telling you."

"Ma . . . you make it all sound so primitive. The old days are gone."

"Aye, but they're no' forgotten, hen. There's a lot of us older ones still living and we don't forget. We don't forget what it was like before the war and what we were all born into."

"Ma, I was born into the same thing. Are you forgetting?"

"Aye, but before you had your right senses the war came and the men all changed. Everything changed. The men had somebody else to fight and the best of them didn't come back. Snakey Holden came back, though, and now they've got him. And there'll be a few old scores getting settled with all they knives and guns they've been bringing back with them."

"Goodness, is that all we can talk about? That's all they were talking about at work yesterday. The stabbing in the East End. Them and their Billy Boys! You should have seen some of them as they spoke about it. They were loving it. They were talking about how so-and-so had got his own back. How someone had put the boot in, as they say. How someone else had 'plunged' him. Yes, that's what they say, 'plunge'. Not a mention or a thought for the person they plunge. And it was almost with glee that they were saying there were about twenty of them all on to the one person. They seemed to think that was good. God, we can be a mean and vicious lot, do you know that? What's it all for? What's it all about? In other countries they do it for wealth and power, not that that's excusable, but it's understandable. Here they all seem to do it to show that they're hard men. To say that so-and-so is the big man . . . the wide-o. And everybody looks up to the hard man, don't they? They looked up to father because of that. Everything is about being hard and being feared. What they're really frightened about is being soft and kind and loving. There's not much of it around here, is there Ma?"

"See that spell you had in the country! Done you no good, Star Nelson . . . coming back here with all your fancy ideas. There's nothing up with the Gorbals folk."

"No, Ma. That's the problem. They don't know there's something up with them. The hard men have taken over their minds. They idolise them . . . everything they do, the way they walk and talk and dress and live their lives. They're our heroes. Not the poets or the writers or the artists or the great things in life. It's the hard men. God, what has happened to us? No wonder we've got the conditions we have. Nobody fights against them. If all your hard men got together and battled against the people that mattered, you and I wouldn't be living in a single-end with rats running about the back close and sharing the stairhead lavvy with forty other people."

"Oh, for heaven's sake, lassie . . . you've an awful head on you, have you not? I've seen a' them that's argued to get us better conditions, going round with their wee pails and writing slogans on the streets at night. They just end up in the same kind of houses as everybody else. And the hard men end up in them as well!"

"Ma, that's exactly what I'm trying to tell you. Everybody seems to end up the way they started . . . the men with their pub on a Friday, their football game and a fight on the Saturday, the long lie on the Sunday; and the women surrounded with weans in a room and kitchen for the rest of their days. No doubt that's how my father would have ended up had that man Holden and his gang not got him. The great hero. Their fantastic hard man. And living out his days in a single end or a room and kitchen. Even their heroes end up with nothing."

"Don't you go saying anything against your father, Star Nelson."

"Mother . . . do you not understand? I'm not saying anything against my father. It's the system I'm against and the way the people have been so browbeaten by it that they merely accept it. I'm sure my father must have been rebelling against something. The trouble was that he didn't know what. So, like the others, he took his venom out on his own kind to become what he did . . . the hard man of the hard men. And with nothing to show for it except respect from those who either feared him or worshipped that kind of violence. He was like that because he had never been away from the Gorbals: it was all he ever knew and he thought he was the best part of it . . . the king of the hard men. And he ends up in a gutter in Crown Street. Now this one Holden is found in the middens down the road. And the boy Docherty is left lying in the middle of the street, stabbed and kicked to death, just like you told me they did to my father. Do you understand it all, Ma . . . for I don't?"

"Understand! Do we need to understand? It's just the way . . . isn't it?"

"Aye, I suppose you're right. It's just the way . . . isn't it! Just the way."

Sally Hall returned to her work on the Wednesday. The police had released her and most of the other youths they had detained for inquiries. A group of the girls immediately surrounded her when she came into the big room where the machinists worked, anxious to hear about her experience. She had always shown the tough girl image, rarely smiling, tight-lipped, with the graceless walk of that kind of tenement girl who wanted to show that she was from the hard school, her head and shoulders moving in time with her jaunty small steps, like the way the wee flyweights used to take the ring at the National and the Grove. She was enjoying the attention and laughed as she ridiculed the police for not being able to charge any of them with the murder of Docherty.

She didn't attempt to speak to Star until they were about to start work and got a surprise when, just as she was about to tell her story, Star turned on her. She had only known her as the quiet girl who was her nearest machinist and the cold stare and the angry words took her aback. "Never," said Star, repeating the word for emphasis, "never you do anything like that to me again. Never ever you get me involved in any of your ways. Keep them and your friends of the street to yourself. Do you understand?"

Sally lowered her head, unable to meet the angry eyes of Star staring fiercely at her. Her only reply, head bowed, was to ask if she had the bayonet . . . "My fellah says he wants it back."

"You've a damn cheek to even mention that after what I've said. Well, the answer is, he's not getting it back. No one is. It's been destroyed. And that's the subject closed."

Sally Hall got the message and never spoke about the incident again.

No one was ever charged with the two murders, that of the boy Docherty and of Snakey Holden. The police knew all the names of the gang who had attacked the boy and they knew the names of the two who stabbed him, one with a bayonet, the other with a butcher's knife. But while their informers had been accurate, there were no witnesses and no forensic evidence to connect them with the death. Of the ten youths who had been taken into custody, six were released, including Sally Hall, without being charged, and the remaining four, including the two killers, were charged with mobbing and rioting and breach of the peace. The charges were later reduced to disorderly conduct and they were each fined £10 with the alternative of sixty days imprisonment.

There was even less success with the Holden murder. The usual batch of anonymous calls led to four suspects, all with previous convictions, who were interviewed. But none of their fingerprints matched those taken from the grooved wooden grip of James McLean's bayonet. Because they hadn't come by one identical to it, the big Winchester bayonet ended up on display in the Black Museum, a harshly lit room two flights up in the police headquarters at St Andrew's Street. There it was labelled with the details of the incident in which it had been involved and put on show in the company of a bizarre and deadly collection of daggers, swords, machetes, knuckle dusters, spiked and evil, pick axes, whips of cable wire, home made coshes, a unique collection of chains, some with razor edges, a chain bolas, and pikes, all collected in the aftermath of Glasgow street battles, together with a framed piece of broken glass with the fingerprint which had sent John Caldwell to the gallows the year before and the Luger used by Charles Templeman Brown in the sensational Pollokshields East Station double murder the year before that.

They kept Holden's body for a week in one of the forty-five chrome doored chambers on the side of the room in the City Mortuary which the chief attendant said were for his "short term customers". The ones on the other side, he would point out, had their cooling systems twenty-seven degrees below the freezing point of the others . . ."my long stay residents", he would fondly call them. Holden's younger brother, Freddie, an honest and respectable tradesman, claimed the body for burial after the post mortem which established he had died instantly from a bayonet thrust driven into him at such force that it had gone right through him, from the base of his neck to his throat, severing all the vital arteries, including the spinal cord, on its way. A duty minister conducted a brief service in the little chapel next to the green tiled post-mortem room before a Rolls Royce hearse from the Co-operative and one car took the body and the mourners to the final destination point of generations of Gorbals folk, the Southern Necropolis.

Only four people, his brother and three cousins, were at the service and travelled in the car behind the hearse. Another mourner was waiting by the fresh grave in the west end of the cemetery, Snap McLatchie, the confidence photographer. As they walked from the cemetery one of the cousins, who had run with the gangs in the 1930s pointed to a light granite memorial stone just three graves away from the family lair where they had buried Holden. "I wonder what Steve would have said if he had known he was lying there almost next to him," he said. He was referring to the last name inscribed on the small gravestone . . . JAMESIE.

24

A SURPRISE FROM THE PAST

THE involvement with Sally Hall and the murder of Steven "Snakey" Holden had a profound effect on Star, even though she didn't know and never was to know that it was she who very nearly became the victim that fateful foggy night. What did it matter if this man Holden, as her mother reminded her, had been the one who had killed her father and, as the papers had said, was a well-known small-time criminal? That didn't lessen the impact of such a brutal death occurring just yards away from her very own home. And it was that very same night that she had carried the murder weapon that had been used on the boy Docherty. She could have been stopped by the police outside Gordon's and if she had . . .? The ugly web was closing around her more and more. She felt insecure and unsure about herself and her future. Unless she was to do something about it *now* she would become completely entangled and then . . . trapped.

She came home more cheerful than usual that Tuesday night, and the heavy and musty smell of the lobby which led to their house was laced with the more homely aroma of mince and potatoes as it always was on a Tuesday, the only day of the week when her mother made a proper meal. She smiled to herself knowing her mother would say, as she always did when she served the dish "And I've put a wee onion in it. Gives it a great flavour, you know." And Star, as she always did, said "Oh, what a great smell Ma," when she went into the house. Before she could reply Star anxiously gave her the news of the day.

She wanted to tell her how she had left work early in order to enrol for nightclasses to improve her School Leaving Certificates as she had made up her mind to take a career of some kind, perhaps nursing, in order to get away from Gordon's . . . and the Gorbals. She broke off after only a sentence or two because of her mother's disinterest. "What is it, Ma? Are you not well or something?"

"Oh Star . . . how did you never tell me?"

"What?"

"About the boys. The Fordyces."

Star gaped in astonishment, the colour vanishing from her face with the stunning impact of the news. She took a seat and leaned her head on a hand and was silent for about a minute before she spoke. "How," she said softly, pausing, "how did you get to know?"

"One of them was here the day."

"Here," she gasped incredulously.

"Aye. Here. He's a sojer. But wi' a collar and tie. You know . . . an officer. Says he's in the HLI and just back from Palestine and that he hasnae been in Scotland since he joined up in the war. Oh, my God, lassie, how did you never tell me? Me . . . your very own mother. You never said . . . "

"No . . . and I never would have. It was something I had to live with . . . and sort out for myself. I wanted to put it completely out of my mind. And it's only very recently that I've begun to feel that I'm getting over it. Even what you've told me isn't the shock it would have been a year ago . . . or worse, two years ago. They're right. Time does heal."

"Oh, I never realised what you had been through, darling. Never. And all these years you never said a word. I cannae understand that."

"Which one of them came here?"

"You know me wi' names, Star. Maybe he said but I was that taken aback. Anyway he wants to meet you. He wants to say he's sorry."

"Sorry. Good God!"

"I told him I didn't know what to reply. He was that nice about it. I told him where you worked and that the best place to meet you was at the Suspension Bridge. He said he would know you."

"Know me! Aye, Ma . . . he would know me all right. Damn cheek of him . . . wanting to see me. After . . . "

"I was thinking the same . . . but he was such a gentleman."

"Gentleman! Some gentleman. God, what the hell brought him back? To say sorry! For God's sake . . . sorry! And when is he supposed to be coming to say he's sorry?"

"He said he was on duty till Friday, but would be there at the bridge at five o'clock. He'd be in his uniform so you would know him."

"Know him? I'll never forget him . . . them. And I'll tell him . . . tell him how he and his brother devastated my life. How they made me live through my own murder . . . That's what it's like, you know. Like you are being murdered. A nightmare that is real; real yet you can't believe it's real. A horror you can't understand. They say your life flashes before you when you die. Well, it does when you're being raped. And remember, it was much worse for me. For I had that experience when I was a little girl . . . you know? I had got over that more easily though, what with being so young and having all those great years at Glenmulloch with all the nice people I met there. They helped me although they didn't realise they were. But what happened to me that night at Lydeburn has left a permanent scar. I'm like those razor victims . . . the way my Da must have been. Scarred for life. Only you could see their scars and feel for them. You can't see mine. They're in my mind. And I'll tell Fordyce that when I see him. If I see him that is."

"C'mon, hen. We'll have a bite to eat. I've cooked a lovely pot of mince. Put a wee onion in it, you know. A' the good cooks do that. Gives it a lovely flavour."

Star smiled. And for a moment the shock of the Fordyce boy's return was forgotten.

The rest of the meal passed in silence, Star deep in thought about the unexpected visitor, her mother still appalled and confused at what she had learned from him. She stared at her in pity from time to time, coming near to tears each occasion she did. It wasn't till later in the evening when Star was settled by the fire with a book that the subject of her decision to go to nightschool came up once again.

"And what's this about you wanting to be a nurse?" said Isa, almost out of the blue.

"Goodness . . . it went completely out of my mind when you told me about the . . ." and then she paused before adding "the visitor." She closed her book and brightened for the first time since she had come in. "I've been thinking about it for some weeks now but it was only today that I actually did something about it by enrolling at nightschool. By next Spring I'll have another two certificates, giving me three Highers and three Lowers."

"Do you need all that education to be a nurse? I know a lot of lassies I went to school wi' that went to the nursing and they had as many certificates as me . . . nane."

"Nursing is only one of the things I'm considering. But whatever I decide, the more education I have the better."

Isa, however, had it fixed in her mind that she was going to be a nurse. "Would you go to the Royal or the Victoria?"

"I'm not thinking of Glasgow, Ma."

"Where then?"

"Well, to be truthful, I don't really know. I just know if I have a better standard of education, the better the job I'll get. God, I would hate to be a machinist the rest of my days. But you know how unsettled I've been since I came home. I don't know why I haven't done something about it before now. You can move around a lot in nursing . . . but there are other things. I'll decide on that once I pass my exams."

"I would miss you, hen."

"I would miss you, Ma. But you're all right, really. Look at the friends you've got. Goodness, you're hardly in at night."

"You're right, Star. I enjoy my life. Did I tell you I'm going out the night? It's Sarah Paterson's menage night. And some of us are going out for a wee refreshment afterwards. And . . . Annie Mooney has asked us up for a wee singsong after that. You'll mind o' Annie . . . her that lives in the Lane, the Cumberland Lane, the wee street that's so narrow they cannae even turn a horse and cart in it. Her man's on the boats and she has great wee nights for the lassies when he's away."

"Ma . . . you might miss me, but you'll never be lonely."

25

A BEAUTIFUL GUN

THE window on the ground floor of the closemouth of number 188 Florence Street was open and an elderly woman was leaning from it. She moved quickly when she saw the well dressed man approach and the window closed with a sharp thud. Sammy Nelson laughed to himself as he knocked on one of the unwashed panes, knowing that the woman who had been there was lifting lines for the local bookmaker, a common occurrence at specific ground floor houses whose residents allowed their windows to be used as collection points for the illegal bookies. "What is it?" she shouted querulously from behind the drawn curtain.

"Open the window, missus."

"No afore you tell me what you want."

"I'm looking for the Bairds, you know Isa and her daughter Star." The window opened cautiously. "What do you want them for?"

"I'm the lassie's uncle."

"Oh! I thought you were someone else. One up, first on the right at the end of the lobby. Are you Jamesie's brother?"

"Aye . . . thanks hen. Am I too late for a bet on the three o'clock?"

"Cheeky messin." And the window banged shut again.

The heavy smell of decay and squalor quickly took the smile from Sammy's face as he climbed the spiral stairway, turning off on the first landing to go along a dark passageway, so dark that he had to fumble for the door at the end of it. It was some minutes before his knocks were answered and he only waited because he could hear someone moving about the house. The door opened cautiously at first and a shaft of light filled the dark lobby. The woman who answered clutched at a cardigan she had obviously just put on. Her hair was unbrushed and she had all the appearance of someone who had just awakened.

"You'll be Isa . . . Star's mother?"

"Aye . . . and I know you. You're Sammy . . . Jamesie's brother."

He was surprised when she said that. "You've got some memory."

"Oh, I've seen you about and people have pointed you out to me. Come on in."

Isa moved the near-boiling kettle to the middle of the range to make some tea and when she saw Sammy looking around the room she said, "You'll have to excuse the mess. I was having a wee lie down after dinner. Don't work on a Wednesday now. We get the Tuesday half-day for working on a Sunday morning and I get Wednesday for working on a Saturday. No' like the old days when I was in the shop seven days a week." She kept moving round the room as she spoke, tidying newspapers and items of clothing that had been draped over the chairs at the dining table and putting some unwashed dishes into the badly chipped enamel basin on the wooden draining board by the sink. "You'll be thinking I'm a right untidy one . . . but I just didn't feel like doing anything. We were late getting to bed last night. I normally have my floor washed by this time, you know. It's not even swept. And look at the time . . . it's by three."

"Stop your fussing, Isa. I'm not here to inspect your house. I still can't get away with you knowing me. We met just the once, didn't we?"

"Aye . . . that time in Rutherglen Road."

"That wasn't yesterday."

"No . . . more than twenty years ago."

"That long?"

"Aye . . . 1926 to be precise, for it was the year before Jamesie died. And there was me . . . madly in love wi' a married man and walking along the street wi' him like he was my ain man. Then we bumps into you and your wife. Peggy isn't it? You didn't half gie me a dirty look Well deserved, I might add."

Sammy smiled. "Aye, he was a bit of a lad."

"Was he no'! I often think about him, even though it's all these years. I wonder what would have become of him had they no' got him?"

"He'd have won the war single handed," replied Sammy. "Like this Audie Murphy they're all talking about. They say he killed 244 Jerries in the one battle and he's got more medals than anybody. That would have been our Jamesie, so it would." They laughed together as they thought of that.

Only the sweet memories came back as they recalled various characters and incidents of their young days in the Gorbals, both of them enjoying every minute of their reminiscences. Then Isa asked, "What brings you here, Sammy?"

"I heard about the lassie. Your lassie. I could hardly believe it when it was mentioned to me that our Jamesie had a girl and that she was living right here in Florence Street. We just always assumed that Jamesie and his wife Nell never had any weans and that was it. I've been meaning to come and see you for ages . . . but you know how it is. What between one thing and another, I just never got the chance. And then, recent like, I had a few wee problems. Anyway, I'll tell you all about that later. The girl's more important right now. Is she at her work . . . machinist . . . is that right? How is she? What does she look like? And you call her Star?"

Before he could ask her any further questions, Isa intervened. "Sammy, I've been worried sick about the lassie. I couldn't sleep last night for thinking about her, poor thing. You've no idea how pleased I am at seeing you . . . at seeing a man that's one of us. It's at times like these that you need a man about the house for I don't know what to do. Oh, it's a terrible story, Sammy. I've never heard one like it and it's left me that confused. I even felt pity for the boy. He was such a nice fellow. But it wasn't right, Sammy. It wasn't right what the boys did . . . it wasn't right that it should have happened to my Star."

"For God's sake, woman, you'll need to calm down and tell me what it's all about. You're talking in circles."

"Oh dear . . . I'm sorry. My mind is still reeling at what I heard. I wish I had a wee drink to offer you . . . you've been in the house all this time and all you've had is tea. I finished what we had last night. I was that upset, you see."

"C'mon . . . get ready, Isa. It's nearly five and we'll go down to the Moy."

The drink helped. Before returning to the subject which had so obviously upset her, Sammy spoke briefly about his own life, how he was now a publican, that his son John was hoping to graduate from University soon and that Peggy, his wife, was "in a nursing home . . . nervous breakdown, Isa. It's a long story . . . I'll tell you sometime." Before she had time to sympathise, he said, "Right, you were telling me about Star."

Isa had relaxed considerably and was able to speak much more coherently. The story was obviously going to be a long one, for Isa, like so many of her friends, preferred to retell entire conversations and events as they happened, one sentence beginning, "Well, he said to me," and the next one "And I said to him." And, along the way, all the various asides were included, every little detail recounted. Sammy settled down to listen.

"You see, yesterday, Tuesday, was my half-day. I work up in Duncan's . . . you know, the dairy right at the top of the hill in Batson Street . . . your wife used to come in when you lived in Carfin Street, but she didn't remember me, although I knew her. Awfy nice customers, you know. Oh, the stories I could tell you about some of them! Anyway, it was my half-day and I'd just got home when there was a knock at the door and who should be there but this sojer. Oh, but he was smart . . . had one of they fancy Sam Browne belts a' polished up and a collar and tie as well. You could tell right away he was an officer. 'I'm Captain Fordyce,' says he. And then he asks for Star. So I says to him 'Come in, son' and in he comes, sits doon and I make him a cup of tea. 'We've just returned from Palestine,' he says when I set the tea down for him. Then he says, 'Do you not know of me?' and I said I didn't. Then he said he was one of the twins, from Kirkconnel. That's away in the country, Sammy, where our Star was evacuated. And he looks surprised when I says I still hadn't heard of him. I only remembered the Camerons, the people she stayed with. It was a farm on this big estate, see. Then he says to me that he had come to apologise for something that had happened in the past and says he's surprised that I didn't know. 'Know what, son?' I says to him. And then he tells me the whole story."

Isa detailed the Fordyce boy's incredible confessions as he had told the story to her. Sammy gasped loudly in astonishment as the long tale unfolded.

"And there was my lassie . . . back here a' these years, Sammy, and she never told me a word about it. She kept it to herself, brooding about it all that time. I always knew there was something. We women . . . we've got our intuition you know, Sammy. She's that different from the others."

Visibly shocked by the story, all Sammy could say was . . . "Bastard."

"I thought the same masel', Sammy, but he was such a nice fellow."

"Nice, bugger all, Isa. So he was a toff and an officer but that doesn't make him nice. He and his brother have been right bastards. Imagine a pair of boys doing that in the Gorbals? By Christ, they would be sorted out all right. That's what that one is needing."

"Aye, that's how I felt, Sammy, when he started to tell me and that's how I wished she had a father because I didn't know whether or not I was doing the right thing."

"What do you mean . . . the right thing or not?"

"Well, he says he wants to see her. I told him the time she finishes work and where and when he could meet her. He couldn't wait last night as he had to be back at the barracks."

"And so when is he going to turn up again?"

"He said he was on duty till Friday and that he would be there at the Suspension Bridge to meet her that night."

"And is Star going to be there?"

"I think she is, although she hasn't said for sure."

"Christ, Isa, I wouldn't have been telling him, the bastard. He raped my niece! My brother's daughter! Bastard should be shot, so he should. Christ, I didn't expect to hear this the day, Isa. That's given me quite a shake, you know." He looked down, shaking his head. "God, him *and* the brother. Filthy swines. Speaking about his brother, where is he?"

"You know I never thought to ask. I was that shocked, Sammy. Maybe he's up at the barracks as well."

He stared at his drink for some minutes before speaking again. "What did you say his name was?"

"Fordyce."

"Aye, but his first name?"

"I think he said it but I don't mind. I'm terrible wi' names and that, Sammy. All I remember him saying was that he was Captain Fordyce."

"Oh, aye, he'd tell you that all right. He wouldn't have said that had he been a Private, would he? Swine."

"I didn't think it would get you that upset."

"Why not? I may not have met her, but Star is one of the family. You can't get much closer a relative than my brother's daughter . . . can you? My own flesh and blood. And he's meeting her on the Suspension Bridge on Friday. Five o'clock . . . is that right?"

"Aye . . . what makes you ask? You're no' thinking . . . "

"I'm thinking nothing, Isa. Right! And you've told me nothing. Right! You said this is the kind of time you need a man in the family. Well you've got one. Right! Me. Right! Have another half." His eyes flashed angrily as he punched out the words, emphasising the word "Right" with extra venom.

"God, Sammy, you were awfy like your brother there. Frightening, so it was. Jamesie used to talk like that when he said he was going to get someone and when he got really angry his eyes went a' wee, just like yours did just now. Terrifying, so it was. Sammy . . . you're no' thinking about . . ."

"Isa, I don't know what a woman thinks when she hears about a lassie being raped. But I can tell you what a man thinks. At least what this man thinks. It makes me sick, Isa. That's what it makes me. Now I've never heard about it happening to anyone related to me. This is the first time, thank God. And to think he's coming back to see her after all that time. It's unbelievable. It's almost like he's coming back to gloat. I'll gloat the bastard."

"There you go again . . . your eyes a' wee."

His tense face broke into a smile at that. "Isa . . . I'm Sammy. No' Jamesie. And I'm needing a half."

They enjoyed each other's company that night, swapping reminiscences and memories of their younger days and they both

looked at each other in surprise when the 9.30 closing-time bell rang
out. "I don't believe it," said Isa. "Imagine us sitting here all this time.
They'll be talking about us next. Are you coming up to meet Star?
She'll be back from nightschool soon."

Sammy staggered slightly when he stood up. "Oh, Christ, I'm half
cut, Isa. No . . . she's no' going to be meeting her long lost uncle like
this. But you tell her I'll see her right . . . and read what you like into
that." Jokingly, he then added . . . "Right!" And Isa replied likewise.

Sammy Nelson could think of nothing else all that Thursday, the day
after he had met Isa. Nothing had affected him like it since Snakey
Holden . . . and that name over the years had aroused various
emotions within him: fear; suspicion; hatred; malice; revenge. But
there was a parallel, he thought, between the two. Both had inflicted
damage, in one way or another, to members of his family. Both had
perpetrated foul and unforgivable deeds on the Nelsons. If only he had
taken action sooner he might have been able to prevent one of them,
Holden, from going as far as he did. And if only he and not Claney had
taken that action, it would have been he that had the satisfaction of
avenging the havoc which had been brought to his life. Fordyce, it was
true, didn't present a threat to him like Holden had. But, nevertheless,
what he had done was unpardonable, even though it had been years
ago. Hadn't Isa said it had affected the girl's life? Holden had affected
his wife Peggy's life. His eyes glazed when he thought about her and
the years of suffering she had endured by the window of her upstairs
bedroom, dwindling from an attractive and mature woman in the
prime of her life to a haunted spectre of herself; a sad and pathetic
mental wreck who imagined she was a little child. Holden was a
bastard and how he wished he had got him. And Fordyce, for that
matter, was a bastard too. He should be shot, so he should. Shot, so he
should. Shot. Shot. The word ricocheted in his mind and when he tried
to shut it out it returned again . . . and again . . . and again.

Jamesie would have sorted him out all right. By Christ, he would.
His way. But he wasn't Jamesie. And violence wasn't his creed. Yet it
had a place in his society: the problem with Holden couldn't have been
solved unless violence had been used. But why violence for the
Fordyce boy? He was respectable . . . a soldier . . . an officer at that.
What good would violence do to him? He wasn't the loathsome
menace that Holden had been. He would pass from their lives just as
quickly as he had entered it.No matter how he reasoned with himself,
the revulsion of what had happened to his niece prevailed and despite
his efforts to think otherwise, only one objective persisted. Revenge.
He owed it to the girl who, after his son, was his closest blood relative.

He owed it to the memory of his brother, Jamesie. And, more important, he owed it to himself; for Sammy Nelson had everything in life except the satisfaction of having dealt with Holden himself. That he hadn't was something that would nag him to his dying day; his wife, Peggy, poor creature that she was, remained as living proof of that. That was why he needed to do something about Fordyce. He was his compensation. His guarantee of life without further doubts and recriminations about what he should have done but didn't, about what might have been but wasn't. Sammy Nelson had always tried to live with his conscience, to reason out that what he did in life was honest in his own terms. That in itself was honesty, he thought. Others did the things they did without analysis, without considering whether what they were doing was right or wrong. And that, he thought, was not being honest or just. If he shot Fordyce it would be right; for a man who had done what he had done should be punished; *had* to be punished. And if he was then Sammy Nelson's conscience would be perfectly clear. He agonised over that reasoning because he wanted to be sure that what he was planning to do was right. He was in no doubt after he had made his deliberations. His decision was the right one . . . for himself . . . and for the family. And having made that decision he turned his mind to a more important matter — how he was going to execute his plan.

It shouldn't be all that difficult, he thought. It was the third week in November and it would be dark before five o'clock. He turned to the Stop Press column on the back page of that morning's *Daily Record* to check. Yes, he was right. Light-up time was 4.45pm. The weather forecast was cold and showery with perhaps a light fog. A typical November night. Perfect.

He took the little Mauser from the drawer of his twin pedestal Regency writing desk, the one which Peggy had bought at Edmiston's the auctioneers and which she had told him was "a genuine antique" and he, to her dismay, had called it "old fashioned". He held the small gun in the palm of his hand, admiring the ingeniousness of its makers. He had never realised a gun could look so attractive. Hughie Connor had pointed out all the features when he had given him it, pretending to be an expert on the subject: the truth was that he had only learned them himself the day before from Sonny Walsh, the dealer in the Calton who was specialising in guns bought from returning Servicemen. But Hughie had remembered his story well and told it like he was a veteran in handling guns: "A Mauser, Sammy. It's Eyetie. Mauser 7.65 to give it its right title. Notice how there are no nuts or bolts sticking up to spoil its smooth surface. Do you know why they do that, Sammy? Well, it's so you can pull it from its holster or your pocket without it catching on anything. Look," he said pointing to the single countersunk screw in the handle, "that's the only visible screw in the entire gun. It holds the grip in place and the rest of it is held together by interlocking and with pins. Clever buggers, aren't they? Specially for Eyeties. And there's eight bullets fit the magazine. Christ, Sammy, if it's you that's doing the shooting, you'll no' miss wi' eight shots. If you do, let's know. I can get hand grenades as well."

Eight shots! No, he wouldn't need eight shots. Nothing like that. Anyway, there wouldn't be the time or the need if his plan worked out. It would be simple. Isa had said that the girls left the work a few minutes after five o'clock. Fordyce would be at the bridge before then, surely . . . he being the officer and gentleman. There would be no problem in approaching him unnoticed and aiming two or three shots. The getaway would be easy . . . darkness, confusion, a quick run over to South Portland Street and if there were any heroes willing to chase a gunman — and only a bampot would do that — then he could nip up one of the back closes and into the maze of back courts which would take him across to Nicholson Street or Oxford Street. Nothing could be easier.

Could he be traced afterwards? Impossible. No one would know about his mission. He had thought about telling Claney and was glad he had decided not to do so. Who knew he had the gun? Only Hughie Connor had that information. And he wouldn't tell. Not that he would suspect, anyway. He might have thought something if there had been a shooting a day or two or even a week after he had got the gun for him. But even if he had suspected, he wouldn't have said to anyone. Not Hughie Connor.

Fingerprints? Well, he wasn't going to be leaving any, except those on the gun and he would be keeping that. The bullets, of course, could be matched up with the gun. He had learned that in a film he had seen about the American F.B.I. and how they were using science to track down criminals. But they weren't going to get the gun, were they? So they would have nothing to match with the bullets.

What if they traced Fordyce's movements? Would he have told his pals at the barracks that he was going to meet a girl called Nelson from the Gorbals? Like hell he would. Officers didn't go to the Gorbals, did they? The only one he had ever seen in the area had been in charge of the Military Police patrol, looking for deserters. Wait a minute! Fordyce *had* been to the Gorbals; just two days previously to speak to Isa. He must have asked a few folk for directions and a few nosey buggers would have spotted him. Aye, somebody could nark to the Busies about that. Sell their granny for a half and a pint from the plainclothesmen, so they would. But supposing they did find out the officer had visited Isa Baird's house? Well, she wouldn't mention that he, Sammy, had been there. Supposing they questioned the girl? She wouldn't tell them anything either. She couldn't. She hadn't even met him. That was why he had decided not to return to see her until . . . until he had finished with his appointment with the officer. So Sammy's plan really was infallible, with the single exception of being caught on the scene. And he would time his movements on the bridge to make sure that didn't happen.

He held the gun in his hand once more, remembering Connor's words, "Look at that wee barrel, Sammy. Just a fraction more than three inches. And feel the weight, Sammy! A pound and a wee bit. See having a gun like that, Sammy . . . makes you want to go out and shoot somebody so it does." He turned it over in his hands another time then slipped it into an inside pocket of his jacket where it rested without making any bigger bulge than the thick crocodile wallet he had removed to make room for it. He wouldn't be carrying it there, of course, when he walked up to Fordyce. It would be in his overcoat pocket then . . . no, not the camel one; something much more commonplace than that; his old gaberdine coat. Aye, that would be a fine description for the Busies to be hunting for, he mused . . . a man of medium build, medium height, in a gaberdine raincoat and cloth cap. That was Mr Everyman in Glasgow.

The news wasn't good when he phoned the nursing home on the Friday morning to enquire about Peggy. The matron explained that she had wandered into the grounds in her night attire the previous evening and contracted a chill. They were worried about "complications", she said and advised him not to come to the hospital because they wanted her to have complete rest. "Can you phone back later in the day?" asked the matron. "Maybe at about six?"

"Six o'clock? Oh, yes, six is fine . . . I'll phone then." Yes, six o'clock would be fine. Everything would be fine for Sammy Nelson by six o'clock that Friday night. If he had needed any reassurance about his appointment at the Suspension Bridge that night, the news he had received on that phone call was it. It reaffirmed all his thoughts, attitudes and plans of the previous day. Five o'clock, Friday, November 12, 1948 — the day after Martinmas — and he would have atoned for what he had failed to do in the past. Five o'clock. Aye. Everything would be fine after five o'clock.

He didn't go out for a drink that lunchtime for fear that it might affect his aim in some way, although he was only an average daytime drinker — a couple of halfs, small ones, and pint chasers and he was happy. Instead he drove his new two-litre Riley to the Cathkin Braes, a small ridge of wooded hills close to the southern suburbs of the city. It was a popular place for schoolchildren to picnic and play in the summer months but on a grey November day the woods would be deserted. He couldn't find an old tin can to use for target practice, but a big stone, about half the size of a man's head sufficed and he placed it on top of a fence post. The gun had come with fifty rounds of ammunition, about half of which he had already used when he had tried similar target practice prior to the night he had gone out to look for Holden. He had been surprised then for it was the first time he had ever fired a gun and he hadn't expected it to jump as much after pulling the trigger, although, in fact, it didn't jump nearly as much as some other pistols. He had been pleasantly relieved that the noise hadn't been as loud as he had anticipated, more of a crack like the little gun caps children were always exploding in the street. He hoped that's what they would think they were when he fired off his shots tonight. He fired fourteen rounds at the stone in a methodical programme of target practice; five shots at fifteen paces, missing with every one; another five at ten paces, hitting the fencepost twice; and four shots at five paces, two of them hitting the stone, raising little puffs of blue smoke as they did.

That confirmed his plan. He would stroll up to Fordyce to ensure that he was , in fact, an officer and a Captain at that, then walk past him, exactly five paces, turn round quickly and fire. If he could hit the stone at that range, there would be little problem in hitting the real target. No longer was he questioning the morality of what he was going to do. That had all been gone through; it had all been thought out. His mind was settled and only one thing was uppermost in it, that the job be accomplished properly, efficiently and without Sammy Nelson being caught.

His target practice over, he drove back to St. Andrew's Drive and had a short sleep on the big four-seater divan in the lounge. At three o'clock he synchronised his dress-pocket Canadian Hamilton, the one Peggy had given him for their fifteenth wedding anniversary, with the time signal on the Home Service. Then he began to figure out when he should leave home. He knew by heart the route and the times it took for that regular walk to the Gorbals. From his house in St. Andrew's Drive at the corner of Nithsdale Road, it took four minutes to walk to the big villa called Barrochan, where he turned right into Maxwell Drive, which became Maxwell Road. By the time he got to the long and handsome tenement block dated 1880, it was twelve minutes. Another eleven minutes after that, passing the gas works and the timber yard by the railway sidings at the far side of the suburb, he would be at Eglinton Toll. From there to the Gorbals Cross took a further fourteen minutes and the Suspension Bridge was only five minutes beyond that — a total of forty-two minutes walking time.

He decided to leave the house at five minutes to four o'clock. That should get him to the bridge a good few minutes before 4.45. Hopefully, Fordyce would be there . . . waiting.

On his way down Main Street Star came into his mind. It would be great to see her, he thought. And he would ... soon. Aye, why not that very night? He could take her and Isa out for a drink. Still a good-looking woman was Isa. Jamesie knew his talent all right. And again he was thinking about Star. She would be good-looking too, he thought, what with Isa her mother and Jamesie her father. "Aye, she'll be a right beauty, I'll bet. Wonder if she plans to meet this Fordyce one, cheeky bastard that he is, coming back like that? Funny ... I never thought about that. I hope she doesn't get a fright when she sees ... No. Don't be silly. He'll be away by then. They'll have taken him away. The ambulance. Aye, the ambulance would have come. But supposing she did see him ... lying there, like? Well, she hated him, didn't she? Aye, she had to hate him. Hate him so much that when she hears what happened it would be good news to her. Wouldn't it? Wouldn't it? Christ it would ... wouldn't it? She would approve. Wouldn't she? Wouldn't she? Jesus, what if she didn't? No, she couldn't possibly. Uncle Sammy was right ... wasn't he? Of course he was. Of course he was. Oh Jesus Christ what am I thinking like this for? My mind is bloody well made up ... isn't it?"

It was just leaving twenty-five minutes to five on the four big roman-numeralled clocks high on the standards above the underground toilets with the sign 'Lavatory for Gentlemen' which marked the Gorbals Cross. There was already a small knot of men gathering outside J McConnell's "The Cross Tavern" beneath Campbell's big pawn offices, readying themselves for an early drink when the pub opened at five o'clock. Everything was going to plan; he would be at the Suspension Bridge before the clocks reached the quarter to. On down Main Street after the Cross, then left into Carlton Place by the river and in the distance, as though magically suspended, were the six lights of the big lanterns which lit the Suspension Bridge, each hazily reflecting the thin cloud of housefire smoke. And, as he got closer, he could see the little coasters, the *Polythene* and the *Prase*, one in from the Mersey with a cargo of I.C.I. chemicals the other from Creetown with granite, both busily discharging the loads he had seen them arrive with when he had reconnoitred the scene the previous day.

And he hoped that Fordyce would be there ... waiting.

As he passed Nicholson Street, about twenty-five yards from the southern end of the bridge, he paused by a street light to take the little gun from his inside pocket. Turning the small safety catch which put the firing pin assembly in line with the hammer, he put it in his right coat pocket. He wondered for a minute which side of the bridge Fordyce would be on. The north side would mean a longer exposed run for him for he would have to come back along the full length of the bridge. He might be on the south side, however, which would be perfect, for then he would merely run across the road to South Portland Street and vanish into the night. The unknown assailant.

26

THE HEART OF THE GORBALS

THE letter had come for her that morning but she had left the house before the postman called. The Maryhill postmark puzzled her for she couldn't think of anyone she knew who lived in that northern suburb of Glasgow. A warm flush came over her when she opened the envelope and took out the small bundle of pages, each with its bold crest of elephant and bugle and the words Highland Light Infantry. It was dated Thursday, November 11, and she was glad Isa hadn't come home yet from the dairy for it was a long letter and she wanted to be on her own as she read it.

Dear Star,
As you read this I will be on the overnight train to the South. I was only warned three hours ago that some of us have to be off tonight to strengthen the garrison in Berlin for this big Air Lift operation which everyone seems to be getting a bit desperate about. And I haven't even had my disembarkation leave from Palestine yet! But that's the Army for you.

Star, I so much wanted to meet you tomorrow night. I know that no amount of words or excuses or apologies will ever explain or account for the actions of myself and my brother that horrendous night six years ago. But at least I had to try. That was why I came to see you on Tuesday. I was absolutely amazed to learn that your mother had never been told. I do hope it wasn't too great a shock, although it must have been an awful experience for her. I found her a most understanding lady. She took it all so bravely. Please bear with me as my story is fairly long, but I do wish you to know it . . . from the beginning.

My visit and, indeed, this letter, was inspired by my 'little' brother Robbie. Robbie, you see, was killed in the Sachsenwald Forest at Hamburg just three days before the war ended in 1945. We had thought we were going to make it together . . . but it was not to be. After a short while in Germany following the end of the war I was posted to Palestine and this is the first time I have been home to Scotland since we left together in 1942. Before he was killed Robbie spoke a lot about you and was deeply concerned about everything in the past. It was his idea to come and see you as well as all the people who had been friends of our family in and around Kirkconnel. I disagreed with him and told him so at the time. But it was firmly in his mind that we should try and restore to our family the honour we had taken away from it. I argued that it would serve no purpose whatsoever; that what was done could not be undone. We had been a disgrace to ourselves, our parents, and everything that Lydeburn had stood for in the community; and no matter what people say in these changing days, my father did try and stand for something; for respectability; for the continuity of our heritage of freedom and democracy; for the care and welfare of all those who worked for him or who were his tenant farmers; and for the preservation of the beauty of our area. We could never restore that lost image, I thought. But Robbie insisted that the very least we could do was show them we still had some honour.

When Robbie died my whole world changed. Losing a twin brother is different from losing any other member of your family. For a twin is part of you. It's as though you have lost a part of your very own body. We had very different personalities but we each relied on the personality of the other. Robbie's weaknesses were my strengths. My weaknesses were his strengths. And when we were together our character seemed to mould into a single entity, each bolstering the other. I was shattered when he was killed; and that's putting it very mildly. It was as though half of me wasn't there any more. For a while I thought I was going to go out of my mind for I needed him, my other half, more than I ever knew. We had often spoken about how we would go our own ways one day; but it had only been talk . . . something that would happen in the distant future. But for it to happen as it did! I think if it hadn't been for the discipline of the regiment I would have gone to pieces. But officers don't show men their feelings; at least, not officers in the HLI or Glasgow Highlanders.

Then strange things began to happen to me. My whole personality began changing . . . as though it was me, Andrew, who had died and Robbie had lived. It's difficult to explain, I know. It was weird enough to me.

Getting back to yourself. Robbie had spoken to our Padre about you. He told me this one night after a particularly nasty battle we had come through. He had made up his mind that as soon as the war was over and he was demobilised, he would go straight back to Kirkconnel to seek everyone's forgiveness and after that he was going to find you to do the same. I told him he was crazy . . . stupid . . . that it was all in the past and should be left there. But, like me, he wouldn't be swayed in his thoughts. He was so happy that day we moved into the big forest, for the Germans were surrendering everywhere and he said we would soon be home. It was a Wednesday . . . Wednesday, May 2, 1945, when Robbie and another soldier were hit by a sniper. They were the last men in our regiment to be killed in the war. Three days later it was all over. We buried Robbie and the other man in a little clearing at the edge of the forest.

Everything seemed to change after that. I discussed it with the Padre. God! Me . . . confiding with a Padre! I would never have done that before. But it seemed so natural for me to speak with him; as though it was something I was used to. Then, almost unthinkingly, I began to make plans about returning to Kirkconnel, about who I would see and what I would say to them, and how I would go about finding you. I was doing it all as a matter of routine . . . as though I had never thought otherwise. Then I was posted to the Middle East which delayed everything, but I never wavered from the commitment I had strangely inherited.

It was fairly hectic in Palestine, what with the Jew being your enemy one minute, the Arab the next, and it wasn't till the voyage home that I got the time to think. I thought about the experience I had undergone in assuming the character of my brother; but it didn't seem all that important any more. For I had so completely changed that it was as though there had never been 'another' me before and that I had always felt the way I did now. None of my plans had changed . . . I would go to my Mother's, then to Kirkconnel, and finally to see yourself. I've been to Maxweltown to see my Mother. What can I say about her? Mother was Mother; as always, kind and understanding, comprehending fully the story of what I call 'my experience'. Women do seem to have a special understanding in matters such as these. Then I went to Kirkconnel. I saw the Camerons. What a lovely couple they are. Willie's rheumatics are pretty bad now and he walks with a stick all the time. But they were full of compassion and paid me the compliment of saying I have restored honour to my family. They've got a very smart smallholding, by the way, not far from the Guildhall place. I saw Wull Andrews as well. He's on the railway now . . . a surfaceman and looking fitter than ever. Says it's the easiest job he's had in his life. I can believe that knowing the way he used to work. And I went to see the Walkers at the Tamsmiddy, the Douglas's who used to be at High Mulloch and are now at Merkland, the Scotts who were in the Home Farm and are now at Polquheys, and to Lydeburn to speak to the Howiesons, but that was just a formality really as I had never met them before. I saw everyone I could and they were all so kind to me . . . and not just because of Robbie and that. I couldn't have wished things to go better than they did . . . although there's no doubt a few tongues will be wagging. Wull Andrews joked that there would be a fair crack, as he put it, going on between Wull Moffat's the cobblers and Bell Mushet's the sweetieshop. Aye, and when McGlone's butcher van and Erch McMath's mobile shop do their rural rounds, not forgetting Sam Grieve the postman, there'll be a few more 'guid cracks' I'm sure. But I can accept all that; where would country folk be without their crack?

I am so disappointed I didn't see you. A letter does seem like the weak way out. And I did *not* want it to be that way. I wanted to look directly at you and tell you that what happened that Martinmas night is something I cannot explain. Of course, I should offer some kind of explanation . . . but believe me I have tried so hard to find an answer without success. It would be so easy to say to you . . . we were young, irresponsible, spoiled brats . . . whatever. But none of these or any other terms offer an explanation of what we did and why we did it.

I would not dare to simply seek your forgiveness. How can one forgive the shame of what we inflicted on you? How can one be expected to absolve the sinner merely because of his expression of a few appropriate words? I ask neither of these. What I do ask of you, Star, is to believe that what was in my brother's heart when he died is in my heart now — the deepest contrition for our actions. If good does come from evil, then that contrition will be a guiding light to me for the rest of my life. As I said, I did want to tell you this personally and I apologise for having to resort to conveying this to you by letter; but my immediate posting to Berlin was totally unforseen.

Please tell your mother that I greatly appreciated her kindness and understanding. I do hope this letter achieves something; at least it has given me the chance to let you know my feelings. Do take care of yourself.
Yours sincerely,
Andrew Fordyce.

The bridge had been quiet when Sammy Nelson arrived at exactly eighteen minutes before five o'clock. He had expected Fordyce to be there at about quarter to five at the earliest, five to five at the latest. There were few people around as he approached the southern archway and he stood there for about seven minutes, waiting for the officer to turn up. At ten minutes to five he then crossed to the city side of the bridge, but there was no one there either. When he saw that, he turned round and returned quickly to the Gorbals side. There was still no one waiting. His mind began to race as he tried to visualise precisely where the captain might be.

"It *would* be the city side . . . the other side . . . that he would turn up," he thought. "He would come in the red tram from the Barracks, the one that went to Mount Florida and Clarkston. It came down Stockwell Street and he would get off at the Fishmarket stop and walk along Clyde Street. Of course he would. Why didn't I think of that before. Christ, maybe he's just decided to wait for her at Gordon's factory instead of coming along to the bridge. Jesus . . . three minutes to five. The girls will be out in five minutes."

At that he ran from the bridge towards Gordon's, only getting as far as St Andrew's Cathedral, the one that was simply called "the chapel" and only a few yards along Clyde Street, at which point he became breathless and had to resort to walking. It was almost a minute before five when he arrived at the factory entrance and already some of the girls from the various premises in the big building were coming down the long and wide staircase. "Jesus Christ, where is this bastard? Back at the south side of the bridge? Aye, Christ, he must be. That's the only place he can be if he hopes to meet her now."

He turned to hurry back once more to the Gorbals end, not even attempting to run this time as he was still breathing heavily from his exertions, the cold night air tingling the beads of sweat on his forehead and the back of his neck. From the second set of lamp standards on the bridge he could see the opposite archway . . . and still there was no one waiting. Sammy Nelson had never felt so frustrated. "Bastard," he said to himself. "Bastard."

He checked his Hamilton once more. "Five past five . . . oh, Christ, here they come." Across the bridge he could see the walkway filling with the girls from the factories and other workers from that side of the river. And from the south side too, from offices and bakeries, and dyers and cabinetmakers and distillers and confectioners and ironworks and stables and blacksmiths and bonds and warehouses they came, workers of all sorts pouring into the streets, many of them heading for the bridge and their homes on the north side of the river. All of a sudden Sammy Nelson was lost in a noisy tide of bustling work people: a lonely man with a beautiful gun and an unrequited quest.

Star had finished reading the letter when her mother arrived.

"He wrote, Ma. The Fordyce boy. There's only one of them now. Andrew. Robbie was killed in the war. He couldn't meet me tonight for he's been called away for this Berlin Air Lift thing in Germany. It's a rather surprising letter . . . here, I would like you to read it."

Isa read it slowly, pausing now and then and asking help with some words, saying she couldn't understand the writing, although it was written with a bold and legible hand. She cried as she read the final sentences and when she had wiped the tears, turned to Star. "You see. I told you he was a nice boy. What do you think?"

"Does it matter what I think, Ma? Does it matter that he wrote? Does it matter what he wrote and how he feels? No, Ma, it doesn't. Not a bit. For no matter what he thinks or how he feels, it doesn't help me. Does it? His letter will make his conscience feel a lot better but it doesn't do me any good or make up in any way what I have suffered. Only time has been a help to me. Years and years of time at that . . . years when I was deprived of the pleasures of normal girls. It's only recently that I've started to get my confidence back again and to feel free of the horrible nightmare which haunted me night and day for so long afterwards. What Andrew Fordyce wrote in that letter is for him; it did him good to write it; it makes him feel good to have got it off his chest. He's accepted again in Kirkconnel for he has made his peace with everyone. Well, if it has done him good then I suppose I can feel happy for him. But nothing . . . *nothing* could ever make up for what I was made to endure. No amount of letters or . . . "

She stopped suddenly at that point to answer a knock at the door. The caller was a well-dressed man with a friendly broad smile. She didn't recognise him, but he knew her. "Hello, Star," he smiled. "I'm Sammy . . . your Uncle Sammy." The three of them spoke excitedly when he came into the house, Star giving him a tight hug and a kiss like she was welcoming a long lost friend and Isa, overjoyed at the occasion of them being together, said it was just like "the bells" . . . when they kissed and greeted each other with the bells which announce the arrival of a new year.

Sammy changed the mood of the occasion suddenly and dramatically when he asked, "And what happened to him? The sojer. Fordyce?" When Isa explained about the letter and about him being called away, he let out a loud gasp of astonishment then shook his head in dismay saying, "That bastard will never know how lucky he is," and then, turning to Star, apologised for swearing. Isa asked him to explain what he meant and he confessed he was carrying a gun and what he had planned to do with it less than an hour earlier. Star was visibly shocked at the revelation.

"You were going to do *that* . . . for me? For me, Uncle Sammy? For God's sake . . . why me? Good God, we've just met tonight. And you were actually going to shoot a man in cold blood . . . all because of me. Not only that, you were going to risk your own life in prison. Oh my God . . . it could actually have happened. And for what? Why, Uncle? Why?"

Sammy was surprised at his niece's reaction. "I'm amazed," he said. "I didn't think for a minute you would take it like that. I thought it would be the other way about. And you ask me why? You're family, Star. That's why. And you're Gorbals family. We stick together here. When I was a wee boy we stayed in the Cumberland Lane for a while.

Poorest street in the Gorbals, so it was. With other wee boys we would go round to Eglinton Street station at night time to meet the men coming home from work and hold out our hands to them shouting 'piece . . . piece'. The men used to bring back with them what pieces they had left over from their dinner breaks. They could easily have thrown them away but they brought them back for the wee boys that needed them. And after we ate what we needed we used to take what we had left to the worst-off families in the Lane. We needed each other, you see — needed each other just to live at times. And do you know what we used to do if we saw a drunk on his own in the street? We would go up to him and take him by the hand. Know why, Star? For the polis wouldn't arrest a drunk as long as he was with somebody else. So we even made sure our drunks got help. It was our way, Star. Wives would take in weans and look after them even though they weren't related to them: if some lassie was unfortunate or if there were weans being neglected or some wife had too many for her house, others would help and look after them. There were more women called granny and auntie in the Gorbals than in any other place in Scotland. And see if you were family, real family I'm talking about, then the others that were related would do what they could for you, no matter what your problem. You never let your own be neglected. I'm no' saying we were all saints. Far from it. But we did look after each other. And as soon as I heard about you and that boy, well, I thought I had to do something. God, Star, you're my very own niece . . . my brother's lassie."

Star was silent after he spoke and looked at him fondly, reflecting what he had said. The Gorbals hadn't been explained to her in that context before. It was always the other side, the hard side, she had been confronted with since her return from the country. She was more than impressed with the sincerity and the warmth her new-found uncle was showing towards her, even though he had been so misguided. "Your answer explains a lot to me, Uncle Sammy. I think I'll understand a lot more now: a lot more about everything. But do promise me one thing . . . that you'll not be violent or take revenge or even consider taking it for me. I seek no revenge. I wish none. The very thought of violence makes me feel ill. I have been the result of violence and I wish it on no one. Do promise me . . . Uncle."

Sammy nodded and smiled. "That's a promise, Star. I'm glad now the boy didn't turn up."

"Just as well you're not like your brother, Sammy," said Isa. "He would have been out there tonight looking for some of his enemies to make up for not having got that boy."

"Ma, that's a terrible thing to say."

"Aye, I know, but it's true," she replied, laughing. "Your Da was a right terror."

"But I'm nothing like Jamesie, Isa. You know that. In fact, I've been terrified ever since I got this gun."

"Did you get it just for that boy?"

"No. There was somebody else."

"Then you *are* a bit of a lad!"

"No . . . no, Isa. Don't misunderstand. I'm not like that at all. Star said violence makes her ill. Well, it does the exact same to me. I do things other ways, but never violence. The gun . . . well. It's an awful long story, believe me. I'll tell you one day. But as for the boy . . . well, as I said . . . I thought I was doing the right thing. Gees, I really am glad he didn't show up. For his sake . . . for Star's sake . . . for everyone's sake. Anyway, I could never go through again what I did today. See my nerves when I walked away from the bridge! God, if some wee boy had said 'boo' to me I would have dropped dead with fright. I thought I was a bit of a big man with the gun, and that. But I wasn't really. Thank God it's all over. C'mon, let's all go down and get a drink."

Star stood still as her mother, almost instinctively, reached for her handbag and coat. "That means you as well, dear," said Sammy.

"I don't . . . I . . . "

"Aye . . . fine . . . They say a sweet sherry can be nice."

"This is Star's first time in the Moy," said Isa when Sammy served up the drinks in the little Sitting Room, separated from the main drinking area of the bar which was for the men. "In fact, it's her first time in a public house."

"Uncle Sammy must think me a right oddity. Anyway, I've been in the Whitehall uptown . . . with the girls when we went dancing to the Locarno . . . remember?"

Sammy asked about her plans when she finished nightschool.

"I just want to get on at something . . . perhaps nursing. I'm not really sure yet. I'm leaving Gordon's for sure and I was hoping to get away from the Gorbals."

"Why don't you two come and live with me in the 'Shields? I've got a house that's bigger than your tenement . . . and half of it is lying empty. And I might have a job for you, Maggie, when you've finished nightschool. You see, I hope to get a third pub in the next round of licences and I'm thinking of branching out into restaurants. I met this Greek guy. He's just arrived here. And he was telling me there's going to be a fortune made in this city from restaurants. That's what he's going into . . . and he can hardly speak a word of English. When you think about it, we've got hardly any good ones for the ordinary folk."

"What about Knotts?" said Isa, almost indignantly.

"I'm not talking about ribs and cabbage places. Good restaurants up town, like, but no' with the fancy prices they've got in Ferrari's and Guy's and the Rogano. Gees, it's a week's wages they're looking for in some of these places just for a meal. Anyway, I'll be needing someone for the office I'm going to open up to organise the buying and the books and that kind of thing for the new enterprise. How would you like that, Star? Be my company secretary . . . aye, that's it. Company secretary. Sounds great . . . doesn't it?"

Star smiled enthusiastically. "Well . . . let's think about it. I'll know better when I finish my nightclasses. But as you say it sounds good. Great in fact. Imagine me being offered a job like that!"

"I couldn't live away in the Pollokshields. I would miss the Gorbals,"Isa said.

"Don't be daft. You don't need to miss the Gorbals where I live. I have the best of two worlds. I sleep in peace with plenty of space about me and all the comforts I could wish, and when I want my friends and a drink in good company, a half hour's walk sees me here in the Gorbals."

"Is that all it is?" said Isa. "You know, I've never been there. I thought it was miles away."

"Well, think about it you two. Godsakes . . . you're not getting much of a life living in a single-end. Are you? Seriously though, I really want you to come and stay in my house. From what the doctors have been saying, it looks as though Peggy is going to be in the home for years . . . maybe for the rest of her life." At that he looked up startled at the pendulum clock on the wall. "God, it's by six. I said I would phone. I'll go round to the boxes in Cumberland Street."

He hadn't gone long when he returned and from his face it was obvious the news was bad. "She's in a coma," he said slowly and softly. "Pneumonia. She's critical, the matron said."

Isa had brought a fresh drink when he was out and he downed it quickly, after which he sat for a few minutes without speaking, staring vaguely into space. He closed his eyes for a brief moment as though snapping out of a trance, then began speaking slowly and softly. "Funny . . . I was just saying that I wanted you both to come and stay in my place. Now it's more than wanting you to come . . . I'll need you to come. I'll need company about the place. My God, what a day this has been."

Star reached out and held his hand . . . "Never mind, Uncle Sammy. Everything will be all right. You're family. Gorbals family."

And they smiled fondly together.